W9-AUU-770

BOOM!

In that moment Manny felt the explosion lift the car and saw its flash as he heard it. The electric car jerked and rolled over on its long axis, up and away from the bridge's centerline.

Below him, out the side window, Manny glimpsed the gargantuan red-orange steel rope that was the bridge's east side suspension cable, as the car spun above and beyond it.

For a heartbeat, gravity balanced the bomb blast's upward force. The bomb blast that Manny realized, too late, a fleeing assassin had triggered with his phone. The Galvani hung in space, nothing between it and the Golden Gate Channel's black waves but rain and wind.

The math was simple, but facts recovered from an eidetic memory boiled up quicker in Manny's mind, and delivered the bad news accurately enough.

The blast had tossed the Galvani over the bridge's side. The height above water of the Golden Gate's upward-arching deck at the span's midpoint, plus the distance the Galvani must have risen to clear the side suspension cable, had to total over three hundred feet.

A human body, or a car containing one, would take maybe four seconds to fall that far, accelerating while it fell as inevitably as Isaac Newton's apple.

The Galvani tumbled through the storm.

Manuel Colibri didn't spend his four airborne seconds wondering why or who. He didn't spend them wishing his engineers had built some secret-agent escape mechanism into this car. He only thought it ironic that after so long it would all end for him where it had started. In the water.

BAEN BOOKS by ROBERT BUETTNER

ORPHAN'S LEGACY SERIES
Overkill
Undercurrents
Balance Point

The Golden Gate

To purchase these and all Baen Book titles in e-book format, please go to www.baen.com.

THE GOLDEN GATE

ROBERT BUETTNER

BAEN

THE GOLDEN GATE

This is a work of fiction. All the characters and events portrayed in this book are fictional, and any resemblance to real people or incidents is purely coincidental.

Copyright © 2017 by Robert Buettner

All rights reserved, including the right to reproduce this book or portions thereof in any form.

A Baen Books Original

Baen Publishing Enterprises
P.O. Box 1403
Riverdale, NY 10471
www.baen.com

ISBN: 978-1-4814-8294-3

Cover art by Dave Seeley

First paperback printing, November 2017

Distributed by Simon & Schuster
1230 Avenue of the Americas
New York, NY 10020

Pages by Joy Freeman (www.pagesbyjoy.com)
Printed in the United States of America

In Memoriam

David Frederick Richards

Cleveland, Ohio, 1943—

Portola Valley, California, 1998

The Golden Gate is a work of fiction. All characters and events portrayed in it are fictional, and any resemblance to real people or incidents is purely coincidental. Particularly, the U.S. Army's 18th Infantry Division is fictional, as are locations and situations in central Iraq associated with it.

HOWEVER, background astronomic, biologic, geographic, historic, legal, medical, and technologic facts, places, and organizations portrayed are accurate, including all specific life-extension science advances *The Golden Gate* describes.

THE GOLDEN GATE

The Golden Gate's view leads the eye west, all the way to the sunset. It's a metaphor for life, which also leads inevitably to a dark end. Unless you buy heaven. Fortunately, there's no third choice. I mean, if the Golden Gate led to living forever, consider the mess.

—Note recovered in the Pacific, west of the Golden Gate Bridge, in 1995, associated with human remains believed to have been the bridge's one thousandth suicide

ONE

On New Year's Eve, 2019, a bearded jogger, shivering visibly in orange Lycra tights, chased after a plaid fedora that a frigid night wind swirling in off the Pacific had snatched from his head. He vaulted the fence that separated the Golden Gate Bridge's pedestrian walkway from its outbound traffic lanes, snagged one running shoe on the fence's top rail, then sprawled into an onrushing Mercedes' path.

Panic-braking, shrieking tires smoking, the Merc stopped inches short of crushing the man's skull.

Behind the Mercedes, Manuel Colibri, CEO of the world's most valuable, and arguably least public, corporation, watched the drama from his driver's seat. But he held tight with both hands to the steaming mug beneath his nose, as his Galvani prototype stopped itself feet short of the Mercedes.

Deceleration nodded Manuel's head forward just enough that warm liquid wet his lips with hints of clove. But not a drop of chai spilled.

Ahead, the bearded man snatched up his hat, recrossed the fence, then squinted into the headlight stream he had interrupted.

The workaholics behind those headlights now raced to escape downtown San Francisco before a phalanx of city police closed the bridge approaches.

The jogger waved his FitMitt monitor glove, which blinked red like a timer ticking toward zero as it announced his rapid pulse. "My bad, drudge-monkeys!"

The jogger backpedaled on along the walkway toward the crowd ahead of him and smacked butt-first into one of the gold-and-blue helmeted Highway Patrol officers deployed, hands on hips, every ten yards along the bridge proper.

The CHP cop scowled, caught his balance, and ignored the whole incident. Tonight, Manuel Colibri thought, hipsters ranked last on a policeman's list of preventable evils.

Pop. Pop-pop.

Isolated raindrops rattled off the Galvani's twenty-first-century windscreen, like sixteenth-century grapeshot.

Ping.

The car's console weather widget lit, chimed, and announced, *"Manny, a storm is arriving earlier, colder, and stronger than forecast. If you wish to know more, say 'More.'"*

Wind swirled more rain in through the car's open side windows, and the droplets needled Manny's neck and cheek. The wind also pricked his nostrils with the sour odor of rubber scorched off the Merc's tires.

Manny smiled.

Not at the cold or the wet or the smell of burnt

rubber, though he had come to relish piquant airborne sensations. Manny smiled at the irony. He already knew a storm was coming, but a storm that bid to change not the weather but the human race.

The jogger had delayed traffic for barely longer than it took to send a text. Nonetheless, behind and alongside the Galvani, horns bawled.

Manny shook his head.

The longer he lived, the more it amazed him that every human soul on Earth rushed toward the future's uncertain promise, when the only certain promise that had ever awaited there was death.

The diesel Mercedes lurched forward, and the electric Galvani, silent and unbidden, glided behind it.

The outbound traffic inched toward a flashing red LED board suspended above the bridge's deck. The closer Manny approached the board, the more densely the joggers alongside him packed the bridge's pedestrian walkway.

The board read:

START LINE

RUN FOREVER NEW YEAR'S 5K,

PRESENTED BY ELCIE, THE EARTH

LONGEVITY COALITION

BRIDGE WILL CLOSE TO VEHICULAR

TRAFFIC 11 P.M.–1 A.M.

Some of the fun run entrants jogged in place, heads bent over their phones' screens. Others cupped hands around glowing joints, as much to warm fingers as to get high.

They wore crayon-bright tights, matched to even

brighter sneakers. And bought with wages paid them by the tech and biotech employers who chauffeured them daily to cubicle farms, which sprawled south from the Golden Gate to San Jose, where ideas grew wild.

These bourgeois idea farmers were turning San Francisco's diverse, gritty six and a half square miles as white and as hip as a designer phone, and they had gathered tonight to party, not to mount the barricades of ELCIE's revolution. But all of them were party to that revolution, bound to it as tightly as the insurgents in any revolution in human history. They not only expected to live forever, the work they did every day was bootstrapping their own expectations toward reality.

Before 2010, serious gerontologists ridiculed predictions that the first person who would live to age 150 was already alive. Five years later, in 2015, biogerontology's paradigm had shifted so far that Google had announced a $1.5 billion investment in its California Life Company affiliate. Suddenly, predictions that the first person who would live, not just to age 150 but to age 1,000, was already alive were debatable rather than ridiculous.

Tonight, five more years of explosive progress after Google announced Calico, immortality appeared as inevitable, at least to this visionary crowd, as the continuously accelerating fall of Isaac Newton's apple had appeared to him.

Not that revolution immunized revolutionaries against *objets bourgeois*. Most of the crowd wore flashing FitMitt monitor/safety gloves, like the one the hipster jogger wore.

FitMitts were wrist candy, not miracles. But Manny's life had taught him that, at least in the short run, candy outsold miracles.

As Cardinal Systems CEO, his last act before he'd left his office minutes earlier had been to announce a year-end bonus for every employee of Cardinal's wildly profitable FitMitt unit. Each bonus was big enough to buy a Mercedes. Or a more-coveted Cardinal/Galvani from FitMitt's affiliate, if one chose to endure the order backlog.

In 2019, every other Cardinal unit had been just as profitable as FitMitt and Galvani. And Manny had rewarded all his employees just as lavishly. Indeed, Carlsson had argued Manny into declaring January 2020 a paid sabbatical for all hands. *Forbes* reported that each day, seven of ten consumers connected to the world by their C-phones, or played with, drove, or otherwise benefited from, a Cardinal product. And that nine of ten of the world's advanced-degreed workers rated a position at Cardinal as their dream job.

The outbound traffic lanes squeezed right into one single lane at the race start line, bottlenecked so cops could stare down into each car before releasing it to cross the bridge.

The officer who waved Manny through frowned in at him.

Not, Manny thought, because he looked like a terrorist. Like a million other bronze-complected men of indeterminate age and small stature who wore off-the-rack suits and cut their own hair, Manny Colibri just looked too ordinary to drive a Galvani.

He smiled again. He also looked too ordinary to hold the immortality revolution's fate in his hands.

Once past the start line, the cars sped up, rain or not. The walkway stretched, nearly empty, alongside them out across the bridge's center span.

Two khaki-vested photographers, posted to record the impending stampede, bent over cameras, sheltering them from the onrushing weather. Beyond the pair, an elite African racer warmed up, bounding like a slim, brown gazelle.

Abruptly, the sky so blackened with rain that the deluge eclipsed the light from the bridge's street lamps.

Distant thunder boomed. Somewhere a transformer popped. The bridge lamps flickered, then quit completely.

The Galvani widened the angle and intensity of its headlights, its sensors groped forward, and it crept ahead, independent of the bridge's feeble emergency lights.

On the bridge's unsheltered center span, howling wind rocked the car on its suspension and drove rain in torrents through the Galvani's windows.

Bing-bing.

The Galvani chimed and its synthetic voice warned, "*Manny, it's too wet in here. Please watch your hands and arms while I close my side glass.*"

The windows hissed closed and cut out the storm.

Manny gasped as lightning, a meteorological Bay Area rarity, cracked above the Golden Gate's north tower and lit the car's interior like the noon sun.

Boom!

The thunderclap echoed and Manny so stiffened that his lap belt pre-tensioned itself across his thighs.

Darkness returned and Manny could see barely twenty feet in any direction. But the Galvani's display showed that the distance to cars ahead and behind had grown.

Yet Manny wasn't alone. Lightning flashed again, and

he glimpsed the elite runner, now huddled shivering and wide-eyed, beside the walkway fence.

The next flash illuminated another man fifty yards ahead. Dressed in a jogging suit, face protected by a ski mask, he stood erect at the fence, leaning into the wind as he peered back at the traffic creeping toward him.

By the time another bolt flashed, the Galvani had closed the distance to the man to twenty yards. He was too beefy to be a racer. In one gloved hand the man cupped against his chest a dark object. A phone? Perhaps a race photographer's camera?

The rain closed down like a drawn curtain across the Galvani's windscreen, and Manny moved both hands onto the Galvani's steering wheel.

A needless precaution. If the man ahead leapt into the traffic lanes, like the bearded jogger had, the Galvani would stop itself before Manny could even twitch.

Manny flicked his eyes to the rearview, remembering the nervous cops. Could the object the misfit man held be a gun?

Manny snorted softly. He had long ago conquered both naiveté and paranoia. Nonetheless, caution had always served him well, and his fingers regripped the wheel.

The Galvani reached the span's midpoint, where the bridge's main suspension cables curved down almost to the bridge deck. Through the rain the massive cables, just yards to Manny's right, were just dark shadows. But ahead the flailing wipers cleared the windscreen and the car caught the man in its headlights. His eyes, dark and narrow, stared in at Manny. The object in his hand was blocky, black, the size and shape of a phone or a small camera, not a gun.

Manny's fingers relaxed a millimeter. Once the man was behind him, Manny pursed his lips, then said, "Rear. IR. Magnify."

The white-on-gray infrared image produced by the man's body heat against the cold night flickered on the center console screen as Manny spoke, then swelled and sharpened.

The man spun, ran toward San Francisco, and turned his head to stare back toward the Galvani. He raised the object in his hand, as though he were dialing a phone.

Manny's brow wrinkled. Why—?

In that moment Manny felt the explosion lift the car and saw its flash as he heard it. The car jerked and rolled over on its long axis, up and away from the bridge's centerline.

Below him, out the side window, Manny glimpsed the gargantuan red-orange steel rope that was the bridge's east side suspension cable, as the car spun above and beyond it.

For a heartbeat, gravity balanced the bomb blast's upward force. The bomb blast that Manny realized, too late, a fleeing assassin had triggered with his phone. The Galvani hung in space, nothing between it and the Golden Gate Channel's black waves but rain and wind.

The math was simple, but facts recovered from an eidetic memory boiled up quicker in Manny's mind, and delivered the bad news accurately enough.

The blast had tossed the Galvani over the bridge's side. The height above water of the Golden Gate's upward-arching deck at the span's midpoint, plus the distance the Galvani must have risen to clear the side suspension cable, had to total over three hundred feet.

A human body, or a car containing one, would take maybe four seconds to fall that far, accelerating while it fell as inevitably as Isaac Newton's apple.

Galvanis performed industry-best when DOT crashed them at forty miles per hour. But Manny and the prototype would strike the water at seventy-five miles per hour, give or take. The car would crush under a force greater than one hundred G. Pilots blacked out at less than twelve G. An average human body suffered certain fatal damage when subjected to sixty-five G.

The Galvani tumbled through the storm.

Manuel Colibri didn't spend his four airborne seconds wondering why or who. He didn't spend them wishing his engineers had built some secret-agent escape mechanism into this car. He only thought it ironic that after so long it would all end for him where it had started. In the water.

TWO

Acting United States Secretary of the Department of Homeland Security Arthur Petrie levered up the seatback of his leather recliner as he scrubbed sleep from his eyes with the heels of his hands.

The C-37B's engines spun down and died after a long night's work, and Petrie squinted out through the executive jet's oval side window. On the wet tarmac outside the parked aircraft a stretch Lincoln sat, glistening with rain from a just-tapered downpour, and bookended front and back by two black Suburbans.

Petrie turned to the other person in the jet's passenger cabin, who stood in the aisle dripping rain onto the carpet. "Modesto? Shepard, why the hell am I in Modesto?"

The acting secretary's aide had been out here in the Bay Area since the bombing, and his eyelids drooped as though he had been awake the whole time.

Ben Shepard brushed with a three-fingered hand at rain that had soaked his suit when he had dashed through the downpour from the Lincoln and boarded the jet. "The storm's still sitting across SFO and San Jose like a gorilla, Mister Secretary. The Golden Gate's still closed, so accessing the city from the north is terrible. This was as close as we could get you, sir."

Petrie frowned. "How close is that?"

Shepard shrugged wet shoulders. "With the escort, you should be in your suite in an hour and a half. The rest of the staff's there now, preparing a full brief for you."

Arthur Petrie kept frowning. He didn't want a full brief. He wanted a full breakfast. Thirteen hours before he had been hustled out of a New Year's morning meet-and-greet brunch in Paris, introducing him to his opposite numbers in the NATO countries.

Hustled out because California had been attacked, and somebody in the West Wing had decided that the Department of Homeland Security needed to look concerned about a state that later this year would cast fifty-five electoral votes for the next president of the United States.

So instead of quality Frog food and wine, Arthur had eaten too many airplane peanuts from a jar, washed them down with blended scotch from the plane's galley that proved the government really did buy from the lowest bidder, then tried to sleep sitting up, in his clothes, for most of the flight.

He stood, stretched, rubbed his eyes, and sighed. "Can you tell me enough during the drive over so I can tap out of the briefing?"

Shepard rubbed his own eyes, nodded. Dark circles painted the skin beneath them, and blood let by a razor nick had dried on his collar. "I thought you might be anxious to get into the loop, sir. I worked up a prebrief summary during the night."

The secretary stepped forward to the plane's open doorway, and paused. Outside, the rain now merely trickled through the chill air, a few wide-spaced drops wrinkling the puddles that glistened on the tarmac. He sighed again.

He had brought Shepard along with him when he moved from the Senate to the cabinet. Ben Shepard was his second ex-infantry aide, and the first with a Purple Heart, plus a visible dismemberment that advertised Petrie's Sincere Support For Our Troops.

Grunt vets were as loyal as Labrador retrievers. But brighter, at least if they had been officers. They worked themselves to exhaustion without complaint, said "sir" if you so much as farted, and the brownie points for hiring them were off the charts. Petrie had fired the first one only because the guy had not only the loyalty of a Labrador retriever but also a similar political IQ.

The more universal problem with ex-grunts in government as a class wasn't that they believed bad food and staying out in the rain were small prices to pay for the privilege of serving their country. The problem was they assumed everybody else in government believed the same thing.

The secretary turned to his drenched, shivering aide. "There are still drops out there. Next time, remember to bring me an umbrella."

As the three-vehicle convoy sped toward San Francisco it ran again under rain that thundered on the Lincoln's roof. Petrie chewed Tums from the accessories bag that Shepard carried for him, while Shepard leaned across the Lincoln's rear compartment from his jump seat and passed executive summary pages to his boss.

The lights of the Suburbans ahead and behind flashed in through the Lincoln's windows, so Shepard's drawn features turned from paste white to pale blue and back to white six times every second. Jet lag, a peanut gut bomb, and cheap scotch were already making Arthur ache from his brain to his ass. The disco show made it worse. He squeezed his eyes closed.

Shepard said, "The instant wisdom was that it was Boston Marathon copycats, sir."

Secretary Petrie opened his eyes, then unwrapped a granola bar from Shepard's bag. "The instant wisdom was wrong?"

Shepard nodded. "In the first place, there was only one casualty."

Petrie chuckled. "The average terrorist's too stupid to plan a good crap."

Shepard shook his head. "Actually, the inference the response team's drawing from the casualty is this incident wasn't terrorism, sir. And the bombers weren't stupid."

The secretary wrinkled his brow. "Five-thousand-person footrace event. Bomb so big it blows a car sky-high. Defiles a goddam American landmark. How's that not terrorism?"

Shepard rubbed his gimp hand with his good one. "The bomb wasn't actually that big. Not even a bomb, really. Explosively Formed Penetrator emplaced under the bridge deck. Sort of a cannon shot up into the car's belly. Neither we nor our correspondent foreign intelligence services saw the spike in terrorist community chatter that usually precedes an attack. And none of the usual suspects, foreign or domestic, have claimed responsibility. Besides, the casualty doesn't seem random."

The secretary raised his eyebrows at that last. "Oh?"

"Manuel Colibri."

"Who?"

"I'd barely heard of him myself. But everybody's heard of Cardinal Systems. Apparently he deflects the spotlight onto the people in his organization who do good work. But he's—was—the CEO."

The secretary's eyebrows rose higher. "I missed a sixty-one *Chateau Latour* because somebody whacked a one-percenter?"

"Maybe. I mean, the thing still *seems* like terrorism. We're hitting it hard like it is, sir. Yes, if it hadn't been for the storm, there could've been more casualties. But not massive losses. The bomb was planted a half mile from the crowd. If the idea was to kill and maim people the same explosives could have been planted in a backpack full of nails near the start line. And the race start wasn't until fifty minutes after the detonation, so the north end of the bridge was nearly empty when the device was set off."

"Set off how?"

"Remote transmission. Basically, dialing a number on a cell phone." Shepard rubbed his hand again and stared at the rain. "So simple a twelve-year-old Iraqi can do it."

"So foreign nationals *were* involved?"

Shepard shook his head. "Only if you count Kenyans."

"What?"

"Between the rain and the power outage there's

no useful imagery from the traffic and surveillance cameras on the bridge. The only significant eyewitness evidence we've got so far comes from a Kenyan distance runner who was warming up out on the bridge when the storm hit. He was sixty yards away from the bomb when it blew."

"He saw something?"

"He saw there was nobody in Colibri's car but the driver. He saw, beside the traffic lane, what he describes as a heavy man. To a Kenyan, that could be anybody who weighs over one forty. The man was wearing a ski mask and jogging clothes. When the device detonated, this man was running back toward the crowd at the starting line, but looking over his shoulder. He apparently got lost in the panic after the explosion."

"There was a footrace. He was wearing jogging clothes. It was cold. He was wearing a ski mask. There was an explosion. He ran the other way. What's suspicious?"

"The Kenyan said that, as the guy ran, he threw something the size of a phone over the side of the bridge."

Petrie's jaw dropped so far that he drooled granola crumbs. "We found it?"

Shepard shook his head again. "The storm chased the police boats and helicopters that would have been below and above the race. We can't even find the car. Speaking of which, if the sun ever shines again, the water under the Golden Gate turns out to be three hundred feet deep. And the currents pump two million cubic feet of water under the bridge every second. So there's no telling where what's left of the car or of Colibri ended up, Mr. Secretary."

Petrie drummed his fingers on his armrest as his convoy blew past snarled California traffic. "Mr. Secretary." He liked the sound of it even better than he had liked "Senator."

Arthur Petrie got this job because he had called the loudest and most visibly for his predecessor to quit it after the Port of Savannah fiasco. Also because Petrie's poll numbers had convinced him that another Senate campaign was as promising as jumping off the Golden Gate Bridge. And mostly because Arthur Petrie knew where just enough bodies were buried on Capitol Hill that he could get nominated and confirmed.

Pending hearings, he had drifted in interim limbo for six weeks, with the compromise title of Acting Secretary.

He swallowed.

The prospect of being on the witness's side of the confirmation hearing room table made him even dizzier. Arthur had a few buried bodies of his own.

He knew real estate. He knew politics. About terrorism he knew dick. But he had assumed that, Savannah notwithstanding, the Department of Homeland Security had people for that.

He yawned, tossed his crumpled granola bar wrapper to Shepard, then closed his eyes and leaned back for a minute while his intestines made gas and his head pounded.

He fervently hoped that those *people* at DHS were managing his first crisis more competently than Shepard was managing his diet. Arthur was tired enough that he dozed anyway.

❖   ❖   ❖

"Sir?" Shepard's voice woke him.

Petrie's aide hung up the rear cabin phone that connected to the stretch's driver, then raised the Cardinal C-phone that he held in his other hand. "Sir, they say they may have him."

"Have who?"

"The guy the Kenyan saw. The guy running away on the Golden Gate Bridge."

THREE

Arthur Petrie sat up in the limo's back seat, head pounding, but eyes wide, and blinked at his aide. "What do you mean they have the guy? Just like that? How?"

Across from Arthur, Shepard squirmed in the limo's jump seat like he was about to confess to chopping down a cherry tree.

Arthur sighed. Shepard's pussyfooting when he had to share classified information with his own boss always made Arthur's head hurt, which was the last thing he needed just now.

Shepard said, "The unclassified euphemism in the mid-2000s was 'The Find.'"

The acting secretary turned up his eyes and scanned the limo's headliner. "Does this look like a fucking TV studio to you, Shepard?"

"Sir?"

"I want an answer, not a *Jeopardy* question."

Shepard pressed his lips together, then said, "Yes,

sir. By my second tour in Iraq, among other intel methods, the U.S. was already tracking insurgent's phones by their GPS chips, and eavesdropping by a 'backdoor' built in to most phones to defeat their encryption systems. Even when the insurgents thought their phones were off. Not that anybody admitted it then. When I asked why we were finally getting decent intel, one guy just told me 'The Find.'"

Shepard frowned. "A few years later, it turned out the NSA was doing more or less the same thing to people here in the U.S. Sort of made some of us wonder what kind of government we'd been fighting for. Today most of the manufacturers have stopped building in backdoors. Or at least they've stopped admitting it."

Arthur cocked his head. He had never understood why government surveillance offended otherwise clever people like Shepard. Government's *job* was screwing over the governed, and it couldn't do its job if it didn't know what the governed were up to.

Shepard said, "We knew from what the Kenyan saw that the bomb was detonated by what we assumed was a phone that was located somewhere between the center of the Golden Gate and the bridge's North Tower. At the time, there were thousands of phones behind the start line at the south end of the bridge, but just the one near the north end."

"But he threw his phone away."

Shepard shook his head. "This phone's not in the bay at the moment. So he threw away something else."

"What was that?"

"This guy improvised a radio-controlled explosively formed penetrator. If he was smart enough to build and deploy an RCEFP, he was smart enough to know that a high-profile event like this race might rate shutting off the cellphone towers in the neighborhood. Exactly so a phone in a bomb couldn't receive a detonation command from another phone. The towers weren't shut off, but he couldn't have planned on that."

"Then how—?"

"Kids' walkie-talkies can do directly what two phones do via cell towers. Especially if the guy holding the transmitter's fifty yards from the receiver, like he was. Amazon'll deliver a pair of walkie-talkies that don't have tracking chips for under sixty bucks."

Arthur stroked his chin, nodded.

Shepard said, "What NSA's tracking is a *phone* the bomber probably had in his pocket while he waited for Colibri's car."

The secretary narrowed his eyes. "Why would he have a phone in his pocket? If he's so smart, he knows about tracking chips. Does this guy *want* to get caught?"

Shepard said, "Actually, that's exactly what he wants. At least the psychologists say that's the most probable scenario. Or maybe he's just not that smart. Bomb building's not simple, but it's not rocket science."

"But NSA's rocket science *is*. For whatever reason he's carrying this phone? And they're tracking it?"

Shepard nodded. "They place it in a house in Redwood Heights. That's a residential neighborhood on the south side of Oakland. Local SWAT's clearing the area and surrounding the place right now."

The secretary's eyes widened. Whether smart, stupid or suicidal, Arthur Petrie wanted to kiss this guy right through his ski mask. The confirmation hearing narrative had just changed. Now, the story would be how in six short weeks Arthur Petrie had flipped a dysfunctional agency like he had flipped all those on-the-skids malls of his. Terrorist bomb hurts nobody except some rich guy. Terrorist nabbed within forty-eight hours. Case closed.

Arthur Petrie had transitioned from real estate speculator to politician in the first place by being shocked—shocked!—at problems he knew dick about, then blaming them on somebody else. The tactic had propelled him from the House to the Senate and now almost into the cabinet.

But these circumstances were new to him. Government was actually about to do something efficient and useful. Better yet, he could take credit for it.

Arthur drummed fingers against his chin.

Of course, there was always the danger that whoever had actually done the work might get the credit, and he would look like a clueless bystander.

Suddenly the forward Suburban blipped its siren, then Arthur was thrown left in his seat as the convoy cut to the right across traffic and shot down an exit ramp.

Shepard said, "Sir, before I woke you I took the initiative to redirect us to the field operation command post in Redwood Heights. Apparently the media's got wind. I thought somebody in authority, like you, should be on site to keep the media informed."

The acting secretary rubbed his chin stubble. Shepard's bag contained an electric razor reserved for Arthur. He didn't ask for it. Haggard warrior was the better look. He could even get the protective detail boys in the Suburbans to Velcro him into one of those bulletproof vests they wore.

He reached across the compartment, slapped Shepard's knee, and smiled. "Now that's political IQ, Shepard! A politician's aide puts himself in his boss's shoes."

Shepard squirmed in his seat. "Actually, sir, I was just putting myself in the shoes of the grunts on the ground. When the Congressional junkets came to Iraq we'd use the politicians as bait."

Arthur straightened, brows-up. Shepard didn't seem that devious. Maybe he had underestimated the man. "You put members of Congress in the line of fire?"

Shepard shook his head. "No, sir! Not bait for the insurgents. Bait to draw off the camera crews. So we could go to war in peace."

Seven minutes later the Lincoln and the Suburbans, their lights and sirens long since off, were waved over on a steep street of fifties-vintage bungalows. The landscaping was mature but overgrown, and most of them had the curb appeal of dog kennels.

The cop who waved them over was black, younger than Shepard, and wore a rain slicker. One of those clear plastic shower caps covered his cop hat, and a walkie-talkie's stubby antenna protruded above the raincoat's lapel. The last person Arthur had seen dressed like that was when he was twelve, and the person had been a school crossing guard.

Arthur's protective detail piled out of the Suburbans, heads on swivels, cleared the area, then waved him and Shepard out of the Lincoln. Nobody even offered Arthur a bulletproof vest.

Shepard, who was nothing if not a quick study, hopped out, popped open the golf umbrella in his hand, then held it above the car door while his boss climbed out quite dry. Also quite bravely, considering his torso was unarmored against sniper fire.

The cop in the rain slicker approached them, saluting like a Boy Scout. He leaned close and spoke up to be heard over the drum of rain and the rush of runoff down the curbside gutters. "Mr. Secretary, I'm Officer Gerald Waters."

"*You're* in charge, here?"

"Of outside agency liaison for this critical incident, yessir. The incident tactical commander's closer to the objective while the other elements move into position."

The secretary looked around.

A black SWAT van, rear doors open to a depopulated interior, was parked twenty yards further up the street. Another slickered cop closed the van's doors, then scurried back inside the van's cab.

What the hell? Arthur Petrie was the Secretary of the Department of Homeland Frigging Security, but instead of the command post he was out here in overflow parking with a PR flack dressed up like the safety patrol.

The black cop cleared his throat. "May I orient you to the area of operations, Mr. Secretary?"

That sounded professional. Arthur nodded.

The black cop walked them across the street with two of the protective detail's members trailing behind.

The lot that the cop led them across was vacant except for a worn concrete slab and a rusted roll off hopper, overstuffed with a jigsaw of shingles, plaster, and slabs of sledgehammered brick.

When the black cop reached the slab's back edge, he stopped and pointed out and down.

Below, streets just like this one snaked and climbed

the side of the wooded rise they stood atop. On a clear day, Arthur supposed, this lot had a view of Oakland. But a teardown in this shithole neighborhood was stupid, as whoever was flipping this property was about to find out. Arthur had fled the private sector because the marketplace punished human stupidity. Whereas government was based on the proposition that human stupidity was infinite.

The black cop pointed. "That one."

A football field down and away from them, Arthur made out through the gauze of rain the red tile roof of a smallish single story.

The view plus the slab provided a perfect vantage to see whatever the hell was going to happen, and also a spot with a stage and a backdrop from which to give interviews after it did happen.

The black cop, whose name Arthur now wished he had remembered, said, "The surrounding residences are clear. Nobody home on workdays when school's back in."

The secretary pointed at the red roof. "You're sure the cell phone that was on the bridge is in that house?"

The black cop shifted, foot-to-foot, nodded. "Your people told us that, sir. They also said the phone's moving around in there, not stationary."

Shepard was listening with his own phone to his ear, then held it to his chest and said to Arthur, "We're just now getting a profile of this guy. Well, of the guy who owns the phone and rents that house."

The secretary peered down and sucked a breath in horror. What if they had surrounded only a phone? What if the phone's owner was escaping into Mexico right now? While a decoy beagle waddled around an unmarketably outdated kitchen with a phone taped on its ass? Arthur asked, "Has anybody actually *seen* a person moving inside that house?"

Before the cop could answer, his walkie-talkie crackled. "I got eyes on a target. Left front window. White male, bald, camo T-shirt. He just pulled a curtain back. Still peekin' out."

The secretary exhaled. At least he wasn't going to have to read headlines like "DHS Surrounds Pooch While Bomber Escapes."

"Weapon?" It was a different voice. Authoritative.

"Nothing visible."

"Range?"

"One six zero. But—"

"But what? Hostage?"

"No evidence of one. But—damn!"

Static crackled for as long as it took Arthur's heart to thump twice. It was chilly here, but he was sweating and the cannonball in his gut throbbed.

Arthur, Shepard, and the cop leaned forward, staring down like tourists through the downpour at the red-roofed house surrounded by wet greenery, while rainwater coursed off their umbrellas.

Arthur blinked back dizziness, shook his head to clear it.

He couldn't see any sniper, and the dizzier he felt the less he cared.

"Lost target. He dropped the curtain. I think he's moved away from the window. I think he might've made us, Lieutenant."

Silence, then the sniper said, "Front door opening!"

Arthur's heart thumped and his head throbbed worse.

The sniper said, "Never mind. He just let the dog out."

Below, a tiny, gray speck of a dog ran out from beneath the trees and crossed the street.

The authoritative voice said, "I don't like—"

All in one instant the red roof tiles a football field away parted and bloomed as a flash like the risen sun startled the crap out of Arthur Petrie.

It seemed to take forever for his heart to beat again, and dizziness blurred his vision.

Then he felt nothing.

FOUR

Arthur Petrie lay flat with his back against something cold, hard, and wet. His head ached, and liquid trickled off his face and into his open mouth.

"Mr. Secretary?" The voice in Arthur's ears was familiar, urgent.

Arthur opened his eyes, blinked away streaming rain, and coughed it from his mouth. "What happened?"

Shepard and one of the protective detail men knelt over him, tight-lipped faces silhouetted against the clouds behind them.

The PD man said, "The house blew up, sir."

"I knew *that*." Arthur moved arms, legs, wiggled fingers and toes. "I meant what happened to *me*. Am I alright?"

Shepard took Arthur's face in both hands, then cocked his head and peered into the older man's eyes.

The ex-platoon leader nodded. "I'd say when you fainted you cracked the back of your head on the concrete." He smiled. "You got your bell rung pretty good, sir. But I've seen plenty of worse concussions."

Arthur blinked again, then Shepard grasped his elbow to help him up.

"Ow! Fuck."

"Sir?"

"Let go! I think I hit my funny bone when I fell." Arthur sat up on his own and rubbed his elbow until the numb burn in his arm faded. "How good did my bell get rung?"

"You were out six minutes, Mr. Secretary."

Someone was shouting in the distance, and the protective detail man stood and turned toward the shouts.

A flint-eyed, helmeted man wearing black SWAT gear, with a silver lieutenant's bar on his uniform, muscled past the protective detail man. The cop stood, booted feet apart, while he pointed down at Arthur with a trembling finger. "You didn't even ask where my people were! We weren't even in position yet. You could've killed my guys!"

Arthur recognized the authoritative voice that had crackled out from the black cop's walkie-talkie.

Arthur stood, then touched the back of his head and discovered a lump that felt as big as a Titleist. "What?"

The SWAT unit's commander stalked to the edge of the concrete slab and stared down, waiting with hands on hips until Arthur joined him.

Where the red-tile-roofed bungalow had been was only a circle of flattened, smoking vegetation. At the circle's center yawned a crater filled with flaming rubble, including scorched red roof tiles. The windows of neighboring houses were shattered, and a water spout fifteen feet high jetted from a broken pipe near the crater's center.

The SWAT commander said, "Don't bullshit me. You called a fuckin' drone strike down on Oakland!"

The Acting Secretary of Homeland Security turned to Shepard, who was back on his C-phone. "We did?"

Shepard rolled his eyes. "No! That's ridiculous! The guy in that house didn't let his dog out to save it from a Hellfire missile he didn't know was coming. He blew himself up."

The pity, Arthur thought, was that, based on what he had seen of Oakland, if he *had* blown it up no jury would ever convict him.

The SWAT commander drew a deep breath as he stared down at the smoking crater, then turned to Shepard. "You're telling me that was a suicide?"

Shepard held his phone against his chest, and nodded at it. "I am. The billing name on that phone is Eli Abney, Jr. A Specialist 5th Class Eli Abney, Jr., served three tours in Afghanistan as an Explosive Ordnance Disposal tech. He was discharged for medical reasons three years ago. VA records show he was meeting a contractor therapist from San Francisco at a VA outpatient center on MLK in Oakland, for PTSD treatment. But he missed his last three appointments. The third miss should have triggered a follow-up, but didn't. He was fired from his job for excessive absenteeism, but applied for unemployment benefits anyway three months ago. That house down there has been in and out of eviction proceedings since he moved in."

The SWAT commander crossed his arms and nodded slowly. "So. Adios to the psycho who bombed the 'Gate."

"Psycho? He probably—he did—kill himself." Shepard pointed below at the wreckage. "But it's a stretch to say he was a danger to anyone but himself. Why would a guy who wouldn't hurt a dog murder some tycoon?"

Shepard's phone pinged again, he listened, then his shoulders slumped. "The employer that fired Abney contested his unemployment claim. It was Cardinal Systems."

"Oh." Arthur stared down at the rubble as the rain snuffed the flames to black smoke. Then he sighed. "Don't suppose we'll be lucky enough to find a suicide note from this guy in *that*."

Shepard scowled as he peered at his C-phone. "We won't have to. I'm looking at the note he texted to his therapist ten minutes ago."

Arthur turned toward an approaching vehicle's roar, and saw a local-news SUV, antenna mast folded along its roof, squeal to a stop thirty yards from him.

A blonde wearing a purple parka sprang out the front passenger's door. She flipped up the parka's hood so that it covered her hair, then turned back to the open door and began unpacking a microphone and its coiled cord from a black canvas shoulder bag that she had placed on the SUV's front seat.

In the distance, an even bigger media truck lumbered up the residential street's hill.

Arthur's heart skipped. The moment called for decisive leadership and immediate action. He spun and faced the smaller of the protective detail men, who was about Arthur's size, and pointed at the man's black protective vest. "Take that off and show me how to wear it!"

FIVE

The Honorable Maureen Dunn stood between the US and state of California flags arranged on pedestaled staffs in front of the paneled wall of her San Francisco city hall office. Seated in a chair at her side, Arthur Petrie motioned Shepard, who was holding an ice bag against the back of Arthur's head, to step out of frame.

The photographer, kneeling in front of Arthur and the mayor, motioned her closer to him, then he reached forward and smoothed the fabric of the black cloth sling that supported Arthur's arm.

Hitting one's funny bone was, strictly speaking, nerve damage, and one couldn't be too careful.

The mayor looked down at Arthur, brow furrowed in concern, while Arthur stared up at her, tightening his lips as though his head ached more than it usually did at eight a.m.

The photographer's flash flickered and the camera whined as he shot a cluster of photos. He reviewed the images by scrolling through them, then held a thumb up to the mayor.

The photographer and Shepard left the two politicians alone in her office.

The mayor lifted the morning's *San Francisco Chronicle* off her desk with both hands and read the front page headline aloud. "Mission Accomplished! DHS Secretary Wounded on Front Line as 'Gate Bomber Siege Ends." Unsmiling, she shook her head. "Well, you found *yourself* a pony in this manure pile, Art."

The soon-to-be-confirmed DHS Secretary wrinkled his forehead at his old friend. Seven years before they had shared not only party affiliation and a business-to-politics career path, but side-by-side broom-closet freshman House of Representatives offices. "Why the long face, Mo? The manure's not stuck on you. Six counties run that bridge."

"There are nineteen directors on the board of the Golden Gate Bridge, Highway and Transportation District. Nine of 'em are from the city and county of San Francisco. I'm the only mayor in the six counties who gets to appoint a director. Did you read the subhead?" The mayor of San Francisco brandished the paper. "'Local Preparedness Questioned.' Local government can't do very many things that outrage average voters, Art. Screwing with their commute is one of them. If this thing goes to more shit, don't tell me where it won't stick!"

Arthur shrugged out of the sling and raised his palms. "Okay! What do you want from me?"

"First, tell me why DHS is 'confident' this psycho acted alone. I want the truth and I want details. Not the crap you're peddling the morning shows."

Arthur shifted in his chair as he pulled the mental string in his neck and unleashed the knowledge that Shepard had briefed to him during the drive to city hall.

Arthur Petrie was not a stupid man. He learned quickly and perfectly anything that interested him. However, the only thing that interested him was himself. Fortunately, Shepard seemed to realize this, and his briefings transferred his knowledge to Arthur with an easily regurgitated clarity that made Petrie wonder how the man had been dumb enough to have gotten himself blown up.

Arthur said to Maureen Dunn, "Pretty good. Seriously."

"Why?"

He corkscrewed his face. He had a jet to catch. "The DNA they collected from what was left of him in the house matches DNA on bomb fragments embedded in the bridge structure. He was an EOD tech, so he knew enough to build a bomb this fancy without help."

"And he got it up under the bridge without help?"

"They found fragments of coveralls in the house debris that match the ones that one of the district's maintenance contractors issues its workers. And pieces of melted nylon rope with those little metal climbing thingies attached." Arthur shrugged. "Stealing laundry and an ID badge doesn't take a conspiracy. The explosive was commercial blasting gelatin. It's plastic, like military C-4, so it can be molded into a shaped charge. It's waterproof, it's cheap, and obviously it was powerful enough to do this job. Most importantly, because it's commercial it's easier to get."

"ID badge or no badge, he couldn't just carry a bomb onto the bridge."

"No piece of the bomb as we reconstruct it was too big to be carried past any checkpoint inside a good-sized toolbox, then hidden. Then all of the pieces could have been reassembled. Some of the bridge employees remember his face. He appeared briefly in some surveillance video from the bridge, and he graduated from the army mountaineering school, so he could have emplaced the device. And he had night time access."

"But the phone. Wasn't that so somebody could call and alert him Colibri was on the way?"

Arthur shook his head. "The short answer is NSA says the cell phone towers around the bridge were turned on, but there were no calls or texts in or out on that phone during the relevant interval. And the only calls in or out on the phone since he bought it were routine stuff and to his therapist at the VA about appointments. And the suicide note."

"Then how did he know when Colibri was coming?"

"The shortest drive between Colibri's office downtown and his home in Marin County is across the Golden Gate. Colibri's administrative assistant said he normally worked 'til ten thirty, seven nights a week like clockwork, climbed into his car parked in a secure garage, then drove himself home alone by randomly alternating routes. Except, of course, for the bridge, for which there was no practical secure alternative. When he got home, he pulled into another secure garage. His admin's recollection matches the records of Colibri's movements that night based on recordings from building cameras and the swipes of his company ID.

"The pre-race publicity warned that outbound bridge traffic would be squeezed into only the curb lane after ten p.m. Apparently one thing the army teaches morons like this guy is set your ambush where the terrain channelizes the target. And this target was a one-of-a-kind prototype car. So this guy didn't need coconspirators. All he needed was patience and the ability to recognize a tangerine metallic orange electric car that looked like nothing else on the road."

"Then why did he keep the phone on him?"

"He wanted to get noticed, but he didn't want to get caught and imprisoned. I mean, if *I* was suicidal the last thing I'd want is to wind up alive and facing a lifetime of prison food and sex with men. The psych people say it's all consistent with the vanilla suicide note he texted, and why he kept the phone with him."

"He kept the phone with him to communicate with coconspirators. Or he and the conspirators used separate, burner phones. Most of the drug dealers in this city use burners every day. That's what the talking heads will say it's consistent with. That's what every cabbie and bartender in San Francisco will say it's consistent with."

"Well, if they're right it's a murder conspiracy, not a terrorist conspiracy, Mo. There's no ongoing threat to the public at large."

The mayor dropped her jaw. "DHS is declaring victory and blowing town? That's where I was afraid you were going."

Arthur knew where he was going, but resisted the urge to glance at his watch.

A brief window had opened in the weather so his jet had been flown closer, to San Francisco International. The C-37B, now catered as lavishly as the Gulfstream executive jet it actually was, beckoned.

Arthur wanted to take his victory lap live and uncut on the evening network news shows from D.C. Because back there some Beltway-centric reporter would undoubtedly ask whether Petrie had considered the possibility that a stalemated convention might turn to him. And Arthur could say he was too busy keeping America safe to think about politics. To realize that springboard moment, Arthur had to wrap up with Maureen and get outta Dodge before the thunderstorms grounded him.

"Art, at the very least, we need wreckage and a body for closure. Otherwise I'm gonna be dealing with comparisons to Amelia Earhart and the Kennedy assassination for the next three election cycles."

"You want a visible DHS presence?" Arthur stopped short of saying, "So there's another place for any shit to stick?"

The mayor of San Francisco nodded. "Better for both of us."

Arthur nodded back. More likely only better for Mo. But Arthur was late to his rendezvous with destiny already. And if this thing took a turn for the better, somehow, he wanted a piece of the cheese. What he needed in order to have it both ways was what everybody in Washington always kept in their back pockets. A visible minion loyal enough to fall on his sword, or expendable enough to be thrown on it, if things *did* turn back to shit.

Arthur said, "The guy who I came in here with? Shepard? How about he stays? He can stand behind you at the pressers as DHS liaison."

Mayor Dunn snorted. "Your gofer with the mangled hand?"

"He's smart enough. He looks strong and handsome. He's a vet, so he follows orders and keeps his mouth shut. Christ, Mo. I'm offering him as a decoration, not a typist."

The mayor crossed her arms, half nodded. "If he's

the most I'm gonna get. The most Manuel Colibri is gonna get."

"Your heartfelt empathy for the world's richest dead guy touches me." Arthur snuck a glance at his watch, then at the mayor's stony face. "Maureen, back in Washington we have real terrorism problems to deal with. The briefing tablet they hand me every morning would scare the crap out of you. Our real pros are chasing real terrorists. This really, truly isn't DHS business."

The mayor stared at him, silent and still disgruntled. As usual in politics, speaking the truth wasn't worth the time it took to tell it. When the truth failed to set you free, a last resort was to argue that the problem just didn't matter. Arthur said, "Besides, Colibri's grieving widow's not crying out for justice on the cable shows. The guy was a damn recluse."

The mayor frowned. "Well, I had a personal phone call from one guy who does want justice."

"So does Batman. Why's this guy entitled to it?"

"Because he's David Powell."

Arthur whistled. Then he cocked his head. "Why does *he* care?"

"Don't all you tycoons get nervous every time people see how easy it is to kill one of you?" The mayor finally smiled.

Arthur frowned. He had noticed that, for some reason, contemplating his death often evoked that reaction in people.

The mayor said, "But why does David Powell care about Colibri? David told me he and Colibri got friendly when David recruited him to join the Powell Charities Coalition's Board last year. For as long as I've known him, David's been introducing new money to philanthropy like AA has been introducing drunks to coffee."

Arthur nodded. "Everybody knows how much David Powell gives to cancer research." He waved a hand. "For all I know, he just eradicated toe fungus in Zimbabwe, too. What I don't know is how much does your Batman give *us?*"

"Plenty. Piss off David and his PACs today, kiss off California next November." The mayor raised her palm. "I'm one hundred percent serious about that, Art. I've seen the numbers."

Arthur raised his eyebrows. "Well, all right then. What does this fine citizen want for himself? And how much will it cost us?"

Maureen Dunn rolled her eyes to her office's high ceiling. "What David wants from us isn't really even for himself. But even so he says he'll pay all the bills himself."

"Mo, even I know that's illegal."

The mayor shook her head. "Not if I appoint a special investigator. I have discretion to bless independently funded blue ribbon inquiries."

Arthur nodded. There was no better excuse for doing jack squat about a problem than saying you were waiting for a blue ribbon investigation to complete its work independent of government pressure that could compromise its integrity. "You're telling me Powell is the last Boy Scout?"

The mayor shrugged. "Art, just because we're ambitious, self-absorbed pricks doesn't mean everybody else is."

Arthur Petrie sighed. "At least we know his checks won't bounce."

SIX

The Bentley turned right off Beach into Hyde Street, then paused at the curb.

A cable car, packed with poncho-draped tourists outbound from Fisherman's Wharf, clanged and rumbled past as it departed its turnaround in Aquatic Park. Neither vehicle had been deterred from its mission by the pelting rain that had persisted throughout the first three days of 2020.

Paul Eustis glanced out the Bentley's rain-smeared side glass, at the windows of the corner bar to his right, then frowned into his rear-view mirror at the slim, gray-haired man in the back seat. "Mister Powell, do you really think you'll find Mr. Boyle at the Buena Vista? In all those years he never struck me—."

David Powell peered through the rain at the bar's double doors and smiled. "As a tourist? Paul, Mrs. Boyle was a tourist and Jack was a law student waiting tables the afternoon he met her. Right in there at the Buena Vista. Marian would have turned sixty-three today. I like my chances."

Paul Eustis smiled. Not at the memory of Marian Boyle. That gentle woman's passing remained too profoundly sad for anyone who had known her, even two years on. Paul smiled because David Powell had never forgotten Paul's birthday, or the birthday of anyone he employed, or even their partners' and children's birthdays.

David Powell turned up his topcoat's collar, then laid his hand on the rear compartment's door handle. "Two hours. Unless I call."

The driver reached for the umbrella on the seat beside him, as he prepared to limp around to Powell's door and hold the umbrella over his boss.

But David Powell raised a calf-gloved palm. "Stay put, Paul. Silly for us both to get wet."

SEVEN

Jack Boyle had beaten the crowds, and sat alone at the skinny four-top farthest from the Buena Vista Cafe's wood and glass double main doors. The café's interior formed an L-shape, with the doors angled across the apex where the L's legs joined. The L's long leg paralleled Beach Street, and squeezed age-darkened wood tables between a tile-fronted bar along the inside wall and arched windows along the outside. Beyond those windows cold rain wept, as it had for days.

Jack had chosen the table not in order to avoid the damp drafts that would whistle in as the exiting brunch diners held the doors open for the entering lunch crowds. Though the older he got, the colder and wetter San Francisco winters seemed.

He chose this table because it was the one that he had cleared for the fragile, alabaster-skinned red-headed girl who had sat there, quiet and alone, while she read her Fodor's guide.

Marian had ordered Irish coffee even though

41

everybody did, and laughed at his crappy jokes even though nobody did. And she had waited 'til he got off that night because when he carded her, and noticed that it was her birthday, he had asked her to dinner.

He looked away from the rain, stared down into his second neat scotch of the morning, and didn't move until somebody bumped against the table.

Without looking up, Jack lifted his glass. "Again. And a menu."

The waiter didn't budge. Christ, the staff here had gone all the way to hell in forty-two short years.

Jack glanced away from his glass far enough to realize that the person standing alongside the table wore a topcoat, not a waistcoat. Cashmere, at that.

A grey-gloved hand withdrawn from the coat's pocket pointed at Jack's neat scotch. "What? No Irish coffee? You know, they invented it here."

Jack kept his head down. "I know they invented it in Ireland. So do you. Christ, David. What're you doing here?"

David Powell tugged off leather gloves as thin as cocktail napkins and pocketed them. "Pleasure to see you, too, Jack. Mind if I sit?"

David Powell slipped off his coat, folded it across the back of an empty chair, and sat down opposite Jack.

"Apparently I don't."

A waiter materialized, neat and smiling, reset the table for two, then gathered Powell's coat to hang and stood by silently.

Maybe not all the way to hell.

The kid peered down as Powell looked up. Fifty-eight, imperially slim, with silver hair brushed back to frame a tan, unlined face, David Powell looked the patrician he was.

David pointed at Jack's glass, then at the empty spot in front of himself and held up two fingers. Then he brought his palms together, pantomiming a menu being read, and cocked his head at the waiter with a smile.

The kid nodded and disappeared.

"Still a man of few words, I see."

David shrugged. "The difference between the right word and the almost right word is the difference between the lightning and the lightning bug. Mark Twain said that."

"He said San Francisco weather's crap, too. So what brings *you* out in it?"

"You do. My office has been calling your home and leaving messages for days. Not a word back. And you don't even have a mobile number anymore. My admin asked me whether you were antisocial."

Jack shrugged. "Lack of a smartphone doesn't make somebody antisocial."

"True. What makes somebody antisocial is pigheaded cynicism. When I interviewed you thirty years ago, phones were dumb but you were already a pigheaded cynic."

"Then you should've told me to fuck off thirty years ago."

David smiled and shrugged again. "I figured your intelligence and work ethic would be worth the aggravation. They were. They still are. Jack, problem solvers are like words. The right one's hard to find."

The kid returned with scotches and menus.

They drank the scotches, they ate omelets. They

talked about the shitheads who still protested at every hospital wing dedication and fund-raising ball that David paid for, even though he spent a smaller percentage of his net worth on personal consumption and a larger percentage of it on charity than any busboy, accountant, or cardiologist in San Francisco. They talked about the Powell Gallery's new Impressionist exhibit. They talked about how the Giants needed better short relief and about Wall Street's speculation on why Powell Diversified was sitting on far too much cash. It was, Jack realized, the longest conversation he had had in two years, and the first time in two years that he had laughed.

Finally, the kid brought coffee, cleared the table, and David grabbed the check.

Then he rested his elbows on the table, leaned forward, and frowned. "Jack—"

Jack rolled his eyes, puffed out a breath. "If Mark Twain's the one who said there's no free lunch, it was right after you picked up his check."

David raised his palm. "Hear me out."

Jack sat back in his chair and crossed his arms.

"Jack, have you heard about the Manuel Colibri business?"

Jack rolled his eyes again. "Christ, David. I read the papers front to back every morning. I just don't read them on a tiny little phone."

"You know I didn't mean it like that."

"You know I didn't take it like that. The bridge is fixed. The bomber's dead. His neighbors even adopted his goddam dog. They got new windows free from HGTV. Everybody's happy except the billionaire looking up from the bottom of the bay."

David's frown deepened. "That's what Maureen Dunn told me, too. I disagree."

"With the mayor?"

"With everybody, apparently. Jack, I didn't know Manuel Colibri well, or for very long. Nobody did, apparently. But he seemed better than just some billionaire. You know the rumors about Cardinal and life-extension research."

"I don't. Why the hell would somebody with my life care about extending it?"

David blinked, then said, "And killing Manuel Colibri at what amounts to an ELCIE rally's just too coincidental."

"Don't know about that either."

"And the story ties up the loose ends just too tight."

Jack metronomed his head. "Maybe I am skeptical when a story's too good to be true. But police departments have professionals for that. They're called detectives."

"Maureen says her detectives are too busy to chase conspiracy theories. And so are the feds."

Jack snorted a laugh. "You want me to play detective?"

"No. I want you to solve a problem. When you lawyered for me, every time I gave you a poorly drafted contract or an insoluble problem you didn't let go 'til you choked the shit out of it."

Jack waved his hand. "That was my job."

David raised his index finger. "I'm only asking that you do that job one more time. Just look into Colibri's murder. Your hourly rate will be Pullman Hartwell's current senior partner rate, plus twenty percent—"

Jack shook his head. "Which was rapacious even

when I was reviewing their bills. I don't need the money. Or your charity."

"Thought you'd say that. I'll send the money to a charity that does need it. You choose one, or I can choose for you."

"I choose you to butt out of my life."

"Jack, I'll pay any costs you incur. I've already talked to Maureen Dunn. She'll appoint you a special investigator. She's promised you'll get government cooperation anytime you need it, even from the feds. If you find something, we turn it over to the authorities. It's that simple."

"No. Contract law is simple. Outwitting embezzlers who try to steal money from a man who's got too much of it is simple. Exposing a murder conspiracy? That's hard. Especially an imaginary one."

Jack stared up at the saloon's ancient tiled ceiling. Like most of this planet, it was older and wearier than he was. But every day the age gap seemed narrower. "David, what part of 'I quit' did you misunderstand two years ago?"

"Jack, you never quit anything in your life. You don't know how. You just needed time."

Jack let his mouth drop open, then wagged a finger. "Ah! This isn't about justice for your new, dead friend. It's about rehabilitating a withdrawn widower who's been drinking his lunch lately."

Powell lowered his voice. "It's about helping an *old* friend. Who is very much alive. I know you. And I never knew a couple closer than you and Marian were. But you're like a shark that drowns if it stops swimming, Jack. It's time to reconnect with the world."

Jack shook his head. "I read the news off paper.

I still drive a car that doesn't talk, with a carburetor I can adjust."

"Jack, this Luddite posturing of yours merely announces that you're stubborn."

Jack said, "I'm not a Luddite. I'm a paranoid. I turned in that damn iPhone when I quit. Those phones are spies."

"The Fourteenth Amendment protects us against government spying. Apple stopped building spying capabilities into iPhones years ago. That's one reason we started using iPhones. And why would a commercial enterprise bother? Anything they want to know about a customer the customer will happily tell them in exchange for a free latte. Jack, we're getting off track."

"Not really. David, the longer we talk, the older I get. I'm too old to reconnect with the world you want looked into."

"Perhaps. But you don't have to do it alone. You've got an expert right in the family. Who'd be happy to help, if you let her."

Jack's jaw dropped. Then he slapped the table with one hand so hard that coffee erupted from his cup, while he stabbed at Powell with the other hand's index finger. "That's not helping, David! That's meddling!"

"Kate didn't think it was. She said you two haven't spoken since the funeral."

"I told you. I can't answer a smartphone I don't have."

"What about that antique of a landline you *do* have? And is your mailbox carnivorous? Kate says when you wouldn't answer the phone, or respond to the messages she left, or even the doorbell, she sent you letters. And they came back marked 'undeliver-able' in your handwriting."

"The funeral wasn't my best day."

"I recall. So, I'm sure, does the priest. And every-body else who was there. You don't think Kate would understand and forgive you that?"

"Of course she would. Kate is her mother's daugh-ter. She'd forgive a germ for giving her a cold. But *I* don't forgive me that. I don't want to talk about it."

"Fair enough. Put it behind you. Put the whole terrible business behind you. Kate's ready to, I'm sure. But Jack, Kate's the closest thing to Marian left on this Earth. You need her. And she needs you, perhaps even more. If you love her, don't shut her out."

Jack swallowed and the lump that grew in his throat made his voice croak. "You had no right to speak to my daughter without my permission."

"She's a grown woman who I've known since she and Marian sold me Girl Scout cookies. And I don't need your permission to speak to a columnist for a magazine that Powell Diversified has advertised in for years."

"Yeah. Well. Fuck off. Both of you."

David nodded. "Exactly the reasoned, articulate initial response I'm used to from you." He slid back his chair and stood.

Jack waggled his hand. "Maybe I'll think about it a while."

"I'm used to that, too. How long a while?"

"How much scotch is left in San Francisco?"

As David stepped past he patted Jack's shoulder and whispered, "Give my very best regards to Kate."

The kid waiter reappeared with a towel, lifted Jack's

overturned cup, and sopped up the spilled coffee. "This mess'll be gone in a second, sir."

Jack watched through the window as David Powell's Bentley pulled in to the curb, picked him up, then disappeared into the rain.

"No. No, this mess is just getting warmed up." Years before, in still, cold darkness above the North Atlantic, when David and Jack had shared the cabin of a Powell Diversified jet homeward bound from London, David had confided that he saw the world as a vast, multidimensional chess game.

Jack had smiled and asked whether, if it *was*, David was always six moves ahead of everybody else. David had stretched, yawned, then said, "Usually eight."

Jack had no doubt that Kate would show up on his doorstep soon enough. He dreaded that moment. Yet he ached for it, too.

The kid nodded, smiled, and left Jack Boyle alone to boo-hoo about an immutable past that shouldn't have turned out that way and a lonely future in which the only sure thing was a hole in the ground. But then, he thought, who had anything else?

EIGHT

Seated alone at a table in the St. Francis hotel's bustling, high ceilinged, lobby breakfast bar, Ben Shepard turned the complimentary *San Francisco Chronicle*'s pages.

The article was all the way back on page three, headlined: SFPD, DHS TO SEEK DERANGED VETERAN'S VICTIM.

"Deranged?" Ben slapped the paper shut without reading the article, then tucked it into his rollaboard's front pocket before he day-checked it.

Ben's C-phone, resting on the granite table top, trilled and the caller ID lit. Petrie. The secretary had arrived back in Washington the prior afternoon.

"Good morning, Mr. Secretary."

"Did they send you the draft regulation on Canadian border security?"

"I got the email early this morning, sir."

"How long will it take you to boil it down to a four-page memo?"

"It's a very large file, sir."

"Large? It's four hundred goddam *pages* large. Why do you think I forwarded it to you? I need the summary in my inbox by noon tomorrow."

Ben stared up at the ceiling. So much for seeing the sights.

Petrie asked, "What's the print coverage like out there?"

"The story's already dropped to the inside pages. The *Chronicle* article was biased."

"Bastards."

"Not about DHS. About veterans."

"Oh. I meant about the candidacy rumors."

Ben wrinkled his forehead. Candidacy?

Petrie said, "Veterans are the VA's problem. And the media out there are Queen Maureen's problem anyway. Remember, we're putting on this dog and pony show to give Mayor Dunn an exit strategy. Let her decide where she wants the spotlight to shine. Just don't let her eat my lunch on the way to the exit."

"I know why I'm here, sir." And it's not to ungarble your metaphors. You think I'm here to be your dog or your pony or both. I'm beginning to think I'm here because veterans shouldn't be just the VA's problem. "Actually, I'm on my way now to meet the person in charge of the marine search. He works for the mayor."

"'Til he fucks up. Then he'll say you were in charge and that makes it my fault. They all will. So watch your ass with them."

Petrie cut the call.

Ben stared up at the lobby ceiling again.

Petrie thought the world had stuck an IED up his ass and everybody had a detonator but him. Some days the difference between working for the federal government in Iraq and working for the federal government in California seemed to be only the price of breakfast.

Ben peeked inside the leather check folder that the counter attendant had brought with his pastry, and swore.

With tip, he had already burned through too much of his Government Services Agency per diem on coffee, a warmed danish, and a newspaper that suddenly seemed less complimentary.

Ben returned his attention to his own exit strategy. He couldn't charge breakfast to his room, because he'd already checked out. Petrie had tasked his aide to remain in San Francisco to "liaise with local authorities indefinitely" so Ben was no longer part of a cabinet officer's traveling circus. Ben needed to find GSA-approved cheaper lodging, preferably with breakfast included, or go broke.

Ben slid his last three tens from his wallet into the check folder, made a mental note to find an ATM, and stepped to the register.

The counter attendant who had brought over the warm danish and the check was pretty, and had smiled more like a woman interested in him than like a server interested in maximizing her tip. Long journeys began with first steps. Just because so far they had ended in stumbles didn't excuse him from trying.

The silver tag on her vest read: CASSANDRA.

Grand hotels like the St. Francis justified their rates with perquisites like free newspapers and chatty, attractive staff who wore built-in conversation starters.

He matched her smile, handed the check folder to

her, and opened his mouth to ask how she got such a pretty name.

Her fingertips brushed his hand, her smile froze, and she recoiled. She looked up at an invisible point beyond his shoulder, said, "Have a nice day, sir." Then she turned to the next customer.

Ben splayed the index, middle, and ring fingers that remained on his right hand on the counter while he balled his left hand into a fist.

Compared to the legs and lives his comrades had lost, the stump of his missing little finger was an unworthy dismemberment and he was an unworthy survivor. Maybe veterans were the VA's problem, like Petrie said, but the VA didn't even count a lost finger or toe as a major amputation. Not that Ben disagreed.

He couldn't complain that it really handicapped him. The lack of a small finger discouraged only occupations that weren't on most people's short lists anyway. Neurosurgeon. Violinist. Quarterback.

But a hand couldn't be covered by a pant leg, or hidden beneath a table napkin for the duration of a first date. And he couldn't blame women who opted out of a second date with Captain Hook. It wasn't just eligible women who cringed. The right hand was the only part of another human being that people deliberately touched on a routine basis.

Suck it up, Shepard. Do your job. If you had... He shook it off, the way he had been taught to, the way he should have learned to long before he did.

Ben checked his bag, app'd a car, then stared out its window at thousands of ten-fingered people surging through Union Square, and wondered why he worked for Petrie.

It wasn't the money, although, GI Bill or not, this year off to accumulate savings would ease Ben's last two years of law school. It wasn't the workload, which was unreasonable even for a cabinet staffer. And Petrie treated Ben like a pony only when he ran out of ways to treat him like a dog. But then, Petrie treated people like dogs no matter how many fingers they had. On balance, being pitied or avoided was worse than being treated just like everybody else.

The car climbed, then descended, through the city, and deposited Ben in the small parking lot of a low brick government office whose windows looked out on the Hyde Street Pier and San Francisco Bay beyond.

An SFPD Marine Unit cop led Ben out of the building, let him through a locked gate, then pointed him down a sloping, railed walkway. The walkway ended at the beginning of a concrete sidewalk on stilts that held it a foot above San Francisco Bay's wave crests. A hundred zig-zag yards along the pier Ben's objective bobbed in its slip, among dozens of other boats.

Water. Why did the damn car have to fall in the water?

Low lead clouds scudded across the morning sky driven by a wind that smelled of creosote, fish, and diesel.

Against its chill, Ben zipped his jacket, turned up his collar, then slid one foot out onto the pier as though it were mined. Raised a Kansan, he had never set foot in saltwater, a life experience deficiency he had no desire to fix. Although the student in him had spent two hours the night before Googling nautical vocabulary.

By the time he reached the boat it had become

clear that piers were less deadly than they looked, and he walked normally, albeit near neither edge.

San Francisco Police Marine 1 was nearly fifty feet long, gleaming white-painted metal, and the bow that pointed at him was painted with a diagonal swath of police blue that extended from the deck to the waterline, overprinted with a blue and gold San Francisco Police shield.

The boat's foredeck stood six feet above the water, four feet above the pier, and its antennaed, canopied superstructure rose like a stepped pyramid another ten feet above the deck.

A boat was, really, little different from a combine or an armored personnel carrier. All three were heavy-gauge metal folded and welded around a diesel that deafened you when it ran right, spit oil on you when it didn't, and that would maim or kill you if you disrespected it.

But this machine bobbed and wove even when shut down. And if you fell off it could drown you.

The only person visible stood on the boat's heaving deck near the bow. His back was turned to Ben while he clung with one hand to the bow's waist-high rail and polished it with a rag gripped in the other. Balding and gray, the man wore black rubber boots with the tops turned down, and blue coveralls.

Ben walked until he stood on the pier opposite the man, then shouted over the waves' slap and boom and the screeches of gulls that wheeled overhead. "I'm looking for the officer in charge of the San Francisco Police Underwater Recovery Unit!"

The man glanced over his shoulder. "You Shepard?" He waved Ben forward, then turned away and shouted, "Come aboard!"

Crap. Ben's heart thumped. Can't I just wait here until you come back to land?

The boat's forward deck was a moving target, its handrail set back perhaps a foot from the hull's edge. The wave-churned gap between the pier and the deck constantly shrank, then grew, fluctuating between a foot and two feet wide. The water's translucent depths and the perils within them were unknowable.

Ben took two steps back, gauged the boat's movement cycle, then gathered himself to run, then leap.

The gray-haired man turned his head. "Holy Jeez!" He spun toward Ben and rushed forward, arms extended and fingers splayed. "Whoa!"

The man pointed twenty feet farther down the boat's hull, where a cutout in the vessel's flank brought the bobbing deck level with the pier. Boat and pier were held apart by inflated, floating fenders so that the shifting gap between them was only a foot or two. "Step aboard down there at the recovery well."

The man led him from the deck through a hatch and two steps down to a compartment in the boat's gut that reminded Ben of an armored personnel carrier: fold-down metal seats in a cramped metal box, in constant, unpredictable motion. One thing that this boat offered that no APC did was a built-in coffeemaker.

The man poured two mugs, sat down across from Ben at a bare metal table that extended out from the hull's inner surface, and handed him one. "Mick Shay. I suppose you could call me the officer in charge of the Underwater Recovery Unit. But these days my title's Marine Unit Maintenance Officer."

Shay's eyes twinkled behind wire-rimmed glasses, and above a brushy moustache. When the two of them shook hands, if Shay noticed Ben's missing finger, he gave no sign.

Shay had peeled off rubber gloves, and his thick, bare left forearm was tattooed "USN" across an anchor design.

Ben pointed. "Navy man?"

"Destroyer man. Much better class of people than the rest of the outfit. Master Chief Petty Officer, retired. Based on the way you board a vessel, I'd say you're not navy."

Ben smiled. "Army. Infantryman. Much stupider class of people than the rest of the outfit. First lieutenant honorably discharged."

Shay smiled, bowed his head a notch. "Flattered to make your acquaintance, Lieutenant. Most folks aren't so anxious to meet me that they'd broad jump the ocean to do it." He shifted in his seat. "Mr. Shepard, may I ask whether the DHS believes the driver might be alive?"

Ben stuck out his lower lip. "Why does that matter?"

"Turf. Jurisdictions in the Bay area overlap more than a fat man's love handles. If you think the driver's alive, or he died accidentally, it's a rescue. San Francisco Fire Department's got jurisdiction over aquatic rescue. In which case I go back to polishing boat rails and you continue this discussion with some Fire Department lifeguards who mostly polish their Speedos. If crime evidence underwater needs recovering, SFPD Marine Unit Dive Team's in charge."

Ben narrowed his eyes. "Rescue? Are you saying that you believe Colibri could have survived?"

Shay shook his head. "Hell no. Suicides jump off the 'Gate literally every other week. They hit the water at seventy-five miles an hour. Five percent survive the sudden stop, then drown or die of hypothermia. And the papers say the bomb blew Mr. Colibri and his fancy car to bits before he even hit the water, anyway."

"Actually, maybe not. The only eyewitness said the car went over the side in one piece."

Shay cocked his head. "New Year's Eve. Sober witness?"

Ben smiled. "Probably. Turns out he may have been right. This bomb was designed to blowtorch through the floorboard of a conventional car, then spend its energy burning out everything inside. Like an RPG guts a tank. The hulk and the driver's body should have wound up a smoking pile on the pavement."

Shay grunted, sipped his coffee. "Why didn't they?"

"Because a Galvani's not conventional, Mick. It runs on a tray full of batteries. The tray forms the whole underside of the car. It's also the car's backbone. In this prototype, the tray was titanium and the body was carbon fiber. Even stronger, and also way lighter, than the tray and body in a production Galvani. The experts think this bomb was designed to break a conventional car's back. But the prototype was too rigid and too light. So instead the explosion just pushed the whole car up like champagne bubbles pop a cork."

"Mr. Shepard, I'm a sailor, not the highway patrol, but I've seen tin-foil balls that were perfectly good cars going seventy-five before they hit a wall. Conventional or not. The channel there's three hundred feet and change deep."

"Mick!" Ben raised his palm. "You had me at 'Hell no.'"

"All right then." Shay pumped his fist, grinned, and inclined his head. "Mr. Shepard, the founding officer of the URU is at your service."

"Oh. Then when will the URU divers start?"

"They won't. URU started as a conduit to use civilian volunteer divers to fish murder weapons and dope baggies out of golf course ponds. The only paid employee it ever had was me. Marine Unit's got its own full-time divers now. URU's just an excuse to make my real job more fundable, 'cause I'm too old to dive and too stubborn to retire for the second time. I earn my check painting bulkheads when there's no evidence to recover, and offering grandfatherly advice when there is. Which, by the way, is why they stuck you with me instead of somebody in the unit who has a real job."

"Oh."

"Second place, three hundred feet's for seasoned, saturation-certified specialists with oversized life insurance policies. Which Marine Unit's divers aren't."

"Then—"

"And even for pros the channel bottom under that bridge is a sandstorm in the middle of the desert in the middle of the night."

"Then how—?"

"Side-scan sonar first. The Marine Unit's got pole-mounted sonar equipment that might work. But I found an outfit out of Houston that wants to test a prototype towfish designed to operate in high-energy environments like the Golden Gate Channel. They'll work for free 'cause if their prototype locates the wreckage they'll brag about it to the paying customers. Marine 1 here can tow the fish, and she needs the hours of sea time to justify her existence."

"You said first. What's second?"

"Then we'll need a saturation dive spread, or if I

have my way a remotely operated vehicle, to poke around and take pictures. Or raise the wreck. Not cheap. Could take weeks."

Ben sighed.

Weeks? If Ben couldn't find some visible activity that at least looked like progress, Petrie would demand something idiotic to advance his political ambitions. Ben frowned. "Can't we do *something* else in the meantime?"

Shay shrugged. "You could hire a recon drone to survey the ocean seaward of the bridge and hope to spot a floater."

"Sounds also not cheap. What are the odds?"

"Pretty good."

"Really?"

"Not of *your* floater. You'd be surprised how many drunks and suicides think they can swim."

NINE

Kate Boyle backed her Corolla down the steep, narrow cul-de-sac in Russian Hill, hemmed in on both sides by unaffordable condoized three-story row houses, and by the equally unaffordable sedans that the condos' techie owners and renters wedged nose-to-tail along the curbs in front of the houses.

Kate had been prowling for four blocks and nine minutes after inching past the house where she grew up, in search of a close parking space. Though the last time she had actually found a space close to home the Giants had a decent closer.

She hadn't been up into the city from Palo Alto since the week after the funeral, and the truth, she admitted, was that she had felt relieved when she couldn't immediately find a spot today. Because it delayed the confrontation for a couple more minutes.

Ten spaces downhill, and on the opposite side of the street, she spotted a fender twitch in her rear view and squeezed her steering wheel's rim.

From the opposite direction, a lurking silver Beemer sprang uphill, turn signal flashing to lay claim to the space.

"Bastard!" The Beemer had her by four car lengths.

She floored the Corolla and caught a break when the exiting Maserati reversed after clearing its space. She plunged the Corolla's tail into the void that the Maser had left, before the Beemer could get within ten yards.

After the Maser cleared out the foiled Beemer slam-braked to a stop a foot from the Corolla's already-dented door panel.

The Beemer driver blipped down his passenger side window and screamed so loud that she heard every syllable through her own closed windows. "That shit box have a turn signal, bitch?"

Kate extended the appropriate finger, then smiled to herself and softly recited aloud what her father had said when he taught her how to drive in San Francisco. "Never signal, Katy. That's just givin' aid and comfort to the enemy."

She waited, angled across the narrow street with her doors locked, until the Beemer driver bowed to the inevitable and backed away. She toed off her heels, squirmed into her Nikes, finished parking, then hoofed it. Four blocks, and every step felt uphill.

By the time she reached the house, she had to set the quiche that she had bought before she drove in from Palo Alto on the sidewalk, while she wheezed, hands on knees, and stared up at the place.

Mom had loved the house's view out to the Golden Gate from the upper floors. He hated housework even more than he hated organized religion. But he scrubbed the windows to sparkling transparency every Sunday that Kate could remember, while Mom attended mass, and when he would have preferred to be watching the early games underway on the East Coast. Because he knew it would make her smile.

Apart from Jack Boyle's many Neanderthal qualities, he possessed a few that his daughter admired. Foremost his unconditional and unending devotion to the few people about whom he gave a shit. That made her father unique among men. At least among all the men Kate had trusted since puberty.

But as Kate peered up today, the third-floor windows were black with grime.

Regardless, the place was distinguished by two bay-windowed stories over a one-car garage. By now, there couldn't be more than a half dozen family homes left in Russian Hill that hadn't flipped. If Dad ever sold, the location and view alone would draw silly-money bids from redevelopers, who would split the place into flats, then rent them to the twenty-something video game designers and app developers who were the only San Franciscans who could afford them.

After four minutes, Kate knew her pounding heart wouldn't slow further if she shivered there 'til dark. Like she had a week after the funeral, when he pretended he wasn't home.

She straightened, muttered, "David Powell, if you're wrong I'll castrate you," then stepped to the door.

Kate balanced the quiche in one hand, rang the bell with the other, then held the quiche between both hands, chest-high in front of her. Less as a peace offering than to finesse the awkward moment. Dad didn't hug.

The door opened, and he stood there looking the same, mostly. Same pilled, unbuttoned cardigan. Same thick brush of gray hair. Cut the same short length as it had been when short hair mortified one's daughter. Less paunch than a sixty-something man was entitled to. But the eyes that always twinkled at the sight of her were dull, unlit stones.

She extended her offering.

He snorted. "Quiche?"

"Eggs. Ham. Cheese. Pie crust. You loved Mom's."

He tilted his head back, read the label through his bifocals, then snorted again. "Mom's wasn't organic and gluten-free."

"Dad, those are dietary positives."

"Those are code for 'cardboard.'" He stood aside from the doorway, then sighed. "Put it on the dining room table."

"On top of the pizza boxes or under them?" When she passed she smelled alcohol on him, old newspapers, and something thick in the air that may once have been cheese. And Holy Christ there wasn't a square foot of table or counter not piled with clothing, magazines, or dishes. "Okay. We're skipping the quiche."

"Fine. Scotch doesn't need embellishment."

"No scotch."

"What?"

"We'll go out for pie. When I was little you used to take me out for pie."

"There's no pie in San Francisco since Bepple's closed."

"Bepple's closed in 1993."

If a man mourned a pie store for twenty-seven years, how long could he mourn the loss of half of himself?

When David Powell had told her that he thought her father was ready to reconnect with her and with the world, she had expected a delicate, painful journey. She should also have expected that on the journey she would have to drive the bus all by herself. "Find your coat, Dad. It's four blocks to my car."

"The Ford's in the garage. I'll—"

"You're half-bagged. The fresh air'll do you good."

Kate and her father stood, hands in coat pockets, in the pie shop on Mission. They stared up at the overhead menus while the aroma of the pies, arrayed in the old-wood glass cases to their front, and of strong coffee, drifted across them. This place had been to her and her friends as, she supposed, Bepple's had been to him. How long before the Hispanic family that ran it were displaced by a glass box filled with people who could pay sixty bucks for a reindeer moss salad?

Jack read aloud, then snorted. "Vegan Avocado?"

The counterman smiled. "Señorita?"

"The Pear Raspberry with brown rice crust." She jerked a thumb at Jack. "He'll have the Dutch Apple."

"Only if they're free-range apples."

Kate sighed and raised two fingers. "And black coffees. Extra large."

Once they sat, Kate's father inverted his first forkful of pie as though he expected to find scorpions crawling its underside, then tasted and raised his eyebrows. "Not bad. Not Bepple's."

"Dad," She closed her eyes, opened them, "Nothing will ever be Bepple's again. But the world's still got good pie."

He grunted, cut another bite.

She took a deep breath. "I'm sorry about the funeral."

"You?"

Of *course* not me. "I should have pushed harder to let Kirk deliver the eulogy for you. You know, he debated for Harvard. And you hadn't passed beyond the anger stage of grief. People understand it's hard for a spouse to hold it together."

"Kirk the Jerk? He never even met your mother."

"True, he never did." And also true you turned out to be right about Kirk, whose fidelity didn't match his rugby shoulders and his velvet tongue.

Jack said, "And I held it together."

"You did. Mom was a practicing Catholic and you're agnostic but—"

Jack pointed at her. "But we made it work! You're the living proof." He sipped coffee. "I just expressed my doubts. It was no time to lie."

Oh God, it was exactly time to lie.

Kate nodded anyway. "Dad, there may be a time and a place to debate the proposition that religion was invented by extortionists to peddle afterlife to suckers who couldn't deal with their loved one's deaths. In front of two hundred Catholics and Mom's sister the nun wasn't it."

"Oh?" He pointed at the ceiling. "You believe your mother's sitting on a cloud listening to this conversation?"

Of course not. I'm your daughter. I've grown up just as cynical and secular as you are. Except I'm Mom's daughter, too, so, I dunno. And it's too soon, far too soon, for the two of us to talk about Mom. "Dad, neither of us needs to get into that right now."

"You know that priest?"

"Father Alvarez? The one you turned to at the pulpit and called a lying mackerel snapper?"

Jack rolled his eyes. "I didn't call him a pedophile, for chrissake!"

"Oh. Full marks for restraint there, Dad."

He pointed at her again. "You didn't get that sarcastic tongue from your mother!"

"Well that narrows it down."

"Did you know that hypocrite came to the house the week after the funeral? To forgive me because we all say things we don't mean in times of stress." Jack Boyle scrubbed his eyes with his paper napkin, then wrung it as though squeezing out nonexistent tears. Then he rolled his eyes again. "And to thank me for the twenty thousand your mother left them."

"And that pissed you off?" She felt her cheeks burn. You opened your door to someone you considered a pedophilic hypocrite, but not to your own daughter?

"When he came in he looked around and nodded and said Marian and I had created a beautiful, loving home."

Father Alvarez must have arrived before the mozzarella in the pizza boxes turned black.

"Wow, Dad. What an awful thing for him to say." Kate rolled her eyes. She hadn't realized until this conversation how often her father did that. Or where she had picked up the mannerism.

Jack pointed at her again. "Don't you roll your eyes at me, young lady! Your mother's twenty grand wasn't enough for the snappers. They expect me to leave the house to them instead of to you. Don't you get that?"

What I get is you're the only person left in this world I can count on. Or at least you used to be.

And we have a long, long bus ride ahead of us to get back to that place. And in the meantime I need a subject change before I lunge across this table and choke the crap out of you.

She tasted her pie, chewed, swallowed. "David Powell got my managing editor to cut me loose on indefinite special assignment. To research a bio piece about Manuel Colibri. On condition that you help."

"You do see what David's doing? He's manipulating us both. This special investigator business is crap. There's nothing special here to investigate. He just wants his Eagle Scout badge in family counseling."

"Speak for yourself. Dad, Cardinal Systems is the mysterious black hole of the industry I cover. And Colibri built Cardinal. But people know even less about him than about the company he built."

"Well, he's not going to build it any bigger. He's old news."

"No. This could be the kind of story I got into journalism to write. I can feel it. It could be a steppingstone that would get me back to where I left off at the *Post*. You know what I write now? Profile pieces about millionaire computer geeks whose idea of hardship is acne. If I'd known, I would've gone back to Washington after Mom . . ." Christ, you just said we weren't going to get into that. Kate sucked in a breath. "Dad, I'd eat dirt to write this story even if—"

"If what?"

"Dad, I'll put it this way. If this assignment was algebra story problems I'd still do it," her eyes moistened, she blinked, swallowed, "to get our life back. I miss Mom, too, Dad. But now I miss the way you were even more."

Kate watched her father stare into his empty coffee cup and her heart pounded while she waited for a reaction.

"Algebra? That D you got in Algebra II was a gift to you from Mrs. Walker. So you'd graduate with your class. She showed me your grades. The final didn't bring them up to passing but she gave you extra credit for coming in for tutoring."

"You never told me that."

When did you start digging boots out of the memory locker, then kicking your only child with them? This may be hopeless.

"Of course I didn't tell you that. That's the point. I wouldn't tell Willie Mays he was a lousy violinist, either. You already had early acceptance at Columbia. All you needed was to graduate. I swear I didn't ask her to pass you. She thought you earned it."

"Oh."

"Your gift was journalism." He looked up and smiled. "Still is. I read your column every week. Every word. Three times. Haven't found a single one that needed changing yet."

"You never told me that, either."

His eyes glistened. "Should have. Just did." He swallowed. "You really want to write this article, then?"

Kate nodded. "Not just want to. Need to. Bad. You didn't put me through Columbia so I could leave the world the same."

"And you only get to write this article if I throw in with you?"

She nodded again. "That's David's deal."

Jack shook his head. "You may need this aggravation. But I don't."

Kate's heart skipped. "Yes, you do, Dad. Even worse than I do."

He stared down at the crumbs left on his empty plate. Then he patted both palms on the tabletop, looked up, grinned, and for that instant his eyes shone like they had on sunny Saturday mornings when he dragged her out of bed for swimming practice. "So, where do we start, Katy?"

Her throat swelled and she bit her lip. You haven't called me Katy since...

Kate looked down at the table top and blinked back tears, then looked up. "Where do we start, Dad? Depends. What do you already know?"

"About Cardinal? I don't even know why they call it Cardinal. It sounds like they sell bird feeders."

She smiled. "Cardinal actually didn't start as an information systems company. And that certainly isn't all it is now. It was founded by Frank Cardinale. He was a boat radio repairman down on Fisherman's Wharf, kind of an eccentric loner. In the mid-sixties he started his own business on a shoestring to manufacture a fish finder he'd patented. But he was afraid Americans wouldn't buy a complex electrical product from an Italian so he dropped the *e* from the company name. He must have been right, because fifteen years later he'd built Cardinal Systems into the powerhouse of marine electronics, without going public."

"I thought Colibri was the rags-to-riches story."

Kate nodded. "He was Cardinal's *second* rags-to-riches story. 'Til the eighties, all people remember about Manuel Colibri is this quiet little guy who knocked around the waterfront doing odd jobs. Then he landed a full-time position as a janitor's assistant at Cardinal. The legend is that Colibri worked hard, worked smart, and Frank Cardinale identified with Colibri's humble beginnings. As Frank aged, his mental acuity diminished, and he gradually passed control to Colibri. By the time Frank died, Colibri was running the place. Colibri immediately sold the marine electronics business. He reinvested the proceeds buying new assets and new ideas all over the Silicon Valley almost before people started calling the valley that."

"Smart."

Kate shook her head. "Nobody thought so at the time. Smart entrepreneurs risk *other people's* money looking for the next big thing, not their own. But a trillion dollars later, everybody thinks Colibri was a genius for staying private and self-funding. Self-funding meant that when a bet paid off, the payoff was bigger. And nobody knew *how* big the payoff was, or what he'd reinvest the payoff in next. And everything he invested in next seemed to turn out to be the next big thing."

Kate's father laid down his fork, narrowed his eyes. "David mentioned this ELCIE. That people thought it had to do with what Colibri was betting on next."

Kate pushed back her chair and nodded. "That is what people thought. That's what I still think. And that's the kind of story problem I'm good at, Dad. Based on my instincts and training, I vote we start with a visit to ELCIE."

Jack stood, then stared at the display case. "I vote we start with a cherry pie to go."

TEN

Ben Shepard stood and squinted into the wind on the fly bridge atop the police boat where he had met Mick Shay the day before. Shay stood alongside him, his legs adjusting effortlessly to the deck's roll, which was gentled by the curved pier that separated Hyde Street Harbor from San Francisco Bay.

Ben clung with both hands to a chest-high grab bar and looked out across the water. Beyond the sea wall, whitecaps salted the bay. In the distance ferries large enough to swallow a half dozen of this boat, and freighters vast enough to swallow a half dozen of those ferries, cut smoothly through the waves. But, despite the clear sunshine, boats as small as this one were scarce, and the few that Ben saw bobbed on the waves like drifting corks.

Ben ran one hand over his life vest's clasps. "Mick, is a police boat big enough to go out there today?"

Shay covered his moustache with one hand and coughed. "Police boat? Mr. Shepard, this is a Textron

MLB 47 self-righting, self-baling motor lifeboat. The finest foul-weather rescue vessel God ever put on water, and the pride of the United States Coast Guard. A twenty-foot wave can capsize her and she'll right herself and bale herself dry before a Coastie can pee his pants."

"Oh." Ben swallowed. Was there a less reassuring vessel in which to go to sea for the first time than one expected to capsize?

Shay winked and clapped Ben's shoulder. "Mr. Shepard, you'll live to tell this day's tale, I promise. But if you don't like the water, stay here. We can handle this."

Shay knew as well as he did that Ben was just here for show. They both were. Ben could wave the DHS flag from dry land as visibly as he could wave it from the deck of this death trap. And Ben was connected with this underlying crime only by the accident of common service with the criminal. But it had stained Ben and every vet, and Ben had learned the hard way that the only way to deal with some irrational fears was to confront them.

Ben shook his head. "I'm going."

The third person on the bridge stood by the helm, which consisted of an adjustable high-backed armchair set on the fly bridge's right, starboard, side. In front of the chair were controls and instruments, and to its right were hand-operated throttles that controlled the boat's two diesel engines. The principal control, of course, was a steering wheel. This boat's wheel was the size of, and set at the flat angle of, the kind Ben was used to seeing on a city bus. The coxswain wore the same uniform as Shay and the other three members of the boat's crew did, blue police utilities and an SFPD Marine Unit ball cap crested with oars crossed over a life ring.

She looked up, frowning, and asked Shay, "Mick, you wanna see how much longer your contractor needs to turn my beautiful boat into a damn tug?"

Ben followed Shay down a ladder to the bob-tailed boat's afterdeck and asked, "The crew's unhappy they're pulling this duty?"

Mick shook his head as he jerked a thumb toward the coxswain on the fly bridge. "This ain't the Army. Mr. Shepard, the best way to turn unhappy cops into happy cops is pay 'em overtime. Which we are. She just thinks towing sonar behind her MLB 47 is like using a racing catamaran to haul garbage. Which is a fuckin' horselaugh since ninety percent of this boat's operating hours are chuggin' around McCovey Cove outside the ballpark during Giants games, tellin' people to put on life jackets."

"But is she right about this boat?"

Mick ran his fingers across the superstructure's smooth white skin. "Marine 1's a thoroughbred hooked to a beer wagon, for sure. She's got newer electronics and engines than a Coastie MLB. But the alternatives to using her were using up hours on a workhorse boat that already gets too many, or requesting a hydrographic survey boat from NOAA. National Oceanic and Atmospheric Administration paper pushin's slow as traffic. And the People's Republic of San Francisco don't invite Washington into its business unless hell cools to room temperature. Present company excepted, of course."

On the afterdeck knelt a slender, curly-haired man in a logoed tan windbreaker and matching cap. He bent over a yellow, rear-finned torpedo decaled with the same logo as his cap. The sonar towfish was as long as the contractor's representative was tall, and was as thick as the man's arm.

A yellow, braided electrical cable was plugged into the torpedo's midsection, then lay coiled on the deck and connected through a second device, a delta-winged yellow glider as wide as a man's shoulders. From the glider the cable curled up and through a pulley that hung suspended from an A-frame hanger of tubular metal that the sonar contractor's representative had affixed to the deck. The pulley hung out over the water beyond the boat's stern. The cable snaked back from the pulley to a horizontal cable spool like a motorized and oversized fishing reel. The reel, too, was affixed to the boat's afterdeck. The mechanism would allow the yellow fish to be towed through the depths like a fisherman's lure.

The sonar contractor's rep stood and stretched. "Towfish is good to go. If I run the predeployment tests while we're underway, we might have time to find what you're looking for yet today."

Ten minutes later, Ben and Mick stood again on the fly bridge alongside the coxswain as she idled the rumbling police boat past the opening in the harbor pier.

The lifeboat cleared the pier and the coxswain pushed the throttles forward. The boat accelerated and its bow lifted as it sped toward the Golden Gate, orange and majestic in the morning sun.

The wind flushed Ben's cheeks and he grinned at Shay. "Do they always ride up here outside when the weather's good?"

Mick nodded. "Even more when it's bad. Or when there's serious business to do. Better visibility, and us old salts prefer the wheel to a joystick. Which is how you steer from the other control stations."

Ben kept grinning. There was joy in this assignment all.

Ten minutes later, Ben's grin had faded as the lifeboat rose, fell, and pounded through wave after wave at twenty-five teeth-rattling knots.

The coxswain leaned toward Ben. "Sir, you don't look too good."

"Don't feel too good."

"Sorry. MLBs are stable for their size, but they're built for buoyancy, not comfort."

An interesting fact. Not therapeutic, but interesting.

"The survivor's compartment below is the most stable space aboard. And there's Dramamine in the aid kit. If you can keep it down."

A half hour later, Ben staggered out on deck from the compartment with the coffeemaker, leaned over the boat's rail, and evacuated his complimentary hot breakfast, and probably the aid kit's Dramamine, into the waters of San Francisco Bay.

Shay laid an arm across Ben's shoulders. "I know, Mr. Shepard. But don't jump. The swim to shore's too far."

Ben wiped tears from his eyes and drool onto his windbreaker sleeve. "When I die, it won't be in the water." He waved his hand at the hatch from which he had emerged. "Prefer to die indoors." Whoever named it the survivors' compartment had a keen sense of irony.

"Stay up here in the fresh air, sir. Keep your eyes

fixed on the horizon. That helps. And maybe some of that Dramamine stuck."

Ten minutes later, Shay proved a prophet, and Ben staggered, weak but relieved, forward.

Unlike a car, the MLB could be operated from multiple driver's seats. The coxswain continued to drive from the fly bridge while Ben and Mick Shay stood below her, in the wide windowed, and currently underutilized, enclosed bridge. The curly-haired sonar operator sat in front of his laptop, set up on a stowable chart table, while they peered over his shoulder.

The sonar rep pointed at one of two rectangles displayed side-by-side on his laptop's screen. "This one's the GPS feed. Actually, I just plugged my phone in here, and the nav app's not much different from what you use to find a coffee shop. In fact, it's all Windows-based plug-and-play software."

Shay looked at Ben and shrugged.

A ship outline crawled bottom-to-top of the GPS feed's blue rectangle like a red beetle.

The rep shifted his finger. "This is the feed from the towfish."

The other rectangle resembled a two-lane high-way viewed from above that scrolled slowly from the screen's top down.

Ben pointed. "The centerline's—"

The rep nodded. "The axis the boat's moving along. We're towing the fish parallel to the bottom. To record in water this deep, we tow the fish behind the depressor wing you saw lying out on the afterdeck. It forces the fish deeper. The wing's like the plane that tows an advertising banner above a ballpark. Side scan sonar's transmitting sound energy from the fish at a specific frequency, in a pattern like a Chinese fan was hanging below the fish. When the energy encounters an object, the object bounces some of the energy back and the fish hears it."

Ben said, "Ping?"

The sonar operator nodded. "Ping. Like in the movies, more or less."

Ben asked, "What have you found so far?"

"So far I've been tuning up, not finding. The depressor wing keeps the fish down, but the currents in this channel make keeping the fish stable difficult. And we have to adjust for the velocity of sound through the temperature and composition of the water the fish is moving through. Then we correct for noise, adjust boat speed for the frequency the fish is set to transmit and receive. Then we're ready to take pictures."

"How sharp are the pictures?"

"Depends. If we ping at lower frequencies we can search wider areas with a single pass. But the resolution's lower, too, so the imaging's fuzzier. If we ID something of interest, we mark the location as a target then make another pass across it at higher frequency."

Ben asked, "How fuzzy are we talking about?"

"Once we know what we want to look at, under the right conditions, 1600 Kilohertz can show you details less than a centimeter wide. Half the width of a dime."

The rep spoke to the coxswain over the ship phone. "Good to go. Come about and let's start working through the grid."

Ben's heart ticked up a beat and he leaned on the rep's chair back and stared. The bottom of the Golden Gate Channel, pitch black and three hundred feet beneath and behind him, glowed on the screen like a yellow-brown desert, visible in every wrinkle and dune.

He pointed at the screen. "That curved, floating line?"

"An actual fish. At least its reflective parts. This thing's really just a glorified fish finder."

Ben had never caught a fish, much less tried to find one. He shook his head slowly as he whispered, "Amazing!"

He was here to cover Arthur Petrie's ass and to bear witness. But now he was hunting buried treasure, and it bordered on fun.

An hour later, Ben straightened, stretched, and peered out the enclosed bridge's tall windows at the Golden Gate's red arch, and far beyond the bridge the needles and blocks of San Francisco's skyline. Most of the time, this view out the window was more amazing than the view of the bottom of the sea, after all. The real fish turned out to be scarce, and he hadn't seen a doubloon yet.

"Hmm." The rep grunted.

Ben flicked his eyes down from the Golden Gate Bridge to the laptop's screen. A squared off corner of something crawled into view at the edge of the yellow-brown road. They said the rarest thing in nature was a straight line.

Ben squeezed the rep's shoulder. "What's that?"

Mick had been napping in the enclosed bridge's right-hand seat. At the sound of Ben's voice he swung to his feet and stood behind the rep.

The sonar technician opened another screen window in which the object showed larger, and had been frozen. He moused a cross-shaped cursor over the corner of the image, dragged it to the opposite corner and clicked.

"Eight feet, six inches." The rep turned to Mick and shrugged.

Mick shrugged back. "Yeah. Fuck it."

Ben's mouth hung open. "What? You can't even see what it is."

Mick said, "Standard intermodal shipping container's a steel box eight feet by eight feet six inches in end dimension. Ten thousand of 'em fall off container ships every year."

"But—"

"Full of doubloons?" Shay shook his head. "Cheap plastic crap from China, Mr. Shepard. And it sure ain't your electric sports car."

Shay settled back into his chair and tilted his cap's bill over his eyes.

Twenty minutes after Shay's dismissal of the shipping container, Ben stood, pouting, at Marine 1's bow as he clung to the waist-high rail with one hand while he unzipped his fly with the other and relieved himself. Marine 1 was faced about toward the open ocean as it trolled the towfish, moving so slowly that the wind blowing off the land pressed against Ben's back. One common denominator between Kansas and the Pacific Ocean was the folly of pissing into the wind, which Ben had concluded his current assignment here at the bow amounted to.

Shay came forward and stood beside him. "Spotted any grays yet, Mr. Shepard?"

Shay had sent Ben forward to watch for whales, and insisted it wasn't the maritime equivalent of a snipe hunt. "It's bullshit, isn't it, Mick?"

Shay shook his head as he raised his palm. "God's

truth, Mr. Shepard. Night and day from November to March every year twenty thousand gray whales migrate past the Golden Gate south from the Arctic Circle to the lagoons off Baja California. The single girls are lookin' to get lucky, the pregnant ones are lookin' to drop their calves, and the cows who already have calves just want to dodge the orcas."

At that moment, a hundred yards ahead, a pectoral fin larger than a car's hood broke the water as casually as a swimmer's arm, gray and crusted in white.

Ben pointed. "Ah!"

Then a grouping appeared where the flipper had been. A half dozen hillocks bulged the sea's surface upward as they moved right to left, or as Ben corrected himself, starboard to port. Then the hillocks parted as the great, glistening gray snakes of six whales' backs, large ones and small, rolled forward, then vanished.

Ben's jaw hung slack.

"That's what I thought you'd say. They're a sight you never get tired of. They mostly hug the shoreline, but when they have to cross the open water of the mouth of a bay, like this one or down at Monterey, they pack into groups."

"Why?"

"Orcas—killer whales—try to squeeze in between a cow and her calf and cut the little one away from the pod."

At that moment Ben felt and heard the diesels' pitch change and the boat's progress toward the huge animals slowed abruptly.

Shay said, "The cox just throttled the engines back. Federal buffer's three hundred feet, unless they swim up."

Ben frowned. "You mean they swim at us?"

Shay laughed and shook his head. "Yes, Mr. Shepard. *Moby Dick* was based on a true story. But grays swim up to tourist boats all the time looking for a nose pat, not a fight. I think they're more interested in us than we are in them. The buffer's not to protect us from the whale. But a full-grown gray's longer than this boat. If we did T-bone one, the fine and the misdemeanor would be the least of our worries."

Ben and Mick stood at the bow, scanning the sea, then a gray breached ten yards off the starboard bow, water coursing off its vast black body as its great head rose ten feet above Ben's eye level. The whale expelled its breath with a roar, crashed back into the water, then vanished again beneath the sea. A blink later the only evidence of the whale's existence was the drifting mist cloud that settled onto their skin, their clothing, and onto the boat's deck.

Shay whooped.

So far today, Ben had vomited over a boat rail, discovered a pirate's treasure chest as big as a GI's Containerized Housing Unit, but less valuable than a losing lottery ticket, and had been sneezed on by a whale. All things considered, in terms of seeing the world's wonders, today beat the best day he ever had in Iraq.

Two hours later, Ben stood on SFPD Marine 1's afterdeck and stared at a reddening sun dipping toward the western horizon. The taut towfish cable cut down into the waves behind the boat. Breaching whales and sunken treasure aside, he was beginning to wonder whether this voyage was just pissing into the wind.

The MLB's coffeepot was empty, and the boat

had just come about and begun to sweep another overlapped swath, as though the boat were mowing a vast lawn, but guided precisely along its path by its GPS. The boat continued through the water as slowly as a riding lawn mower, so the towfish could transmit and recover its pings. The litter the towfish had found on the channel bottom consisted of another shipping container, a half-buried truck chassis that Shay opined, based on the curve of its rotted hood, dated to World War II, and undecipherable bits of chain, cable, building materials, and miscellaneous machinery so numerous that Ben had stopped counting.

"Hey." The pitch of the sonar man's voice was elevated as it drifted out through the enclosed bridge's open hatch.

By the time Ben reached the enclosed bridge, the sonar man had opened a window on his laptop's screen that showed a "snapshot" of a target lying flat on the bottom.

It was a disc, perforated in a pinwheel pattern, and by the scale the size of an automobile wheel without a tire.

The sonar man called up an internet image of the Galvani prototype on a stage at the 2019 Detroit Auto Show. It showed the sleek, orange car in profile, and an equally sleek, short-skirted model caressed its low roofline.

The sonar rep enlarged the image, then maneuvered it until the prototype's front wheel, an elaborately sculpted, unique alloy masterpiece, covered the fuzzy image of the object on the sea floor. Identical. The rep whispered, "Bingo!"

Shay stood alongside Ben and slapped his shoulder. Ben's heart pounded. "We found it!"

The sonar man removed his glasses and rubbed his eyes. "Well, we found a wheel. Might have come loose when the car hit the water, then floated on the current until the tire went completely flat, got torn loose by wave action, then the wheel sank here. Or this wheel may have broken loose when the car hit bottom in one piece, and the whole wreck's lying ten yards from it, in the next furrow we're set to plow. Truth's probably something in between. All I'm sure of is the cox says we're headed for the barn after one more pass. And tomorrow the seas'll be higher. When the boat moves up and down the towfish tries to move up and down. It won't make things easier."

Ben asked the sonar man, "What if the car *is* close?"

The rep cocked his curly-haired head. "If you're a gambler in a hurry, we could run the last track at sixteen hundred K. The coverage's narrow, so there'll be more passes to make tomorrow, in rougher water. And even if I'm working free I don't know whether this boat is. But that wheel didn't sink out of sight, so the bottom silt's not deep here. If we capture an image tonight, it'll be a beaut'."

The wonder had worn off for Ben. Except for the whale-watching prospects, another day of this in rougher water held little appeal. The quicker they found this body the quicker he could return to D.C.

If Petrie was actually thinking of running for president, absurd as the notion was, Ben could do more for veterans in D.C. than he could do floating around San Francisco Bay.

"Well, Mr. Shepard?" Shay winked. "I'll leave it up to you. Are you a Beltway bean counter? Or a riverboat gambler?"

ELEVEN

By the time Marine 1 came about for the last time, with the towfish behind, far below, and set to record at its highest resolution, both the Golden Gate and the city beyond the bridge sparkled as their lights winked on in pre-evening twilight.

Ben peered out at the lights, arms crossed, and suffered buyer's remorse at his decision to record this last pass of the day at high resolution. Life had taught him that gambling was foolhardy. Of course, life had also taught him that playing it safe was even worse.

Two minutes later, the sonar man whistled. "Mr. Shepard, next time you visit Vegas, take me along."

Ben stared at the screen as hair rose on his neck. There was no need to overlay a photo of the Galvani. Its lines shone in ghostly, mottled brown silhouette as clearly as any stylist's drawing.

It lay on its driver's side, sunk perhaps six inches into the bottom silt. Both passenger side wheels were missing and suspension bits and disc brakes dangled in the empty wheel wells. The driver's side wheel wells were obscured by the silt, so the other wheels' fates were uncertain, and the battery tray floor pan was marred by an enormous dimple just left of its center.

Otherwise, the car could have been resting on an auto show stage, but turned up to display its aerodynamic underbelly.

As the boat ran out the rest of the track, Shay said, "The body's—."

"Still inside." Ben pointed at the frozen image. "It has to be. Look. These doors are intact. And closed. The windows, windshield, too." He asked the sonar man, "Is there a way to look inside?"

The rep removed his glasses again, rubbed his eyes, and shook his head. "Solid surfaces reflect sound energy. Far as the towfish knows, windows, especially coated with precipitated solids and bottom slime, which these probably are already, are as opaque as metal door panels."

When the boat came about again, Shay and the rest of Marine 1's crew began reeling in the towfish while the sonar man disconnected the cables that sprouted from his laptop and its pedestal. Then he coiled them and packed everything away in a foam-lined plastic case.

Ben asked him, "What do you make of the detached wheels?"

"Well, I've seen it once before. Pickup ran off a bridge and sank in a river two years ago. Hit the water in a perfect belly flop. The suspension and tires took so much of the shock that they disassociated from the chassis."

"What happened to *that* driver?"

"Not really my department. But the wheels didn't take enough of the shock. I heard when the divers got to the body he looked like a building fell on him. And that bridge was only *sixty* feet above the water."

As the MLB passed beneath the Golden Gate, Ben craned his neck and peered out the side glass and up at the span.

The Haji Hilton had five flights of stairs, and its roof had surveyed out at sixty feet above ground.

Ben had read that a twenty-story building could fit between the Golden Gate's deck, at midpoint, and the water. Maybe it was just as well the sonar couldn't look inside the Galvani.

The sonar man went aft to check on his towfish and passed Shay as Mick entered the enclosed bridge, unsmiling, but waving his phone like a trophy.

Ben wrinkled his forehead. Except for the puking, this had been a very good day. So far. "Now what?"

"The drone we hired? Found a floater."

"I don't think we're looking for a floater anymore, Mick."

"True. But it's gonna take time and money to get down on that car and sort through the nuts and guts inside."

"Okay. For the sake of argument, why might this floater be Manuel Colibri?"

"Currents, mostly. That's why we started looking for the car seaward of the bridge. This body was in a tide pool in the Farallons. Mostly-uninhabited islands thirty miles west of here. Jumpers that don't get fished out right beneath the bridge get carried out there, if they don't get eaten or drift south towards Monterey. And the timing's right."

Ben closed his eyes. "We don't have to go pick up this corpse, do we?"

"Nah. The Coasties had a boat in the area. They fished him out an hour ago."

"Him?"

"That's about as specific as the description gets." Mick handed Ben his C-phone. "Read it for yourself."

"One leg severed?"

"Lotta sharks in the Farallons."

"What's SMD?"

"Severe Marine Depredation."

"Don't tell me."

"Crabs have a taste for eyeballs. And they love cheek flesh."

Ben winced. "Do they eat the teeth, too? Or can we match dental records?"

"Mr. Shepard!" Mick rolled his eyes and waved a hand as though flicking flies off a dead body. "Easier these days to just match DNA. The tests run eight-fifty a pop, but this case isn't overtime parking. If we get a sample of Mr. Colibri's DNA, and it matches up to this body, your mystery's over."

TWELVE

Kate switched off her Corolla's ignition. From the curbside parking space she peered across the street at four Victorian row houses in Lower Haight, newly renovated and connected to form Earth Longevity Coalition headquarters.

She yawned. This audience was such a plum that she had snapped up the seven a.m. time slot, dragged herself north from Palo Alto, and picked up her father. Even though Kate Boyle agreed with her mother that nothing good happened before ten a.m.

Early-arriving ELCIE employees bounded up the stairs between the sidewalk and the houses with energy that Kate found subversive, as Kate's father sat beside her, bright-eyed and whistling.

Jack Boyle was a morning person, which made the lifelong bond he had shared with Kate's mother all the more antiquely miraculous.

Jack peered at the Levis-clad staffers. "So the hippies have come home to Hashbury after all these years."

"You think the Golden Gate Bridge closes for a hippie cult festival? Dad, ELCIE's a mainstream foundation."

He pointed at the brass plaque on the wall next to the main entrance: EARtH LONGEVItY COALItION.

In each of the three words the letter "t" was emphasized in gold, set in lower case, and the letters' vertical shafts above their cross strokes were formed by an inverted teardrop.

"Then why are they hiding peace symbols in their name?"

Kate rolled bleary eyes. "Those are ankhs, Dad. Egyptian hieroglyphs. They symbolize eternal life."

"Well, Julia Madison's a hippie. While I was waiting tables for tuition she was across the Bay at Berzerkeley leading demonstrations."

"She's a feminist legend. She's been a cabinet secretary twice. And nobody's called anybody a hippie in this century."

"Oh. Are we finally calling 'em self-indulgent dope fiends?"

Kate sighed as she flipped down her vanity mirror and checked her face again. She had resigned herself to interviewing boy-millionaire geeks whose lives boiled down to one-hundred-forty-character tweets. Julia Madison was not only a witness to history, she had made history. History makers didn't suffer unprepared reporters gladly.

"Remember, Katy—"

She rolled her eyes again. "'Be prepared! A good lawyer never asks a witness a question she doesn't already know the answer to.' Good advice, Dad. But I'm not a lawyer and interview subjects aren't witnesses under oath. So today I'll do the asking. You and Mom paid the full freight to get me a masters from the place that hands out the Pulitzers. Let me use it, okay?"

"So I'm a potted plant?"

At least you're not potted. That's a start. In fact, you've cleaned up great this morning. But after two years of geeks and video games I'm interviewing an accomplished historical figure, one intelligent woman to another.

"Just for today *please* be a potted plant. Julia will know you worked for David. And David gives ELCIE real money. That got us in the door, and that's why I brought you along. But if you're abrasive and tactless she'll dump us to some staffer. We'll go home with nothing from this but a brochure. So play nice."

Victorian as ELCIE's restored row houses looked from the street, its headquarters' interior décor was top-dollar leather and Bauhaus chrome. Kate and Jack waited less than a minute, then Julia Madison herself walked around the still-empty reception desk into the lobby, wearing a polite but serious interview smile.

"Ms. Boyle? Kate, is it? The first thing I read in *Gizmo* is always your column."

Kate smiled in spite of herself. It was as probable that Julia Madison read *Gizmo* as it was that Jack Boyle read *Rolling Stone*. But really good politicians made everyone they met feel like the most important person in the room.

ELCIE's president may have been as old as Jack Boyle, but she was better preserved. Tailored, slim, with short hair dyed blonde, the taut skin around her eyes and across her high cheekbones announced work done. Although done damn well.

Kate said, "Madam Secretary, your pictures don't do you justice." An ex-secretary wasn't entitled to the honorific, but sucking up couldn't hurt.

The legend's handshake conveyed genuine energy.

And apparently you're a morning person, which must be the only thing besides age that you and my father have in common.

Madison led them from the lobby. "Please call me Julia." She turned to Jack as they walked down a short hall and squeezed into a phone-booth-sized elevator. "Mr. Boyle—"

Kate held her breath.

"Please. Call me Jack." He actually smiled like he meant it.

Kate exhaled.

"Jack, the Powell Foundation's a significant source of our funding. I understand you were David's special counsel for thirty years. Though from where I'm standing you hardly look old enough." Where Julia Madison was standing was even closer to him than the tight elevator required, she returned his smile more warmly than the moment required even of a good politician, and she smelled like two hundred bucks an ounce.

Apparently you clean up even better than I thought you did, Dad.

Kate shuddered. Visualizing Dad horizontal with Mom had always creeped her out. Visualizing Dad horizontal with a former *Rolling Stone* cover girl went way beyond creepy.

The elevator opened on the renovated mansion's tiny second floor lobby. To the left was the ELCIE president's suite. Ahead was a steel exit door, labeled as connecting to listed offices located in the adjacent houses.

Also taped to the steel door was a hand lettered cardboard sign that read: THIS WAY TO THE *METH* LAB.

Jack paused, pointed at it. "Supplemental funding?"

Madison laughed as she led them into a paneled conference room with a round table and four chairs, which adjoined her office. "The Meth is the staff's abbreviation for the Methuselarity. The biotechnological breakover moment when living forever becomes reality." She turned and poured three coffees from a pot on a sideboard. "When I was introduced to the staff on my first day here I referred in my remarks to the 'Singularity Lab.' I haven't lived it down. ELCIE is not a 'laboratory.' We're a trade association. For a trade that doesn't even exist yet."

Kate sighed, then fished her recorder out of her bag, laid it on the table, and raised her eyebrows at Julia Madison. "Madam Secretary?"

Madison nodded. "Kate, can we agree no questions specifically about the New Year's Eve unpleasantness?"

Kate hated sideboards, but Madison must have answered every bombing question a hundred times and Kate hadn't planned to ask one, anyway.

Kate nodded. "No problem, Madam Secretary." She pushed "record." "On the record. In 2015 you left government. Why then?"

"It's a great question." Madison leaned back in her chair and cocked her head. "2015 was the moment when the idea of attacking normal aging as just one more treatable disease went mainstream."

"You mean the Calico announcement?" Kate flicked

her eyes to her father. See, Dad? I do know the answers to my questions.

Madison smiled, nodded. "I'm no molecular biologist. But an old prosecutor knows how to follow the money. When Google made the California Life Company a one and a half billion dollar reality I realized that someone who knew how to follow the money also knew that life-extension science had arrived at the cusp of commercial viability."

"And at that time Google wasn't alone?"

"Correct. But most of the other entrepreneurs' vision went beyond commercial viability. It still does."

Kate knew the answer to this one, too. "And what is that vision?"

"Money is a powerful motivator. But survival is even more powerful. Billionaires don't need to make more money in their lifetimes. Billionaires need more lifetimes to spend the money they've made. Most of the others who jumped into the field, even though they largely avoid admitting it, have their own skin in the game, literally. They want to live forever. And they've awakened before the rest of us to the new idea that life-extension science is advancing explosively. So explosively that a person alive today may become able to buy immortality in his or her lifetime."

Jack said, "It's not a new idea. When Ted Williams died, he got his head frozen."

Kate narrowed her eyes. Dad? That's the *stupidest*—

Madison pointed at Jack and smiled. "That's an excellent anecdote that illustrates my point. Cryonics, the Holy Grail, the fountain of youth. They used to be the only life-extension game in town. The field was quackery and myth. Today the Methuselarity—the moment when man on average begins cheating death faster than he dies—may be so close that the first person who will live to be one thousand is alive today."

Kate sighed. B.A. and M.S. in journalism from Columbia? Two-seventy large. Night law school degree, a baseball card collection, and smiling like you mean it? Priceless.

Kate asked, "If ELCIE's not a lab how can you say that?"

Madison sipped her coffee. "We *have* said that. *I* have said that. But ELCIE doesn't make scientific predictions so much as it promotes and publicizes others' work, and the predictions that flow from it. Our objective is to alert society, so mankind will be ready for the social challenges that life extension will bring."

Jack cocked an eyebrow. "Like what to do with all those frozen heads?"

Madison nodded. "That's an important distinction. Reanimating the dead is for horror films. And no matter how ageless we make the human body, you won't live forever if you step in front of a bus. Life extension also isn't about prolonging our time in nursing homes. It's about reengineering our bodies so we don't grow old in the first place."

Kate smiled. "ELCIE's not in this to bankrupt Social Security?"

Madison nodded again. "But that's an example of the kinds of issues in play. The technology may be the lesser challenge. Everybody who's seen their smartphone obsolete itself within months after it's unboxed understands the accelerating pace of change in information technologies. Life sciences may be less visible, but the rate of progress in the field may be even more rapid. The human genome was sequenced two years faster and three hundred million dollars cheaper than predicted. And that was at the 1990s pace of technological change. In 2016, work began not just to map and edit human DNA, but to synthesize it from scratch. Not only does change outrace predictions, the *rate* of change outraces the predicted rate, too. Even five years ago lab mice that were fed restricted calorie diets and Rapamycin were living two centuries in mouse years. Roundworms with reengineered genes were living six centuries in worm years."

Jack snorted. "Mice and roundworms aren't people."

Julia leaned forward. "Jack, life-extension research focuses on mice and roundworms because their normal lifespans are short enough to allow testing over multiple generations." She glanced down at her boob job. "You don't think I'm suggesting this body looks like a roundworm's?"

"Actually, it looks fine from here."

Julia Madison batted her eyes.

"Eeewww!"

Jack and Julia straightened and turned to Kate, eyes wide, and Jack said, "What?"

Kate felt herself redden as she pointed at the cup in her left hand with her right index finger. "Coffee. Was a little strong." She patted her chest. "I'll be fine."

Julia and Jack turned back to one another and Julia said, "Although actually, at the molecular level, mice and roundworms are more closely related to humans than you or I might think. Rapamycin was actually developed for human use, as an immune suppressant in organ transplantation. But when someone fed Rapamycin to mice, the mice stayed young."

Kate cleared her throat, glanced at her notes, and changed the subject. Finally we get to the reason we're here. "You're saying the Methuselarity's arrival depends on continuously accelerating progress in biogerontology. But since the fanfare in 2015, Calico has announced nothing groundbreaking. Google's health care investments lately have been in things as conventional as heart disease research. The other players have been just as quiet. Can that deafening silence possibly be just normal industrial security?"

Madison's face went blank. "Kate, ELCIE's a trade association. Trade associations promote their trade as a whole. They don't take sides within it."

"The rumors are that the other players in the field, besides Cardinal Systems, are so quiet because Cardinal's been locking up all the talent and all the patents. True?"

Julia Madison shrugged. "Rumors are rumors. I don't comment on the ones I hear. I can't comment on the ones I don't hear."

This interview was suddenly looking like three hours of perfectly good sleep wasted.

Jack rolled his eyes and sawed the air with his palm. "What kind of political bullshit is that, Julia? When you were at Berkeley at least you answered questions like you had a pair!"

Kate felt her jaw drop.

Julia Madison froze and stared at Jack.

"Dad!"

You just called the most prominent feminist in Northern California a spineless liar, and threw in a crude and biologically absurd sexual stereotype for good measure. She may shoot you. Hell, I may shoot you first.

Julia Madison turned to Kate. Teeth clenched, she said, "We are off the record, Ms. Boyle."

Kate switched off the recorder, and stared at it.

Katy, if you bring a hog to the prom, wear your boots. Good advice, Dad. Wish I had taken it and left you at home.

Kate reached down to pack up her bag. "Madam Secretary, I'm so very—"

"Jack, your political incorrectness is breathtaking." Julia Madison ignored Kate and spoke to Jack. "However, too many years in politics can make someone forget how much more liberating honesty is than political correctness. Thanks for reminding me."

Jack said, "If we're being all liberated and honest, I said I admired your frankness. I still think your politics are crap."

"I'm hardly surprised, Jack." Julia turned to Kate. "Still off the record. But you want to know what I really know about Manny Colibri? And what I think about what I know? Listen."

Kate sat dead still. Katy, when the judge indicates he's about to rule in your favor, shut up.

Julia Madison said, "Yes, of course I know what's really going on in the world where I make my living. I survived two decades in Washington. Yes, it is one hundred percent true that Cardinal's outbid not only Calico but every other major and minor player between here and San Jose for every decent mind and idea in the life-extension field over the last four years. Cardinal's been spraying money out through a fire hose. That's good. But they're washing the competition down the drain. That's bad. The prosecutor in me calls what Cardinal's been doing predatory, monopolistic behavior. But how can you monopolize an industry that doesn't even exist?"

Kate wrinkled her brow. "What's Cardinal been doing with all those minds and ideas, then?"

Julia Madison said, "That's the odd thing. The people over at Cardinal do whatever they want. No direction. No accountability. Nobel-class molecular biologists while away their days breeding wine grapes for fun and playing billiards. 2019 was a good year, so Manny Colibri just gave the company January off with pay. That's a preposterous perquisite, even in the tech industry. Top management's off on a penguin-watching sabbatical because it's summer in Antarctica. And the patents seem to have wound up in some electronic wastebasket."

Kate squinted. "But somebody must get tired of watching penguins."

"The few walkaways haven't left pissed off. They've left so rich they'll never bother to work in their fields again. None of it sounds conducive to accelerating the Methuselarity. And I left government to accelerate the Methuselarity, so that pisses *me* off."

Jack said, "Sounds conducive to bankruptcy to me."

"Perhaps, Jack. But Cardinal has no shareholders to complain about earnings or dividends. At least I don't think it has. Now that Manny's gone, I'm not really even sure who really knows who Cardinal's actual, beneficial owner or owners are."

Kate said, "I understand why *you're* not in a position to speak on the record. But would any of the walkaways be willing to talk?"

Julia rubbed her chin. "Not really. Tech industry exit settlements come with pretty sophisticated nondisclosure requirements. But you might try Quentin Callisto. You've heard of him?"

Kate raised her eyebrows. "Heard of him? I interviewed Quentin once before. On a completely different topic. He never mentioned Cardinal."

"Quentin's connection to Manny Colibri isn't really on point to your interest. But for that very reason his confidentiality constraints may be laxer. And in any case, Quentin's always flattered to be noticed. Even if he can't or won't help you directly, he may open a door to someone who can and will." Julia Madison consulted her Rolex, then smiled. "I'm afraid that's about as big a can opener as I'm willing to give you just now, Kate."

Julia walked them to the elevator. As the door between her and Jack and Kate whispered shut, Julia called, "Jack, if you want to discuss honesty and politics over dinner, call me."

THIRTEEN

Kate and Jack jaywalked from ELCIE headquarters back to her parked car, and she chucked her bag into the back seat as she slid behind the wheel. "Well. That didn't go the way I expected."

Jack rolled his window down and inhaled a morning breeze that smelled of nothing more narcotic than fresh bread. Mom had told her that even the *Lower* Haight smelled like weed in the mornings when Dad had dragged her out of bed to walk there when they dated.

Jack said, "Sure didn't. Julia smelled better than any hippie I remember."

Kate sent a text, then before she shifted to drive she frowned. It turned out that the prospect of Jack Boyle moving on from the only woman who he'd ever been with, and with someone who had been Kate's best friend, wasn't all a breath of fresh air. It came with a puff of creepy and a whiff of betrayal.

Kate's father said, "Julia seems to think that a lot of

Colibri's fellow billionaires jumped on this life-extension bandwagon so they could live forever. Personally. You think Colibri did, too?"

Kate shook her head. "Well, if he did, things couldn't have worked out worse for him, could they? And Julia's not the only one who thinks the billionaires are in it to win it for themselves, personally. A couple years ago Bill Gates rejected life-extension research as legitimate philanthropy, because it was too egocentric."

Jack crossed his arms. "But if Julia knows what she's talking about, Colibri's investment wasn't helping him live forever. Even before somebody blew him up."

"Dad, people have been looking for the fountain of youth for centuries. Failing to find it is no surprise."

"The surprise is that he wasn't even *trying*, Katy. Besides, I understand why most billionaires would want more lives to enjoy their money. David Powell races horses and vintage Ferraris and antique motorboats. He collects first editions and impressionists and antique chess sets. But Colibri? He was an ascetic. Why would a guy who didn't waterski behind one yacht want to survive to ski behind fifty of them?"

Kate smiled. "What would be the use of immortality to a person who cannot well use half an hour?"

"That's what I just said."

"No, that's what Emerson said a hundred and forty years ago. But the other thing Colibri was failing at with all this investment was making money on it." Kate wrinkled her forehead. "Maybe because Colibri had stopped trying to make money on this project his shareholders fired him with a bomb."

Jack shook his head. "Maybe one of Colibri's VPs got a lousy review. I'd like to know which one of his minions thought up the penguin-watching trip, because being in Antarctica's a little too perfect an alibi. But Katy, a conclusion based on incomplete facts is a guess."

"You're saying we need to figure out Cardinal's structure?"

Jack nodded. "Julia's a bright gal. Like she said, we follow the money. If somebody put that guy up to killing Colibri, it was probably somebody who stood to cash in on his death."

"Cardinal's closed for January. But we can access its government filings online."

Jack frowned. "Waste of time."

"Dad, the internet isn't—"

Jack shook his head. "The internet's not the problem. Take it from an old corporate lawyer, one reason private companies choose to be private is because their public filings don't have to disclose very much. But I have an idea where I can get the information we need. Meantime, how about we visit with that friend of yours. The one Julia mentioned?"

"Quentin Callisto? Way ahead of you, Dad." But after this morning, I've learned my lesson. "We" aren't visiting Quentin.

Kate checked her phone. No answer to her text. She dialed a number, snorted at what she heard. "I just texted Quentin. He didn't answer, and normally he would. And I just called him and his voice mailbox was full."

Jack grunted. "By the way, what the hell kind of name is Quentin Callisto?"

"Not his real one. He legally changed it from Quentin Pinkleberg."

"He picked the name of a goddess who got changed into a bear?"

Kate smiled. "Not for Callisto from Greek mythology. Callisto is a moon of Jupiter that orbits out of step with Jupiter's other moons. Quentin considers himself out of step."

"Out of step with what?"

"Mundane humans. Who include everybody except him." Kate eased out into traffic. "I'll drop you back at the house. You work the corporate structure problem while I go see Quentin. We'll meet up tonight back there, compare notes, then we'll sleep. Late."

"You're moving back in?"

"I can't handle driving back and forth from Palo Alto every day. Unless you rented out my room?"

"No. It's just like you left it."

Kate swerved into a parking space in front of a small hardware store.

"What are you doing?"

"Buying Windex, Lysol, paper towels, trash bags, rubber gloves—"

"Katy, I know what I always said. But your room was never really that messy."

"My room's not really the problem."

Kate's father snorted, then read aloud a sign in the store window. "'We have PETA-approved cockroach traps.' Now you know that you've come home again to San Francisco." He cocked his head. "But you just said you don't know where Callisto is."

"No, I said he wasn't answering texts and his voice mail was full. That tells me *exactly* where he is. But that means we can't wait for him to come home again to San Francisco."

"Why not?"

"Because he never visits just one planet at a time."

FOURTEEN

"This is unbelievable." Ben Shepard looked up from the curled-paper facsimile sheets that Mick Shay had handed him. The brisk breeze off San Francisco Bay tugged at the papers as Ben and Mick walked along the Hyde Street Pier and drank their morning coffee.

However charmless Shay's windowless corner in the SFPD Marine Unit offices at the Hyde Street Pier was, the bay view outside the door was unbeatable.

Mick said, "I know. But I didn't used to be too good with the email, so some comedians rescued a fax machine from the dumpster and hooked it up in my workspace."

"I mean what the report says."

"The Belvedere Police Department claims it's believable."

"I'm no cop, but I watch enough TV to know there's DNA anyplace people spit or bleed or defecate or shed hair. But they didn't find any in Colibri's house?"

Mick shrugged. "I'm not one to speak ill of another

department. But Belvedere Island's not what you'd call a high crime area. The property values over there make Beverly Hills look like subsidized housing." He flicked his coffee dregs into the water. "The BPD's a chief, two sergeants, three full-time officers, and a secretary."

"You think they're incompetent?"

Mick shook his head. "Didn't say that. I just think an officer could put in his whole twenty at the BPD and never have to learn to spell DNA. Maybe they outsourced the job. Maybe they tried to do it on their own and got it wrong."

"So now what?"

"So I called a SFPD lab rat I know who's ex-navy. She's sharp and careful and she's a single mom who needs the overtime. Brenda's gonna give Colibri's house a do-over, personally."

"When will we get the new report?"

"Depends on her duty schedule. Maybe couple hours. Maybe couple days."

"So 'til then the Farallon body remains unidentified?"

"Yes and no. Yes we don't know who he was. No he wasn't Manuel Colibri."

"But you said—"

Mick pointed at the fax. "See back on the first page?"

Ben ran a finger across the collection particulars. "This says they collected samples of possible hair and skin from the clothes in Mr. Colibri's closet. But you think they lied?"

"Don't know. Don't matter. You see what it says about the trouser labels?"

"Dockers? We already knew he wasn't flashy. What's that tell you?"

"It tells me that sometimes a policeman can see more by looking than he can by playin' with a chemistry set. Those pants have a thirty-inch waist and a twenty-seven-inch inseam. I asked around. Turns out Mr. Colibri stood about five foot two. That matches the pants, more or less."

"Then at least the report's not made up."

"Jury's out on that. But the floater stood *six* foot two. Even on the one leg he's got left."

"Oh. So now what?"

"So we're gonna have to recover enough of Mr. Colibri from his car to match against the rest of his DNA, after all."

"How do we do that?"

Shay pointed out to the Golden Gate. Lit by the morning sun, a vast ship, low in the water and tiny in the distance, inched slowly in from the Pacific toward the opening between the bridge's orange towers. "That bulker's just about over top of Mr. Colibri's car right now. The flood tide she's riding in on is the Moon tryin' to pull the biggest ocean in the world through a channel a mile and a quarter wide and three hundred feet deep. Later today, when the tide ebbs, all the water that's drained down west from the Sierra Nevada mountains into San Pablo and San Francisco Bays is gonna try to squeeze back out through that same funnel."

"You're saying examining the car is going to be harder than finding it was?"

"That side scan sonar search took a next year's model towfish and one fella from Houston in a polo shirt who could fit all his gear on two airport luggage carts. The Marine Unit's got its own ROV. But the ROV we *need* is a Tether Managed Heavy Work Class

ROV with enough oomph to manipulate a two-ton dry weight object, and operators who're used to doing it every day. Preferably premounted on a DP2 or better dynamically positioned dedicated ROV tender boat. Those are three or four times the size of Marine 1, which is the biggest boat Marine Unit's got."

Ben's mouth hung open. "Is that really necessary?"

Shay crossed his arms. "Friend of mine died saturation divin' at three hundred feet because somebody thought a robot spread wasn't really necessary."

"Oh."

Shay waved his hand. "An ROV's just a refrigerator-shaped robot with headlights and claws. A crane lowers it over the side of the boat. A pilot topside drives it with joysticks and a TV screen, like playing Pac Man. There's more Remotely Operated Vehicles workin' in oil fields every day than there are tourists lined up for the Hyde Street cable car. One ROV just came off hire this morning. It's as just-right for this job as the baby bear's porridge."

"Great."

"Except it's in the South China Sea. The mobilization time and charges would eat us alive. There's another DP ROV boat that's fishing up a dropped blowout preventer off the bottom of the Santa Barbara Channel. That one should come available in a couple days."

Ben's phone juddered in his trouser pocket. Petrie.

"Yes, Mr. Secretary?"

"Maureen Dunn's benefactor wants confirmation."

What benefactor? "We definitely found the car, if that's what you mean, sir. But that's old news."

"CNN's quoting sources that say you found the body, too. Were you planning to tell me that, Shepard?"

"The drone found *a* body out in the Pacific. That was paragraph three of the summary I sent you yesterday." Ben rolled his eyes. If Petrie read an email longer than four lines at all, he missed, on average, two out of three salient points. Ben could almost see Petrie clicking back through his mail while he talked.

"I never got—oh."

"But that body is definitely not Manuel Colibri. That's new as of five minutes ago." Ben raised his eyebrows at Mick Shay and cocked his head.

Mick nodded.

"My marine liaison here confirms that. CNN's source either jumped to a conclusion or lied. But the story is just wrong. Sir, it may take a few days to get the submersible equipment that will allow a positive identification of the remains inside the car. I was just thinking I could use the slack time to look into the suspect's background."

"He's not a suspect. He's a wrongdoer that we already brought to justice. That part of the case is closed, and it needs to stay closed. And you don't have slack time."

"Sir?"

"Mayor Dunn says the donor who's bankrolling this investigation wanted quick progress on recovering the body."

"Sir, there's nothing more I can—."

"Yes there is. You're out there as a liaison. Take down this name and address and phone number. Then go liaise your ass off with these people. Persuade them we're making progress."

"Sir—"

"Shepard, politics is fifty percent making gridlock

look like progress and forty percent ass kissing. The other ten percent is knowing whose ass to kiss. Just go do it."

Petrie hung up, and Ben swore while he dialed the number that his boss had just ordered him to call.

FIFTEEN

Parked on the two-lane asphalt road's shoulder, Kate lowered her car's windows and breathed in cold, pine-scented air. As she flexed fingers stiffened by four hours clenched on the wheel since she left the Oakland Bay Bridge behind and headed northeast from San Francisco, she smiled.

Her watch showed she had beaten her GPS's estimated trip time by twenty-four minutes. And except for one winding stretch of two-lane and some idiot in front of her who insisted on driving the speed limit, she would have beaten it by twenty-six.

Kate rubbed her eyes and looked out through the windshield at the surrounding scrub pine country. Sparkling beneath a blue afternoon sky, January snow dusted the wooded hills and the distant mountains that bordered the flat land. A four-strand wire cattle fence separated pastures from the road. So far as Kate could see, the cattle fence didn't have to work very hard. Then somewhere a cow mooed. Nothing

111

had changed here since her first visit with Quentin Callisto, when his legal last name was still Pinkleberg.

Fifty feet ahead of her a paved driveway framed by open metal gates led to her right. Alongside the gate a painted metal sign read: HAT CREEK RADIO OBSERVATORY.

The Search for Extraterrestrial Intelligence had built its own dedicated radio observatory because conventional radio astronomy, which dismissed SETI as a long-shot sideshow, hogged too much time on the big dishes, like Arecibo in Puerto Rico. SETI had built its observatory in the Hat Creek Valley, sheltered in the electronic dead spot between the Cascade mountain range to the west and a fault scarp to the east. The telescope array shared the Hat Creek Valley only with cows, and with trout fishermen as indifferent to electronic connection to the world as the cows were. So the Hat Creek Valley was also free of the electronic background noise generated by cell phone service.

Like most of the geeks who Kate Boyle interviewed, Quentin Callisto may have been out of step with the real world, but he remained addicted to it 24-7. When Quentin hadn't hit Kate's text back, and hadn't tidied up his voicemail, it meant he was either up here at Hat Creek, or was bound and gagged at the bottom of a well, or was dead.

Kate drove through the open gates and parked in front of a single-story house and outbuildings.

A petite, mocha-skinned girl wearing jeans and a faded red sweatshirt that read "Space Is Freaking Awesome," trotted from the house, then rested her elbows on the sill of Kate's rolled down window. "Welcome to Hat Creek. We're still open to the public 'til three today. Tours are self-guided, so help yourself. But if you've got questions, I'm the resident astronomer."

"Andrea, is Quentin Callisto around?"

The girl's mouth opened as she nodded in recognition and grinned. "Now I remember. Kate, is it? You're the reporter who interviewed Quentin last year. Actually, he hikes every day after lunch. But he'll be back at the array," She eyed her C-watch, "in a half hour. It's a ways. You'll want to drive out."

The Hat Creek Radio Observatory's resident astronomer pointed back at the house. "Meantime, I'm making chai. Come in and wait?"

Ten minutes and a ladies' room visit later Kate sipped tea with Dr. Andrea Chaudhury, nominee for the Sagan Medal for her contributions to the Search for Extraterrestrial Intelligence. But it was just as well that Jack Boyle wasn't here or he would have noted that Andrea Chaudhury looked as though her father would have to drive her to the awards banquet.

The distinguished Dr. Chaudhury sat across from Kate in a kitchen that looked like time had stopped during the Eisenhower administration. The sink held unwashed dishes and on the table between the two women a scented candle burned. Probably a cloaking device disguising the smell of snack debris too long forgotten.

Hat Creek resembled less the sleek Silicon Valley cafeterias and campuses where Kate interviewed her usual suspects and more resembled a roachy off-campus flat that Kate had shared with two other undergrads.

Research in the noncommercial sciences was the underfunded stepchild to profitable fields like pharmacology and information technology. And lately, to the field of life-extension biology. Unlike those potential moneymakers, radio astronomy, particularly radio astronomy devoted to the search for extraterrestrial intelligence, survived on scraps begged from hobby philanthropists like Paul Allen, Yuri Milner, and Quentin Pinkleberg.

Andrea's lower lip twitched in a veiled pout. "You're writing *another* story about Quentin?"

Unlike Dr. Andrea Chaudhury, and unlike most of Hat Creek's staff, whether old or young, Quentin Pinkleberg wasn't a prodigy who had earned an advanced degree from a selective university. Neither was he an internet billionaire like Allen and Milner.

Quentin Pinkleberg was an anorexic, self-taught computer geek who collected comic books while he squatted in his parents' basement. Or he had been, until a video game he developed, which he set in putative subterranean oceans of the moons of Jupiter, caught commercial fire. Nintendo bought *Aquanaut*, and Hollywood tentpoled a blockbuster movie series around it.

Quentin Pinkleberg had changed his name to fit his fortune and his fame, but he couldn't change his résumé. He was still a self-taught computer geek who collected comic books. However, he had succeeded Paul Allen as Hat Creek's principal funding source.

Dr. Chaudhury's pout was understandable, if uncharitable. It was easier for Hat Creek's distinguished but impoverished astronomers to accept Quentin's money than it was to accept Quentin.

Kate shook her head in answer. "I'm not here to interview Quentin again. I just want to see whether he can help me with an unrelated story."

Kate pointed at one kitchen wall, which functioned as a bulletin board, labelled "EXOPLANET ROUNDUP." The wall was push-pinned with printouts of artists' conceptions of planets that orbited stars beyond the solar system, grouped around an autographed photo of Mr. Spock.

Kate asked, "But is there a story *here* I should do? Everybody loves to read about aliens."

Andrea smiled the smile of an unexpectedly acknowledged stepchild. "Unfortunately, there's not much that's concrete enough to love yet."

"Try me."

The astronomer stood and walked to the wall. "When I was a kid, the only way astronomers could search for life outside the solar system was to point radio telescopes at random stars in a sky full of billions of billions of them." Chaudhury shrugged. "Then they just listened for years for some sign of intelligent life, without result. Does that sound like a waste of time?"

Kate said, "It sounds like being a political reporter in Washington."

"The problem was that if extrasolar planets were out there orbiting stars, the planets weren't big enough or bright enough to see from Earth. And the Milky Way alone contains at least a hundred billion, and probably multiples of a hundred billion, stars."

"Big haystack, small needle?"

Dr. Chaudhury nodded. "But by 2009, optical astronomy had telescopes orbiting outside the atmosphere. They still couldn't see planets. But they could detect the drop in a star's brightness when a planet transited the star's surface and cast a shadow." The astronomer passed her hand between Kate's face and the flame of the candle on the table between them, circled her hand around behind the candle flame, then obscured the flame again. "Like this, but the shadow's the size of a rice grain, not a hand. We've improved our methods. Now we can identify Earth-sized planets that are neither too hot or too cold for liquid water. And spectroscopy's going to let us spot other telltales. Plants aren't the only way to generate atmospheric free oxygen, but if we *find* some, eyebrows will raise."

Kate swung her arm at the wall. "Wow. All of these?"

Andrea laughed and shook her head. "No. There isn't a wall big enough for all the earthlikes anymore." She stepped to the wall and tapped her index finger on a yellowed sheet showing a blue-brown ball. "Kepler 186f. This was the first habitable-zone Earthlike planet NASA identified. That was in 2014. A year later, we had eight confirmed Earthlikes and we were impressed. But Kate, since then we've found so many Earthlikes that we estimate twenty billion Earthlikes are orbiting yellow suns, and twice that number are orbiting red dwarf suns, like Kepler 186f does. To say nothing of brown dwarf stars and Earthlike moons that orbit planets, like Quentin's moons of Jupiter."

"But with all those worlds, we haven't heard anything?"

The astronomer shook her head. "Not a peep. In sixty years of listening. But we haven't come close to listening to all those places. But now that we *know* Earthlike planets are a dime a dozen, other civilizations almost certainly are, too."

Kate narrowed her eyes. "And Quentin Callisto is devoting his life and his fortune to listening?"

Andrea wrinkled her forehead. "We're grateful to

Quentin for his support. But you know Quentin. He'd probably prefer to tell you directly what he expects to do with his life and his fortune." She eyed the wall clock. "If you drive out to the array now, you should catch him."

"Thanks." Kate lifted her cup. "I owe you a drink."

"No, I owe you one, if you'll give me a chance to sell you on writing an article about what we do up here. Tomorrow I'm going down to San Francisco to sell SETI to the public with a lecture series. You have my mobile number. Give me a call."

Five minutes after Kate left the resident astronomer, she drove out onto the road through the meadow across which were sprinkled the radio telescope dishes of the Allen Telescope Array. A silvery forest of them, each as tall as a two-story house, sprouted from concrete pedestals near and far, each arranged and pointed in directions and at angles that to Kate looked random.

From the telescope grove's center rose a white fabric box, a tent, big enough to hangar a small blimp. Open at one end, the tent housed telescopes during assembly and maintenance. Inside the tent one of the satellite dishes lay concave side-down, like an inverted saucer.

As Kate stopped her car, a goateed scarecrow, wearing jeans and a blue sweatshirt that flapped on his torso, shambled out from behind the dish, walked toward her, and waved.

He smiled as he peeled off thick wire-rimmed glasses and scrubbed them with his sweatshirt's hem.

Kate extended her hand and Quentin Callisto shook it. "I liked the story, Kate."

"So did my editor." She turned and pointed at the

telescope dishes that dotted the meadow. There had been perhaps fifty when she had interviewed Quentin about his foundation's gift to this program. Today, she stopped counting at seventy. "You've been busy."

He shrugged. "I'm no astronomer. It's only my money that's busy."

"You earned your money."

He shook his head. "I'm proud of *Aquanaut* 1.0. But 2.0 and the movies are just corporate crapware. The beauty of this place is the suits can't get to me up here." He wrinkled his forehead. "But you did. Why?"

Kate nodded. "I want to ask you about a different matter."

He frowned. "That Comic Con business was a total case of mistaken identity. I was not the only Klingon in that room."

"It's nothing like that. Quentin, somebody told me you knew Manuel Colibri."

Quentin's frown deepened. "I heard they found Manny's car on the bottom of San Francisco Bay."

"Yes, apparently. How did you know Manny?"

Quentin shifted foot-to-foot.

Most interviewees wanted to tell their stories. The reluctant ones just needed a reason not to hold back.

"Quentin, is there any reason to hold back now?"

"I suppose you're right." He wagged his head like it was a balloon on a stick. "People wonder how some penniless geek could develop and market *Aquanaut*. The answer is it was easy, because Manny paid for it. Not Cardinal Systems. Him, personally. Cardinal used to host a retreat for science fiction writers to get seed ideas. Manny actually approached me because he had read a fan fiction story I had written online called *Aquanauts*. He thought the idea of civilizations in the aquaspheres of planets and moons would make a cool game. He offered to pay one hundred percent of the initial development, manufacturing, and promotion costs. But I got to keep eighty percent of the venture." Quentin shrugged. "I made obscene profits. Manny made semi-obscene profits."

Kate pursed her lips. "Did you keep in touch with him?"

"Sure. He still hosted the meet-and-greets down in the city. The idea was cross-fertilization."

"Did you ever cross-fertilize about the Methuselarity?"

He cocked his head. "In a way."

Kate's heart skipped. "In what way, Quentin?"

Quentin Callisto pointed at the saying printed across his sweatshirt:

186,000 MILES PER SECOND
The speed of light:
It's not just a good idea, it's the law!

"As an absolute matter of physical reality, nothing can outrun light. In science fiction, man crosses interstellar space as quickly as sailing ships used to cross oceans. But warp drives, and diving through black holes, and mile-long generation ships, and astronaut crews that travel flash-frozen like corn dogs? Man will never reach the stars in those ways, Kate. The very best we will ever do is accelerate vessels of economically feasible size to a fraction of light speed."

Kate laid a hand on Quentin's bony arm. "You said this had to do with life-extension biology, not astronomy."

"It does. Kate, I'm listening to pick out the Earth-like planet I'm going to visit before I die."

"You just said we can't get there from here."

"No. I said man can't reach the stars by outrunning light. But a man doesn't have to outrun light. He just has to outrun death. Once mankind can outrun death, the only obstacles to interstellar travel are perfecting the nonchemical propulsion technologies we already know about and combatting boredom enroute."

"You're saying that you, personally, plan to visit exoplanets?"

"Correct. Extrapolating current progress both in propulsion science and life-extension biology, I estimate that I will be one hundred fifty-one years old when usable antimatter or plasma drive vessels become available."

"You're serious."

Quentin Callisto nodded. "If a ship can accelerate to one third of light speed, and its crew can live for hundreds of years, then thousands of Earthlikes are reachable. The only problem will be boredom."

Kate raised her eyebrows. No wonder Andrea wanted Quentin to answer Kate's questions directly.

Quentin said, "You think I'm crazy."

"I think you're a visionary."

"So did Manny."

"You talked to Manny about your plans?"

"Sure. And he agreed with me."

"That people would do all that you plan?"

Quentin shook his head. "Not exactly. He just agreed that it would be a long, boring trip."

Kate asked, "At these meetings did you cross fertilize with any of Manny's partners or ex-partners who were more *directly* connected with life-extension research? Especially any who might be willing to talk to me about it?"

Callisto tugged his goatee. "Maybe. Most of the division presidents were as nice as Manny. The only real prick was Victor Carlsson. People said Manny only put up with Carlsson because C-phone was such a cash cow and the phone business was such a shark tank. But C-phone's got nothing to do with the life-extension stuff. Nolan Liu was in charge of Cardinal's whole life-extension research operation right up until he left. He's kind of old, and kind of private, but I always got along with him. Tell him I sent you and maybe he'll talk to you."

Kate drove back southwest toward San Francisco as the afternoon sun slanted in through the windshield.

It had been a long drive just to get an entrée to this Nolan Liu. But Kate had gained an insight into why Manuel Colibri may have been cornering the life-extension market. Maybe he didn't want to ski behind more yachts. Maybe he wanted to survive until the Methuselarity, so he could play science officer on the *Enterprise*, like Quentin Callisto wanted to.

If Colibri had his head beyond the clouds, instead of on business, maybe his shareholders, if he had any, had decided to have him blown up. Or an ambitious subordinate, like this also-private Mr. Liu, had.

Or Carlsson the cutthroat phone prick had.

At the moment, her father would say there were still too many unknowns to formulate a working hypothesis.

As she drove, she tugged her phone from her purse, started Googling, and began solving the story

problem one phrase at a time. Quickly she discovered
that Manny Colibri and Nolan Liu may have been shy,
but plenty of Cardinal's other executives, especially
Carlsson, loved the spotlight.

An hour later, she paused, dialed the house and,
as usual, got no answer, then sighed.

The best way to communicate, whether with aliens,
with geeks, or with Jack Boyle, was face-to-face.

She had coaxed a little truth out of Quentin just
by getting face-to-face. With Jack Boyle the truth was
blacker, and it was buried deeper. But getting face-
to-face over a couple of beers was a way to begin,
at least. Kate leaned forward as she regripped the
wheel, then put her foot down harder.

SIXTEEN

Powell Hall rose near Nob Hill's summit like a stone behemoth scarcely contained by a spiked iron fence twelve feet tall. Today the latest in the line of Powells who had owned Powell Hall was away at another of the family homesteads, on the shore of Lake Tahoe.

Jack Boyle cranked the Ford's window down, reached out and poked the call button on the wall of the mansion's empty guard box.

The speaker above the call button crackled. "Mr. Boyle? I'm sorry nobody's on the gate. Since Mr. Powell's out of town I gave most of the staff a thirty-six hour pass. I thought when you phoned you said quarter past."

"I did, Paul. I'm early."

The gate box speaker buzzed, and as motors swung the gates open the head of David Powell's household staff said, "I'll meet you at the front door, sir."

Jack slid the Ford into the visitor's space in the tiny, cobbled courtyard, which was wide and long enough to fit a couple of catering trucks or stretch limos. On Snob Hill's tiny crest, square footage devoted to occasional parking was the very definition of regal exclusivity.

Jack squinted up at the neoclassical stone palace as he crossed the courtyard to the front doors. Powell Hall looked exactly as it had on his last visit, three years before. In fact, it looked exactly as it had in the predawn of April 18, 1906, before it, like all save one of the mansions on Nob Hill, and much of the rest of the city, had then been destroyed by the earthquake and fires that recast San Francisco forever.

Today luxury hotels rose from the ashes of the Nob Hill mansions that the likes of Leland Stanford had abandoned. The sole surviving original mansion had long ago been sold, and now housed the exclusive Pacific Union Club.

Only David Powell's grandfather had rebuilt the house on the hill that his own father before him had constructed. He had rebuilt with replacement Connecticut brownstone imported, again, 15,000 miles around Cape Horn from the New England quarry from which the original stone had been cut.

And only the spiked high fence altered the house's original external appearance. David had been forced to add it during the recession, in 2011, after one of a mob trying to "occupy" Powell Hall, "symbol of the One Percent's greed," set himself and the shrubbery on fire while scaling a drain pipe when he fumbled his Molotov cocktail. The irony of it was that updated equipment, funded by the Powell Foundation at the St. Francis Hospital Burn Unit, saved the guy's life.

Jack climbed the last step to the front doors and heard their locks click open like a rifle salute.

Paul Eustis, militarily precise in a morning coat, striped trousers and spats looked as much a throwback as did the mansion that he ran for David Powell. "Mr. Boyle, you are lookin' well."

The Georgian, a head shorter than Jack, turned and led the way across the two-story foyer's familiar marble toward the inconspicuous door, around the side of the grand staircase at the foyer's end, that led down to the great house's utility level. The two men's footsteps echoed in the chandeliered silence. The Georgian's steps quieter, even though he walked with one leg stiff.

"You look good too, Paul. Leg's better?"

"Well, they say the winter's gonna be wet, and that won't help. But the wettest winter in San Francisco's dryer than the driest summer in the Mekong, sir."

From the paneled wall to Jack's left, gilt framed oil portraits of David Powell's great-grandfather, grandfather and father stared down at Jack. Each painting was larger than the door of a more common family's refrigerator, and the stern eyes that peered down from each face could easily have been David Powell's, save for differences of fashion in facial hair and clothing. If any family bloodline in San Francisco qualified as royal, it was the Powells of Nob Hill.

Paul paused to rest his leg and leaned against the foyer's only freestanding decoration, a chest-high wood and glass case, set on the floor beneath the central chandelier.

The case contained a simple carved chess set and board, with the pieces forever arranged so that badly outnumbered white had checkmated black.

David had told Jack that David's grandfather had

bought the set because it was the very one on which Anderssen and Kieseritzky had played an exhibition, that came to be called the "Immortal Game," in London in 1851. Jack had asked why, if the game was immortal, the board's varnish had faded.

As the retired staff sergeant recovered, he asked, "How can I help you today, sir?"

"You said David mentioned I might call?"

Paul inclined a head of close-cropped gray hair. "Yes, sir. Mr. Powell instructed me to render you any assistance you deemed necessary."

"Anybody home back in the foundation office today?"

Eustis pressed his lips together as he shook his head. "I'm afraid that Mr. Powell's absence has prompted Ms. Haggen to give herself the day off as well."

Jack rubbed his cheek to hide his smile. Gloria Haggen administered the Powell family charities from a tiny office in a remodeled toolshed behind Powell Hall, that was accessed from the lower kitchen and laundry level.

In thirty years association with the Hagg, Jack Boyle had learned three lessons about her. The first was that she would never share anything about the family's Byzantine philanthropies with some snot atheist night school lawyer who worked on the opposite side of the incorporeal firewall that separated the Powell charities from Powell Diversified. The second was that the Hagg never missed a chance to dodge an honest day's work. The third lesson was that she never missed a chance to openly criticize the hick crippled veteran who had replaced her as head of household, when she was kicked downstairs to look after the Powell charities.

Jack said, "I just need to borrow a couple foundation files, Paul."

Paul Eustis pursed his lips. "I'm afraid Ms. Haggen keeps her office locked. She's easily upset if her files are disturbed."

Jack sighed. "Yeah. I suppose somebody nosing around in her files would really piss her off."

Eustis reached into his waistcoat pocket. "Actually, now that I think on it, I do believe I have the key to that office." He spun an about face. "Follow me, sir."

By the time Jack arrived back home in the Ford, with the stack of borrowed files on the seat beside him, the day had slid into twilight. Beneath storm clouds, the setting sun's reflection died in his rearview mirror while he waited in the street as his garage door opened.

Rain began to sizzle on the Ford's roof. Paul Eustis was right. The newspapers were forecasting that *El Nino* would bring with it the stormiest January in ten years for San Francisco. But for the first time in two years, Jack's house greeted him with interior lights glowing yellow and warm.

SEVENTEEN

When she heard the car door slam out in the garage, Kate turned back from the 'fridge.

Her father stepped through the connecting door from the garage, then plopped a stack of manila file folders onto the kitchen table. He raised his face and sniffed. "Is that moo shu pork?"

She smiled at him. "I stopped in Chinatown. There's a six-pack in the fridge."

Jack wrinkled his nose. "What's that other smell?"

"Clorox. I cleaned a little."

He dragged a finger across a countertop, eyed it, then nodded. "You cleaned a lot. You were never this industrious when you were eighteen."

Kate set two beers from the 'fridge on the table beside the Chinese food cartons, plates and utensils, then turned to him, hands on hips. "We had an internet connection when I was eighteen. What the hell happened?"

"I stopped throwing away money on something I didn't use."

Kate's jaw dropped. "Dad, everybody uses the internet now."

He pointed to newspapers stacked on the kitchen counter. "No. If everybody did then I wouldn't still be able to buy those every morning when I go out for my coffee. And Columbia would have to give away their journalism degrees."

"Most of what we did at Columbia assumed the product would be created and consumed electronically. And by the way you throw away a lot more money on those papers than you would on internet subscriptions. And you kill trees." She puffed a lock of hair out of her eye with an upward-directed breath.

Her father plopped into his chair at the kitchen table.

Kate rested her elbows on the back of the empty chair across from him. "So the landline's your only connection to the world, now?"

"No. The message machine's still connected."

"Not exactly. Dad, when the tape fills up you have to turn it over. But I fixed it." Kate extended her hand, palm up, and wiggled her fingers. "Gimme your cell phone."

He cocked his head. "What's wrong with yours?"

"I used up my battery because you don't have an internet connection. My charger's in my car, it's five blocks away, and it's raining. So I need to borrow your phone."

"My iPhone was company issue. I turned it in when I quit Powell. Those things are just little spies anyway."

Kate rolled her eyes. "So we're cut off from the world?"

Jack drew back. "No. I have cable."

She shook her head.

"Katy, would it be so bad if we had to talk to each other for one night?"

She sat down and smiled at him. "No. No, that wouldn't be bad at all, Dad."

They sat at the table and ate in silence until he said, "So, Katy, what did you learn today?"

It was what he had asked her every night at this table. She said, "It turns out that not every business Colibri invested in was part of Cardinal. The guy I went to see got rich enough that I wrote an article about him because he developed a video game. It turns out he got his seed money from Colibri. He also gave me a connection to a former Cardinal employee who might talk about the life-extension business."

"Former employee? Did he leave mad enough to hire a mad bomber?"

Kate shrugged. "Not according to anything I can find. But suspects don't usually advertise."

"Nope." Her father swigged his beer.

"Except for Victor Carlsson."

Jack Boyle raised his eyebrows. "And who might he be?"

"None other than the guy who's leading the penguin-watching expedition. Colibri hired him away from the biggest phone manufacturer in Sweden, and Carlsson built C-phone into Cardinal's most profitable business. At the expense of the market shares of the iPhone and all the Droid phones. He's regarded as a management genius. And maybe Colibri's heir apparent."

"If he's such a genius why pick such an obvious way to create a vacancy at the top?"

"He wouldn't be the first genius who overestimated

his wisdom and his goodness. And Quentin says he's a prick."

"Too bad we can't talk to him."

"Actually, we can. The reports are the police and the feds *have* via C-chat video and a satellite link to the ship."

"This is where David's connections will come in handy. I suppose there's a videotape of the interview in a cabinet someplace that David could get us a peek at."

"Video yes. Tape no. Dad, information's stored as electrons in the Cloud, now." Kate pointed at the files stacked on the table. "Mostly. What's in those?"

Her father shrugged. "Answers, I hope. To Cardinal's real structure and Colibri's estate plan."

He slid a file off the top of the stack, flipped it open, then flicked his eyes across the pages. "This summarizes Cardinal's structure. Cardinal Systems is a holding company for the shares of a hundred sixteen subsidiaries. The subs own all the physical and real and intellectual property. Cardinal Systems' shares are owned by the Frank Cardinale Trust, administered by Manuel Colibri as trustee."

Kate frowned. "Colibri just administered a trust? Like some bank vice president?"

Jack raised his index finger. "Actually, not much like that at all. As trustee of the trust, Colibri would own legal title to all of the stock. So he could vote to make the company do whatever he wanted it to. He could vote that the company should pay him a salary. He could vote to buy a patent or to sell one. Hell, he could vote to serve free lobster in the company cafeteria. And from what I read in the papers he did. But he didn't own the stock for his own benefit."

"Then whose benefit did he own it for?"

"Well, let's keep reading and we'll find out." Kate's father closed the first file, set it aside, then lifted the second file, which was the thickest one, off the stack and without opening it laid it atop the first one.

Kate pointed at the unopened file. "That's the fattest one. Why did you skip it?"

"Because it's Pullman and Hartwell's bill for generating all the rest of these files."

Kate narrowed her eyes. Pullman and Hartwell was the old line law firm that had done the Powell family legal work since the Powells had been exporting California rock oil and importing peasant labor from China and bootleg whisky from Canada. P and H lawyers were the cream skimmed from America's elite law schools, and they had chafed at taking orders from an in-house Powell Diversified lawyer whose degree had been earned after he had finished his day job. "P and H helped you out? They hate your guts and you hate theirs."

Jack shook his head. "They wouldn't have given out confidential client information even if they loved me."

"So where did you get these?"

"Paul Eustis let me borrow them from the Powell Foundation office."

Kate cocked her head. "The chief butler at Powell Hall? The little southern guy who walks like a penguin?"

"He walks like a penguin because a North Vietnamese Army sentry shot Paul's kneecap off while Paul was slitting his throat. There's an automatic in the Bentley's glove box in case Paul has to shoot some protestor's kneecap off."

"Dad, he's still just a *butler*. You always said there

was an impenetrable legal information firewall between the Powell charities and Powell Diversified. And that David was too much of a gentleman to ever breach it."

"David is. But I'm not. So I went over to Powell Hall today, while David's up at Tahoe."

Kate's jaw dropped. "Dad!"

Kate's father held his hands out palms down. "Take it easy! David and I have worked together long enough that I understand that David wouldn't *want* to know if I breached the firewall. The only person who logically might give a shit now is dead. I think Colibri would be pleased that somebody's trying to figure out whether somebody had him killed. Don't you?"

"You could have asked Cardinal. Or the police."

"The reason we're doing this is because the police don't care and Cardinal's management is chasing real penguins. Besides, I doubt that Cardinal's employees would have access to Colibri's personal affairs."

"Well, if Colibri's own company doesn't even know his estate plan, why the hell does the Powell Foundation have all this stuff?"

"Because the foundation paid Pullman and Hartwell to examine and make recommendations about Colibri's estate plan."

"I don't understand."

"You understand that David Powell gives away money."

Kate nodded. "You always said he was just trying to atone for the way his ancestors made the family fortune."

"There are worse motives for investing in good causes than a desire to be loved, Katy. David's been preaching philanthropy to every Silicon Valley instant millionaire he could find for as long as I've known him. David offers to have the foundation's law firm review their estate plans, at his expense."

"Why?"

"Because he explains to them that a good estate plan can save a lot of money and a bad one can waste a lot more. Most of them eventually return the favor by contributing to charities that David likes."

Kate pointed at the rest of the stack. "So is the answer really in those files?"

Her father opened the next file. "We'll see." He ran a finger across the first page and read aloud. "'EXECUTIVE SUMMARY: At the request of the Powell Foundation our estate planning section has reviewed documents in attachment A, provided to us directly by Mr. Manuel Colibri."

Jack skipped forward. "'We have also reviewed applicable statutes, regulations, and judicial precedents, applied them to the facts developed from the materials reviewed, and summarize our findings, conclusions, and recommendations as follows:

"'1. The principal property to be considered consists of the common stock of Cardinal Systems . . . currently valued at approximately one trillion dollars.'"

Kate whistled. "That much?"

Jack shrugged and kept reading. "'The only other notable property for which we were separately provided information are those items enumerated in a handwritten schedule of property dated July 16, 2018, and provided by Manuel Colibri. We make no estimate of value of these assets except to note that they are likely immaterial in comparison to the shares of Cardinal Systems.'"

Kate wrinkled her forehead. "If they're immaterial why mention them?"

"The notable property question's a catchall some firms ask. It's to remind clients who may be losing their marbles to make disposition of assets of sentimental value. Like the brooch Aunt Minnie always promised to her niece."

"Oh."

Jack nodded. "The schedule will clear up what Colibri thought was important enough to make a specific disposition of. We'll get to that in a minute. The important question is who gets a trillion dollars worth of stock."

Jack ran his finger faster through the pages, skimming phrases. "'The Current Estate Planning documents appear to be executed with all requisite formalities and would in all probability be given effect as written if presented to a court of competent jurisdiction.'" Jack raised his eyebrows. "Well, P and H may be pricks, but they're good lawyers. If they say the documents will stand up in court, they will." He flipped a page and read as his finger moved. "Irrevocable Trust dated and effective July 1, 1983, appointing Manuel Colibri as Trustee... the Trustee possesses an expressly unrestricted power of appointment..."

"What does that mean?"

"A lot. Colibri didn't have to continue as just a trustee. He could have owned the company outright anytime he wanted to. All he had to do was appoint himself owner of the stock. Or he could have given the stock to somebody else, just by appointing them."

"How could he do that?"

Jack shrugged. "He could execute a formal document.

He could write a letter. He could provide for it in his will. These days I'd bet a court would let him get away with a video recorded on one of your little phones, as long as he did it with the right witnesses and the right recitals."

"Then why wouldn't he just *do* it?"

"I told you a good estate plan can save a lot of money. The reason the stock was put into an irrevocable trust in the first place was probably so when Frank Cardinale finally died, he didn't own it, the trust did. So Frank's death wasn't a taxable event for federal estate tax purposes. There are plenty of taxes that *would* have to be paid, and plenty of ways to finagle them, and eventually a taxable event would occur. But on the face of this the federal estate tax on a trillion-dollar estate, that could be deferred, could be about four hundred billion dollars."

"Oh. Wow."

Jack kept skimming the lawyers' letter. "'If Trustee does not exercise said power during his life or competency, the Trust corpus would vest per the beneficiary clause, which clause is fully discussed below. THEREFORE, WE STRONGLY RECOMMEND THAT MANUEL COLIBRI CONSIDER IMMEDIATELY EXERCISING HIS POWER OF APPOINTMENT AND/OR OTHERWISE COMPREHENSIVELY PROVIDE FOR DISPOSITION OF HIS ESTATE.'"

"What's that mean, Dad?"

"If Colibri gave the stock to himself, there would be a big tax to pay, sure. But if he *didn't* give the stock to himself, or to somebody else, before he died, he would lose control of the whole enchilada. Whoever's named in the beneficiary clause would own the most valuable company in the world. Worst case, after tax, that could still be worth six hundred billion dollars."

"Dad, with so much at stake, surely Colibri tidied this mess up."

Jack wagged his finger. "This summary memo was only written two months before Colibri got unexpectedly pushed off a bridge. So far as we know he had no living relatives. Katy, people put off decisions about their death unless it's staring them in the face."

Kate stiffened. Her father didn't see the irony.

Jack said, "There's nothing in this file that says Colibri tidied up the power of appointment or wrote a will or executed a codicil to any will he might have had outstanding."

"Then where does the stock go? Who's won the lottery?"

As Jack flipped to the end of the executive summary he paused at the tab labeled "Schedule of Notable Assets provided to us by Manuel Colibri."

Kate stepped around the table and read over her father's shoulder. The "schedule" was just a copy of a single handwritten sheet that read:

> Manuel Colibri
> July 16, 2018:
> OMC H4282.606
> LOH EDA 2018.5
> APB 272
> CJM H1
> CAS TE21
> DRB 833

"What are those, Dad? Symbols of stocks he owned? Numbered bank accounts?"

"Maybe. Most stocks symbols are three letters. But I don't see any blue chips I recognize and the numbers don't look like share positions."

"Numbered bank accounts?"

He shook his head. "Not enough digits."

Kate snapped her fingers and pointed at her father. "He *did* change his estate. And those are safe-deposit boxes. And after he changed his will he put it in one of them!" She wrinkled her forehead. "Or a copy in all of them. Or something."

Jack shrugged. "Whatever it's a list of, it's dated a year and a half earlier than this opinion. Katy, lets come back to that after we see who gets the big money."

Jack flipped to the beneficiary tab then read aloud, "Archdiocese of San Francisco." He sat back in his chair, mouth agape. "Son of a bitch!"

"Dad, Colibri wasn't even Catholic, as far as anybody knows."

"But when the trust was written in 1983, I'm guessing Frank Cardinale was as good an Italian North Beach Catholic as your mother was a good Boston Irish one."

Kate stared at the ceiling. "Colibri put off appointing himself owner, because he didn't expect to be murdered and he wanted to keep deferring a four-hundred-billion-dollar tax bill. And now the Catholic Church inherits a trillion-dollar company."

"Very convenient for the mackerel snappers."

Kate shook her head slowly. "Dad, don't go there."

He narrowed his eyes. "Why not?"

"Dad, the Catholic Church did not have Manuel Colibri killed so it could inherit his money."

"The Catholic Church has been having people killed for two thousand years for a lot less."

"Apart from the fact that absolutely nothing whatsoever supports your suspicion, people are only motivated by something they know. You practically stole this file, so why would you think the Church knows about the trust's terms?"

"The trust dates from 1983. Over the course of thirty-seven years I'm thinking the Church got wind of this. Who knows, Frank Cardinale may have confessed it to some priest. Hell, your mother told them years ago that she was leaving them twenty grand."

Kate reached across the table and took her father's hands in hers. "Dad, look at me. You are not going to pursue some delusional Catholic Church murder conspiracy theory. Because it is batshit crazy. Got it?"

He ground his teeth and his eyes glistened. "Those bastards made her think she could buy heaven, Katy."

The day had been long and stressful. So had the last two years. Now wasn't the time to finally deal with this.

Still Kate felt her heart rate climb, her breathing rasp, and the words spilled out anyway. "Dad! Listen to me. In the early stages maybe Mom kept too much to herself and her priest. And maybe she underrelied on chemo and overrelied on prayer and holistic medicine. But we both know that in the end that wasn't what killed her."

Jack Boyle shook his head at his daughter, his face blank. "Katy, what are you saying?"

He still didn't accept it. Maybe he never would. Maybe he never should.

"Never mind. I'm not saying anything, Dad." She

stood and pressed her hands palms down on the table until the trembling subsided and her breathing slowed. Then she gathered their plates and empty beer bottles and turned away. "I've had a long day." And a long two years. "I need a rest. So do you."

EIGHTEEN

The door chime woke Kate Boyle in the dim morning light that filtered through the drawn shade. She stared up at the ceiling of the bedroom in which she had slept for the first eighteen years of her life. The discolored rectangle above her head marked the spot where she had Scotch taped Jimmy Kocurski's junior picture forever. Or until he asked Kate's BFF Meagan Degenbach to the prom, a tragic betrayal that had occurred sooner.

The chime rang again.

Kate wrapped her pillow around her ears. "Dad! The doorbell's ringing!"

No response. The most likely explanation was that her father was not responding so that she would be forced to drag her ass out of bed. This would cure her of congenital laziness, of ennui preached by hippies, and of the other uncountable weaknesses that Jack Boyle believed had rotted the ruin that American culture had become.

At the third ring, she rolled onto her side, squinted at the nightstand clock, and moaned. "Nine a.m.?"

Her father's failure to answer the door was, in fact, none of the above. Her father was already hours gone for the morning papers and for his coffee, as always.

Fourth ring. The only thing more annoying than a morning person was a persistent morning person.

She kicked back the comforter and stumbled down the stairs wearing the high-school leftover cutoffs and T-shirt she had found in her dresser, then cleaned house in, then slept in.

At the landing she paused and pressed her fingers to her temples, before a three-beer hangover could crack her skull open.

Despite whatever indeterminate number of nightcaps her father had consumed after she had crashed last night, he had risen from the dead like Lazarus, on four hours sleep. As he always had.

From her father Kate Boyle had inherited skepticism and pugnacity. From her mother Kate had inherited a disaffinity for early mornings and a constitution incapable of absorbing even three lousy Heinekens. In assigning Kate Boyle her genes, Mother Nature had been as traitorous a bitch as Meagan Degenbach had been.

As Kate reached the front door, the bell rang again.

She leaned against the door jamb. "If you're Jimmy Kocurski you're too damn late!"

"I'm not—"

"Obviously, you moron! Who the hell are you?"

"Benjamin Shepard. With DHS."

"Leave it on the step."

"You don't understand—"

She stood tiptoe in her bumblebee-striped kneesocks and peered out the peephole. A tall, broad-shouldered man wearing a suit held some sort of cardboard box in both hands. She called through the door, "I have to sign for it?"

"Not—"

"Where's your uniform?" This visitor was obviously no delivery man, which meant he was a liar. He also was obviously an early riser, which was even worse. "I'm dialing 9-1-1 while I'm talking. So if I were you, I'd beat it."

"Not DHL. DHS. I'm with the Department of Homeland Security, ma'am."

Kate flicked her eyes to be sure the deadbolt was closed, then leaned her weight against the door. "And I'm with the Justice League of America."

"Yes, ma'am. Are you Katherine Boyle, by any chance?"

She stiffened. "What if I am?"

"I've been trying to leave phone messages for Jack or Katherine Boyle since yesterday. Nobody answered so I decided to drop by."

"In the middle of the night?"

"It's nine a.m., Ms. Boyle."

DHS? Something drifted at the back of her mind. One good thing Kate Boyle had inherited from her parents was a damn good memory. "Just a minute."

Kate shuffled to the kitchen, then riffled through her father's recent newspapers until she relocated the article about the Golden Gate bombing. A fuzzy photo of the mayor of San Francisco, seated with a group, was captioned "Mayor Dunn meets with her staff and DHS Liaison Benjamin Shepard."

A cold knot formed in Kate's belly as she padded back to the front door. She hadn't spent much time as a journalist in Washington. But she had spent enough to treat a federal agent's unannounced knock on her door as a visit from a KGB death squad. "You have a warrant?"

"Ms. Boyle, I'm not here to ask you questions. I'm here to answer any questions you may have."

"Why?"

"I was hoping you could tell me that. All I got was an address, a phone number, and an assignment direct from the secretary of the Department of Homeland Security to contact you and Mr. Boyle and answer your questions."

"Fine. I'll think some up. Come back at noon."

"Ms. Boyle, a car dropped me off here. I brought coffee and doughnuts. By noon they'll be cold."

She'd never heard of a death squad that brought doughnuts.

Kate slid off the chain, unsnapped the deadbolt and opened the door.

Benjamin Shepard looked to be her age, as tall as Kirk, with better shoulders, shorter hair, and softer brown eyes.

She stood aside and as he passed she smelled coffee and fresh bakery and a very cute man who had obviously just stepped out of the shower. Maybe good things did happen when you got up before 10 a.m. Kate raked at her hair, pinched her cheeks, and wished she didn't smell like Clorox.

She motioned him to sit at the kitchen table, sat across from him and leaned forward on her elbows. "I'm sorry for the paranoid attitude. It's congenital. Please, tell me about your—case."

He wrinkled his forehead. "You don't want to wait for your husband?"

"I don't have a husband. Jack Boyle's the paranoid I inherited the attitude from. He goes out at six every morning to read newspapers, drink coffee, and wait for Ronald Reagan's third term."

"Oh." It seemed that Shepard's eyes lit, and he smiled.

"So it's just you and me, Mr. Shepard." Kate flicked her eyebrows.

"Ben." He smiled, then cocked his head. "I'm confused. Why are you and your father—?"

Kate said, "You've heard of David Powell?"

"Of course."

"He was a friend of Manuel Colibri's. He's also a friend of the mayor of San Francisco. David wanted the bombing looked into more aggressively than you folks seemed inclined to do. So he asked my father and me to help out."

"You're criminologists?"

Kate shook her head. "My dad was a lawyer for David for years. I'm an investigative journalist."

"Then think of me as a forthcoming source."

Kate sat back and crossed her arms. In her mind the person she wanted more information about, after Colibri himself, was Victor Carlsson, the ambitious prick with the too-perfect alibi. "Okay, Mr. Shepard. Let's see whether your definition of forthcoming matches mine. Ever heard of a Cardinal executive who's headed for the South Pole named Victor Carlsson?"

Shepard pulled his phone from his pocket with his left hand, thumbed it on, then laid it on the table between them. It was a C-phone GIGA, more a tablet than a phone, but in Shepard's hand it looked as small as a domino. He said, "The FBI interviewed Carlsson aboard the ship he's on via satellite phone video link, yesterday. I made a highlight reel of the interview for the secretary."

Kate's mouth hung open. "You're willing—?"

Shepard smiled. "Don't worry. I always edit out anything that could remotely be considered classified from any summary material I turn the secretary loose with. He can be...expansive when he recommunicates. And his instructions to cooperate with you were explicit and open-ended."

This was like having your own Terminator. Kate smiled back.

Shepard entered passwords, poking his phone with his left index finger, then said to Kate, "I'll spare you the boring parts." Then he tilted his head toward his phone and said, "Play VF 1/20-9335. Highlight Reel. Begin fourteen minutes eighteen seconds to end."

And a Terminator with a Boyle-quality memory.

The face that appeared on the phone's screen was scraggle-bearded, blue-eyed, and frowning. But it was obviously the guy she had seen in online photos.

Carlsson said, "Yes, we did argue on occasion. Manny expected pushback from his subordinates just like I expect it from mine."

An off-camera voice said, "What did you argue about, Mr. Carlsson?"

"Product design."

"Can you be more specific?"

"I can. But I won't. The mobile electronics business is very competitive."

"This is a secure link, Mr. Carlsson."

"I think I'm in a better position to judge that than you are. Look, the crew says there's weather coming and they need this uplink."

"Very well, sir. We can continue this later."

"We can continue this when I get back to the office. And after I've consulted counsel."

"If that's your preference."

"My preference is you drop the tone that says I had Manny blown up. Because it's ridiculous."

The phone's ringer cut in and Shepard stopped the video. Peering at the caller ID, he frowned, then raised the phone to his ear and said, "Answer."

Kate stood and pointed at the kitchen. "I'll wait in—"

Shepard shook his head. "Please. Stay."

He spoke into his C-phone. "Mick?" Shepard listened, nodded. "Be there in an hour." He rang off, then looked up at her. "Ms. Boyle, would you like to accompany me to a meeting with a forensics analyst about developments in the collection of Mr. Colibri's DNA?"

She laughed. "Only a policeman asks a woman to the morgue for a first date."

Shepard blushed right down to his dimples, then shook his head. "I wasn't—" he paused. "I'm not a policeman. I'm a law student."

Kate wrinkled her brow at Shepard, who should have been as many years removed from postgraduate education as she was. "Taking you a while to get through, isn't it?"

"I took time off after college." He shrugged. "To do something that seemed important at the time. Then life happened. At the moment I'm kind of interning as Secretary Petrie's aide."

"Arthur Petrie?" Christ. She had forgotten that buffoon's nomination was still pending.

Shepard shrugged his big shoulders. "The job opened up just after I finished my first year at Georgetown Law School. I got lucky."

Shepard unpacked three coffees and a bag of doughnuts from his cardboard box. He did it with just his left hand, as inefficiently as would a rich snot who had never bussed a table in his life.

Kate narrowed her eyes as she pried the lid off her coffee, and stared at Shepard through the steam that rose from it.

Her time at the *Washington Post* had taught her that patronage jobs like Shepard's didn't go to the lucky; they went to the children of the wealthy and of the connected.

Her blushing policeman turned out to have more in common with Kirk the Jerk than great shoulders. The two of them probably shared a III after their names, a soft pass into and through an Ivy, and the luxury of knocking around the world for a few years after college, skiing the Andes and surfing the Maldives. All bankrolled by their trust funds.

The idle rich pedigree was disappointing enough. But even in the clown show that was Washington, a rich kid who could probably intern for anybody chose Petrie, a bombastic ego on feet?

Kate stood and said, "Stay put there, Shepard. Eat a doughnut."

His brown eyes turned sad as his forehead wrinkled. "Did I say something wrong?"

Whatever Shepard's personal shortcomings, he apparently was willing and able to provide her fast-track access to information that would be hell to get once Carlsson, who seemed not only the prick that Quentin Callisto said he was but a guilty prick to boot, got back to his office. Once he did, his corporate lawyers would launch a legal shit storm while he covered his tracks.

As she left the room she said over her shoulder, "It'll keep you out of trouble while I get dressed. Then I'll drive us to this meeting of yours."

Shepard straightened. "Oh. You're coming? I'm happy to call us a car."

Kate shook her head. "I'm in a hurry, whether you are or not. And I do my own driving."

NINETEEN

Jack Boyle stared up at the ordinary office building, dim in San Francisco's early morning shadows. Catholic as Marian Boyle had been, her husband had never seen the Archdiocese of San Francisco's offices. He had expected a fluted slice of St. Peter's. After all, these people could afford it.

The archbishop of San Francisco's outer office proved to be as disappointingly un-Spanish Inquisition as the archdiocese's exterior.

"His Grace will see you now, Mr. Boyle." The archbishop's secretary, who except for his turned collar could have been any other administrative assistant in a black suit, smiled, stood, led Jack into the archbishop's office, and left the two of them alone.

It was a cavernous office, as large as David Powell's in the tower on Market Street, but with less inspiring views.

The archbishop was in his fifties, gray and balding.

Like his assistant he wore a vested black business suit. Except for a clerical collared shirt and a little cross on a silver chain that hung round his neck, he could have been a stockbroker.

He smiled as he shook Jack's hand. "Mr. Boyle, my pleasure." He led the two of them away from his desk to a pair of upholstered chairs divided by a table set with a coffeepot and cups.

His Grace sat, poured for both of them, opined on *El Nino,* the Giants' prospects, and the quality of the coffee. He smiled all the while, and never once suggested that he had a direct line to the guy in charge of any of his small talk topics.

Then the archbishop crossed one leg over the other, laced the fingers of his hands over his knee, and leaned forward. "Jack, I understand from the mayor's office that you may have a question about Manuel Colibri's relationship to the archdiocese."

"I do. What was it?"

The cleric shook his head. "So far as our records show, nothing. Of course, a company of Cardinal's size supports various Catholic charities around the world, and I'm sure many of its employees share our faith. But no more than would be the case with any multinational corporation."

"How about his predecessor at Cardinal, Frank Cardinale?"

The archbishop nodded. "I had the matter researched after your call. Actually, Mr. Cardinale was an active member of the congregation at Saints Peter and Paul Church in North Beach when I was an associate pastor there. Although I'm afraid I have no specific recollection of him."

"Have you heard anything about what's going to happen to Cardinal since Colibri's death?"

The clergyman furrowed his brow. "I haven't. I trust the company will choose new leadership." He smiled. "If they chose a Catholic I would be delighted."

"What if they chose someone bent on accelerating Cardinal's life-extension research?"

The archbishop sipped his coffee, then frowned. "I'm afraid I don't understand the question. But we like to think we've been in the business of life extension, one way or the other, for two thousand years."

"Exactly. If people started living forever, your product would be obsolete, wouldn't it?"

The archbishop grinned and shook his head. "The Church has always welcomed medical advancements that prolong and enhance Earthly life. There are more hospitals named for or founded by Catholic saints than there are for or by pharmaceutical companies. We don't see biochemistry as the enemy, if that's what you're suggesting. We've always found Satan a sufficiently robust adversary."

"You haven't heard where Cardinal Systems' ownership might be headed?"

The cleric wrinkled his forehead. "Mr. Boyle, I really don't know. And frankly I'm surprised that you think I would know. Or that I should care."

The guy was good. Every tick and signal Jack had learned to read in people said the archbishop was telling the truth, the whole truth, and nothing but the truth. So help him, God, of course. If Jack were on a jury, he would hold out for acquittal. But then, the archbishop had been trained by an outfit that had successfully peddled the biggest whopper in history for two thousand years.

"Mr. Boyle, if I may, I have a question for *you*." He shifted in his chair. "When I was contacted about your request for this meeting, I did some checking about you as well as about Mr. Cardinale. I learned that, like Mr. Cardinale, your late wife was a practicing Catholic. The loss of a spouse is perhaps the most difficult loss any of us must endure. And I understand that her loss was, perhaps, unusually painful for you."

"Is there a question in there someplace?"

The archbishop clasped his hands in his lap as he nodded. "I also learned you were a lawyer, and by reputation a good one. No, I failed to deliver a question in there. It was more an offer. If the Church can in any way assist you in dealing with Marian's passing, please know that you are welcome in our house."

Jack blinked back a tear, nodded. "Thanks. But I wasn't raised a Catholic."

"Neither was Jesus, but we still think highly of him around here." He smiled. "If you have no other questions, I do have other appointments this morning." He stood and walked Jack to the door to his outer office.

As Jack passed by the archbishop's assistant's desk, he noticed that one of the outside lines' buttons had just lit. He shook his head to clear it of the knee-jerk suspicion.

Kate was right. The idea that these people went around bumping tycoons off, either for the money or to get rid of the competition, was batshit crazy. It would take a boatload of evidence to persuade any judge or jury otherwise.

TWENTY

Jerry Chisholm blinked as he stepped from the dim interior of Saints Peter and Paul Church into the sunlight that flooded the lawn and bare trees of Washington Square, just across Filbert Street.

On the sidewalk he turned, looked back at the church, its twin spires resplendent, and smiled. His mood had lightened, as he had been told, and as he had found, it would. Without medication. He had come to despise the medication.

Jerry had returned to the Church even though he had been far from a perfect Catholic. As he had been reminded, DiMaggio hadn't been a perfect Catholic either, and without an annulment of his first marriage had been denied the opportunity to marry Marilyn Monroe in Saints Peter and Paul. Even so, Joe DiMaggio had been a hero. Jerry Chisolm intended to be a hero, too.

Jerry basked in the sunshine, eyes closed and face upturned, for a moment, then turned and walked down Filbert until he arrived back at his car, parked in the shadows in the alley where he had been told to park it.

He glanced at the car's Nevada tags. He had been driving on them for months, since he had moved. He needed to get California plates. Jerry did not consider himself above the laws of man. Although there were some men who considered themselves above God's law. Jerry didn't like that.

As had become the custom, he had left the car unlocked, and a manila envelope had been tucked beneath the front passenger seat.

He sat in the car, opened the large envelope and shook out the contents. The letter-sized white envelope inside contained the cash stipend that covered both his rent and car payment. The other item in the manila envelope was a new phone. Like his current phone, it was a cheap grocery store prepaid.

Before he pulled away from the alley he stepped back out of the car, smashed the old phone with his heel, then dropped half the pieces and the blank envelopes into a dumpster. The other bits of the old phone he would dispose of miles away. They said they were precautions that would prevent identity theft. It seemed to him to be overdramatic, but hardly an unreasonable ask from the people who had given him his life back.

He thumbed the new phone's on button. Already, he had a message. He hoped it would involve nothing more taxing than the previous one had. But if it did, Jerry was prepared.

Jerry Chisholm's life up to this moment seemed to him to have prepared him for what he assumed lay ahead. He wasn't particularly frightened or excited. After all, life by itself lacked intrinsic value. A life's worth could only be determined after it ended, and the world could judge what was left behind.

TWENTY-ONE

Ben and Kate Boyle sat shoulder to shoulder on gray plastic chairs that filled up the remaining floor space in the corner Mick Shay called home in the offices of the SFPD Marine Unit at the Hyde Street Pier. The rest of Mick's space was stuffed with Mick, his desk, and the forensic technician that Mick had persuaded to retest Manuel Colibri's home.

She was a thin African-American woman named Brenda who wore her hair cut as high and tight as an infantry private's, and her face looked so tight that it could break if she smiled.

Brenda held a clipboard in one hand while she adjusted black-rimmed glasses with the other and spoke to Mick. "Okay. I retested the whole place." She tugged a sheaf of papers off the board and slid it across Mick's desk. "Here's your copy of my full report. Now, I'm gonna give you the quick and dirty." She raised her index finger. "You know I know what I'm doing, Mick. And I redid perfectly good work as a favor. So don't give me attitude if you don't like hearing what I found. And what I didn't find."

Mick twisted back and forth in his swivel chair and it creaked while he frowned. "What's wrong? You said on the phone you found somebody's DNA."

"I did. But I didn't find Colibri's DNA."

Mick said, "We don't *have* Colibri's DNA. So how do you know that?"

"I know because what I found matches the DNA of Leslie Pumphrey."

"Who the hell is—?"

"Leslie Pumphrey was convicted of burglary three years ago, so his DNA's in the database."

"How the hell—"

Brenda paused, then tilted her head forward so she could stare at Mick over the tops of her glasses. "Mick, if you keep interrupting, this won't be the quick and dirty. It'll just be the dirty."

Mick crossed his arms and grunted.

Brenda cleared her throat. "Before I visited the premises, I checked for any prior official activity related to the address. It seems Mr. Colibri's contractors pulled all necessary permits for a complete teardown and rebuild, which was completed six years ago. However, some of the inspections of finished work remain open because Mr. Colibri is rarely home during normal business hours to admit an inspector."

Mick fidgeted and Brenda shot him a look. "I agree. There's some building inspectors over in Marin County that need to get off their asses. But if I were a building inspector, it's the last place I'd worry about. According to the inspections that *were* completed it's earthquake proof and environmentally friendly and the construction is top drawer.

"The only other activity is that back on July sixth of 2018, Mr. Colibri reported an attempted burglary of his residence. The investigating officers found that the place is as secure as Fort Knox—which I verified when I was there, by the way—but somebody had apparently gotten over the compound wall and around the alarms and made an attempt to force a window in the home's laundry room, apparently while Mr. Colibri wasn't home. He told the investigating officers that his home is designed to maintain itself, and anything it doesn't do he attends to himself. He also rarely entertains visitors, so there wasn't really a question of an inside job. The window latch had been damaged, but no entry appeared to have been made. Mr. Colibri told the investigating officer that nothing inside the residence appeared to have been disturbed."

Brenda shifted in her chair. "With all that in mind I examined the laundry room window latch and found a small quantity of what appeared to be dried blood. DNA in dried organic fluids can be some durable shit. I collected a sample and tested it. I got a match to Pumphrey."

Brenda tugged her report off her clipboard and turned to the next page. "I sampled the usual locations, including but not limited to those locations the previous investigation sampled."

Mick opened his mouth, closed it.

"And a bunch more places that they maybe should have sampled. The samples were analyzed thoroughly and precisely in accord with all applicable protocols. The results were that no sample returned a result other than the blood on the window latch." She looked up at Mick. "The end. Now you can talk."

Mick pushed out his lower lip. "What do you make of it, Bren?"

Brenda shrugged her thin shoulders. "Theoretically, somebody could have hosed the whole place down with bleach and destroyed the DNA. But I didn't notice the smell, and neither did the other investigation the first time through. Besides, it's nearly impossible to scrub a whole house perfectly clean, especially when somebody like me knows where to look."

"Any other possible explanations?"

"I ran an unrelated sample, just to be sure nothing was wrong with our equipment. *Those* results came out perfect."

Kate asked, "Would it matter if Colibri was a germaphobe? Like Howard Hughes? What if he wore surgical gloves and scrubs and booties around the house?"

Mick shook his head. "Unless he did all his business in plastic bags, right down to spitting out his toothpaste, Bren would've found something in a house he lived in for six years."

Brenda said, "I hate to agree with Mick, but yeah. And he had no reason to be a germaphobe. He was healthy as a horse."

Ben wrinkled his forehead. "How can you be sure of *that*?"

Brenda shrugged. "Well, Cardinal's got a health plan that's platinum plated plus. You want your DNA tested to see whether you have increased breast cancer risk? All you have to do is give up some spit, a concierge explains your results, and it's free."

"Nice," said Kate.

Brenda nodded. "Cardinal voluntarily integrates the results into the National Health Care Database if the employee doesn't opt out. Colibri never opted out. But his DNA's not in there."

Mick said. "Figures."

Brenda raised her index finger. "But what doesn't figure is nothing else of Colibri is in there either. He's in the plan, but he's never submitted a claim or taken a free physical. Not so much as a hangnail or a headache."

Kate said, "I wonder where he buys his vitamins."

Brenda shook her head. "He doesn't. At least, his bathroom medicine cabinet and kitchen cupboards were bare. Not an aspirin, much less prescription anything."

Mick said, "It's California. Maybe he chewed willow bark for a headache."

Brenda actually smiled as she shook her head. "Didn't see anything like that, either. Maybe the billionaires learned their lesson about herbs and acupuncture from Steve Jobs."

Mick said, "So that's it?"

Brenda shrugged again. "Could the hairs I pulled out of the sink traps have been synthetic materials like brush bristles? I saw a kid make that mistake once, but I know better. Were what I thought were skin flakes on clothing just pocket lint instead? No way." She shook her head. "I wish I could give you a better answer, but the only one I have right now is I don't know."

"So, what would you do next, Bren?" Mick asked.

"If I were you? Fire us experts. Fish up the corpse and identify the body the old-fashioned way."

Mick nodded. "Thanks Bren. I owe you."

As Brenda tucked her clipboard into her shoulder bag she paused. "One odd thing. Doesn't have anything to do with the test results, though. When I keyed in Colibri's gate combination and drove into his driveway, it was already dusk. I thought I caught a glimpse of somebody disappearing around the side of the house."

"What kind of somebody?"

"Smaller rather than larger. Something funny in the walk, like a limp. Just a flash. It could've been nothing. It could have been a big dog."

Ben said, "Could it have been the burglar? And *that's* why you found his DNA on the window? With the owner dead, coming back for a second try at an empty house may have seemed like a good idea."

Brenda shrugged. "Maybe to *some* burglar. Colibri had nice furniture. Nice AV system. A couple nice-looking paintings on the walls. In the living room there's a lockable glass display cabinet. Almost more a glass safe than a cabinet. But it's empty. All of that is exactly the same description the first investigation catalogued. Except for the laptop they picked up, which had nothing on it but business-related material. And the photos they took when they were there match what I saw yesterday."

Mick nodded. "Ah!"

Brenda shook her head. "But if anybody or anything was actually there the other day, it wasn't Pumphrey. Since the last incident he was reincarcerated for a parole violation. He died in San Quentin of complications from pneumonia three months ago."

After Brenda left, Ben asked Mick, "So where do we stand on the robot boat? My boss asks about it three times a day."

"So does the mayor. The vessel's underway north from Santa Barbara. How soon the ROV goes in the water depends on weather and on how soon they can redeploy the equipment after their last job." Mick stood and stretched. "Meantime, if you'll excuse me, I got a date with a rusty bulkhead.'"

Ben sat buckled in to the passenger seat of Kate Boyle's car as she dodged through traffic along San Francisco's waterfront toward the Bay Bridge ramp that led to Oakland.

Ahead, a Volvo's left turn signal flashed and she swerved right, only to encounter a delivery van ahead, that had the audacity to creep down the adjacent lane at the posted speed limit.

Kate braked, Ben pitched forward against his shoulder belt and she hammered her horn with her fist. "Go, you moron!"

Ben said, "My appointment's open-ended. Please feel free to slow down."

"I'm driving. Please feel free to shut up."

Ben settled back into the passenger's seat and tried to distract himself from the accidents waiting to happen by staring at Kate Boyle.

Ben found her an easy distraction. Kate Boyle made him believe the expression that a woman could take your breath away. And it wasn't just her driving. Her hair was red and fine, her skin was as fair as fresh milk and her wide blue eyes glistened above high cheekbones. And she filled out her business suit more like an athlete than a soft girl who lived behind a desk.

A motor scooter buzzed up the white line between the lanes of cars and she hissed, "Idiot!"

In a peculiar way Kate Boyle's hostility toward random traffic reassured him. There had been a moment, after she refused him entry and before he had mentioned Petrie, when she had seemed delightful and pleasant toward him. He was certain it wasn't about his hand. He didn't advertise it and she hadn't seemed to notice.

But for whatever reason, since that turn in their conversation she had treated him with disdain. But no more disdain than that with which she treated anonymous panel trucks.

Once they climbed the ramp onto the Oakland Bay Bridge, they cruised in steady, solid traffic multiple lanes wide, high above San Francisco Bay, and bound for Oakland, on the Bay's north shore. The absence of an alternative route seemed to relax her.

Kate Boyle asked, "Why are we going to the VA, Shepard?"

"The veteran who planted the bomb was being treated for PTSD. His therapist moves around to various facilities. She's at the Oakland VA Outpatient Clinic today. I want to learn more about him."

As she drove, Kate pulled a folded page from a pocket, smoothed it over the center of her steering wheel and began reading. "Well, I want to learn more about Manny Colibri, the man so private he hides his DNA."

Her car rapidly closed the few feet between itself and the rear bumper of a Mazda ahead while her eyes were off the road.

Ben gasped and stiffened, as though pressing his foot through the floor would arrest their progress.

Kate flicked her eyes up, braked so hard that her tires chirped. "Whoa!"

Ben pointed at the paper. "Ms. Boyle, can I help you with that?"

"This page is a verbal puzzle, not a rugby match. I have a hunch that this is a list of places. Probably safe deposit boxes. I think Colibri wrote a will or something and put it into one of them."

"He's dead. Why the hurry?"

"The asshole who I think had him killed, that smug dick in your video, Carlsson, is going to start covering his tracks in a couple days." She nodded at the paper. "But if a Columbia graduate can't figure this out—"

"Then maybe Columbia needs to graduate less condescending students."

She looked away from the road and stared at him. "Okay, smartass." She handed the page across the console as the traffic in all the Oakland-bound lanes stopped so dead that she put the car into park. "This is a list of stuff Manuel Colibri owned that he jotted down when he had his estate plan evaluated. Take it from there."

Ben exhaled, and realized that he had been holding his breath. He peered at the list, which was a copy of a handwritten page. After a minute he tugged out his C-phone and surfed the internet. After another minute he said, "Ah. Got it."

"Bullshit."

"Yes I do."

"Shepard, don't be smug. You people are always so smug."

"What people? All I said was—"

"Your *tone* was smug. And I bet you're wrong, anyway."

"Bet?"

"Smug loser buys coffee. Gracious winner picks the place."

"Done."

Kate Boyle said, "I call. Whaddaya got, Shepard?"

"This list is dated July 16, 2018. That's ten days after somebody tried to rob Colibri's house."

"It's also twelve days after Fourth of July. So what?"

"There was an empty display case in Colibri's living room, but nothing had been stolen. What if somebody getting past his wall as far as a window that led into his house spooked Colibri? So he was scared his stuff might get stolen?"

"What if he was?"

"He might have loaned his stuff to museums."

"And monkeys might have flown out of his butt. How is that a logical inference?"

"The wealthy do it all the time. Last year I wrote a paper about the deductibility of charitable gifts in kind, for a federal income taxation seminar. But I suppose you're already an expert on that."

"Now who's being condescending?"

Ben sighed. "Anyway, they get a tax deduction for the appraised value, and eliminate expensive art from their insurance. They get credit for being civic-minded. They can even set the donation up on a cycle. They can split possession time, and get a deduction for the time when the museum has the art. And museums have better security systems than most private homes, possibly even better than Colibri's."

Traffic rolled forward.

As her car lurched ahead Kate said, "Maybe. But that doesn't get us anywhere."

"Actually, it gets us everywhere." Ben held up his

phone and displayed its screen. "The very first entry on the sheet is OMC H4282.606. OMC? How about 'Oakland Museum of California'? And H4282.606? That reads like a museum catalog number to me."

Ben was tossed left as Kate floored the throttle, hurled the car across two lanes of accelerating traffic, and darted onto an exit ramp.

Behind them horns blared.

Ben extended his arms and braced himself against the dashboard. "What are you *doing*?"

"Proving you wrong. The Oakland Museum of California's a couple miles detour from the VA." Kate swerved right around an eighteen-wheeler. The truck blasted its horn as she cut back left in front of it.

Ben gritted his teeth and pressed his palms harder against the dash.

TWENTY-TWO

The receptionist led Ben and Kate to the open door of the office of the director of the Oakland Museum of California.

The office's occupant looked up from the screen at his desk, then stood, came around and greeted them. He was in his fifties, with pink, chubby cheeks, and wore a tweed jacket with leather patches on its sleeves.

The director smiled. "Mr. Shepard?"

"Ben." Ben smiled. "You're Doctor Brown?"

"Call me Ben, Ben. Unless you think it will be too confusing." The director frowned. "Actually, I'm already confused by a visit from the Department of Homeland Security. If there's an imminent threat to the museum, you should have been directed immediately to our security staff."

Ben shook his head. "Nothing like that. We—"

Kate unfolded Colibri's list, elbowed Shepard aside, then held it up in her left hand. She shook the director's hand with her right. "Kate Boyle, Dr. Brown.

This line item? H4282.606?" She rolled her eyes. "Could that *possibly* refer to an item in the museum's collections?"

"Well, that number matches our alphanumeric pattern, but we use a common system. Our catalog contains nearly two million items, so—," the director pursed his lips while he unfolded horn rimmed glasses and put them on. "Ah! Mr. Colibri! His morion."

Kate's eyes widened. "You know it?"

As the director stepped past them out of his office he motioned them to follow him. "I do. It's terrible what happened to him."

Ben leaned down and whispered to Kate, "I take my coffee black."

She whispered back, "Bite me, Shepard."

As they followed Brown, the director said, "The number of the item I would have had to look up. But as soon as I saw Mr. Colibri's name I recognized it instantly. Not so much because of the donor's celebrity as because of the quality of the donation. He brought it in personally. It's probably the finest morion in any public collection in the world."

Kate said, "I aced art history, but I don't recognize the artist."

"Ah." Brown smiled as he stopped at an elevator and pressed its call button.

They boarded and he pressed the button labelled "Level 2, History Gallery," not the one labelled "Level 3, Art Gallery," which was the level they were already on.

The elevator opened on a hushed, dim, and nearly deserted gallery of glass cases filled with dramatically lit artifacts, and placards that described them and their roles in various episodes of California history.

Brown led them to a display area signed "Cultures Meet." The area's centerpieces were free-standing glass cases opposing each other, each containing a single object. One was a feathered Incan headdress.

Facing the headdress, spotlit from above, mounted atop a thick glass rod that raised it to eye level, the object in the other case was a polished metal helmet, with a wide brim that rose at front and back to points like a boat's bow and stern. A rounded blade of a peaked crest traversed the helmet's crown from front to back, and segmented metal cheek guards, connected to the helmet by what looked like tattered leather binding, dangled below the helmet's brim.

Every surface of the object was decorated with scenes, etched into the metal, of warriors engaged in combat, against one another and against animals.

Gold rivets, shaped like flowers, ran along the helmet crown's base just above its brim.

The plaque beneath the helmet read:

MORION (HELMET) CIRCA 1570
Steel, Etched, with Gold Ornamentation
Anonymous Gift, 2018

Kate Boyle's mouth hung open in a beautiful, tiny "O." She said, "A conquistador helmet?"

Brown grinned as he nodded. "And such a special one that we moved the excellent morion we had on display off and replaced it with this one."

Kate cocked her head. "Was there anything with it? A document?"

Brown said, "Of course. An appraisal, for tax purposes. And the terms of the donation."

"Not a will?"

Brown pursed his lips as he shook his head. "Nothing like that. I'm quite certain. I could call up the file."

Ben said, "You said it's special. Why?"

Brown drew a ballpoint pen and pointed through the Plexiglas as he said, "Well, the extensive etching and gold overlaid riveting indicate its owner's high social rank. The Cross of Burgundy flag etching identifies the owner as Spanish."

Brown stepped to the case's opposite side and his visitors followed while he pointed again. "The dent near the comb on the left side is consistent with a blow by a right-hand wielded blunt instrument. It raises the possibility that the wearer utilized the helmet for more than ceremony. But I should point out that it's a high-comb morion helmet. Pizarro's conquistadors are often depicted wearing comb morions during early battles with the Inca, but the style didn't appear until the late 1540s, during the Incan Empire's death throes."

Ben wrinkled his brow. "It's real. But the owner wasn't Pizarro?"

Brown nodded. "Precisely. This piece's significance is as a tragic reminder of the fate of a people descended, according to legend, from the sun god. Who died out just three centuries later, unable to survive contact with the children of a different god."

Ben asked, "The anonymous donor, that's Manuel Colibri?"

Brown nodded. "But obviously you already knew that."

Kate said, "It's unusually valuable?"

"Value is a relative term. The presence of the cheek plates, still fastened by apparently the original leather hinge and headliner after four and a half centuries, is almost unique. The dent adds speculative romance, even if in fact someone may have added it with a baseball bat rather than an Incan war club. To a man of Mr. Colibri's means, a seven-figure value artifact may be trivial. But to a historian, it's priceless."

"You're saying that not only was it not Pizzaro's, it wasn't even worn in battle?" Ben asked.

Brown smiled. "Mr. Colibri believed it had been, or at least that's what he told me when he brought it in."

Kate said, "You're saying he got cheated?"

"Hardly. It's a genuine mid-to-late-sixteenth-century masterpiece. I'm saying that Mr. Colibri, like many novice private collectors, may have been swept away by the romance of the detailed provenance recounted to him by whoever he bought the piece from. But the helmet could as easily have been dented falling off a shelf in some armor shop, and spent the last four hundred fifty years sealed in a chest in a European cellar."

Brown turned toward the helmet, gleaming in the darkened gallery, and the three of them stared at it as he said, "It's every historian's wish that a piece like this could speak the truth of its history. But of course it can't."

TWENTY-THREE

Squire Eduardo Diaz de Oropesa stepped out of the single file of Spanish and native troops laboring up the steep, narrow trail. In the frigid early morning he dropped to one knee, gasping. Light in his head, he bowed it.

Ahead of him and behind him marched an expedition of two hundred fifty Spaniards, two thousand natives, and their four cannon.

On April 1, 1572, the Viceroy of Peru, Francisco de Toledo, Count of Oropesa, provoked by the murder of his ambassadors, had dispatched this force to carry a war to Tupac Amaru. Now the rebel king of the remains of the Incan Empire awaited them in his mountain stronghold in the valley of Vilcabamba.

The native soldiers, accustomed to these mountains, trudged past Eduardo, and so even did those other Europeans, older than Eduardo, who had lived among these hideous green peaks for years. The months that Eduardo had traveled after departing the bosom of his family in Oropesa had not acclimated him to the New World. Nor had the scant months since he had arrived in Lima, now two hundred leagues distant. And certainly neither had his ascent into these gigantic mountains, fully one league higher than the level of the sea at Lima. This ascent had, however, brought Eduardo one league closer to heaven.

A hand slapped Eduardo's morion. "Praying won't make that monstrosity on your head lighter, boy. Neither will your friend the viceroy."

Pedro el Galeote de Venecia stepped round to face Eduardo, then knelt himself. He tugged at the simple cloth cap he chose in preference to a soldier's morion.

Pedro was easily this expedition's oldest Spaniard, but he possessed a bear's hairy arms and torso. His accent was common and coarse, though no more coarse than his pox-ravaged cheeks, where his cheeks could be seen above his gray beard.

His surname was not, in fact, "el Galeote de Venecia." In fact, if he had a surname at all no one here knew what it was. The younger men mocked him with the name "el Galeote de Venecia," "the galley slave of Venice," because he claimed to have made passage to the New World as a sailor, and to have served once as a hired rower aboard galleys of the Venetian Navy.

Pedro stood, then dragged Eduardo to his feet, and the pair struggled to rejoin the column.

The further the expedition traveled from the already mountainous terrain around the city of Cusco, the higher and steeper rose the great, green sentinels that had guarded the remains of the Incan empire. An empire that had outlived its conqueror, Pizarro, who had died even before Eduardo's birth.

As the sun, from which the heathen Inca claimed direct descent, rose to its zenith, the column was halted and Pedro was called forward. Eduardo followed.

At the column's head a local man, dressed in what Eduardo considered rags, sat cross-legged atop a boulder, surrounded by helmeted Spaniards. The small brown man stared at a captain who stared back. Like Eduardo, the captain wore his morion and the other implements of battle.

The captain turned to Pedro. "Can you understand this one?"

The others may have mocked Pedro's age and his claims of past adventure, but they couldn't deny his command of the natives' diverse tongues.

Pedro exchanged a few sentences with the local man, then nodded to the captain. "He says his people don't follow Tupac. And they don't like him."

"Ask him what lies between us and Vilcabamba."

"He says he wants to be paid with gold."

The captain laid a hand on his sword's hilt. "Tell him if he doesn't tell all the truth, and quickly, I will pay him with steel."

One hour later Eduardo, Pedro, the captain, and a party of twenty-five Spaniards crept on hands and knees from the narrow, ascending path that the local guide had revealed to them. The party halted at the edge of a ledge and stared down into the narrow defile that led to the Incan settlement at Vilcabamba. A mountain wind in their faces carried what small sounds they made up the slope behind them.

A stone's throw beneath them, on another ledge, twenty unalerted Inca warriors, clad in simple cloth, and with their backs turned to the Spaniards, peered down. The gorge into which the Inca warriors peered offered the sole passage through which an attacking army would have to pass in single file, or perhaps by twos, to reach the valley of Vilcabamba. These Inca lay in ambush, with boulders barely small enough for a man to hurl down stacked beside them. Other far larger boulders had been balanced at the ledge's edge, ready to be levered down upon attackers.

Eduardo lay alongside Pedro as the captain whispered, "He was truthful after all. Perhaps I should have spared him."

Pedro whispered, "He said there are a half dozen more of these emplacements along this lower ledge between here and the fort at Huyana Pucara, where the valley widens. And he said that the approach to the fort is planted with sharpened palm stakes tipped with poison."

The captain gathered his men with silent gestures, then whispered, "We will roll up their flank and cut them down as they flee toward Vilcabamba, first one position and then the next." The captain drew his knife and turned it in his hand. "No shouting. Blades only. The more of them we take by surprise the greater their panic will grow as we advance. Forts and poison count for nothing when the enemy is in rout. Pause for nothing!"

As the others moved into position, Eduardo whispered to Pedro. "This flanking maneuver is precisely as Herodotus wrote of the Persians' rout of the Spartans at Thermopylae. I suppose that makes me as sound a tactician as the captain."

"Well, there's the value of a classical education, boy.

Because I'm sure the captain never heard of that, yet he figured it out anyway. But knowing how to kill a man and killing a man, that's the difference all the classics in the world can't teach. You stay close on my heels, boy. And that is all you do."

A moment later the Spanish fell upon the Inca, who turned in astonishment and were greeted with steel as they raised war clubs too late. Some were cut down by swords; others were hurled to their deaths over the precipice.

Eduardo stood shocked and mute, and as one Inca collapsed at his feet, his skull crushed by one of his own boulders wielded by a Spaniard, Eduardo turned away and fell to his knees, sick at his stomach.

In the distance, Eduardo heard the sound of booted feet running, and Pedro hissed. "Come *on*, boy! Pause for nothing, or die!"

By the time Eduardo regained his feet, wiped the spittle from his lips and the tears from his eyes, the ledge was silent except for the sighing wind. The only human presences in view were the twisted, bloody bodies of the Inca.

Eduardo laid a hand atop his helmet to steady it as he began to race forward, desperate to regain the safety of his countrymen. After three steps he tripped over the legs of a fallen Inca warrior, bloody face turned up to the sun and eyes closed.

Eduardo reached to touch the club that remained clutched by the motionless warrior's hand. It was a forked wooden shaft as long as a man's forearm, crowned with a round stone the size of a small cannon's ball.

Eduardo's fingertips brushed the club's shaft and the

Inca's eyes flew open, dark and bright, as he flailed with his club and struck Eduardo's helmet.

Stars burst in Eduardo's eyes, as they had when he had fallen from his father's horse as a child and struck his head on cobblestoned pavement.

When Eduardo regained his faculties, he lay on his back, staring up into the clear, gathering dusk, unsure whether hours or days had passed. His hands were bound in front of him, and a gag that tasted of blood and leather cut across his mouth.

The Inca who had clubbed him knelt above Eduardo, unfastening the leather tie that secured Eduardo's helmet. The helmet that the others had mocked that had saved Eduardo's life.

The Inca's face remained streaked with dried blood, and the skin beneath it, unlike the skin of most of the other living Inca who Eduardo had encountered, was smooth, entirely unmarked by the pox. Otherwise, Eduardo found this man no different in appearance from any other Inca.

When the man tugged Eduardo's helmet off, Eduardo kicked, twisted on the ground, and screamed against his gag. The man was obviously going to finish the work he had begun, crushing Eduardo's no longer-protected skull with the club.

The man raised both hands, palms out, and said, "Lie still. I have no wish to spill more blood here than your friends already have. I'm just waiting for the full moon to rise."

Many of the Inca, particularly those who had not resided within the Spanish settlements, spoke at best halting Spanish. This man's was excellent.

Eduardo closed his eyes and drifted to sleep. If

the man were lying, and clubbed Eduardo dead in his sleep, it would only confirm Eduardo's fears. Eduardo assumed that the man meant that the Children of the Sun sacrificed their captives only under a full moon.

The sound of running feet woke Eduardo, the moon full and bright in his eyes.

The Inca stood beside and above him, Eduardo's dented morion fixed atop his head with the cheek plates fastened beneath his chin. The helmet gleamed in the daylight-bright mountain moonlight as the man peered along the ledge in the direction that Eduardo's compatriots had disappeared.

In the distance Pedro shouted, "Get away from him, you murdering bastard!"

The man turned and fled along the ledge, away from Pedro and away from Vilcabamba. The old man arrived alongside Eduardo, puffing, sword drawn, then halted as the Inca disappeared into the night. Pedro knelt, levered Eduardo to a sitting position, and as he untied Eduardo's gag he said, "It appears that I arrived just in time to save your life."

Eduardo spit out the taste and bits of leather. "And I shall pray for your soul every day of my life that remains. Thank you for returning."

"The death of a fellow Oropesan might displease the viceroy. I would not want that displeasure on my conscience. What happened?"

"He played a corpse. Then when I approached he struck me with his club. The morion saved my life." Eduardo stared into the distance, where the mountains rose black and enormous beneath the moon. "He's running the wrong way."

Pedro shook his head, glanced over his shoulder down the defile toward the last fortress of the Inca. "No. In the other direction lies death for him. We have overrun Vilcabamba, or will in a few days. Tupac and the few who would die for him will be in flight like wounded boar, if they are not already. Within a few days, we will kill him or capture him and take him to Cusco."

"If he is captured?"

"Toledo will have his head on a pike in the square at Cusco as an example. Mark my words well. Killed or captured this is the end of the Inca. But perhaps not the end for your friend there."

"What do you mean?"

"He's clever. When I approached just now beneath the full moon, with its light reflecting off the morion, I took him for a Spaniard. If he travels by moonlight, any sentry will allow him to pass at a distance, or will allow him so close that it will be too late for the sentry."

"But to what end, Pedro? Where will he go?"

The old man untied Eduardo's hands and Eduardo rubbed his wrists. Pedro shrugged, "I suppose anywhere he chooses. That morion saved your life. Perhaps it will prove the charm that saves his as well."

"But there is nothing left for him in the New World."

"Then a fellow so clever may choose to make his way in the Old World."

"But why?"

"Why not? Were I in his predicament I would sooner risk being a galley slave in the Old World than to suffer any longer in this one."

TWENTY-FOUR

Jack Boyle kept the microcassette phone answering machine on the kitchen counter only because Katy gave it to her parents as a Christmas present. Anyone who thought they were too important to just call back later he didn't give a shit about anyway.

However, when he entered his kitchen after his visit with the archbishop the "new message" light on the machine flashed red, because Katy had replaced the machine's tape.

The message light piqued his curiosity not at all, but the object alongside the machine did.

It was a bag of doughnuts, and when he laid his palm on it he perceived they were slightly above room temperature. From this he deduced that they were probably both fresher and more expensive than the day-olds he usually bought with his morning coffee.

Alongside the bag lay Katy's handwritten note and a business card. He selected a jelly, and then read while he ate.

The card announced,

Office of the Secretary,
Department of Homeland Security

Benjamin R. Shepard, Aide to the Secretary

Kate's note read:

Dad—

I have reset your message machine. Please at least listen to your messages.

Because you *didn't*, these doughnuts arrived unannounced with a DHS guy. Have gone with him voluntarily for what he claims is a briefing from SFPD about Colibri's DNA. But if I'm not back for dinner call the ACLU.

—Love, K

Jack licked sugar off his fingers, then punched the answering machine's listen button.

"Jack, it's David. I'm back from Tahoe. I'll be at the Aquatic Park Bathhouse all day. Would you mind stopping by?"

Jack wrinkled his brow. It was unusual for David Powell to call Jack, personally, rather than through his administrative assistant. And David would find it unusual, indeed, if Jack didn't show up as requested.

Not because David Powell expected to be obeyed. But because David Powell played chess with human pieces and knew damn well that Jack would be too curious to stay away.

Before Jack climbed back into the Ford he read the business card again and smiled. This guy Shepard worked for that idiot Arthur Petrie. Worse, Shepard's job sounded like a patronage slot. That meant that Shepard was probably an idiot himself, and worse, an idiot born with a silver spoon in his mouth.

Jack Boyle did not suffer either politicians or, with the exception of David Powell, children of privilege gladly, and his intolerance had rubbed off on his daughter.

Jack smiled. If Katy had presumed as much about Benjamin R. Shepard's résumé as Jack had, then the poor bastard was having a very bad day.

The Aquatic Park Bathhouse had been built in 1939 as a New-Deal depression-buster, a joint project of the city of San Francisco and Franklin Roosevelt's Works Projects Administration. The building was three elongated stories tall, each set back from the one beneath it like a stepped pyramid. The structure's ground level, dug into the shore's slope, opened to a narrow beach that separated it from San Francisco Bay's waters.

Tapered at its ends, its street side studded with round porthole windows, the bathhouse was art deco's architectural interpretation of a ship moored at water's edge, and its portholes opened to interior spaces that had been painted floor to ceiling, by the 1930s' finest muralists, with pastel marine scenes.

In 1978 the Feds had merged their share of the bathhouse into the San Francisco Maritime National Historical Park, with a vision of converting it into a museum, and of restoring mural art that had been painted over when troops had been quartered there during World War II.

Instead the restoration had stalled, and for years

a fraction of the building had been used to display a handful of marine artifacts, part became a senior citizens center, and the rest was shuttered.

The Powell Foundation, after years of San Franciscan protest and counterprotest, had led the drive to relocate the senior center to bigger, better quarters two blocks away, at David's expense. With one more philanthropic facelift, the old girl would at last be ready for her close up.

Today the bathhouse's fresh paint gleamed white beneath a bright winter sun but the building, the parking lot west of it, which was filled with cargo trailers, and the intersection of Beach with Van Ness, were all fenced off behind striped barriers studded with signs that read "CLOSED FOR PRIVATE EVENT."

As the Ford crept along Beach Street toward the barricades it passed two twenty-something couples encamped in folding lawn chairs. The quartet huddled in the wind shadow of a sleek orange mountaineering tent, but still seemed to shiver inside shiny, puffy jackets. A printed cardboard sign flapping beside them read "SOS: SAVE OUR SENIORS." A handwritten sign pinned to the tent read:

The People Demand:
1. Restore the Aquatic Park Senior Center.
2. Reject elitism.
3. Fuck David Powell.

As Jack drove past the protestors, one of the girls waved and shouted to him, "You poor man! Go back! Your place isn't even there anymore!"

A gray-haired National Park Service Ranger in

green uniform and Smoky Bear Hat stood alongside a gap in the barriers, a clipboard in one hand. As Jack stopped and rolled down the Ford's window the ranger bent, then peered at him. "Museum's closed, sir. Can I help you?"

"Have I missed the geezer pinochle game?"

The ranger smiled and shook his head. "Those kids don't get it. The geezers love the new place. It's got faster free Wi-Fi, the plumbing's newer, and the Powell Foundation hosts free happy hours three nights a week."

Jack handed the ranger his driver's license as he pointed to the maroon Bentley, parked in front of the bathhouse entrance, that David drove when Paul Eustis wasn't driving him. "Jack Boyle. David Powell asked me to meet him here."

As the ranger flicked his eyes from the license to Jack's face, Jack jerked a thumb at the protestors. "You expecting more company?"

The ranger handed back the license and nodded. "The prediction's a thousand during the benefit if it doesn't rain. Nothing gripes the ninety-nine percent like the one percent flaunting it."

Jack shrugged. "It's a free country."

The ranger nodded, then tugged the barrier aside. "For all one hundred percent, last I heard. Pull 'er up behind Mr. Powell's car. You'll find him down on the beach."

Jack parked, then walked down the drive that spiraled alongside the bathhouse's curved wall until he reached the beach. There he found that David Powell was less on the beach than he was calf-deep in San Francisco Bay, khaki trousers rolled knee-high exposing bare white legs, his face protected from the sun by a broad-brimmed hat.

David and a half dozen workers bustled around a glistening mahogany torpedo that was a thirty-foot-long vintage speedboat. The beast had obviously just been slid out of a covered trailer backed up to the water's edge, and bobbed in the sheltered shallows inside the Aquatic Park breakwater. A temporary aluminum pier had been anchored to the beach, and stretched alongside the speedboat, which was tied to the pier by nylon lines.

David's now-empty trailer resembled the ones in the upper parking lot, which obviously awaited their own unloading.

David saw Jack, waved, then sloshed ashore; his sockless feet shod in perforated rubber clogs.

Jack eyed the billionaire's feet. "Cold water?"

David shuddered. "This time of year the bay feels as cold as Tahoe."

Jack pointed at the boat. "You brought this back from Tahoe?"

David nodded.

"It looks different. Does it have the right flare gun now?" David Powell collected and restored everything from wounded veterans like Paul Eustis to Duesenbergs to vintage speedboats like this one. David had once lost best in show at the Lake Tahoe Concours d'Elegance because his restored speedboat was equipped with the wrong model of flare pistol.

David shook his head. "This is a different boat."

Jack nodded. The other wooden-hulled speedboat had been named *"Woodpusher,"* chess slang for a mediocre player. The gold script across this boat's transom read *"Fianchetto."* Jack said, "You bought *another* one?"

David shook his head. "Not bought. Inherited. She's been under a tarp at the Whalers' Landing boathouse since World War II. I had her restored by some folks I know up at Tahoe."

"'Fianchetto?' Gave up on the chess names, did you?"

"Au contraire. The Fianchetto is development of a bishop to the board's long diagonal. When my grandfather wasn't bootlegging, he was a fan of the hypermoderns."

"Weren't we all. You do realize that the market doesn't reward paying attention to obscure crap?"

David shrugged. "I didn't restore her to make a profit. If I made money at things like this, they wouldn't be fun, they would be work."

"You know, David, the market will never reward you for working so hard to even the score for your family, either."

"I'd hardly call my lifestyle 'work,' Jack. But expiation of sin through good works isn't a new idea. Or even a particularly religious one. And when you sweep all the familial Powell sins into one pile, it takes a lot of good works to get even."

David's grandfather had built Whalers' Landing at the Pacific's edge south of Monterey, down the coast, and had named it for iron rings bolted into the surfpounded rocks upon which the mansion had been built. Nineteenth-century shore-based whalers had emplaced the rings as mooring points for both their whale boats and for the whale carcasses they dragged ashore to boil down to lamp oil.

"So this boat was your grandfather's?"

David nodded. "I'm not surprised that he hid it. During Prohibition, Powell Line steamers smuggled Canadian whisky down the coast. Rumrunners like this one lightered the bootleg ashore from the ships. 1919 through 1933 were very profitable for the Powells, Jack."

The Powells may have been San Francisco royalty, but like most royalty their empire had been forged in blood and lies, and sustained by ruthlessness. Nobody had ever managed to implicate David's grandfather, but a police chief accused of being his bagman had turned up drowned after an "accidental" fall from a boat crossing the bay one night. From land speculation to bribery to war profiteering to bootlegging, and maybe even murder, David's ancestors had made the family pile by following the rule that they made the rules.

And their play had always been as edgy as their work. David's grandfather's weekend party guests told stories of the old man standing for hours at the balustrade of the Whalers' Landing terrace, fifty yards from the Pacific, shooting migrating whales with an elephant gun as they swam past.

Jack eyed the motorboat stem to stern. David Powell was a captain of industry, a buyer and seller of great enterprises, as well as a philanthropist. But his life, as he had just said, did not resemble work.

The open boat's polished, rounded hull and topside was mahogany, finished as though sheathed in crystal, and studded with glittering fittings cast like fine jewelry. The hull tapered down toward the waterline aft of its two forward cockpits. Like a seagoing vintage Bentley, the cockpits coddled the captain and five lucky passengers on bench seats upholstered in red leather so fine that it would only be ordered by an owner who didn't have to maintain it himself.

Behind the two forward cockpits, the engine bay, with its doors wide open, appeared large enough to swallow a Volkswagen. In fact, the outsized motor that filled the bay looked as large as a Volkswagen. Polished twin exhausts thicker than a man's thigh curled away from an engine block capped with valve covers that shone like silver plate.

The boat stretched so long that behind the engine compartment was a third cockpit, a sort of marine rumble seat. A yellow pennant bearing the Powell family crest fluttered from a chrome standard that angled up from the stern. If the Great Gatsby owned a motorboat, Jack supposed it looked exactly like this one.

One of the workers eased behind the boat's wheel, pressed the starter, and the engine thundered and coughed gray smoke out through twitching twin exhausts that protruded through the rear transom.

When the engine settled into a lumpy burble, Jack shouted, "What kind of boat *is* this?"

David cupped hands round his mouth. "1926 thirty-foot Belle Isle Super Bear Cat triple cockpit with a 675 horsepower 2,000-cubic-inch Hispano Suiza V-12 engine. First time her hull's been wet since the New Deal. Care to join me for a ride?"

"With a name like that you should charge me for a ticket."

Workers held the boat fast while David and Jack clambered aboard.

Once David had thundered the boat up and down the basin like it was a Christmas morning bicycle, he cut the big engine and let them drift.

"Actually, Jack, charging for tickets is *exactly* the idea. Tickets to a little party day after tomorrow to finally wrap up the Bathhouse Museum refurbishment. We've moved the collections crates back into the lower level. All we have to raise now is enough to fund the lower level remodel."

Jack eyed the trailers still up in the parking lot. "A little party?"

"It takes a little money to attract a lot of money, Jack. It's a charity auction. Vintage boat rides, a string quartet, and enough booze to make everyone feel generous. Ten thousand per couple. A few of us are getting together to put it on. Positively everybody will be there."

"So I heard. A thousand protestors?"

David nodded. "Ah. The tragically displaced senior center." He shrugged. "I'm used to it. And you'd better get used to it. Because you're one of the 'us' who are throwing this little party. Since my money's no good at the Boyle household, I'm funding my portion of the costs in your name and Kate's."

"I always wanted a target on my back."

"Which brings me to the primary reason I asked you to stop by, which is a progress report. What am I getting for the money that I'm not paying you to investigate the Manny Colibri business?"

"Kate and I *are* beginning to agree—"

"I'm glad to hear this already."

"That this may have been about Cardinal's handling of life-extension research, rather than about a deranged employee's revenge."

"Meaning there *was* someone else involved?"

Jack paused, rubbed his fingers along the boat's

polished dash. David Powell had always tended to box a little too much according to the Marquis of Queensbury rules to suit his lawyer. David would accept some low punches once the evidence piled up high enough, no matter how the evidence got in the pile in the first place.

But now was too soon to mention that Jack had light-fingered foundation files while David was out of town. Especially when Jack wasn't so sure the mackerel snappers were behind it, now that he had interviewed the archbishop. "We're working on it. You've heard they located Colibri's car."

"But they aren't declaring him dead? It seems to me that's only common sense."

Jack shook his head. "Death in Absentia proceedings in California require five years missing, normally."

David shook his own head. "Jack, that can't be the answer. You know the conventional wisdom about Cardinal. The secret of its success has been that, unlike most CEOs, Manny gave his employees unprecedented freedom to succeed or to fail. But, also unlike most CEOs, only he made final decisions on a range of issues."

Jack shook his head. "Cardinal still operates when the boss is away. Just like any other multinational. Hell, if I'd had to wait for you to come in and sign things Powell Diversified would've gone bankrupt."

"Not the routine stuff. If Cardinal is effectively rudderless for any length of time, innovation and teamwork will yield to an internal power struggle. The business unit managers who reported to Manny will be too busy jockeying for position to provide leadership. The human cost to Cardinal's employees, to say

nothing of the cost of lost productivity to society, will be enormous."

"I said it *normally* takes five years. In a case like an airplane crash, for example, a court can avoid the lack of a body. But proceedings still take time."

"Jack, time is money. That sounds crass, and lord knows money can't buy happiness. But for Cardinal's employees and their families, it will be harder to be happy with less of it."

Jack shrugged. "David, Kate's actually meeting with somebody at DHS today about identifying Colibri by his DNA. The lack of a body may be a nonproblem."

David nodded. "Well, that's encouraging. Speaking of Kate, you're both on this event's guest list."

"Kate doesn't date older men she's related to."

"You're both listed plus one. And prepaid. Just skip the part about telling me to fuck off and say you'll think about it. And you won't need a date. ELCIE's a cosponsor. When Julia Madison saw your name on the list she told me that wild horses couldn't keep her away."

TWENTY-FIVE

The Veterans Administration Oakland Outpatient Clinic's waiting room could have been in any urban clinic in America. Patients slumped in close-packed chairs, the clicks and pings of their phones mingling with coughs and whispers.

Kate scooted herself back into an upright sitting position in her armchair and checked her watch. For the sixth time in eleven minutes she had slid forward when gravity had defeated the friction between her suit's trousers and her chair's upholstery. For the sixth time, too, as she scooted she brushed shoulders with Shepard, squeezed into the adjacent chair, and found his body as warm and as solid as her chair was cold and slick.

And for the sixth time Shepard ignored her touch and kept his head bent above his phone's screen while his left thumb skittered across its keypad. From what she had been able to eavesdrop, Arthur Petrie relied on Shepard to analyze and summarize anything more complex than a lunch menu.

And, to be fair, she didn't blame Petrie for exploiting an unexpected talent. Shepard may have been an overprivileged hedonist, but he was a quick, bright one. Kate suspected that no NSA cryptographer could have cracked the morion helmet's code faster than Shepard had.

While Shepard rolled Arthur Petrie's trivial boulders uphill, like a Sisyphean dung beetle, Kate looked around the waiting room.

However reflective of America this waiting room otherwise was, the veterans who waited in it did not reflect the gospel that had been preached to her growing up in San Francisco and while matriculating within the Ivy League. Kate Boyle had been taught that America had been built, and now stood upon, the backs of persons of color, of the undeservingly poor, and of women. These patients did not reflect those constituencies.

These patients reflected the American military, not the nation that accepted their sacrifices. These patients were overwhelmingly male and disproportionately white. By the speech patterns and accents that she overheard in their conversations, they were educated citizens of the Midwest and the South, places that Kate knew only by looking down on them from thirty thousand feet.

The bodies of many of these men, especially the relatively young ones, were completed by prosthetic limbs. The vacant stares of others, particularly the graying ones, suggested that the parts of themselves that they had sacrificed were visible only if eyes really were windows on the soul.

A lump swelled in Kate's throat, and she looked

away from the veterans and rested her eyes on the bright screen of Shepard's phone.

Petrie was literally tasking Shepard to alphabetize a list of Petrie's laundry, a job for which Shepard was being paid probably more than some of these men had earned in their entire, abbreviated, military careers.

Shepard noticed her leaning in, nodded at his screen, and sighed. "I know. It's ridiculous."

Across the room, a slender man younger than Shepard bent forward in his chair and grimaced as he retied a scuffed jogging shoe that covered a prosthetic left lower leg and foot.

Kate blinked back tears as she felt them well up. She whispered, "Shepard, don't you feel ashamed of yourself, sharing a room with these men?"

He stared at her, mouth agape.

"Mr. Shepard?" A fortyish, slim brunette wearing jeans and a crisp blouse walked toward them, clutching files and a laptop to her chest like a schoolgirl changing classes. She glanced briefly at Kate, then around the room. "As you can see, this facility primarily provides conventional medical treatment and therapies, not psychiatric care. I come over here from the city regularly for my patients' convenience. If you'll follow me I've arranged for a place where we can talk."

Five minutes later Kate and Shepard sat in hard plastic chairs in a bare medical examining room. The therapist sat across from them on a wheeled stool normally occupied by an examining physician.

She said, "I'm happy to discuss this with DHS, Mr. Shepard. But like I told you on the phone, I've answered every question for your DHS colleagues, for the Oakland and SF PDs, for the FBI, for everybody, already. Except the press, of course."

Kate shrank down in her chair. So far Shepard's DHS ID was kicking down doors, to police forensic reports, to the relationship between a museum and its anonymous donor, and to a patient-therapist communication. They were doors that a blabbermouth reporter might not be able to kick down, even if her father was a "special investigator." If people assumed Kate was the big, strong man's assistant, she would zip it and enjoy the ride in silence.

Shepard said, "Sometimes it's not the questions or the answers, it's who fits them together. Eli—Specialist Abney—why were you seeing him here?"

"Why? In general terms, because the world tells my patients they're damaged goods. My job is to show them the world is wrong. As to venue, like I said, I saw him here because he was living in Redwood Heights. Which, I'm sad to say, everybody in the world knows now. Specifically why he was being seen was post traumatic stress disorder. Which I'm also sad to say everybody also knows about now."

She opened her laptop and glanced down at its screen as she spoke. "Eli had served three tours in Afghanistan as an explosive ordnance disposal specialist. EOD's a particularly challenging specialty." She looked up from the file. "Not that there were many soft jobs in the Afghan Theater. I spent a tour in the suck myself, as a National Guard medic, mostly outside the wire. I have invisible scars in places not even my husband will ever know about."

Kate squirmed in her chair. It was no longer only men who could feel guilty for choosing to let somebody else get blown up, while they complained that if they took time to vote they would miss lunch.

The therapist continued. "Apart from physical risk and trauma, Eli had seen comrades, innocent civilians, even animals like trained K9s, maimed or killed. Most typically in horrific fashion by improvised explosive devices. Even one event like that is enough to trigger reexperiencing flashbacks, paranoia, hyperarousal jitters. If the event is extraordinarily traumatic, instead of reliving the event the patient may block it altogether. Hysterical amnesia can persist for years."

Kate squirmed again.

"At all events," the therapist said, "Eli was honorably discharged due to medical concerns three years ago. But I only started working with him five months ago."

Shepard nodded. "He thought it would be unmanly to ask for help. He thought that the losses were his fault. He tried to tough it out."

The therapist cocked an eyebrow at Shepard. "Yes. Exactly. I had another patient who tried to internally manage PTSD related to his experiences during the Vietnam War. He suffered a life needlessly interrupted for thirty years before we began treating it. We resolved it in fifteen sessions, without even resorting to medication. Toughing it out is not a strategy I'd recommend. If by any chance you know anyone who is attempting it, Mr. Shepard."

Shepard asked, "Any idea whether Eli was trying to cope on his own?"

The therapist nodded slowly. "Actually, I think he may have been, simultaneously with our course of treatment. Although you're the first one who's asked about it, and I'm not sure I'd describe his coping mechanism as 'on his own.' Eli didn't say much about it, except to say he was pursuing it vigorously."

Shepard asked, "What was it?"

"He had been raised Catholic, and had recently been encouraged to return to the Catholic Church."

Kate straightened in her chair. "No fucking way!"

Shepard and the therapist turned and stared at her, openmouthed.

Shepard said, "Actually, Kate, in many parts of the United States going to church is still perfectly legal."

Ten minutes later, Kate and Shepard rode down in the elevator from the waiting room to the garage on the way back to her car.

He said, "Would you mind telling me what that Tourette's outburst was about?"

Before she could answer, Shepard's phone rang, he scowled at it, then held it to his ear. "Yes, Mr. Secretary."

After twenty seconds, he rolled his eyes. They stepped out into the dim low-ceilinged garage, and Shepard held his phone to his chest. He pointed out past the auto exit gate toward the daylight beyond. "Sorry. I have to take this, and it's gonna be a while. Would you mind waiting in here while I go outside?"

She nodded, and he walked toward the exit to the street with his phone pressed against his ear.

The elevator door behind Kate whispered open.

"Lieutenant Shepard! Sir!"

Kate turned and saw a man in a wheelchair, brawny arms pumping as he rolled rapidly out of the elevator and spun his chair toward the now-empty garage exit. He stopped, then hung his head, breathing heavily.

Kate touched his shoulder. "You said *Shepard*?"

The man looked up at her. He was fiftyish, with a scraggly salt-and-pepper beard and hair that curled in tangles below a black ball cap. In gold block letters, the cap's peak read: DYSFUNCTIONAL VETERAN; APPROACH WITH CAUTION OR FREE BEER.

He wore a gray zip-front hoodie and sweatpants, and the pants were pushed up above his knees.

His legs ended below his knees in black plastic stumps from which protruded silver metal pipes that connected with feet, toes and all, that looked for all the world to her like the feet of the dolls she had given up at puberty.

He said, "Sorry for putting on the freak show, ma'am."

Oh God. She was staring. She snapped her eyes back up to his eyes. "I—It's alright."

He smiled and nodded. "Believe me, ma'am, I know it is. I've been upstairs for my hundred-thousand-mile tune-up, but if you saw me tomorrow walking around with my pants cuffs at my ankles where they belong, you'd ask me to dance. And I'd accept."

She blinked. "You said Shepard?"

He pointed at the empty garage exit. "Tall fella. Big through the shoulders, narrow through the hips. You know him?"

Kate nodded. "I know that guy. But you called him lieutenant." She pointed at the empty door and smiled. "The closest this guy ever got to lieutenant was captain of his fraternity drinking team."

"Benjamin R. Shepard. My platoon leader in Iraq."

A cold spot grew in Kate's stomach.

The man held up his right hand, fingers splayed

and knuckles toward her, then wrapped the fingers of his left hand around the right's small finger. "He's missing his right little finger."

Kate relaxed, and she waved her palm at the man as she shook her head. "Different guy. This guy has all—"

She paused. Shepard had carried a gratuitous coffee and doughnut offering in front of him, with both hands, when he came to her door. Just as she had carried a quiche that she knew her father would never eat, just so she could avoid an awkward physical contact.

And Shepard had unpacked his offering using his only left hand. Not because he was the rich kid who had never waited table, as she had presumed. But because he didn't want to, as this man had put it, put on a freak show.

Kate whispered, "Oh crap." The cold spot in her stomach swelled until it felt as large as a grapefruit.

She leaned against the man's wheelchair with one hand and he asked, "You alright, ma'am?"

"No. No, I am not alright. What I am is an asshole."

He patted her arm. "Then you're among friends at the VA, believe me."

Kate blinked at him and smiled. "Mr.—?"

"Garvey. Call me Roland."

Kate peered out at the daylight. Shepard was nowhere in sight, and based on what she knew of his boss, wouldn't be in sight for a while. She said, "I'm Kate, Roland. Roland, could you tell me about how you know Mr.—Lieutenant—Shepard? If you can spare a few minutes?"

"Ma'am, this is the VA. Here, time to spare is one thing a man in my position had best possess in abundance." He glanced at his watch. "My ride home's not due for thirty minutes." He glanced around the deserted garage, then pointed at a bench and growled, "Like we say in the infantry, 'Follow me!'"

Garvey spun his wheelchair and rolled a beeline toward the bench, then twirled his chair.

When Kate reached the bench she slid next to his chair and said, "I like the way you drive, Mr. Garvey."

He grinned, then his smile faded. "And *I* like to tell war stories. But not this one. I will, though, because I want the record straight about the lieutenant, Ms.—Didn't catch your last name."

"Boyle. Kate Boyle, Roland." She took Garvey's right hand in hers. Until now, a handshake had always seemed such a simple, insignificant gesture.

TWENTY-SIX

"Garvey! The Good Shepard requests the honor of your presence."

Specialist Fourth Class Roland Garvey concentrated his attention on the task at hand.

"Now, Garvey!"

Garvey stood with his back to his irritated squad leader as well as to the 110 degree wind that blow-torched across the baked and featureless face of central Iraq. He held his breath, because shit still stunk even upwind. Then Roland lit a rolled-up front page of a week-old copy of *Stars and Stripes* with a butane lighter, and dropped the newspaper like an incendiary.

With a whoosh the burning paper ignited the diesel fuel that Roland had puddled atop the anonymous feces that filled the oil drum bottom that he stood alongside. He had wrestled it out from beneath the first of many latrines that he was scheduled to service this day.

Roland called, "On the way, Sarge," then added under his breath, "Fuck." It measured his level of boredom that he regarded being called away from the distraction of burning shit as a greater punishment than having been detailed to burn it in the first place.

He left behind the black, roiling shit storm of smoke he had created, trudged to his platoon leader's tent, and prepared to endure another.

Roland stood at attention, sweat trickling down his cheeks, while First Lieutenant Shepard kept his head down, reading from reports spread out across his desktop.

The silent, sweltering interval braced at attention was a tactic routinely employed by commanders. It allowed the commanded to reflect upon how the figurative, as distinguished from literal, shit of nonconforming behavior into which the miscreant had fallen would defy gravity and roll uphill, soiling the numerous units of the great war machine in which the miscreant was a tiny but vital cog.

At this moment the great war machine in which Roland was a malfunctioning cog included the 2nd Squad of the 1st Platoon of Alpha Company of the 2nd Battalion of the 1st Brigade of the 18th Infantry Division of the Army of the United States of God-blessed America.

Roland knew this reprimand tactic because he had been reprimanded frequently during the First Iraq War, then during the peace that followed, and now during the surge phase of *Iraq: The Sequel*. In fact, Roland knew reprimands so well that he considered Shit Burner to be his actual Military Occupational Specialty, though officially his MOS was Rifleman.

Shepard's BDU sleeves were rolled halfway up his farm boy biceps, so that the sweat that glistened on his forearms caused loose papers to stick to them whenever he adjusted his reading position.

The platoon leader's tent was only marginally cooler than the merciless frying pan outside, even though all platoon leaders at Combat Outpost Apache had been allocated enormous, generator-powered misting fans. In one of the aberrant acts of altruism for which Shepard had become semi-famous, his fan had not been installed in his tent. Instead, Shepard had donated it for the common good, as a supplemental fan to cool the canvas blast furnace euphemistically known as the COP Apache dining facility.

Shepard was also given to spending his evenings pulling engine maintenance when skilled hands were in short supply, at a time when other officers were curled up in their air-conditioned CHUs with their laptops. The other officers viewed Shepard's aberrant altruism as a pain in the ass that made them look bad. Roland, on the other hand, viewed Shepard's aberrant altruism as a tender bond that united the two of them in nonconforming rage against the machine.

Shepard finally looked up at Roland, returned the salute with a requisition form pasted by sweat to his elbow. He tore the form away and crumpled it. "*You* don't decide when it's appropriate to tell the indigenous population that Islam is a crock. The Army does. Goddamit, Roland!"

Shepard did not call Roland Garvey "Roland" because he shared Roland's view of the tender bond between them. Shepard called all of his soldiers by their first names when he was one-on-one with any of them. This was yet another Shepard nonconformity the other officers disliked.

One reason they disliked first-name informality was that it personalized the soldiers whom an officer commanded. It was easier to order a soldier, as opposed to a person, to strap itself into a Humvee and lurch down a goat path beneath which some insurgent had buried an artillery shell. When that shell exploded the Humvee would crumple like a sweaty requisition form. That person's leg would be sundered from that person's body at the hip, and propelled into an olive tree, where it would dangle like a bleeding haunch of beef wrapped in pixelated permanent press camouflage.

Shepard said, "At ease. This isn't about General Order No. 1."

Roland clasped his hands at the small of his back and let his spine curve into an insouciant "S."

General Order No. 1, in its various iterations, had applied to all U.S. personnel in the Iraqi Theater of Operations since Roland had arrived in the theater for the first time, to liberate Kuwait with a pint of bourbon and a *Playboy*. General Order No. 1 prohibited the possession or use of alcohol, drugs or pornography, fraternizing with the local population, doing anything to offend local customs or sensibilities, and a laundry list of less entertaining antidotes to boredom.

Roland Garvey was a fair to middling linguist, a conscientious and courageous squadmate, and a frequent candidate for promotion. Most careerist enlistees with his high aptitude and extensive time in service had by now achieved senior noncommissioned rank. Many even sat behind desks, like Shepard's.

However, it had always seemed to Roland that blowing up locals offended their sensibilities more than *Playboy* did. Therefore, Roland's repeated rebellions against

General Order No. 1 had time and time again caused his career prospects to plummet toward the abyss of a Bad Conduct Discharge, then rebound from the Big Chicken Dinner to the mountaintop of consideration for promotion, as though the gods of war had dangled him for eternity from a cosmic bungee cord.

Shepard asked, "Roland, how's your Farsi today?"

Roland straightened his spine. "But sir, I'm short!"

To be short was a slightly retro term that meant to be mere days from the end of deployment, a status that informally sheltered a soldier from hazardous duty and excused all manner of paranoid or superstitious behavior. In Roland's case he was not merely twenty-six days short of completing his current deployment and departing the Iraqi Theater of Operations whole, but eight months short of completing the twenty years of service that would entitle him to retire.

Roland's command of Farsi, nurtured during his previous tours, was useful when fraternizing with Iraqis in violation of General Order No. 1. Less happily for Roland, it also rendered him a slightly more valued cog in the great war machine when a native Iraqi interpreter was unavailable. Unavailable to assist a patrol outside the wire, where legs wound up dangling amid the olive branches of war.

Shepard sighed. "Roland, I'm six days shorter than you are. So today it sucks to be us."

"How bad does it suck, sir?"

"The spooks say they've identified a high-threat target. Battalion has elected us to go pick him or them up before he or they sneak away."

"Why us?"

"Because we have you. The first two units that

were tasked with this plum claimed they didn't have a 'terp available on short notice."

Roland winced. If an interpreter was so necessary, the objective probably wasn't out in the featureless dirt, where you at least had a chance of seeing the shit coming. This objective was in some claustrophobic Iraqi building in a claustrophobic town or village where every goddam doorknob and floorboard could easily be goddam booby-trapped. "Where, sir?"

"Top floor of the Haji Hilton."

Roland closed his eyes and rolled his head back on his neck. "Jesus."

The Haji Hilton was a concrete slab-sided landmark of a public housing tenement five stories tall. The building rose from the middle of a dusty single-story village in the middle of nowhere for no apparent reason. In the days when Saddam Hussein was the Soviet Union's go-to Middle Eastern sociopath, the Russians had gifted the Hilton to Iraq to demonstrate the majesty of Socialist Civil Engineering. The dump had been erected atop an imperceptible rise in the pancake-flat landscape of central Iraq so that an enormous cistern on its roof could, and in fact did, provide gravity-fed, sun-warmed running water to the building and to the surrounding village.

It was unsurprising that both sides coveted the Hilton, because its top floor was the highest point within a fifty-klick radius. It provided an unobstructed viewpoint from which to observe and report opposing forces' movements. Particularly forces of Americans, who typically rolled so heavy that movements less resembled a Sioux war party than they resembled the Boston St. Patrick's Day Parade.

However, because the Hilton was such a visible and politically significant icon, the Fobbits had decreed that it be secured by local authority, not by U.S. troops. This was not exactly giving the fox the chicken house keys. But it was exactly throwing rifles and civil affairs manuals in the general direction of a herd of chickens and hoping for the best.

The approach to the Hilton's top floor therefore provided a perfect place to lay an ambush, or to plant a series of booby traps, for a bunch of hastily summoned, and therefore poorly prepared, Americans.

"How much recon do we have time for, Lieutenant?"

Shepard shook his head. "Battalion says with a tip this hot only the early bird catches the worm."

Roland said, "Fuck that. Sir. With respect, Battalion can come down here and catch my worm. And so can those NSA fobbits in Baghdad that we're not supposed to know about."

Shepard frowned. "I know. But the real time intel from those NSA embeds has been pretty good lately. Besides, Roland, it's an order, not an invitation to debate."

When they rolled up fast and heavy to the Haji Hilton's entrance with two squads mounted aboard Humvees, the street was deserted. The building looked to be deserted, too, except for a barefoot kid who appeared to be about twelve.

The kid sat outdoors on the building's front stoop, dressed for the climate in dirty white pajamas. He scratched the belly of a squirming brown dog of indefinite breed that was the size of a satchel charge.

Shepard and Roland dismounted and clattered up

to the kid. With their eyes hidden behind ballistic goggles and the rest of their frail humanity muffled beneath the fifty pounds of armor and associated life-and-limb preserving battle rattle upon which Shepard always insisted, they were not dressed for the climate. They were dressed for Halloween on Mars.

The kid had learned, probably by age six, not to threaten the Martians' personal space by eye contact, and kept scratching the dog.

"Roland, ask him where everybody is."

The kid answered, head down.

Roland said, "He says they all left because bad men with guns had moved in upstairs and everybody figured we'd come and there would be trouble."

"Then why's he still here?"

"Says he couldn't find his dog 'til now."

Shepard pressed his lips together, stared into the distance.

The dog was not a favored pet in Middle Eastern cultures, but it had seemed to Roland for some time that the Hajis had figured out that Americans trusted people who were nice to dogs.

At that moment, the K-9 pair dismounted the second Hummer in the little convoy, the handler holding the big German shepherd to heel. The kid's dog yapped at the giant intruder once, then took off down the street with the kid in pursuit.

Roland turned to his lieutenant. "What do you think, sir? A lookout?"

Shepard shrugged. "I dunno. I do know that if we walk away from this and leave an OP up there that calls mortar fire down on one of our patrols, that blood'll be on our hands." He gritted his teeth. "It could all be true. Whether it is or not, our job's to clear the fifth floor, not to ring the front doorbell and leave a brochure."

Shepard stepped off toward the building's front entrance, and the two squads and the K-9 pair piled out and followed without the usual muttered bitching.

Whether due to abundant caution and attention to detail or to sheer luck, the platoons that Ben Shepard had led over the course of his two deployments had never lost a soldier KIA. And not because his units had cowered behind the wire at an FOB in Baghdad. Shepard had always been out here in the suck.

And so his troops called him the Good Shepard and bet their lives every day that he would always find a way to protect his flock.

Still, somebody behind Roland said, "Into the valley of death rode the six fuckin' hundred."

Somebody else said, "Shut the fuck up."

It took them an hour to clear the building. The Haji Hilton may have had sun-warmed running water in abundance, but like most buildings in Iraq, electricity was an unexpected guest, not a utility.

So they crept up through the pitch black stairwells by the light of helmet-mounted headlamps and rifle mounted lights, like disoriented spelunkers, floor by floor, with the canine sniffing every doorknob and stair tread before a GI touched it.

Finally Roland and Shepard, along with the K-9 pair and the three riflemen not dropped off below to secure the vehicles and the lower floors, burst from the dark hallway into the dim-lit last apartment on the top floor.

The six humans gasped as much from the tension

of the journey as from the exertions of climbing under the protective weight of full battle rattle.

Roland surveyed the place as the others poked around cautiously. Like all the corner apartments, it was one room with a sink and bottle-gas stove in one corner and a shared latrine down the hall. Like all the apartment units, regardless of location, that they had cleared on the way up, it was a poorly ventilated pigpen that smelled of cooking and dirty laundry. It had a commanding view, but from a single window at the height of, and no bigger than, a bathroom medicine cabinet's mirror.

Boy, when the commies had designed a worker's paradise, they hadn't fooled around.

What the place lacked was an insurgent, dead or alive, a weapon, or an explosive or other contraband anywhere within view. Or, by the dog's indifferent attitude, within sniffing range.

A soldier snorted. "Man, some joker sold the spooks a load of crap this time."

As Roland felt hair begin to rise on his sweat-soaked neck, Shepard said, "Out! Now!"

As he shoved the others toward the door that led to the stairwell he was on his radio screaming the same order to the soldiers on the lower floors.

Boots thundered below them in the stairwell.

Shepard swept up the rear, last man out, breath rasping just behind Roland's ear.

The initial detonation sounded as distant and harmless as the first thunder peal on a humid July afternoon.

Then the rest of the charges embedded deep within the building's skeleton ripped it in rapid, choreographed succession.

By the time Roland passed the fourth floor landing,

he could feel the stair treads shift beneath his boots, and the roars and howls of a building in its death throes drowned out all other sound.

By the time he reached the third floor landing, the concrete slabs collapsed above and around him. Something glanced off his Kevlar helmet, struck his shoulder like a dropped bowling ball, and drove him to his knees. Roiling dust choked him, and obscured even the helmet lights of those ahead of him as he collapsed. It occurred to Roland that from outside this must be one hell of a show that would become a must-see video on some insurgent website.

Roland considered himself neither religious nor superstitious, but when he regained consciousness it appeared that he had descended into hell, fulfilling the prophecy that his Aunt Patrice had pronounced when she caught him masturbating at age thirteen.

In darkness licked by flickering orange flames, and stabbed by gyrating lightning bolts, men wept and shrieked and the sour smell of mercaptan sulfur curled in his nostrils.

Roland flexed his fingers, moved his arms, but couldn't feel his legs. He felt his face, tasted liquid he found there and recognized blood. He realized that he lay on his back, with something blunt poking between his shoulder blades. He lay inclined, with his head higher than his feet, or at least higher than the place where his feet should be.

The light that flickered came from small fires burning among a jumble of concrete slabs, striped by wobbling shadows cast by twisted steel reinforcing bars. The flames were fed by bottled cooking gas that had leaked from apartment stoves, and the sulfur was odorant infused in gas that had leaked, but not yet ignited. The stabbing lights were the headlamp beams of the men who screamed and wept, and the beams jerked back and forth as the men twisted. Though it was impossible to know whether they were trying to free themselves or were simply mad with pain and terror.

Roland realized that the insurgents had deduced that the Americans they had baited would be alert to the usual suspects. IEDs along the route, snipers, booby traps, ambushes. But to date, the insurgents' concept of asymmetrical warfare had not encompassed bringing down a perfectly good building, thereby blackening their image and rendering hundreds of their country-men homeless, just to kill fewer Americans than it took to play the Army-Navy game. Back in Fobbitland this cluster fuck would probably be hailed as evidence of the insurgency's desperation.

Desperate or not, the insurgency had implemented their concept to perfection. The German shepherd, God rest his canine soul, was neither trained nor tasked to sniff for explosives emplaced within the building's skeleton. Therefore, imploding the Haji Hilton on itself and dropping the Americans and the building's rubble into the building's own basement was as simple as erasing an obsolete hotel from the Las Vegas strip.

A headlamp played on Roland's face and he squinted at it.

"Roland?" The voice was Shepard's. His headlamp shone above and left of Roland, perhaps ten feet away. "Roland, can you move?"

Roland tried his legs again, felt not pain but the stirrings of panic. "No, sir! Help me!"

Shepard's voice quivered. "My right arm's pinned. And my right leg hurts like hell. Hang on."

As they spoke, Roland realized that only a few of the stabbing headlight beams remained visible at all, and now they simply pointed at unchanging angles, their owners still. And silent. In the relative calm a new sound replaced the screams.

It was a muted roar, as though a mountain stream had crested in spring. Against the skin of his crotch, beneath the nad pad that protected his genitals, Roland felt liquid warmth, as though he had pissed himself.

He swiveled his head so that his own headlamp played across the rubble piled in the building's basement until he glimpsed a silver flash of motion, and behind the flash a vast, upward-curving shadow. His panic grew. "Lieutenant! The roof cistern. It's flooding this place!"

As he shouted, he felt the water rise against his body, already at his waist. How much water would it take to fill the interstices remaining between the rubble slabs and debris that filled up the building's basement? How high would the water rise before its flood ebbed? The irony if he drowned in the middle of the desert was that nobody would even notice the irony. Too many armored vehicles had already turned turtle in canals and streams after sliding off of, or collapsing, rural Iraqi bridges designed for donkey carts.

"Hah!" That he laughed out loud at the thought alerted him to how severely he was in shock.

In shock or not, when Roland played his light on Shepard, he gasped. The lieutenant was pinned upright like a collected butterfly, dangling by his right arm, which stretched away until it disappeared into the shadow where one concrete slab lay atop another. His left arm stretched out in the opposite direction as he strained to reach down and across to Roland. No wonder the lieutenant's leg hurt. His right leg hung crookedly down and in front of his left, the right tibia protruding through his BDU trousers above the ankle, a white spike dipped in red blood. He looked as though he had been crucified.

Roland gritted his teeth, then played his head lamp toward his own legs. He felt lightheaded even in mere anticipation of the mangled horror that he would see. Mercifully, his legs were obscured beneath the churning water, but it had now risen to his ribs, at the level of the trench knife he wore on the right strap of his web gear and the holstered 9 mm he wore on his left.

He moved his hand to be sure he could draw the Beretta. If while he was trapped here the gas ignited, or the water rose above his chin, he would have only moments to decide whether to burn alive, drown, or use the pistol.

The water lapped Roland's throat.

He stretched his neck. "Lieutenant!"

Shepard's light played across him. "Oh Christ. Hang on, Roland. I'll be there."

Roland directed his light on Shepard again. The water had barely reached the younger man's boot soles, its rise seemed to be ebbing infinitesimally, and the stink of sulfur had disappeared. Whatever else Shepard would suffer in his future, he was probably not going to drown like Roland most certainly was about to. Nor would either of them burn alive.

As Roland watched, he saw steel flash as Shepard

drew his own trench knife from the scabbard on his web gear with his left hand, then twisted his body to face about. Shepard drew three short, sharp breaths, grimaced, then plunged his knife hand into the dark place where his right hand was imprisoned.

Shepard screamed. Then stabbed again, and screamed again. Then he crumpled to the slab below as his freed right hand emerged from its prison. Shepard cradled his right hand in his left, pressing it to his chest and gasping.

The water reached Roland's lips, and his neck would stretch no further.

He coughed out water, breathed through his nose and tried to scream.

Then Shepard's light swept, for an instant, across Roland's face, inches away, so close that he felt Shepard's breath on his cheek. Then Shepard ducked his head beneath the still-rising water, surfaced, swearing, grasped Roland by the shoulders with both hands, and dragged him up the inclined slab against which Roland lay. The pain caused by Shepard's action swept across Roland and his consciousness flickered and died.

When Roland regained a detached consciousness, he watched through the red fog of emerging pain as Shepard hobbled on his one unbroken leg to the edge of Roland's concrete slab, held a breath and dove beneath the water's black surface repeatedly. Once he emerged dragging someone by the legs, but when Shepard finally got whoever it was onto the slab, it was impossible to identify the soldier because his head was gone.

Finally, the lieutenant surfaced with the German shepherd under one arm, heaved it onto the slab that Roland now thought of as his, and dove again.

The dog's wet black nose was inches from Roland's, and he felt the animal's hot breath as it panted. The miracle of the dog's survival lifted Roland's spirits so high that he wept for joy. Then the animal coughed blood onto Roland's face.

Roland's headlamp reflected off the dog's pleading, glistening eyes, then Roland directed the light along the animal's flank until he saw that the dog's internal organs hung from its gashed belly and puddled in a heap on the concrete.

As Roland's consciousness again flickered he managed to draw the Beretta, press its muzzle into the pink froth that bubbled from the suffering animal's whimpering mouth, and squeeze the trigger.

Pure red pain wrenched Roland, screaming, back to the ragged edge of consciousness. Where the dog had lain, Shepard now knelt, teeth clenched, unlacing with one hand a boot that Shepard held in his other hand. Another boot, already undone, its lace gone and its tongue dangling, lay across Roland's chest.

Both boots looked peculiar, somehow, and Shepard seemed to handle them with clumsy delicacy. His hands seemed to slip on the lace as he tugged it, as though both hand and lace were slippery with something. As Shepard worked, tears streamed down his cheeks.

The lieutenant freed the boot lace at last, laid the boot gently alongside the other, then used the lace to form a tourniquet that he tugged tight around Roland's thigh.

Only then did Roland realize that Shepard, who had been in serious but not imminent danger of dying, had sawed off his own finger in trade for the opportunity to save Roland's life. Only then did Roland realize that of all the soldiers who had entered the Haji Hilton, even including the dog, only he and Shepard remained, for the moment, alive. Only then did Roland realize that the boots were his own, and so were the feet and lower legs inside them.

Whether it was the pain or the shock of realization of his loss, it was the last thing Roland Garvey remembered for a long time.

TWENTY-SEVEN

While she sat on the bench in the echoing dimness of the Oakland VA Outpatient Center's parking garage, Kate laid her arm across Roland Garvey's shoulders as they trembled with his sobs.

He drew a deep breath, then sat up and wiped his eyes. "Sorry."

She smiled at him. "You don't owe me an apology, Roland. I owe you."

He said, "They tell me I had a brief vacation stop in Southern Germany on the way home. But the only souvenir I got there was five quarts of new blood. And it didn't even last. They say I got five complete refills between the Haji Hilton and Walter Reed. When I came back to the world enough to think about trying to find Lieutenant Shepard, I just couldn't gut up to it. I thought what happened to him, what happened to all of us that day, was my fault. By the time I got over that phase, all I could find out was that he'd been discharged. After that, it seemed like he'd dropped off the face of the Earth. Honestly, Kate, until I saw him today, I thought he was dead."

Kate shook her head. "No. Well, obviously. Roland, he has a good job in D.C with the Department of Homeland Security. And he's going to law school. He's fine."

"And you and he are—?"

"No!" She shook her head.

"Oh." Garvey raised his eyebrows. "Because the way you watched him leave—"

"No. We just met this morning. Just kind of working on a project together. Roland, what did the Army do about the whole mess?"

"They awarded me, and I found out the lieutenant, too, the Purple Heart. That's nondiscretionary if you're wounded by an instrument of war in the hands of the enemy. Otherwise, the spooks don't advertise intelligence *successes*, much less intelligence screwups. I'll remember Lieutenant Shepard as a hero to the day I die. If there's a life after we die, I'm sure the men who didn't share our luck that day remember him as a hero, too. But I'm sure the Army remembers Lieutenant Shepard as an officer who let a building fall on his troops. I'm afraid he does too."

Garvey turned his head toward the garage's more distant entry, as its gate swung up and a car entered, then reached forward and pushed his pant legs down over his prostheses. He straightened back up, and waved at the car.

Blocked when another car backed out, the car Garvey had waved to stopped, and its driver stepped out and waved back at him. She was an attractive middle-aged woman wearing a sous chef's whites, her skin olive and her hair covered by a hijab. She smiled, then pointed with the index finger of her left hand at the watch on her right.

Garvey said, "There's my ride."

Kate asked, "Who's that?"

Garvey rolled away toward her and spoke over his shoulder. "Best thing that ever happened to me. My fiancée. Ma'am, have the lieutenant drop me a line. It's my name at GrumpyOldVets.com."

He paused, then turned his chair back to Kate. "Correction. Aala is the second best thing that ever happened to me. Tell Ben Shepard I said he's the best thing."

Then he spun, rolled himself toward the car's passenger door, and a minute later the two of them were gone.

After Roland Garvey left, Kate sat, hands in her lap and stared at the concrete floor in front of her.

She had told Roland Garvey that Shepard was fine. But the truth was that she had only known Shepard for seven hours, everything she had assumed about him had turned out to be wrong, and she had treated him like shit for the wrongest possible reasons. How the hell could she presume to know whether or not he was fine? From what Garvey had told her, how could any human being ever be fine again after what Shepard had been through?

"Sorry. But I think Petrie's finally done with me for the day. It's cocktail hour in Washington."

When she glanced up at Shepard he furrowed his brow, then got down on one knee in front of her. "What's wrong?"

She shook her head but kept her eyes down. If she

looked up, she knew she would stare at his hand and he would think she thought he was part of a freak show. It would be one more shitty thing she had done to him.

He said. "It's about the bet, isn't it? It was stupid and arrogant in the first place. And I know I was just lucky. Look, I'll pick the place *and* I'll buy the coffee. And I shouldn't have criticized your driving. Ms. Boyle, I'm sorry."

She nodded.

He said, "I've been really shitty to you today. But what you said in the waiting room kind of hurt my feelings too."

She put her hands to her mouth as she felt the tears start.

He touched her arm. "What did I *say*?"

She shoved his arm aside. "Stop being so damn *nice*! And stop calling me 'Ms. Boyle.' And stop trying to forgive my debts!"

She stood, wiped her eyes, and straightened her jacket. Then she elbowed past Shepard and stalked toward her car with her chin high.

Shepard hurried after her and said, "I guess this means me offering to drive is off the table."

The drivers headed back into the city from Oakland in the afternoon proved less moronic than usual, and it was only thirty minutes later that she pulled up in front of the street address that Shepard had fed her from an app on his C-phone.

She looked up from the traffic, saw the red neon sign glowing in the late afternoon dimness, then shook her head. "No, Shepard. Not the Buena Vista."

"But the bet was I pick the place."

"You won't like it. It's a tourist trap."

"They invented Irish coffee. And they sell snacks cheap at happy hour."

"They invented Irish coffee at the airport in Dublin." At least that was the story her mother had told a hundred times about how she met Jack Boyle when she stopped in to the Buena Vista. Then this awkward, persistent waiter had told her terrible jokes and insisted on getting to know her. Then one thing had led to another.

"Shepard, of all the coffee shops and bars in San Francisco, why here?"

He shrugged. "Somehow it just seemed like the right place to get to know you."

She sat behind the wheel and felt a shiver run up her spine. Katy, when coincidence T-bones superstition, it's probably a train wreck, not an omen.

She pulled ahead until she found a valet parking sign, then slapped the car into park so abruptly that Shepard's head snapped forward. "Pile out, Shepard. Let's get this train wreck over with before one thing leads to another."

As she stalked alongside Shepard toward the Buena Vista café, eyes straight ahead and her hands jammed into her coat pockets, he cleared his throat. "Does 'happy hour' mean something different in California?"

They sat across from each other at a table by a window as the outside light faded.

Shepard pushed the basket of bread toward her with his left hand as he chewed a slice. "Sourdough. Pretty good."

She shook her head. "Don't do gluten anymore. But thanks."

He raised his Irish coffee to his lips, sipped, set it down, then wiped cream off his lip with his napkin. All with his left hand. He said, "Ms.—Kate, I think you may have the wrong idea about who I am. I—"

If she had expected the Ben Shepard she now knew to run from hard issues, then Roland Garvey's story had taught her nothing.

She reached across the table and pressed her hand against his right arm. "Shepard—Ben. While you were on the phone today at the VA, I met Roland Garvey."

Ben froze, staring.

"He was there to have his prostheses adjusted. Not anything psychological. He told me everything. You don't have to revisit that with me."

Shepard's mouth hung open, and he shook his head. "I wasn't even sure he was alive. How is he?"

"Engaged to a pretty chef. Funny. I think that therapist we talked to would say he's well-adjusted to life on two below-the-knee prostheses." Kate paused. "Ben, Roland had a message he wanted me to give you."

Shepard stared down at the tabletop.

"Look at me, Ben. It's a good message."

Shepard looked up.

"Roland Garvey said to tell you that you're a hero. To him and to everybody who matters. He said you were the best thing that ever happened to him."

Ben Shepard stared past her, eyes glistening, into a place to which nobody like her had ever been. And a place that, she supposed, nobody like Ben Shepard could ever completely leave.

The least she owed Shepard was to be as honest with him as he had been prepared to be with her. Finally, she filled the void. "I didn't know. I was unspeakably out of line in what I said and what I presumed. I can only say I'm sorry. And ask you to forgive me that. And if you can, let me ask you a favor."

He turned his head, looked at her from the corner of his eye. "What favor?"

"Give me your hand. No, your right one."

He shook his head, then lifted his arm and she took his hand in both of hers. In spite of herself, she raised her eyebrows. Ben Shepard's right hand was large and powerful and soft and warm all at once. The smooth scar tissue that covered the spot where Shepard's finger had been felt no different than an elbow or a knee or any part of a person where bone lay just below the skin.

He tried to pull away, but she squeezed tighter. "Ben, it's okay. Believe me. You know me well enough to know I say what I think. And I never thought about it until now. But I don't give a shit how many fingers an intelligent, thoughtful, attractive man has, any more than I give a shit how many appendixes he has."

Shepard sat still there, processing.

Outside, the streetlights came on.

Finally, he cleared his throat. "Intelligent, thoughtful, attractive?" He tipped her glass toward him and peered down into it. "What's *in* Irish coffee?" Ben smiled. "You'd make a good therapist."

"Was that the problem? The reason you disappeared off the grid after you were discharged? PTSD? Survivor's guilt?"

He nodded. "I had all of that. And I made it worse for myself by trying to tough it out without therapy. For eight years I was in and out of work and in and out of a bad place mentally. When I *was* connected I was just doing what I had been doing all my life until I enlisted. It's just that what I had been doing happens to be off a lot of people's grid."

"What was that?"

"Farming. Well, being a heavy equipment mechanic, which is what American farmers have been since before you and I were born."

"Where'd you grow up, then?"

"Texas. Nebraska. Manitoba. Every state in between. Every year we followed the warm weather and the wheat and corn and soybean harvests south to north from Texas to the Canadian border. Then we wintered in Hays, Kansas."

She frowned in concern. "Oh God. Your parents were migrant workers?"

He straightened and tucked in his chin. "There's nothing 'Oh God' about it!"

"I was empathizing!"

Shepard raised his chin. "Farmers don't demand your empathy. Neither do soldiers. Among whom farmers are disproportionately represented, speaking of oppressed minorities." He sat back and crossed his arms. "Define custom cutter for me."

Kate pressed her lips together. She was pretty sure the answer didn't involve a hundred ninety-five bucks with highlights and a blow dry.

Shepard said, "Thought so. American farms spot-hire custom cutters for harvest. My uncle's custom cutting business had two million dollars tied up in combines and support vehicles. Our 'immigrant labor' was white twenty-year-olds with charming accents who flew over for a summer in the States from their parents' farms in England and Australia. Do people like you understand *anything* about the part of America that you fly over? Besides that it makes gluten that you 'don't do' anymore? And community college cannon fodder who you 'empathize' with?"

Kate stiffened. "'People like' me? Now who's stereotyping?" She sat back and stared out the window. "I knew this would be a train wreck."

He uncrossed his arms, sat back, and exhaled. "I'm sorry. I'd really rather talk about you, anyway." He slid his glass aside. "So why does an intelligent, attractive woman still live with her parents?"

Kate inclined her head and smiled. "Okay. Ben and Kate two point oh. I don't live with my parents. I live with my parent." She sighed. "I was a Woodward-Bernstein wannabe at the *Washington Post*. My mother was diagnosed with advanced pancreatic cancer two years ago. I took a job out here to be close. But she died the day I got off the plane." Kate paused.

She had found that those last three brief sentences usually propelled conversations past that topic, but Shepard seemed to be unusually persistent. And unusually quick, which made her rethink her preconceptions about farmers who apparently had community college degrees.

He said, "I'm sorry. I can't imagine losing a parent."

Kate exhaled. She batted the conversation back to Shepard. "Then your parents are living?"

He shrugged. "Maybe. The reason I can't imagine it is my mother dropped me off with my uncle when I was two and never came back."

"Oh." Kate sipped her coffee. If she had pitied Shepard, and she realized he would hate it if she did, the passion in those brown eyes when they had flashed in anger changed what she felt for him. And the power she had felt in those big hands didn't devalue his stock a bit.

She said, "But I don't live in the basement with my comic book collection. I'm just sleeping over for a couple days to work on this business with Colibri. I have a place down in Palo Alto. And an active social life."

"Oh." His face fell. "Oh."

She raised her palm. "Which at the moment only includes you, Shepard."

He grinned. "Oh! So how did you get to the *Post*?"

"I used to interview my mother—she was a librarian—every night about our dinner menu. Then I would write a story reporting about it in a little notebook. Which my father read aloud to my mother every night like it was the front page of the *Chronicle*. Then he'd explain to me what 'burying the lead' meant and why punctuation mattered. When I was five he bought me a laptop with writing software."

"Five? He supported you aggressively."

"Torquemada supported the Spanish Inquisition aggressively. Jack Boyle's in a whole different league when it comes to beating the crap out of things that get in his way."

"Ah. Then he also taught you to drive?"

She stopped talking and stared at Shepard. "You wanna hear this, or not?"

"Sorry."

"Before I turned six I'd figured out that Columbia was the place that gave out the Pulitzers. By the time I was seven my father had figured out that the best journalism school in the country would be an impossible admit for a verbally gifted but undiverse upper middle class white girl who already hated math."

"So where did you end up?"

She smiled. "Columbia. My dad also figured out that even the Ivies cut admissions breaks to stock their athletic teams. I didn't learn to swim fast, but distance swimming's like the rest of the world. If you beat the crap out of it long enough it eventually lets you win."

Ben stared at her, head shaking slowly. "Did the world ever beat you?"

Kate looked away as she shrugged. "I never got my Girl Scout Outdoor Skills Patch. My square knot always looked good but my dad could always untie it."

Ben wrinkled his forehead. "Don't blow off the question. I really want to know. I really want to know about you. I want to know everything about you."

Crap. He was serious. "Shepard, as first-date conversations go, this one's already been pretty intense, don't you think?"

His jaw dropped, then he smiled.

Kate said, "What?"

"You called this a date."

Crap. "No. I said this conversation was intense for the kind of conversation people have when they *go* on first dates." She slid her chair back. "Come on. I'll drop you at your hotel."

His face fell.

"No. I had a nice time, Ben. Really."

He raised his eyebrows. "It wasn't a train wreck?"

She shook her head. "Not even close."

Which only left one other possibility. The shiver ran up her spine again.

TWENTY-EIGHT

By the time Kate got back to the house after dropping Shepard off, she was starving. Shepard had inhaled the whole bread basket, and she never really ate on dates anyway. Although it hadn't been a *date*, for God's sake.

Her father sat sideways at the kitchen table, slippered feet resting on the tabletop and crossed at the ankles. He was drinking a canned beer, still cold enough that it sweated, from a six-pack at his elbow, and he was reading the *Wall Street Journal*. The kitchen was warm, and redolent with the aroma of crust and sauce and pepperoni and mushrooms and extra cheese.

He pointed at the oven. "I picked up a pizza on speculation you'd get here. Fortunately it's still hot."

"If you'd buy a phone, you wouldn't have to speculate." She held up hers. "Cardinal C-phone. Top rated. Top selling. So much memory that it comes with a couple thousand proprietary Cardinal apps downloaded free into the phone. And they're actually not crapware; they're the best on the market."

He snorted. "Which app lets them watch you crap?"

"Exactly. Business isn't interested in watching us crap. Because that doesn't help them sell us anything. Curb your paranoia."

"C-phone? I better get one soon. With the iPhone there are only twenty-four letters left."

"Dad, C-phone is a homophone."

He swiveled his feet to the floor and stared at her with his mouth open. "You're kidding. Now we have to make them special phones?"

Kate rolled her eyes. "C-phone. S-e-e-phone. It's got the most sophisticated video interface on the market. And by the way your homophobia is unacceptable."

"Homophobia? I wrote Charlie Epperson and Keith Spaulding's joint will for free when no law firm in town would. And I was Charlie's best man at their wedding when they could finally make it legal, while you were living in New York. So watch your mouth before you put your foot in it, young lady. Although I'm the one who taught you to put it there."

She plated two slices for each of them, sat, and grabbed one of his beers.

As she rolled up her sleeves above her elbows she pointed at his paper. "What's that right-wing rag say today?"

"The truth. The *Journal*'s won thirty Pulitzers. And they still care about spelling and punctuation."

"Internet manners emphasize speed of information transfer, Dad. People have learned to read around typos." Kate folded a slice and stuffed it into her face. Then she closed her eyes while she chewed, and luxuriated in the warmth of grease as it dribbled down her chin and ran down her forearm all the way to her elbow.

She hadn't eaten real, live, sloppy, decadent, blue-collar pizza since high school. She said, "God, I miss gluten."

"Gobb eyebiss gootun? Do people read around table manners now, too? You didn't talk with your mouth full when you grew up at *this* table."

She swallowed, washed it down with beer. "Easy, Dad. I said 'God, I miss gluten.' You probably don't know that a lot of the people who harvest American wheat actually commute from England and Australia every year."

He turned a page, adjusted his glasses, and nodded. "The custom cutters hire temporary help that's skilled at repairing agricultural machinery. They need the help. Last year the United States supplied twenty-five percent of the world's wheat exports and grew fifty percent of the soybeans."

She stared at him. "How the *hell* do you know that?"

He lifted the paper. "The *Journal. Rolling Stone* miss that story, did they?"

She pouted and pointed at his newspaper. "Well, the *Post*'s got more Pulitzers than *that* rag."

"So what mischief have you been up to with this Mr. Shepler?"

"Nothing!"

Her father peered at her over the top of his glasses, eyebrows raised. "Ah."

"His name is Shepard, actually. In fact, today Mr. Shepard and I found out that Manuel Colibri was so tidy that he didn't even leave DNA when he crapped. Also that the first item on that property list that Colibri wrote is an antique conquistador's helmet, not a will. He donated it to the Oakland Museum of California, probably because he was afraid his house could be broken into. And—" She paused, "Abney, the guy who blew Colibri up? Two months before he died he started attending Catholic Church regularly again."

Jack chucked his paper aside. "That doesn't sound like nothing to me, Katy."

She nodded. "It was a productive day. How about you?"

"Just a little research in the morning." He busied himself extracting another beer from the six-pack while he said it, which meant he had been up to some mischief of his own that he wasn't ready to share with her.

He said, "David Powell called to see how we were doing. Actually, I went down to Aquatic Park during the afternoon and he took me for a boat ride."

She cocked her head. "David? Rubbing shoulders with common tourists at Aquatic Park?"

"He was setting up for a society wingding day after tomorrow down there. You and I are invited."

Kate snorted. "I assume you told him the Boyles don't do fat cat environmental rapist high society."

Her C-phone chirped, she checked its screen, then said, "Dad, it's the guy from DHS. Shepard."

"Really?"

Her phone chirped again and her father sat there. She pointed toward the dining room. "Dad, do you mind?"

"Nope. You won't disturb me. He came to see both of us, didn't he?"

She rolled her eyes, then answered. "S'up, Ben?"

"I enjoyed tonight."

She glanced at her father, who was making a show of refolding the paper.

She said, "Uh, me too."

"Kate, what's the Benefit for the Bathhouse Presented by the Powell Foundation and other Bay Area Charities?"

"Uh. I'm pretty sure it's a stupid society fund-raiser day after tomorrow. Why?"

"Because *my* boss, Petrie, e-mailed me an invitation and ordered me to go to this thing and suck up to *your* client, David Powell."

"Let me check on that. I'll call you back in the morning."

"Sleep tight, Kate."

"Yes. I understand. Thank you."

After she closed the call, her father asked, "How is *Ben* tonight?"

"Dad, he's invited to that stupid fund-raiser too."

"David works in mysterious ways, Katy. I've told you that for years."

"So what do I tell Ben?"

"I assume the same thing you said I'm supposed to tell David. That the Boyles don't do fat cat environmental rapist high society. Then you can sit home alone and catch up on wheat export statistics while your biological clock ticks."

Two hours after Ben's call, Kate, alone in the kitchen, laid her phone down on the kitchen table and rubbed her eyes.

After two hours of Googling the Incan empire, the Catholic Church's history, or lack of history, of brainwashing assassins, the ins and outs of DNA collection and analysis, and the fact that Victor Carlsson's penguin-watching boat was stuck in ice and he and his minions would be airlifted back to civilization within forty-eight hours, she now knew as much about a lot of arcane topics as her father probably already knew. But she was no closer to solving the mysteries of who Manuel Colibri had been, and who had him killed, and why.

She was also no closer to solving the mystery of the Good Shepard. Ben was, in his way, as unshakeable in his devotion to those he was tasked to protect as her father was. But Kate Boyle, Ivy League flyover snob and Ben Shepard, blue-collar warrior from America's heartland, were as different as, well, a gentle Catholic librarian and an agnostic with a serious attitude problem. Which was a good omen, but also a very bad one.

She stretched and rubbed her eyes, cleaned up the dishes and the six-pack carton that her father had emptied, and ascended the stairs.

When she flicked her bedroom's switch, the light spilled out and washed the closed door across the hallway. Beyond the door was the room that had been her mother's reading room for as long as Kate could remember.

She crossed the hallway, laid her hand on the knob and pushed the door open. Her palm came away thick with dust.

When she stepped into the room, she saw, even in the dimness, that it hadn't changed since the day her mother died. Kate averted her eyes from the bay window and the view that lay beyond.

On the wall to Kate's left, the bookshelf remained tight-packed with authors like Proust that nobody in this house would read again, and on the papered wall beside the bookcase remained the gold crucifix. That nobody in this house would depend on again.

To Kate's right was the hospital bed with which Jack Boyle had replaced Marian Boyle's reading chair. The bed's frame remained levered up, so Kate's mother had been able to look out to the bay, but now the bed's mattress was stripped as bare and as white as a naked corpse. The top of the folding table alongside the bed was mercifully bare, too, now.

Kate covered her mouth with her hand to muffle her sobs as she backed out of the dark place and closed the door.

At the far end of the upstairs hallway, her father snored behind the closed door to her parents' bedroom, his dreams a mystery that Kate remained terrified to solve.

In her own room, Kate curled beneath her covers and cried herself to sleep in the dark.

TWENTY-NINE

Kate's C-phone, on her bedside table, exited Do Not Disturb mode at 9:00 a.m. Pacific. On the dot it pinged, announcing a text, in fact two of them. Both from Shepard, Benjamin. She considered getting dressed before she read them, then punched them up. After all, texting while horizontal in your underwear wasn't phone sex.

The first text had been blocked when it came in at 4:44 a.m. She rolled her eyes. Was this early-bird fetish something that farmers and the military had baked in to their DNA?

"Meet me at Mick Shay's office at Hyde Street Pier at 9:45 a.m.? Wear boots and something rubber."

She raised her eyebrows. Maybe it *was* phone sex.

Shepard's second text had come in at 8:59 a.m.

"Are you up? Boat must leave @ 10 sharp with you or not."

She showered and dressed like she was late for class after morning swim and applied her makeup in the rearview as she drove. She had never understood why competing drivers didn't applaud the efficiency in that technique.

Kate skidded to a stop at 9:29 alongside Shepard and Mick Shay, who both jumped back as they stood at the foot of one of Hyde Street Marina's lesser piers. They wore coveralls and rubber boots.

As she stepped out to join them Shay eyed her jeans and sweater and rolled his eyes. Shaking his head, he turned and walked out one of the piers toward a big white, blue-striped SFPD boat. He called back over his shoulder, "Well, when we get out to the job site we can borrow somethin' for you from the ROV pilot. She's about your size."

Kate called after him, although the chill wind off the bay already cut through her thin sweater. "Well, sorry! My whip was at the cleaners, too." She hugged herself against the wind as she turned to Shepard. "Is somebody's hair on fire? What's going on?"

Shepard tugged off a windbreaker he wore over his coveralls and snugged it around her shoulders. "Mick called me last night. He hired a big boat to lower a robot to explore Colibri's car. The boat arrived last night and they're set up and ready to go. It rents by the day for more than I make in a year."

Kate pointed along the pier at the white SFPD boat that Shay was boarding. "Shepard, that's just a crummy police boat."

"That's just our taxi," Ben turned and pointed out across the choppy bay water toward the Golden Gate, "to take us out there to the contract boat."

Seaward of the bridge a light blue boat sat stationary in the distance under wind-driven clouds. The vessel was tiny compared to an outbound freighter that plowed past it. But even in the distance the contract boat was obviously far larger than the police boat. The distant boat's superstructure was set forward on its hull, and from the boat's low, flat midsection, a slim yellow mast, which Kate realized was a crane, projected diagonally out over the water.

Kate shook her head and turned her back to Shepard and the wind. "I'll stay here, Ben."

"I have extra Dramamine. The technology's really fascinating to watch if it's new to you. And Mick's bark's worse than his bite."

She stared down at the pavement. "It's not that. I'm not going near that bridge."

Shepard came around, stood in front of her and grasped her shivering shoulders. "Kate, look at me. Now you tell *me* what's going on."

She looked away, back toward the city. "I told you my mother died the day I got off the plane from D.C."

"Yes. Of advanced pancreatic cancer. Two years ago. The timing must have made it even worse for you."

She shook her head, pointed to a bench sheltered from the wind beside the pier's buildings. "Can we sit and talk?"

"Of course. But you don't have to—"

She took his arm and walked them to the bench. "I do. My father taught me a saying for everything. One of them is that clever truth can be wronger than a lie."

She and Ben sat on the bench, and he took her hands in both of his. "I'm not good with sayings. But I'm a good listener."

THIRTY

When Kate Boyle emerged into the public part of SFO's terminal from the concourse, her rollaboard in tow, her father was waiting, unsmiling, hands in his jacket pockets. He stood tiptoe as he craned his neck looking for her.

She felt the tears well as she touched his shoulder, and he turned, startled. "You're early."

She let go of the rollaboard's handle and tried to hug him, but he reached across her. "I got it, Katy."

"How is she?" Kate asked.

"The first round of chemo starts tomorrow. She's doing that nervous twisty thing with the tissue with her hands. But you know she's solid as a rock inside."

Oh God, Dad. She's always been tough on the outside and flimsy as a tissue inside, but you've never been willing to see it.

He led the way to baggage claim, and while they waited at the carrousel Kate asked, "I mean how is she physically."

"A little pale. I think it's mostly that she's not wearing makeup. Her appetite's not good at all, though. She's maybe dropped a couple pounds."

Christ, Dad, they told you this is pancreatic cancer, not the flu. Her chance of making it a year is one in five, even though they've presumably caught this early.

In the car on the way back up to the city they talked about the Giants and how gentrification was ruining the city's ethnicity and anything except the elephant in the back seat.

While Kate's father unloaded her luggage, Kate climbed the stairs to the reading room. The door stood open and afternoon sun flooded in through the bay window. In the distance, between the Golden Gate Bridge's two soaring orange suspension towers, traffic streamed across the bridge's deck as an outbound freighter crept beneath it.

When Kate stepped across the threshold into the room her mother smiled. "Katydid!" She sat propped upright, wearing a long ivory nightgown, with her red-going-gray hair pulled back and tied with a green ribbon.

She was reading her dog-eared Bible, reclining in one of those hospital beds with the remote control that twisted the mattress any way you wanted, like it was a flatworm.

Kate's mother slipped the blue ribbon place mark into her Bible, then laid it on a bedside table alongside an empty teacup.

Kate's jaw dropped. "Mom—"

"Yes, I know. My chair's on temporary leave. Your father moved it to the attic. Dear, did you know that Proust wrote À *La Recherche du Temps Perdu* lying in bed with a hot water bottle on his feet?"

A little pale? A few pounds? Holy crap, Mom, you're a skeleton with eyes.

Kate shuffled to her mother's bedside, bent and hugged her. Her mother felt as bony as the canvas bag with the bats in it that somebody had to carry back to the dorm after intramural softball.

Kate's father entered the room, crossed to the bed and kissed Kate's mother on her white forehead. He turned back to Kate. "Reporter traveling's taught you to pack light. Just the one case and the rollaboard?"

Kate's mother puckered her lips. "How long are you staying, dear? Did you pack enough?"

Christ. Kate pointed at her mother's teacup. "How about Dad and I go down to the kitchen and make you a refill?"

Her mother smiled. "You're always so thoughtful. There's a jar above the range. Uncle Edgar's Special DeTox."

When Kate and her father got to the kitchen, Kate set her mother's cup on the counter, then shoved her father into the kitchen's far corner, next to the old landline wall phone, and hissed, "Dad! What the fuck? You never said—"

He raised his palm. "Just a minute! I mentioned a couple months ago she was under the weather."

Kate widened her eyes. "Under the weather? Christ, she's almost under the ground! And it's not just physical." Kate poked her finger at the ceiling. "That wuss up there isn't Mom. Mom was sharp and with-it and funny. That person up there is Mary Poppins' lobotomized older sister."

"It's the pills. One minute she's Mary Poppins. The

next minute she's more depressed than the Cuban economy. I'll talk to them about that tomorrow. But really it was the goddam mackerel snappers."

"What?"

"When she started feeling crappy she just said she was having trouble with the runs. And maybe I didn't take it as seriously as I should have as soon as I should have. She talked to that little weasel Alvarez—"

"*Father* Alvarez, Dad."

"And I think he lit more candles than usual or did a rain dance or whatever the hell they do over there when they're not bangin' the choir boys. And she prayed like her hair was on fire and she believed that all of that would bribe God to cure her."

"You blame the Catholic Church. Seriously?"

"And that Chinaman in the choir with the Coke-bottle glasses."

"Edgar Chen. The grocer from Chinatown."

Jack Boyle nodded. "He got her going on acupuncture and detoxifying tea and for all I know powdered rhinoceros horn."

"And you let her rely on that instead of real medical treatment?"

"Of course not! She knows I think all that crap is crap! So she didn't 'bother' me with it until last week when her shit turned white and the jaundice got obvious."

"I read up on this. We're still early. Right?"

He stood silent.

Kate shook him by the shoulders. "Right? Chemo tomorrow? I read sometimes the chemo comes before surgery. Then surgery? Then fingers crossed?"

He shook his head. "They said they couldn't get

it all. They said there's no point taking the risk of cutting. It's too advanced."

"Who's they? Edgar Chen's optometrist?"

"David Powell's on the Board of Stanford Medical Center. Katy, the top pancreatic guy in the *world*'s there now. David made a call and the guy magically found a hole in his schedule and saw her the morning after the initial test results came back. I called you right after those initial results, but before the specialist gave her a hurry-up comprehensive examination."

Kate sank into the kitchen chair beside her, squeezed her head between her hands, and stared at the ceiling through tear-blurred eyes. "Oh, Jesus."

Her father asked, "You really think you brought enough clothes?"

"The rest's coming on a truck."

"What?"

"Not just the clothes. Everything. I got a job writing for *Gizmo*. It's a netzine in Palo Alto that also comes out in slick print. They cover the IT industry."

"How did that happen?"

"With my résumé it was easy."

"How long is your leave from the *Post*?"

"Dad, it wouldn't have been fair to ask the *Post* to hold my job open indefinitely and be shorthanded when there are two hundred qualified candidates who'd donate a kidney to have it. 'If you can't do your job right, be woman enough to admit it and step aside, Katy.' Remember?"

"You *quit*?"

"Boyles don't quit, Dad. Remember? I just told them I was resigning to change jobs for personal reasons that I preferred not to discuss. 'Family business stays in the family, Katy.' Remember?"

"Opportunity never knocks twice, Katy. Remember *that*?"

"Neither does the chance to support the two people who gave me life, when *they* finally need *me*."

"We gave our lives to you, gladly. So you could have a better one. Not so we'd screw up yours just when it's finally taxiing for takeoff."

"What? So now I've screwed up your lives more? By screwing up my own? Jesus!" Kate stood, then banged her head slowly against the wall phone. "Can I *ever* do it right for you? I did everything you ever asked me, just to please you. Everything! I hated swimming. Hated it."

"I saw you smile a lot on the medal stand."

"I smiled because I made *you* smile. Some of my teammates ate up morning swim. They were happy fucking warriors going to fucking war every fucking morning at six a.m. You know what? I did *not* love the smell of chlorine in the morning!"

"If you had told me, we could have found another extracurricular you did like. Or a less elite program than Columbia."

"What? And screw up your opportunity to vicariously trade up to an Ivy League education? Instead of that crap night law school degree? I *loved* you too much to disappoint you like that!"

"Well, now you've thrown away all the work your mother and I did."

Kate tore at her hair with both hands as she shook her head. "Sixty minutes of this and I'm insane. I can't do six months watching Mom die. Neither of us can. And I can't watch it kill you, either. And they don't even *start* poisoning her until tomorrow!" She plucked up the stupid, obsolete paper Yellow Pages on the counter under the phone, turned to throw them at the opposite wall, and froze with her arm upraised.

Marian Boyle stood in the kitchen doorway in her nightgown and slippers, her fingers resting on her cup, eyes wide and mouth agape. "I wondered whether the tea was ready."

"Mom, how long have you been standing—?"

Her mother's lip quivered, she shoved the tea cup across the counter so hard that it fell on the floor tile and shattered. Then she shuffled back to the stairway that led up to the reading room.

Jack called after her, "Marian!"

As Marian Boyle reached the stairs she waved her hand as though she was shooing a fly. "You leave me alone, Jack Boyle! Both of you leave me alone!"

Jack Boyle slammed his fist into the wall. "Now you've done it!"

Kate slapped her palm on her chest. "Me?"

Kate's father snatched the Ford's keys off the peg alongside the garage connecting door. As he slammed the door behind him, he said, "I can't do it either!"

Kate slumped back in the kitchen chair and looked down at her hands in her lap. They trembled, and when she tried to stop them by pressing them together her arms shook all the way up to her shoulders. Her heart raced and her breath came in gasps, as though she had just finished a 1500 Free at altitude.

When the adrenaline finally drained from her, exhaustion mercifully overcame anger and remorse.

Kate dragged herself upstairs. The door to her mother's room was closed, so she stepped into her old room, closed the door behind her, lay down on her bed, and slept.

When Kate woke, it was still late afternoon in San Francisco, even though darkness had fallen in D.C., where she had awakened a nine-hour lifetime before. The house was so quiet that she could hear the wind-up clock in the hallway tick.

Her mother's door was ajar, and Kate remembered she hadn't made her mother tea after all. "Mom?" No answer, so Kate stumbled back down to the kitchen. "Mom? Dad?"

Nothing. She opened the garage door. The Ford was still gone. On the counter beneath the phone the yellow pages were open to the listings for taxicab companies.

Kate frowned, then climbed the stairs again and pushed open the door to her mother's reading room. "Mom?"

The room was empty.

But on the bedside table, propped against Marian Boyle's Bible, was an envelope.

Kate's fingers shook as she tugged out the folded stationery sheet, then read her mother's handwriting:

My Dearest Jack and Katherine,

I dreaded, and I dread, the pain and the inevitable heartbreak that awaits me at the end of this journey. But that is something I could bear. What I cannot bear is the thought of seeing the two people I treasure above rubies suffer even worse than myself, while they tear apart the great love between a father and a daughter, because of the strain of watching me wither and die before their eyes.

Please forgive what I do now, and know that I do it to save you.

Someday we will all be reunited in the kingdom of heaven, because I have faith that God in his mercy will surely forgive even this great sin I am about to commit, because I commit it for a noble cause.

I have always loved each of you more than life itself, and I can think of no greater way to show that love than to spare you a slow end to mine.

Your loving wife and mother,
Marian

Kate felt the heat of tears course down her cheeks, and heard the garage connecting door slam downstairs.

Kate turned and stared out the reading room's windows toward the Golden Gate. The bridge was, as always at this time of day, awash in the glow of headlights, and was now cast in silhouette by the sun that hung behind it, barely above the horizon. But the light stream in the northbound lanes, the lanes alongside the pedestrian walkway that looked back to the city, were dead stopped, blocked behind the flashing blue lights of emergency vehicles stopped near the center span's midpoint.

Kate's father stepped into the room. "Katy, where's your mother?"

Kate kept staring toward the setting sun, its disc blurred by her tears, as she handed the note in her left hand to her father and pointed with her right at the bridge.

Everybody knew that they always jumped off the side that faced the city.

THIRTY-ONE

Ben Shepard sat on the bench beside the Hyde Street Pier and held Kate Boyle's hands as she stared down at a point in the space between them. "Kate?"

"I'm sorry."

"You don't have anything to be sorry for."

"I'm sorry I let you think it wasn't my fault. I'm sorry I can't go under that bridge like you think I should."

"It *wasn't* your fault. It was an unforeseeable confluence of circumstances. It tragically accelerated an inevitable outcome. And the only way you'll learn that it wasn't your fault, just like the only way you'll learn that it's just a bridge, is to confront your misperception of the past. It took me eight years and help from outside of myself to learn that."

"I just can't."

"I understand. That's fair. But at least promise me this. You will go see a therapist. They don't just treat GIs. What you feel's not so different from what a GI feels whose buddy picked up a trash bag that was booby-trapped. The survivor has to pick up a hundred of them before he believes they're just trash bags again. It's not so different from what I felt. I couldn't go up a flight of stairs in a building stairwell. I couldn't pet a dog. I couldn't believe anybody would ever trust me to protect them again."

She turned her face up to him. "You *need* me to trust you, Ben? For you, not for me?"

"No!" He stared past her for a heartbeat. "Maybe."

"Then if I do this—*if* I do this—you'll believe that I trust you?"

"If you do this I will be right there with you every second. And I promise it will be alright. It. Is. Just. A. Bridge. Okay?"

Whhhooooppp!

They both turned as SFPD Marine 1's siren echoed. On the motor lifeboat's flying bridge Mick Shay stood, waving them toward the boat, as he stood alongside the coxswain at the boat's helm.

Kate nodded quickly, eyes down, but she stood.

Ben caught her elbow.

She shrugged him off. "I'm okay. I can do this."

"We can do this."

The windswept deck of the Remotely Operated Vehicle's mothership, upon which Ben and Mick Shay stood, vibrated beneath Ben's feet, although the boat barely moved in any direction as it floated in the gray channel west of the Golden Gate Bridge. The steady deck surprised and relieved Ben after their bucking, rolling half-hour police boat journey.

Ben and Mick sheltered in the wind shadow of the

superstructure two stories below the vessel's bridge, and faced the three-fourths of the boat's main deck that stretched a hundred feet aft of them.

Ben shouted over the gulls and the engines' throb, "I didn't expect this boat to be so stable. In fact, this is what I'd call a *ship*."

Mick pointed past the boat's stern, at the vast bulk of an approaching outbound tanker. "*That*, Mr. Shepard, is what you'd call a ship. Workboats like this one pitch and roll near as much as that MLB 47 we rode out aboard, but," Mick pointed out toward the deck rails then swung his hand in an arc, "this boat's got a dynamic positioning system. Movable thruster propellers all 'round her hull below the waterline. GPS and a computer adjust the thrusters every couple seconds. She doesn't move in any direction farther than a man can piss."

Mick pointed halfway back down the deck's starboard side, at a yellow-painted hydraulic crane arm, the tip of which was swung out over the boat's rail. From the crane's tip a taut cable stretched vertically down into the waves. Mick said, "The robot's already in a garage on the bottom, at the end of that cable." Mick stamped a booted foot on the deck plates, "three hundred thirty feet underneath us."

A hatchway in the superstructure clanged open and a member of the vessel's crew emerged. The bearded guide wore international orange coveralls and a white hardhat that matched the hardhats that Mick and Ben had been issued.

Behind their guide Kate ducked out through the hatch, and behind her came the party's fourth member, who had also been ferried out aboard the police boat.

The other guests, too, wore white hardhats, but also had changed into borrowed baggy coveralls as orange as the guide's.

The other guest, a hollow-cheeked, fifty-something woman who wore her gray hair in a tight bun, raised her arms and peered through wire-rimmed glasses at her sagging sleeves. Judging by the way she wrinkled her nose, she seemed to think that someone had painted her sleeves with crankcase oil.

She frowned at their guide. "My parka was quite windproof. I really don't see the need for this thing."

The guide smiled at her. "It's not mainly the wind, Dr. Bowden. A lot of this equipment's greasy or covered in gull shit. We'd prefer the only souvenir we leave you with is a company brochure."

She sniffed. "How thoughtful."

Their guide pressed his lips together, paused, then said, "And if you fell overboard, the coveralls are no survival suit. But the color could help us spot you."

Bowden sniffed again. "This boat isn't even moving."

The guide nodded. "Ma'am, we are in fact not moving. But the currents in this channel *are* moving, sometimes faster than a man runs. By the time we lowered an inflatable, you could be a half mile gone into the Pacific. And if we couldn't spot you right away the water's cold enough to kill you inside an hour."

Mick shot Ben a wink, stepped between the beleaguered guide and Dr. Bowden and took her arm. "You know, Edwina, that color flatters your eyes."

"Officer Shay, can we for once omit your bullshit? I have a twelve-thirty luncheon engagement ashore in the city."

"Well, he's a lucky, lucky man." Mick guided Dr.

Bowden aft toward the big yellow crane and sighed. "Edwina, if we were a few years younger I'd buy us a drink, myself."

Bowden lifted her chin. "Officer Shay, if you ever bought us a drink I would poison yours."

Bowden's role today was to take jurisdiction of Manuel Colibri's remains on behalf of the San Francisco Medical Examiner's Office. Then the ME's office could determine both the fact of, and the cause of, Manuel Colibri's death. Obviously this was a dance that Mick and Edwina Bowden had danced before.

Kate and Ben fell in behind the guide in the lead, and walked ten paces behind Mick and Bowden. Kate steadied herself by holding Ben's arm as she walked, and she whispered up at him, "Mick's more of a diplomat than I expected. Just like you're more of a therapist than I expected."

Ben looked away and hid his frown. Kate was displaying the immediate buoyancy and bravado that came with successfully reliving a buried mental trauma. She had confronted her approach to the Golden Gate with a single, stifled sob as they had passed beneath the bridge. A start, but not an end. His own life experience had taught him that Kate still felt the world should view her as damaged goods. He wasn't even sure he had gotten past that feeling himself. Kate's progress pleased him, and so did his role in facilitating it, but neither surprised him.

Ben Shepard had been accepting responsibility for lives for as long as he could remember. First for his own life, because his uncle was a single man with a business to run, a taste for bourbon, and no time to parent a kid he never asked for. Ben had been dragged up and down the middle of America, rarely spending time in a school long enough to learn the other kids' names, and from the first day of kindergarten he had been responsible for his lunch, his clothes, his homework, and his self-image.

As an infantry rifle platoon leader, he had simply tacked on responsibility for thirty-eight more lives. Counseling Kate Boyle was as familiar to Ben as counseling a Spec 4 about reenlistment, or counseling a squad leader about a Dear John letter. And now he accepted responsibility even for so undeserving a life as Arthur Petrie's. Ben didn't think of his life as one of hardship, of privilege, or of noble sacrifice. He thought of it as the only life he had.

Mick, Dr. Bowden, and the guide reached the object alongside the crane.

Mick said to the medical examiner's representative, "This here's the twin to the robot on the bottom."

The guide said, "Redundancy."

Mick turned to Dr. Bowden, and to Ben and Kate, then rested his gloved hand on the thick yellow block atop the backup ROV's aluminum chassis. "This here's the floatation chamber. It's filled with foam. The weight's in the lower components, so she stays upright naturally."

Mick pointed to a boxy steel control module fastened to the deck twenty feet from the five of them. "Two pilots in there do the driving."

Mick pointed out the components clustered within the robot's aluminum frame, below the flotation chamber. "They scoot this whole vehicle around down there by swiveling these propellers." He pointed to a bank of lights. "It's pitch black at three hundred feet, so they bring their own sunshine, and these cameras pan and tilt so the pilots can move these mechanical arms."

The medical examiner's representative pointed at the massive hydraulic manipulator arms. "Officer Shay, we are here to recover human remains, not pirate cannons. I suggest we take a few days to devise a less intrusive plan."

Mick shook his head and pointed to a freighter creeping past them. "We're impeding navigation to and from the third largest port on the West Coast. I plan to be in and out faster'n a cabin boy at a brothel."

Bowden crossed her arms. "I see no reason for haste."

Mick raised his hand, then ticked off points on his fingers. "Reason one. This is a limited-term spot hire. We only got a boat like this 'cause she was passing by our front doorstep enroute to a long-term charter in the Bering Sea. Reason two, her spot rate's sixty *thousand* dollars per day. Of course, if the ME's office wants to pay for the standby time, I'll shut 'er down right now for you."

Bowden turned her head. "Don't be ridiculous."

"Reason three, there's a big blow north of Hawaii headed our way. So if we wait we could lose the weather *and* the vessel."

"In that case perhaps you should rethink your methods. Your job is to recover evidence, not beat it senseless with steel fists."

"I've seen a good pilot pick up an egg intact with a manipulator." Mick turned away from the backup robot and marched Ben, Kate, and Dr. Bowden toward the ROV pilot house. "Come on. There's no point brawlin' over a lady 'til you see what's under her skirt anyway."

Robert Boustany

THIRTY-TWO

Ben stood behind Kate and shoulder to shoulder with Mick and Dr. Bowden inside what was yet another way to repurpose standardized steel shipping containers, like the Containerized Housing Units that Ben had sometimes occupied in Iraq.

Like a CHU, this ROV control center was an air-conditioned, elongate box. Unlike a CHU, this container was for working, not sleeping.

The four guests had packed into the container to peer over the shoulders of two coveralled technicians, one male and one female, who were seated side by side in high-backed leather armchairs as though they literally were pilots in an aircraft cockpit. Except that the windscreen to their front was made up of a half-dozen flat-screen video panels, and in front of them their hands rested not on pilot's control yokes but on keyboard touch panels and stubby, button-headed joysticks.

The screen on the upper right displayed a live shot from a camera atop the "garage" in which the ROV had been parked, three hundred thirty feet beneath them. Mick had described the turbulent bottom environment of the Golden Gate Channel as a sandstorm in the middle of the desert, and the image did in fact resemble the churning, obscured view through a Humvee's windscreen during a Middle Eastern sandstorm.

Through the current-swirled silt the ROV, a twin to the backup robot Mick had introduced them to on the boat's deck, crept forward, perhaps two feet above the channel's flat bottom. Trailing the tether cable that connected the ROV to the pilot's instruments, the ROV had advanced perhaps fifteen feet out from its garage, and inched forward guided by tiny corrections that the pilot made by nudging one of her joysticks.

In the dim swirl beyond loomed a dark shape.

The pilot said to her partner, "Can you gimme illumination?"

When the ROV swung its own headlights onto the shape, the Galvani was instantly recognizable, still upturned with the driver's side in the bottom sludge, its orange paint visible through mud that coated both the car's body and window glass.

Ben leaned forward until his chin nearly rested on Kate's head, and he smelled the sweetness of her hair.

Kate stared at the drama unfolding on screen and whispered, "Wow."

The Galvani laid nose-on toward the ROV, and perhaps ten feet away from it.

The pilot swam the ROV up and over the car, then her partner pointed its camera down so it peered at the front passenger side window.

Ben held his breath.

Mick swore. "All I see is mud on the glass."

The ROV circled the car, peeking from every angle, and through every exposed window. Then the male operator shook his head and looked back at Mick. "What do you want to do, Mick?"

Mick looked around at the rest of the spectators, then shrugged. "Omelets don't make themselves."

The male pilot smiled. "Aye aye, Master Chief."

As the female pilot returned the ROV to its position above the passenger's side front window, the male pilot's screen showed his preparations.

Kate pointed at the screen over the male pilot's shoulder. "You're making that claw move with this thingy under your hand?"

"Yes, ma'am. Actually, we call that claw a manipulator, and this thingy's called a joystick."

On the screen, the manipulator reached into a tool rack mounted on the ROV's frame and withdrew an implement.

Kate said, "Omigod! You're going to break the window with that pointy thing that looks like a hammer?"

"Yes, ma'am. Easily. The tip is carbide steel."

"What do you call *it*?"

"A hammer."

Dr. Bowden turned to Mick. "I object."

Mick said, "Overruled." He laid a hand on the male pilot's shoulder. "Do it."

It took one minute to position the hammer, then a single blow with the hammer's point shattered the tempered door glass into pea-sized granules. Four minutes of tugging and breaking away leftover glass shards with the other manipulator passed, then another minute for the disturbed silt to settle before the ROV's camera could see the Galvani's interior.

Ben had seen enough dead and mangled bodies to last two lifetimes. He clenched his jaw and slit his eyes.

No one spoke until Mick whispered, "I don't believe my lyin' eyes. Where'd the son of a bitch go?"

Five more minutes of examination, angling the light into all quarters of the interior, confirmed what everyone saw. The driver's air bag had deployed and its fabric hung limp from the steering wheel hub. The driver's seat belt was unfastened but intact. Silt covered all the interior surfaces, but the interior contained no driver, or anything that resembled, however, faintly, a part of a driver.

Ben said, "If the car was intact, should there have been so much mud inside?"

The female pilot raised one finger. "Good point. We didn't kick up that much silt."

Mick said to the female pilot, "Can you flip the car upright?"

She shrugged, then turned to her partner. "You ever tip cows up there in Nebraska?"

He said, "Omaha actually is very urban."

As the female pilot maneuvered the ROV so it could push against the Galvani's roof she shook her head and muttered, "And my cat actually reads the *New York Times*."

On the third try, the ROV, its manipulator arms extended, toppled the Galvani so that it rotated slowly and plopped belly-down into the silt, churning up clouds that the current blew away within a minute.

The Galvani's driver's side door was missing, the twisted hinges that had held it in place still visible in the door frame.

A search, stirring the silt that had been beneath

the car by blowing the thrusters downward, revealed neither a door torn off nor a body.

The only item of interest discovered in the reoriented interior was a pottery travel mug bearing the Cardinal Systems logo. The male pilot lifted it with a manipulator and laid it in a basket within the ROV's frame, along with a section of airbag fabric torn from the area of the bag that would have contacted the driver's face, so both could be brought to the surface.

In the tight and quiet space, Mick turned to Dr. Bowden. "Well, Edwina? You're the doctor."

The medical examiner's representative tugged off her glasses and wiped her eyes. "Assuming the body was intact when it became separate from the car, once the bacteria in the gut and pulmonary cavity started producing methane, hydrogen sulfide, and carbon dioxide the cadaver would have floated. As our minder pointed out, San Francisco Bay's currents are extremely strong. And so are the appetites of almost all marine life. If Mr. Colibri's remains haven't already been recovered in the Farallon Islands, my opinion is that they never will be recovered in any form that can be connected to him. Perhaps the mug and the airbag contact surface will yield DNA. It can be surprisingly durable. Although that would prove neither death nor cause of death."

Mick looked at Ben and shook his head. "Don't hold your breath on that DNA, Edwina. Mr. Colibri was quite shy about dispensing his."

The medical examiner's representative tugged up her coverall's sleeve and glanced at her watch. "There appears to be nothing more for me to do here. May I turn in these coveralls and get back to dry land?"

The male pilot whispered, "Wait. Did it occur to anybody that he might have *survived*?"

The female pilot shook her head. "About as much as it occurred to anybody that my cat actually reads the *New York Times.*"

Back inside the mothership's main superstructure, Ben removed his hardhat and left it on the counter of a presently unattended half-height window that led to an equipment room.

He pointed to Kate's helmet and floppy orange coverall. "They said we can just leave this stuff here. Bowden's in a hurry to get back to San Francisco. So you can just shuck off that coverall—"

"Shepard!" Kate crossed her arms over her breasts, and then pointed at a hatch down the passageway. "My jeans and my sweater are hanging on a hook in that cabin."

"Oh. I assumed—"

"If you expect to see me in my underwear you're gonna have to work a lot harder than that."

"I—Well, are you busy this afternoon?"

She laughed, and as she walked down the passageway she called over her shoulder, "Actually, yes, I am busy. But don't worry. That means that you are, too. Colibri's ex-life-extension research czar's agreed to see us—well, me—this afternoon."

Ben heard a buzz as Kate unzipped the front of her coveralls. When she stepped into the cabin to change, she paused in the hatchway and stared back at him over her shoulder. Then she bared her shoulder, raised her eyebrows, and said, "But hold that thought, Shepard. Hold that thought."

After the hatch clanked shut behind her Ben stood openmouthed, staring down the empty passageway, and wondered whether he would ever be able to hold any other thought again.

Once the hitch clicked shut behind her, Ben slowly reminded of him driving down the empty passageway, and wondered what ever he would ever be able to build any other thought again

THIRTY-THREE

Behind the wheel of Kate's Corolla, Ben drove through the Napa Valley, north of San Francisco, toward the home of Kate's interview subject Nolan Liu.

Kate fidgeted in the passenger seat beside Ben. They had agreed that Ben should drive because the route from downtown San Francisco crossed the Golden Gate Bridge, and while Kate had sailed under the bridge twice already that day, driving a car across it might have been pushing things.

Although Ben and Kate didn't agree about everything that ought to be pushed today. Ben glanced at Kate from the corner of his eye as he drove. "You know, the speedometer needle doesn't move no matter how hard the passenger stares at it."

Kate raised both hands. "You're driving the *speed limit*."

"If they meant it to be a suggestion, they'd call it the speed suggestion." He pointed at the car's dashboard. "Just like this little 'maintenance required' light. If it meant 'ignore me' it would say that instead."

Kate turned her palm up as she pointed at the amber dashboard warning that Shepard had referenced. "There. You've made my point. I've ignored that thing since last summer and everything's fine." She pulled out her C-phone, stared at its navigation screen, and pouted. "Are we there yet?"

"We're running eleven minutes early. Stop whining like a kid in the back seat."

Kate crossed her arms and looked out her window at the Napa Valley's vineyards. "Shepard, were you *born* a freaking adult?"

"No. I made it to four before *I* gave up on childhood. Maybe it's finally time you climbed out of the pool and dried off too."

She narrowed her eyes at him. "You self-righteous—!" Kate paused and rubbed her forehead. "Look, Shepard. Ben. We've gotten to know each other better in thirty hours than some couples do in thirty months. Maybe we should throttle back the personal stuff, concentrate on the puzzle, and let the system process for a while."

Ben managed to stare straight ahead down the two-lane road, instead of at Kate. He found Kate Boyle a high-maintenance mashup of wit and passion and strength and vulnerability. He also found her the most achingly desirable woman he had ever met. That this extraordinary person thought of them as a couple inclined him to let the system process as long as it took. He relaxed his fingers on the wheel. "Okay."

"I'll tell you about the guy we're meeting." Kate looked down at her phone again and read. "Dr. Nolan Liu. Born 1956 to Chinese immigrants who owned a dry-cleaning store in Newark. B.S. *summa cum laude* from Harvard at nineteen. Ph.D. in biology, also from

Harvard, two years later. Credited academic success to high bar set by his parents." Kate sighed. "I feel his pain there. It also says that by informal poll of his classmates he was voted most likely to win the Nobel Prize."

Ben said, "Apparently Dr. Liu's parents weren't the only ones setting the bar high."

Kate continued, "Liu Molecular Biology Laboratories, Cambridge, Massachusetts, founder and CEO until it was acquired by Cardinal Systems. Owned two hundred seventy-six patents, all assigned to Cardinal when he left three years ago to pursue personal interests outside the field of human biology. Rumored walkaway cash-out low nine figures."

Ben whistled. "Well, I hope his parents were okay about him giving up on that Nobel."

"Hard to say. He's not on Facebook. He doesn't tweet."

"I like this guy already."

"Shepard, my father's gonna *love* you."

Ben smiled as he drove. The system seemed to be processing fine.

When Nolan Liu's housekeeper led Ben and Kate to Liu's home's flagstone back terrace, the doctor was bent, a trowel in one gloved hand, over a flower bed that ran along the sun-warmed terrace's entire one-hundred-foot width. In fact, Ben thought, it was less a flower bed than a grapevine nursery.

Why Nolan Liu needed more grapevines puzzled Ben, because the terrace and the home sat atop a rise, below which stretched what Zillow described as 'seventeen sun-dappled boutique acres of the finest cabernet sauvignon vines in the Napa.' In the distance behind Liu's vineyard rose the green hills that defined the Napa Valley's opposite border. Zillow further described Liu's home as nine bedrooms, one theater, billiard room, one guest house, one wine cellar, one pool, and an appraised value of fourteen million dollars.

When he heard them, Liu stood, turned, and bowed slightly. No taller than Kate, his sparse gray hair curled from beneath his sun hat, and his face was as lined as any other sixty-four-year-old's.

He motioned them to sit with him at a pergola-sheltered table, tugged off his gardening gloves, and wiped his hands with a moist towel while his house-keeper set out a tray with a pitcher of iced tea and glasses. The housekeeper left the three of them alone with the silence and the sweet aroma of grapevines.

Liu rested his elbows on the tabletop, steepled his fingers, then laid his chin atop them and looked at Kate. "Ms. Boyle," he glanced at Ben.

Ben said, "Shepard. Ben Shepard."

Liu nodded, smiled, then continued, "When you called and mentioned that Quentin Callisto sent you, I assumed that *Gizmo* simply wanted to profile an aging nerd. And I was about to turn you down flat. But then you mentioned the Golden Gate—"

"Of course. The Golden Gate," Kate said.

"I realized, as you must have, that with Manny gone and Cardinal's ownership likely in play, the world has to understand the ramifications if the Golden Gate Project moves forward."

Kate nodded. "Yes. The Golden Gate Project. Exactly."

"But I must ask before we continue that you don't

involve the government prepublication. I signed confidentiality agreements when I left Cardinal. My lawyer tells me they were personal to Manny and their binding effect died with him. Nonetheless, if I'm going to hang myself out there, I don't want Big Brother suppressing the story."

Ben cleared his throat. "Dr. Liu, I should explain—"

Under the table, Kate kicked Ben's ankle and said to Liu, "That we realized during our drive up here that the recorder that my intern, Mr. Shepard, operates during interviews has malfunctioned. So I'll have to rely on Mr. Shepard's handwritten notes. He has quite a lot to learn about effective journalism, I'm afraid. So, of course, I'll provide you an advance copy to review to assure you're not misquoted."

Liu nodded. "That sounds fine. Actually, I suppose you could just record the whole thing with a C-phone."

Kate turned to Ben and smiled. "Of *course*! Benjamin, if you had just thought of that, you wouldn't have had to interrupt the flow of the discussion," she bugged her eyes at him, "on this *unexpectedly vital topic*."

Ben smiled back. "Yes, ma'am. I just know how *seriously* you take journalistic ethics. And I wanted to be sure you didn't burn in hell for lying. Like some overambitious reporters I can think of surely will."

Dr. Liu sat back and raised his eyebrows. "Wow. I never realized you people took this ethics stuff so seriously."

Kate pointed at the pitcher. "Benjamin, would you mind getting your phone out and pouring me a tea while Dr. Liu and I get started?"

Apparently Petrie's oft-repeated admonition that

when the truth didn't set you free you should lie
your ass off applied in journalism as often as it did
in politics. Which appeared to be most of the time.

As Ben poured her tea Kate said to Nolan Liu,
"Just tell your story from the beginning."

Nolan Liu nodded. "Well, in the beginning, there
was carbon tetrachloride."

THIRTY-FOUR

Nolan Liu sat back in his chair, looked out across the Napa Valley, and said to Ben and Kate, who sat across from him, "My father and mother arrived in America in 1954 and opened a dry-cleaning shop. I came along in '56. But up until 1954 my father had worked in *his* father's dry-cleaning shop in Hong Kong."

Ben frowned. "He breathed carbon tet every day as a child?"

Liu nodded. "Well before my eighth birthday carbon tetrachloride was a known hepatotoxin, even though *how* it killed liver cells wasn't understood. But on my eighth birthday liver failure killed my father. After a lifetime's exposure. That was the day I decided to specialize in human biology and find a cure for what killed my father. But by the time I got my doctorate people had been testing and rejecting hypotheses about *why* carbon tet killed liver cells for twenty years. Even though dry cleaners actually had stopped using carbon tet during the mid-fifties. But in the meantime people had started taking new over-the-counter pain relievers like acetaminophen, and later ibuprofen, as if they were candy. Overdosing Tylenol or Advil turned out to be hepatotoxic in its own right."

Liu raised a finger and shook it as he spoke. "That's just *one* example, of *one* pathology, that affects *one* organ. But it's the moral of that part of my life story. Bodies break. We fix the damage, as best we can. They break again, somewhere else. We fix them again. Then we find out that the fix for one breakdown causes another. It's biologic whack-a-mole. But it's been the only medicine we had. And while we were absorbed with that kind of medicine, we accepted as immutable the notion that human bodies just didn't last even as long as Great Britain's ninety-nine-year lease on Hong Kong."

Kate said, "But we can also live healthier."

As Ben punched at his phone screen he said, "Ms. Boyle doesn't do gluten."

Liu smiled. "Of course. But all the proactive lifestyle changes and therapies and fads that we presently call anti-aging scarcely move the needle. Consider the spread in life expectancy between two nations with well-developed health care. The difference in average life expectancy between Japan, with its presumed more healthy lifestyle, and America, with its presumed wretched, obese lifestyle is only four years."

Kate said, "You're saying we shouldn't bother?"

"On the contrary. Some very pleasant habits show promise. One of my little projects here is a grape varietal that yields more resveratrol. Resveratrol is a powerful antioxidant found in the skin of red grapes, and therefore in red wine. We understood the value of antioxidants to the immune system. But beyond that we discovered that mice fed a high-calorie, high-fat diet plus resveratrol lived thirty percent longer, and with fewer age-related health issues, compared to a control group."

Kate smiled and nodded. "The French Paradox. Eat more cheese. Drink more wine. Live longer."

Liu smiled back, but shook his head. "To ingest as much trans-resveratrol as those mice got you would have to drink over one hundred glasses of red wine a day. But lots of game changers are out there. One of the reasons we age is that our cells' energy generators, the mitochondria, decay. In 2013 the same researchers who fed the resveratrol to mice found that injections of nicotinamide adenine dinucleotide turned back the mitochondrial clock in the muscle cells of other mice. Information technology now lets us understand and experiment with intracellular structures and processes, down to the molecular level, at rates and in ways we couldn't even think of even a few years ago. My lab was attacking senescence—the deteriorative process of aging itself—as if it was an enemy, not just an immutable part of the battlefield landscape."

Kate said, "But if you were already doing that, why join Cardinal?"

"Resources. The market's a wonderful way to deliver broad, deep solutions. Light bulbs, C-phones, drugs to treat individual pathologies from smallpox to erectile dysfunction. But entrepreneurship just doesn't do narrow-focus, slow-return, truly massive investments very well. The two greatest technological leaps in human history, the Manhattan Project and the Mercury through Apollo Moon landings projects, were driven by existential martial threats to the most powerful nation in history."

Kate said, "Then what could a private company like Cardinal offer that would be different?"

Liu nodded. "Manny offered me my own, private Manhattan Project. I came aboard with absolute control and an unlimited budget and the mission to acquire every life-extension and antisenescence project and talent that appeared on our radar until we had gathered all the eggs in one enormous basket. We didn't rely on one technology, drug, or process. The same way the Manhattan Project created a uranium bomb *and* a plutonium bomb in parallel, we locked them all up. But—"

Kate cocked her head. "But you still must have run out of money, eventually. Is that why you quit?"

Liu shook his head. "Manny's other businesses, the phones, the games, the cars, always threw off more money than I could spend."

"The biotechnology just wasn't out there to acquire?"

"On the contrary. For example, the human body already naturally rebuilds and replaces cells by the millions every single day. As long as the DNA strands in a cell that carry the blueprint to replicate that cell can remake themselves, the cell becomes brand-new also. Aging happens when meaningful numbers of cells cease to replicate, or replicate imperfectly. We knew even five years ago that the problem with the DNA strand packages, the chromosomes, was that their 'end caps,' telomeres, wear out. When they wear out, the DNA strands become shorter. Eventually the cell fails. We also knew that in certain circumstances the body produces telomerase, a sort of telomere repair kit enzyme. Telomerase effectively tacks on a new end cap, and rejuvenates a DNA strand. If we could deliver telomerase everywhere a body needs it, we might master many aspects of aging virtually overnight."

Kate said, "Can you really extrapolate from isolated examples like that?"

Liu smiled and nodded. "The examples were everywhere. The key was that they were, as you say, isolated. Once we consolidated them, their collective promise dazzled us. Not only could you rebuild a better liver cell by cell as its cells reproduced, you could, taken to logical, theoretical extreme, rebuild an entire organism, cell by cell. You could even synthesize DNA, and change an organism cell by cell as you went, into something completely different. Although changing a goldfish into a rabbit wouldn't be much use outside a magic shop."

Without looking up from his phone, Ben said, "You're not saying that one day there would be a pill, and everybody who took one would live to be a thousand?"

Liu shook his head. "No. When the computer folks talk about the Singularity in their field they talk about the law of accelerating returns. Within intervals like years or decades from now we expected that the Golden Gate Project's advances would enable people alive today to celebrate a spry and healthy one hundred fiftieth birthday. But in the meantime, life-extension progress would continue, and continue at an ever-accelerating rate. The new developments would already be propelling them to a healthy two hundred fiftieth birthday even before they reached one hundred fifty, and so on."

"The Methuselarity."

Liu nodded.

Kate said, "You make it sound inevitable."

"Once we had gathered all the methodologies into the big basket I could see that it was going to happen, and it was going to happen within some lives in being today."

"Then what failed?"

"What failed was my moral certainty. The more sure I became that we *could* do it the more I worried about what would happen when we *did* do it."

Kate asked, "What could be wrong with everybody living forever?"

Liu smiled. "Besides people who can't amuse themselves over a rainy weekend having to find something to do for a thousand years?"

Kate smiled and sipped her tea.

Liu continued, "For the first hundred years the technology would be so expensive that it would only be available to the wealthy, the privileged, and the dishonest."

Ben said, "Inequality of result's not new. We've learned to live with it."

Liu raised his index finger. "We've learned to live with inequality because we know that at the end of the day one result is common to us all. Death. Sometimes the good die young, sometimes the rich do, and sometimes the wicked prosper. But we are secure in the knowledge that good or wicked, rich or poor, old or young, in the end the other guy and I are both equally dead."

Kate said, "Unless you buy into heaven. Or hell."

Liu nodded. "Faith in the afterlife helps us cope with the inequality of this life. In the end the good are rewarded and the wicked are punished. But if this life goes on forever where's the justice?"

Ben frowned. "You think society will disintegrate over abstract ideas?"

Liu shrugged. "Over the centuries, abstract ideas have driven more people to kill other people than trade imbalances, mineral deposits, and territorial imperatives. But the issues won't just be abstract issues."

Kate said, "If nobody's dying, overpopulation becomes a problem?"

"Yes. And I don't just mean the crash of Social Security and other programs like it around the world. That's just a political problem of resource allocation, although it would be a massive one. We can achieve a static, sustainable population by closing the door on the front end—no births—or we can kick perfectly healthy, productive people out the door on the back end."

Ben said, "But if we achieve a static total population by terminating perfectly healthy people it's murder. If we do it by eliminating new generations, then where do the new ideas that keep a society vital come from?"

Kate said to Ben, "Maybe we don't need new people to generate new ideas. Think how much more and better music Mozart could have composed if he had written for three hundred years instead of thirty."

Liu shrugged. "On the other hand, think how much more evil Hitler could have visited on the world if he had governed for twelve hundred years instead of twelve. Which brings us to our species' other great ideologues. Virtually all organized religions subsist on the promise of an afterlife. In particular a benign afterlife for the good, and hell for the wicked. Organized religions' carrots and sticks will have diminished value. Will organized religions take that lying down?"

Kate cocked her head. "So you had put all this technological promise and all these ideological conundrums in one basket. Why did you call it the Golden Gate?"

"Names were one part of the business Manny really liked. Take the name of the C-phone. And the Galvani."

Kate said, "Galvani? Cardinal just copied Tesla. They

borrowed the name of an Italian scientist associated with electricity to make an electric car sound sexy."

Liu raised his index finger again and smiled. "But what Galvani *did* with electricity was shoot it through frogs' legs to make them twitch. With that name Manny wanted to celebrate the impending meld of technology and biology."

"What was the Golden Gate Project celebrating?"

"The name was metaphorical. The view from the Golden Gate leads to the sunset. A dark end. But what if we could make the world turn? Then the Golden Gate would lead to endless sunrises."

Kate said, "So that's why you left? You didn't want to proceed with the Golden Gate Project? The endless sunrises would make a mess? But Manny Colibri was full gas on life extension?"

"On the contrary. Manny and I were entirely sympatico. Our reasons may have been different. I can't say I know that because I don't *know* what Manny was thinking. But I always felt that he had no intention of using the big tent we had thrown over life-extension science to do anything but smother it."

"Then why *did* you leave?"

Nolan Liu's housekeeper poked her head out the door to the terrace. "Dr. Liu, you asked me to let you know when it was time for Vivian's lunch."

Liu stood. "Vivian is my mother. Shortly before I left Cardinal and the Golden Gate Project she was diagnosed with Alzheimer's. I believed that if I managed the available therapies personally I could prolong her remaining good time. Three years on, I believe I have. But more importantly I wanted to be there for her whether the time was good or bad."

Kate's eyes glistened. "That's an admirable reason."

Liu blinked. "Sometimes I wonder. My mother has moments of lucidity now when she remembers my father. But the time she remembers is always the day he died. She relives it over and over, weeping. Saying goodbye to someone you love is so difficult that some of us hide behind mental defense mechanisms rather than confront the loss even *once*. I can't imagine enduring that pain over and over for eternity. Which is only one of the tragedies we would face if some of us lived forever and some of us didn't." He pointed to the door. "Thank you both for coming. Now, if you will excuse me, I have to join my mother."

Ben and Kate walked toward her car, mute, as gravel crunched beneath their feet.

Ben said, "Wow."

"I know." They walked on, then Kate stopped and Ben turned to face her.

She said, "Ben, something that Liu said makes me think about something I haven't mentioned to you. Not that I've been holding back. We've just had a lot else going on."

"Okay."

She frowned. "The business about organized religion not taking it lying down if people don't need heaven and aren't afraid of hell?"

"It's an interesting point. But they're not in charge."

"Actually, they are. Or they will be. Colibri died without exercising his power of appointment as the trustee of Cardinal's stock under a trust that was created when his Catholic boss at Cardinal was alive. 'Zat make sense, so far?"

Ben nodded. "That's just first-year decedents' estates and trusts. Keep talking."

"So the Archdiocese of San Francisco gets the whole thing."

Ben frowned. "Whatever Nolan Liu thinks Colibri intended to do about life-extension technology, everybody else in the business thought he was full gas. That therapist said Eli Abney got active in the Catholic Church before he blew Colibri up."

Kate smiled. "You're quick for an intern. One way for the Catholic Church to put a stop to all this was to take it over. And to do that all it had to do was get rid of Manny Colibri. So all of a sudden all the paranoid conspiracy theories don't seem so nuts. So now what?"

Ben said, "Like any problem, keep working it. Which your intern did while Dr. Liu was talking to you. Petrie's sources in D.C. have told him that Cardinal's got Colson and Pell jacked up to Defcon 2. Of course the firm won't say why."

Kate slitted her eyes. "I knew it. Carlsson cut the call with the cops because the penguin-watching ship needed the satellite link. But somehow he found enough of a link to light a fire under his rat-bastard lawyers."

"Kate, that doesn't prove he's covering up a murder conspiracy. Cardinal's about to become a takeover target so big in many fields that almost any deal will trigger an anti-trust inquiry."

Kate sniffed. "Maybe. Either way, we need to keep this moving. Anything else?"

"I've cracked the code for LOH EDA 2018.5."

Kate reached across and shoved him. "Get out! There's not even an 'M' for Museum in it."

"The San Francisco Museums of Fine Art are actually two separate collections."

Kate's jaw dropped and her eyes widened. "LOH. The Legion of Honor."

"You know it?"

"My parents took me when I was little. There's a copy of the Thinker on a pedestal in the courtyard. I asked my mother why we were going to a toilet museum."

"The Legion of Honor has a European Decorative Arts collection. EDA. 2018 is the year Colibri donated his stuff. Bet?"

Kate shook her head.

They reached the car, and as Ben laid his hand on the driver's door handle he eyed his C-phone, then looked across the roof at Kate. "The museum hasn't responded to my texts. And it closes in ninety minutes. We'll never make it."

Kate snorted as she stepped around the car's hood, extended her hand and wiggled her fingers. "Gimme the keys."

Ben and Kate, out of breath and with fourteen minutes to spare before closing, arrived in front of the glass-fronted display case signed "TALISMANS OF FAITH, SUPERSTITION, AND VIOLENCE DURING THE REFORMATION." Among statuettes and jewelry fastened to the case's beige fabric back wall was object 2018.5.

It was a block of age-dulled, light-colored wood, whittled into a simple, one piece model of a sailing ship on a pedestal. The ship's sails were carved as a row of swept-back triangles, arranged along the ship's centerline like sharks' dorsal fins. The banana-sized hull tapered at its prow to a thin spike, to represent a galley's ram, and was cut front to back with diagonal lines arranged in echelon, to represent a galley's oars. A phrase was carved into the model's pedestal.

The placard beneath the little ship and pedestal read:

VOTIVE SHIP FOLK ART CARVING
Linden (Basswood), Spanish, ca. 1577–1588
Anonymous gift, 2018

This carving models a Neapolitan galleass, a sixteenth-century hybrid galley and rowed ram.

The pedestal's inscription reads in Spanish *"Dios salve a la de San Lorenzo y todos los que navegan en su,"* or "God save the *San Lorenzo* and all who sail in her."

At that time, the Catholic Church's blessing of such a model, although most were larger and more professionally constructed than this example, was routinely sought, to protect both ship and crew.

The galleass *San Lorenzo* entered service with Spain's navy in 1588, and was a principal capital ship of the Spanish Armada.

As Kate and Ben stared at the whittled good luck charm, Kate said, "I wonder whether the blessing did anybody any good."

THIRTY-FIVE

During the evening of August 7, 1588, Rodrigo Sanchez de Vega, the galleass *San Lorenzo*'s chief gunner, stood on the ship's forward fighting platform while she swung at anchor in the English Channel. He sought a place on which to lay out the sleeping mat that he carried in his sea bag, because the summer night was fair, the sea gentle, and all the space below decks of any galleass was rank with the products of seven hundred sixty-eight impressed oarsmen, marines, sailors, and the officers who commanded them.

The risen and full moon lit the night so brightly that after Rodrigo seated himself upon his mat he propped his feet upon the rail, took his knife in hand, and resumed whittling his votive miniature of the ship in which he sailed.

Rodrigo's back was to the town of Calais, a league east on the French coast, while he faced into the wind, toward the English fleet and, somewhere in the dark distance across the Channel, England. Close around the *San Lorenzo* over one hundred twenty ships rocked at anchor, the largely intact remainder of one hundred thirty that had departed Lisbon two months before, and now proceeded north in the defensive formation of an impenetrable crescent. So effective had been the tactic that the English were reduced to following after the great navy like starving dogs, picking off the occasional scrap of a ship that had become disabled.

The Spanish ships comprised the Great and Most Fortunate Navy that Phillip II had dispatched from Spain with the mission of delivering onto the coast of England an equally great army, now waiting in Flanders. An army that would wrest control of England from its Protestant heretic queen, Elizabeth, and restore it to the bosom of the Catholic faith.

As Rodrigo shaved away curls of linden wood from his tiny ship's flanks a bronzed hand pointed at it. "What do you make there, chief gunner?"

Rodrigo turned and saw, laying out his own mat alongside, the navigator known only as Mano. Mano was a new addition to the *San Lorenzo*'s complement, employed seventeen days earlier while the great navy refitted at La Coruna. Mano was said to possess extraordinary navigation skill in general, but in particular he had experience of the great Atlantic Ocean, upon which the *San Lorenzo* was then about to embark.

The turbulent Atlantic ill-suited the low freeboard of a Neapolitan galleass, which was built to rule the calmer Mediterranean. The *San Lorenzo*'s oar ports were so close to her waterline that even gentle swells could flood her lower deck to the waists of her rowers. It was said that the *San Lorenzo*'s master, Don Hugo de Moncada, hoped that experienced crew members like Mano would mitigate the *San Lorenzo*'s design shortcomings.

Mano's new shipmates remarked that whatever his experience he moved with a hummingbird's unpredictable speed, and spoke barely more often and scarcely louder than one. He was neither so fair in complexion as a Spaniard nor so brown as a moor. He lacked a moor's broad features and his face was as smooth and as hairless as a page's, though his dark, weary eyes belied a page's naiveté.

Rodrigo raised his carving and turned it in his hand as he answered Mano's question. "I am fashioning a token to receive God's blessing upon this ship and upon us all."

Mano pointed across the Channel. "If the English are such vile heretics as King Phillip says, then has God not already blessed this enterprise ten times over?"

"They *are* so vile. The English deny even the Holy Father's calendar. For them the seventh day of August arrives only ten days hence."

"And such differences are cause to spill blood?"

"We have more strenuous differences with the English than their calendar. Their so-called navy are nothing but seagoing cutpurses. Had Drake the pirate not abandoned his pursuit of us in order to take the *Rosario* as his prize last week, the English could already have scattered this formation, like dogs among gulls. An Englishman will shed more innocent blood for treasure than for God."

Mano stared west into the dark. "I have seen Spaniards spill innocent blood for treasure in the name of their god."

"Mano, have you made the passage to the New World, then?"

Mano nodded as he stared, then yawned. "I know little of this channel or of its currents or of the nation for which it is named. But I have made the passage to this world, and back again to the new, so often that I am weary."

Rodrigo patted his new shipmate's shoulder as he lay back on the platform and closed his eyes. Rodrigo said, "Tonight you may rest. We both may. Neither Moncada nor God will require your hand on the astrolabe or mine on the shot gauges before dawn."

"Rodrigo!" Mano the navigator pounded Rodrigo's shoulder with one hand.

Rodrigo sat up on the platform, stared in the direction where the navigator pointed, and felt the wind that remained in Rodrigo's and Mano's faces. That wind now bore toward them, through the moonlit night, eight ships at full sail. Two were aflame. The other six were dark or showed faint lights.

Rodrigo whispered, "Hellburners."

"What?"

"I warned you the English are demons. They are setting fireships among us. The Dutch heretics set only two fireships on us in the Scheldt and eight hundred Spaniards perished."

Mano said, "They approach in the night like ghosts."

Rodrigo pointed at the fireships as their white sails drew closer, and in that moment flames crept up the rigging of a third ship and her sails came alight. "They approach like ghosts because they are ghosts. Their tillers are lashed and their crews have made away in boats, leaving lit fuses burning. The English have laden those ships with canvas and hemp and rope and tar and pitch and soaked the lot, and the ships' decks themselves, in oil. The ships' guns are powdered and double shotted. When they are among us the heat and flame will cause them to discharge into us in all directions as if each fireship were a great bomb and each ship in this navy a box of tinder."

From the afterdeck Don Hugo shouted orders as the full crew were roused.

A pinnace drew alongside the *San Lorenzo*, and its crew shouted up to them the orders from the Duke of Medina Sidonia that all ships of his navy should cut or discard their anchor cables and make away from the fireships' path.

The pinnace continued on to the next vessel as the *San Lorenzo*'s boatswain called to Mano and Rodrigo to assist him.

But, by the time they reached the boatswain, he had swung an axe and severed the galleass's main anchor. As the cable slithered down into the dark sea like a murdered serpent, the boatswain muttered, "The English call them Hellburners. But it will be these lost anchors that will play hell with us all in the next heavy weather."

As Rodrigo watched, smaller Spanish vessels grappled the two most violently burning fireships and towed them away from the fleet's core.

In haste to maneuver in the darkness, the *San Lorenzo*'s helmsman fouled her rudder on another ship's anchor cable.

Within minutes, the boatswain had pronounced the rudder's damage too severe to repair at sea. Don

Hugo had given orders to make for Calais, maneuvering by oars alone.

An hour after Mano had roused him, Mano and Rodrigo stood on their platform and watched as the six remaining fireships drifted, ablaze but harmless, to ground on the shore of France and burn themselves out. In the opposite direction the lanterns of countless Spanish ships wandered in the English Channel, as aimless as fireflies in the darkness, as the Great and Fortunate Navy dissolved into pandemonium.

At dawn Rodrigo and Mano remained on the forward platform and watched as the English raced to overtake the slowly-rowed *San Lorenzo*. The wounded galleass crept toward Calais borne by the strokes of the three hundred heretics and lesser criminals who rowed her. As the English drew closer, the rowers were exhorted to raise their effort.

A sudden great wrenching and grinding slowed the *San Lorenzo*'s modest progress so abruptly that Rodrigo and Mano were pitched forward onto the prow, beneath the forward platform.

Shouts and screams came from aft and below them.

Rodrigo rose from prone to his knees and felt a great lump begin to form on his forehead. He heard Mano curse as the other man moved his own shoulder.

Mano said, "We have grounded on a sandbar."

Rodrigo rubbed his forehead. "Perhaps as the tide comes in it will refloat her. And if the English come for us she may not be able to maneuver but we shall greet them with fifty cannons worth of Spanish shot."

Mano shook his head. "The tide ebbs and will

continue to ebb for a considerable time. Soon she will sink further onto the sand and list further to starboard. Your starboard guns will be smothered, your port guns will point at the sky like fowling pieces, and your fore and aft guns will be immovable." Mano reached down and lifted an object that lay on the deck, then held it up between them. It was Rodrigo's unfinished votive carving, which had fallen, as the two of them had, upon the impact of the grounding.

Mano raised his eyebrows in the dim light. "Perhaps you should have had this blessed before we left port."

He held the votive model out to Rodrigo, but Rodrigo pushed it away and snorted. "Throw it at the English when they board us. Then it will have been of some use."

Rodrigo watched the English come for the *San Lorenzo*, but not in the manner expected. An entire squadron against one, they were like the scavenging dogs he had predicted them to be. As Mano had predicted, the tide had indeed gone out and the *San Lorenzo* listed so badly that her cannon were unusable.

The English ships drew more water than a galleass. Seeing the *San Lorenzo*'s predicament, the English therefore did not risk grounding their own vessels in the shallows. Instead, they stood off, firing cannon at the *San Lorenzo* from long range, and without effect.

The English then launched longboats, carrying marksmen. When the longboats drew within musket range they began firing upon the wounded galleass.

Rodrigo and Mano sheltered behind the forward platform and watched while Don Hugo directed the *San Lorenzo*'s marines in the return of the English fire.

The marines outnumbered the English in the longboats, and fired down into the unprotected longboats from behind the cover afforded by the elevated starboard rail. In this way, the English were held at bay for the greater part of an hour, and many were wounded.

Rodrigo said, "Perhaps they will abandon this prize, rejoin the pursuit of the remainder of the navy, and we shall be spared."

Mano said, "If their aim is to save England, they will rejoin the pursuit. If, as you say, they pursue treasure, Don Hugo will oblige them. I think he plays on their greed to purchase time so that Medina Sidonia may reassemble his navy. Don Hugo is a brave and clever man."

In that moment an Englishman leapt from the nearest boat, so that he stood waist-deep in the sea with his feet firmly planted on bottom. Another Englishman handed a loaded musket down to him over the boat's rail, and the man in the water raised it to his newly steady shoulder, aimed, then fired.

The Englishman's ball struck Don Hugo full on the face, and he crumpled onto the afterdeck.

Mano ran in a crouch down the long fly bridgeway that overlooked the rowing decks and allowed passage fore to aft. Rodrigo followed. By the time Mano reached Don Hugo, the flagship's surgeon already knelt over the stricken commander of the Squadron of Galleasses, who lay on his back as dark blood pooled around his motionless head.

The surgeon looked up at them and shook his head. "The ball entered his eye and has gone into his brain."

From the lower decks a great wailing rose.

Not for the fate of the brave and clever Don Hugo

de Moncada. The oarsmen trapped below, within the now severely listed galleass, realized that when the tide turned many of their number might perish in the coming flood unless they were released.

In the meanwhile, the leaderless marines began abandoning their firing positions, hurling away their heavy muskets, throwing themselves over the shoreward rail in panic, then wading or swimming for shore as the English boats closed the distance to the *San Lorenzo*.

Mano disappeared below, and scant moments later oarsmen as well as common sailors began to follow the marines in their high-kneed rush through the shallows to shore.

As the first Englishman's head appeared above the *San Lorenzo*'s rail, Rodrigo followed his countrymen in their hundreds in headlong flight toward shore. The English, busy looting their prize, ignored the Spaniards.

A quarter-hour later, Rodrigo slogged ashore, paused calf-deep and panting in the surf, and surveyed the melee. He glimpsed the bronze-skinned figure of Mano, the navigator, darting as nimbly as a hummingbird through the tangle of bedraggled survivors. Many of those were oarsmen whom Mano had liberated from their bondage, and they now had gained both the refuge of the shore and the possibility of a new life.

Mano carried his sea bag in the crook of his arm, and Rodrigo wondered whether it contained, in addition to the navigator's own sparse possessions, the carved ship that Rodrigo had discarded. Rodrigo also wondered whether, if the little carving was in that bag, the votive would bring Mano better luck in *his* new life than it had so far brought Rodrigo Sanchez de Vega and the rest of Spain's Great and Fortunate Navy.

THIRTY-SIX

"Dad! The limo David sent's outside." Kate shouted up the stairs of the Boyle home to her father, then turned to check herself out in the foyer's full-length mirror.

Her dress, purchased earlier in the day, was emerald green and was the only one she had tried on since she stopped swimming that didn't make her ass look bigger than an Airbus. She faced the mirror, tugged with both hands at the strapless neckline, then bent forward at the waist to simulate the view from Shepard's eye level.

Her father's patent leathers thumped down the stairs as he adjusted the collar on the tux he hadn't worn, so far as Kate recalled, since the last David Powell party he and Mom had attended. Jack Boyle stood beside her in front of the mirror, shot his cuffs, and asked, "Is this thing still okay?"

Kate turned and adjusted his bow tie. "Perfect. A little retro, but so's the guy in it."

Her father eyed her cleavage then craned his neck

to check the back of her dress. He sighed. "Well, at least your belly button doesn't show and 'KISS THIS' isn't stamped across your fanny."

"Mom made me take those back before I even cut the tags off. But she also took my Disney princess costume to Goodwill a long time ago, Dad."

"Katy, you'll always be my little princess." He kissed her forehead, then held the door for her.

As the car's driver opened its passenger door for them Kate pouted. A parent in the mix really complicated her plans for an evening that could never be shown on the Disney Channel.

As Kate remembered the Aquatic Park Bathhouse from her Disney princess days, it was a boring, static sideshow among the glitzy and tawdry tourist attractions that peppered San Francisco's waterfront.

Tonight, as the hired car David Powell had sent for them inched forward in the dropoff line to the bathhouse's doors the place finally was dressed up like Cinderella's castle.

And it was under siege.

Demonstrators lined Beach Street three deep for the last hundred yards to the bathhouse, shaking fists and pumping signs demanding that the Aquatic Park Senior Center be returned to the bathhouse.

Whump.

A thrown something struck the limo's roof, Kate winced, then orange glop oozed down the window and blurred her view. She shouted behind the glass at the crowd, "You assholes!"

She turned to her father. "Why does David bother doing this over and over?"

Her dad shrugged. "Katy, you'll never get a coach if you stop buying pumpkins."

Once the limo glided inside the barricades, it left the crowds behind and the bathhouse, its exterior floodlit, gleamed like a palace again. Of course, the footmen who greeted them were parking valets wearing crooked clip-on bowties, and portly park rangers wanded everybody for metal.

Inside the bathhouse building more National Park Service Rangers patrolled in their forest-green uniforms, hands behind their backs, smiling and nodding like Walmart greeters in funny hats, while they waited for somebody to ask them questions.

The party spilled into every quarter of the bathhouse's top three public floors. On the entry floor a string quartet played, while couples dressed for a night at the opera wandered, backgrounded by pastel art deco wall murals, painted before even Kate's father had been born. The partygoers sipped w'hite wine and stuffed their cheeks with *hors d'oeuvres*, passed on silver trays by waitstaff wearing white waistcoats.

When the guests weren't drinking and chipmunking bacon-wrapped scallops, they bent over tiny round tables draped in pressed white cloths, sprinkled among the bathhouse's sparse maritime exhibits. On the tables stood cards that described "silent auction" donations like condos on St. Bart's offered for weeks when it always rained, luxury boxes for games pitting the Warriors against whoever was in last place, and New Age Discovery weekends.

Kate said, "Dad, this sucks."

"What did you expect? David selling Girl Scout

cookies for ten grand a box? He tried to have boat rides to jazz it up."

"Cookies *and* boat rides. Groovy."

"Katy these boats are antiques."

"Exactly." Kate spotted Shepard's head, adrift above a sea of bald and tiara'd ones, and touched her father's arm. "Gotta go. Dad, go find Julia Madison."

"Why?"

"From what you told me this afternoon, I think she's here to sell you her cookies."

Shepard stood looking lost, with his tuxedoed back to her and a stem of white wine in his right hand.

She touched his arm. He turned, his eyes lit and he stared. "You look beautiful."

"Thank you." She turned for him. "It's probably the only dress in here that the wearer hemmed herself. These people are old money. My mother was old school."

"I take it this crowd doesn't impress the Boyles."

Kate shrugged. "My dad says the principal value of an Ivy League education to an ordinary person is demystification of the rich."

Kate stood back, looked Shepard up and down, then touched his jacket's sleeve. "You in a tux *does* impress me. You look like a secret agent."

Ben frowned, then nodded at another broad-shouldered man who stood alone with his back against the wall opposite them. "I'm the only secret agent in here who's not packing. I haven't seen so many jacket bulges and earpieces in one place since I carried Petrie's briefcase at a meeting in the West Wing."

Kate glanced around and counted three more private

security men failing to blend in. "Don't get your paranoia in a wad. The mob outside's lukewarm for San
Francisco. And terrorists don't attack the rich. They
attack soft targets who toil for the rich. The best way
to terrorize this crowd would be a two thousand point
drop in the Dow." Kate snagged a white wine stem
glass off one passing tray, then a canape off another.
She hadn't eaten or drunk anything all day, which
she was sure made her look a half-size thinner. She
swallowed half the wine in a gulp. "So, how's your
day been, Shepard?"

"Busy. Petrie's always eager to work to his staff's
last breath."

A server wearing a white waistcoat passed by holding a silver tray and Ben plucked a cracker from it,
then chewed.

"Shepard, that's caviar. You won't—"

He chewed, swallowed, then cocked his head.
"Osetra. But still good."

Kate's jaw dropped.

Ben shrugged. "Traveling with Petrie has its upside."

Kate glanced around the room, and when she turned
back Ben was staring at a blonde wearing a sprayed-
on, off-the-shoulder black sheath. Her hair was up,
and held in place by a glistening tiara studded with
diamonds the size of raisins.

Kate tapped Ben's forearm. "Those aren't the breasts
you're looking for. Move along."

Ben wrinkled his forehead. "I was wondering
whether the diamonds in that tiara are real."

"Sure you were. Actually, last year her husband
paid six million dollars for a Shakespeare first folio.
So yeah, she can afford real ones. Which, by the way,

those boobs aren't. And I'll bet you another cup of coffee and a Girl Scout cookie that ass is just Spanx."

Shepard turned to Kate and eyed her dress. "I've never had a Girl Scout cookie."

She threaded her arm in his. "All natural, Shepard. And very satisfying." Kate pointed to a male-male-female trio in conversation, drinks in hand, across the room and said, "These are some people who need to meet you."

When David Powell saw Ben and Kate coming he grinned. "Kate! My favorite cookie salesperson." He leaned close to her and kissed the air beside her cheek.

Julia Madison, wearing a floor length red number that was definitely not hemmed at home was already attached to Jack Boyle's arm. She turned to Kate and smiled. "And *my* favorite journalist." She looked Ben up and down, "And *this* is . . . ?"

Kate clung tighter to Ben's arm, "Arthur Petrie's"— she caught herself before she said *right-hand man*— "secret weapon. Ben Shepard."

Ben smiled. "Blunt instrument, actually."

Jack said, "Kate tells me you're only working for that clown to get through law school."

David drew back in mock affront. "I resemble that remark." He winked at Julia, "Jack was *my* secret weapon for thirty years."

Julia Madison said, "Arthur *is*, as Jack suggests, an acquired taste, politically. But some people in Washington whose judgment I trust tell me that he's become a legitimate contender overnight." Julia narrowed her eyes at Ben. "Where would you see yourself fitting in a Petrie campaign, Ben?"

Ben smiled and shrugged. "I wouldn't. I committed

to a year with the senator, which is turning into most of a year with the secretary. All I want to fit into on election day is my seat in the second-year class at Georgetown Law School."

The former cabinet secretary wagged her finger at Ben. "Ben, you listen to your Aunt Julia. The experience and contacts an intelligent, handsome young man could earn, whether Arthur wins or loses, would be worth more than graduating quicker."

David took Jack and Julia by their elbows and steered the three of them to another group. "Julia, a couple of people just arrived who you need to sell on ELCIE."

As Kate and Ben walked upstairs to see more of the party, she felt too much wine on an empty stomach, leaned against him, and they paused on the landing halfway up the stairwell. Kate said, "Well. Your new aunt sees something in that tux, too."

"It's called a night school mentality. Like your father's." Ben took Kate's shoulders and faced her toward him. "Kate, even in a few seconds with your father I noticed a lot of you in him. So I like him very much." Ben paused. "But I also noticed that you've never mentioned how he adjusted to your mother's death."

Kate stared at her stilettos. "You notice a lot that people don't want you to see."

"Eighty percent of surviving as a platoon leader is noticing a lot that thirty-eight other people under stress don't want you to see. So, how is he?"

She shifted on the damn stilettos, they pinched her toes worse, and she shoved his chest with her free hand. "You can be a pushy little fucker, too."

"If your platoon sergeant doesn't notice either, and you're not pushy, somebody gets killed."

"Okay. My father blamed her death on an over-reliance on prayer and holistic medicine. And the inevitability of cancer. It's like the other thing never happened."

"Hysterical amnesia? Like Abney's therapist mentioned?"

"That's my guess. If Googling's a substitute for a psych degree. My parents were so close, Ben. I think my dad couldn't accept the reality of how he lost her. And I'm scared to death about how he'll react when he finally does see it. Why else do you think I've stayed out here for two years writing for a crappy niche magazine after I left home to change the world?"

Ben nodded. "I'm no shrink either. But I don't think there's any way to know when and how the wound opens up. What does his therapist say?"

"Therapist? The man drinks whole milk instead of two percent because bad cholesterol's just a bunch of tree-hugging hippie crap." She blinked back tears, shoved Shepard further away and crossed her arms. "Dammit, Shepard, stop trying to be *my* therapist! Just be my fucking *date*, okay?"

"Okay." Ben stared down at the floor, then looked up and smiled. "Please believe me, Kate. That's all I was hoping for tonight." He paused, lips parted, and his cheeks turned pink. "Not in the sense of the entire expression, of course."

She turned her face and choked back a laugh, then took his hand and led him the rest of the way upstairs, where the murals were more abstract, the music was less antique, and the crowd was closer to their age.

She towed Ben to one of the auction tables, behind which a baggy, hooded red suit hung on the wall like footed pajamas, then lifted the survival suit's ragged-ended sleeve. "Ooo. Designer neoprene. And Mick's girlfriend complained about orange coveralls."

Ben read the item description, then said, "The boats look pretty cool. But after setting all this up all the rides are postponed because it's cold in January? And nobody thought about that? How did these people make fortunes?"

"Shepard, they didn't make fortunes. Their parents and their grandparents made fortunes. What these people do is figure out how to dissipate their inheritances and get patted on the back for doing it. Restoring a cool boat costs more than a regular family's mortgage, even though the boat is an obscene luxury and the mortgage is a necessity. Even rich people know it's cold in January. But it's like you said about donating art to a museum. If you commit your boat enough for charitable purposes, the obscene luxury is as deductible as the interest on the regular family's necessity. And everybody thinks you're a hero."

Ben pointed at the survival suit's ragged sleeve. "Did somebody ruin this for the hell of it, then?"

"Well, David Powell's grandfather used to shoot whales from his porch for the hell of it. But no. What was the first thing that happened after you walked through security?"

"Uh. A waiter brought me a big glass of very good wine."

Kate nodded. "My father says a sober patrician is an asshole, but a drunk patrician is a philanthropist. They cut the mittens off the survival suits so people could keep drinking and writing down auction bids. So the donor and the donee could each deduct part of their costs."

"You know, my only assignment here tonight was to meet David Powell, and now I've done that. The only part of staying here I'm enjoying is being with you."

"At last we agree. Shepard, you could enjoy me even more if we weren't here."

"You mean go have coffee together?"

"Shepard, we've already had *coffee* together."

Kate plucked his wine glass from his hand, then set it on a bare table covered with a pressed, floor-length white cloth.

Ben pointed at his glass. "I'm not finished with that."

"Oh yes you are. Shakespeare said in that six-million-dollar folio that drink provokes the desire but takes away the performance."

His mouth hung open. "You're seducing me?"

"Or assaulting you. I can go either way."

He looked down at the long, covered table on which she had set their glasses. "I don't think we can fit under there."

Kate rolled her eyes. "Shepard, you have a hotel room."

Ben winced. "It's cheap. It's borderline dirty."

"That describes the current state of my libido perfectly. Let's go." Kate took Ben's hand and tugged him around a fishing dory exhibit.

As he passed a wall mural alongside the stairway that led back down to the main floor he gawked at it like a three-year-old being dragged past a basket of puppies. He said, "The invitation said 'bathhouse.' But this place is actually a museum, isn't it?"

"That's right. The Aquatic Park Bathhouse Museum at the San Francisco National Maritime Historical Park. Can we move this along, Shepard? I only have a couple decades left before menopause."

He reached into his trouser pocket, tugged his phone out with his free hand, and thumbed it. "APB 272." He slapped his phone against his forehead. "It was so obvious."

Kate paused and turned on him with her hands on her hips. "What's obvious is that somebody in this relationship had no idea what somebody else in this relationship had in mind for tonight."

Ben brandished his phone and rolled his eyes. "It will only take me a minute to finish."

"And that definitely wasn't it."

THIRTY-SEVEN

The green-jacketed National Park Service Ranger at the front doors pushed his hat back on his head as he studied Shepard's DHS ID in its flip-open wallet. "Of course, Mr. Shepard. The stuff's all boxed up downstairs. Most of it's been in storage for years. Funding's a terrible thing to waste, but not having the funding to put items on display seems worse. Number 272, that would actually be a fairly new item."

Ben said, "The donation would have been made in the middle of 2018. Generally, what kind of stuff is it all?"

Kate asked, "Are there papers and files?"

The ranger shrugged. "It's a maritime museum. There's items in storage from cannonballs to stuffed marlins." He pointed a finger around the auction room. "I'm supposed to be available out here to answer questions. But you're welcome to help yourself."

The ranger led them, winding through the crowd, to the doors that led out to the wide, open-air balcony that looked out over the bay. When the ranger held the door open for them, the chill night air dizzied Kate. She eyed her half full second wine glass and left it on another white-clothed table.

Ben asked, "The wine bothering you?"

Kate whispered, "I'm fine. Let's get this over with and I'll prove to you it didn't kill *my* performance."

The ranger handed them a flashlight he carried, pointed them down the exterior stairs that led to the space that had housed the senior center, and returned to his rounds among the guests.

White-jacketed *hors d'oeuvre* passers scurried past them, both climbing and descending the exterior staircase. At the stairway's base, a wide aisle, dimly lit by a single, dangling overhead bulb, had been cleared through the vast stacks of museum crates moved into the bathhouse's lower level. The aisle was wide enough for servers carrying full trays to pass others returning from the party with empty ones, and periodically they bustled back and forth up and down the aisle. As Kate's eyes adjusted to the dimness she realized that the bottom level space had been gutted to the bare concrete walls and floor for renovation, and at some points the stacked crates reached all the way to the lower level's ceiling, like coarse-paneled wooden walls.

Kate clutched her bare arms with her hands as she began to shiver. "We're back indoors. Why am I still freezing my ass off?"

Ben pointed down the crate-walled aisle, thick with servers. "Because we're in a wind tunnel. It comes in there and goes out up the stairs."

At the aisle's end, double doors stood propped open to the outdoors. Beyond the doors a catering truck was backed up to within a few feet of the open doors, its own rear doors open wide.

Kate sheltered behind Shepard. As she pressed against his warm, wide back she felt the muscles beneath the layers of his tux jacket and shirt's smooth fabric. Shepard's quest for item 272 was becoming an existential threat to her plans for the evening. Maybe she should have dragged him under that tablecloth upstairs and had her way with him while she had the chance.

Ben wandered down the dim aisle of wooden crates, craning his neck up, then bending down, using the ranger's flashlight to read stenciled numbers on individual crates.

When Ben reached the first cross aisle in the crate wall, he paused and stared down the main aisle at the catering truck, and at the wide-open doors. As a female server turned sideways to maneuver her tray past them, the ID hang tag around her neck twisted in the frigid breeze.

Kate pointed at the truck. "You looking for more caviar, Shepard?"

He shook his head. "It's nothing."

"Nothing's ever nothing with you, Shepard."

He shrugged. "The security upstairs is tight and professional. But the outside perimeter people I saw holding back the crowds at the barricades were unarmed rangers whose job was to avoid making waves. It looks like anybody could sneak past the barricades and just walk in here past that truck."

Kate stepped into the cross aisle then hissed back at Shepard, "We just had this discussion. Tonight you're my date, not a security consultant. Remember?"

Kate rubbed her arms with her hands again. The cross aisle was darker than the main one, and the boxes stacked along both of its side walls left just a person-wide opening between the stacks. The whole place was cold, dark, smelled like wet cardboard and old wood, and this space wasn't even wide enough to do it standing up. She said, "Well, this is disappointing."

"No. We're good. The numbers are getting closer." Ben shined his light high, then reached atop one stack and tugged down a three-foot-long plastic mailing tube labeled on its end cap "272."

Ben shuffled boxes to make a waist-high work space, then used a ballpoint pen to pry the end plug from the mailing tube.

The object that Ben slid out was a rusted iron rod. One end flared out, as though it was designed to fit as a cap over a piece of larger diameter. The other end was a barbed spear point, with the barb joined to the spear point by a rivet, like an axle, that allowed the barb to rotate. Ben flicked the barb with his index finger, so that it either lay flat against the spear's shaft or stood out nearly at a right angle to the shaft.

Ben tipped up the tube, then tapped it until a handwritten index card slid out and fluttered onto his improvised table top.

He shined the flashlight on the card. The handwriting read:

> Per whaling expert: Based on condition and
> style, this is the iron portion of a genuine,
> original "Temple Toggle harpoon." Should
> be held and displayed with other whaling
> artifacts.

Hand-forged in New Bedford, MA, between 1848 and 1852 by Lewis Temple, African-American free man and blacksmith.

The invention is regarded as "the single most important invention in the whole history of whaling." But Temple never patented it. So even though thousands and thousands of whales were harvested with toggle harpoons mass-produced by others, Temple died destitute.

Kate sighed. "Another minority screwed over by corporate America. Stories like this are why all those protestors upstairs are right about David and his friends."

Ben sniffed. "Really? Kate, to a whale, Lewis Temple wasn't a victim, he was an accessory to genocide. It all depends on how you look at it." Ben rotated the rusty harpoon in his hand as the two of them gazed at it in the dimness. "How do you suppose Manny Colibri looked at it?"

THIRTY-EIGHT

At noon on June 1, 1851, George Weeks sat in the bar of the inn on Walnut Street in New Bedford, Massachusetts, to which he had been dispatched by the first mate of the whaler *Corinthian*. George had chosen a seat that afforded him a view out across the inn's sparsely occupied public room, to the door from Walnut Street through which George's quarry would have to enter.

George pressed his fingers to his temples in the hope of relieving the pressure of the headache that had driven him to take refuge in drink. Rather, to take refuge in a mixture of sarsaparilla and gin that the innkeeper assured him would not only ease his headache but would also purify his blood, relieve scrofula, scurvy, and dyspepsia, cleanse his body of mercury, and eradicate the peculiar weakness to which the female body became subject upon the onset of warm weather.

George tipped his glass up, drained its last drops, and reflected that he had yet to experience any of the promised benefits. Or to understand why the innkeeper might feel that George had need of the last benefit enumerated.

A man entered from Walnut Street and selected a seat in the public room's far corner, near the window where the light was better. He unfolded, held before him, and then began to read, the broad sheets of the *Whalemen's Shipping List*.

Like the public room's other occupants, the man wore a seaman's monkey jacket, but of a finer cut and fabric. He was slight of build, and a bit less than average in stature. George would have ignored him, but for one readily observed fact.

George set aside his glass, approached the stranger, and bowed slightly. "Sir, I am Seaman George Weeks, of the whaler *Corinthian*. Have I the pleasure of addressing Mr. Manwell Coalbeard, late of the Marquesan Archipelago?"

The man folded down the top of his paper, peered at George through dark eyes set in a bronze-tinged face, and smiled. "Sir, you have not."

George straightened, looked round the white faces in the public room again, turned back to the man who read the *Whalemen's Shipping List*, then said, "But you are the only negro in this place."

The bronze-skinned man stiffened, then said, "Sir, I am an Englishman, not a negro."

The man spoke with a precision that George might have expected in a schoolmaster's voice, but not the voice of a harpooneer, and certainly not in the voice of a Marquesan cannibal.

The man peered at George's monkey jacket, and then extended a small hand toward the settee beside himself. "Although I may not sound it, I have spent years before the mast, as it appears that you have. So please sit. And tell me how I may otherwise be of service."

George sat where he was bidden. "The *Corinthian* was scheduled to depart New Bedford five days ago, bound via the Azores and Cape Horn for the Pacific. She remains here owing to the failure to appear of a certain harpooneer."

The brown-skinned man raised his brows and smiled. "I assure you sir, I am not your missing harpooneer. I arrived in Boston from Liverpool aboard the *America* only yesterday."

George shook his head and smiled. "I did not take you for that liar, sir. I am here to meet a replacement harpooneer who has already completed negotiations, through the keeper of this establishment, with the *Corinthian's* first mate." George's smile drifted into a frown. "My task is to conduct him back to the *Corinthian* with all deliberate speed."

"I have some experience of Marquesans. You may find him disinclined to deliberate speed, particularly when commanded."

George shook his head again. "I hope not. The mate says that if Coalbeard is lost so is my share."

In that moment another man entered the public room from the street. He did also wear a seaman's monkey jacket, although so broad were his shoulders and so massive his arms that the jacket's sleeves had been cut away.

But his biceps, although round and hard as coconuts, were not the features that caused all eyes in the public room to fasten upon him.

He stood easily a full six feet in height, his skin gleamed as dark as anthracite coal, and swirls and circlets blacker than his skin made a pattern on his cheeks and chin where a white man's beard would be. In one outsized fist he clutched the iron shaft of a harpoon's business end.

The Englishman said, "Mr. Weeks, I believe you have found the man you seek."

George stood and raised his palm. The fierce black giant nodded, strode to George and thumped his great chest with a fist. "Man Well CoalBeard." He pointed a thick index finger in the direction of the waterfront. "Corrint—ian?"

George stood and pointed at the harpoon. "Temple iron?"

To a whaleman, the shop of the free negro blacksmith Lewis Temple, where Temple crafted harpoons of his own ingenious design, was as appreciated an address on Walnut Street as the address of any inn.

The Marquesan grinned and flicked the harpoon's tip, so that it rotated about a bolt that penetrated the harpoon shaft. Then he clenched his fist. "Whale pull. This hold whale tighter."

The small Englishman stood and leaned to examine the harpoon as he said to George, "In England they say that when the Royal Navy sails to the ends of the Earth, it finds Americans hunting whales already there."

Manwell Coalbeard pointed to the heavens, or more probably to the room in which he slept, which was located on the floor above the public room, then said, "Sea bag. Then go Corrint-ian. Then go kill whales."

As the giant savage departed, George nodded to the Englishman, "When the English arrive at the gates of hell they will find a New Bedfordman lighting the porch lamps. But he may be a cannibal like that fellow, rather than an American. The streets of New Bedford are awash in black foreigners in the way that a whaler's decks are slick with oil when her pots are lit. Is that what brings you here? To seek a berth aboard a whaler?"

The Englishman who did not look like an Englishman shook his head. "They say that today New Bedford is the richest city in the world. I have come up from Boston to see it for myself. Then I am bound from here south to New York. And from there aboard the steamer *Prometheus* for San Francisco, thirteen days from now."

The Englishman sat, and returned to his paper.

The door from Walnut Street opened again, and two full-bearded white men entered. Neither wore a seaman's monkey jacket or pea coat, but rather both wore broad-brimmed hats and long, loose coats the color of sailcloth that reached below their knees.

The pair took seats in the corner opposite George and the Englishman and conversed in low tones.

When Coalbeard appeared again in the public room, his sea bag under his left arm and his new harpoon in his right hand, one of the men stood and walked toward the bar.

As Manwell stepped forward and allowed the bearded man to pass behind him, the man drew an object from beneath his coat, drew back his arm, and struck Manwell behind the Marquesan's left ear. The blow caused Manwell to stagger and to drop his sea bag to the floor.

The bearded fellow seemed shocked that Manwell remained upright. He fell upon Manwell from behind, the arm in which the man held his truncheon now barred across Manwell's throat. With his other hand, Manwell's attacker clutched the hand in which Manwell gripped his harpoon.

As Manwell bent and spun, the man was lifted off his feet and his legs dangled behind Manwell as if the large man were no more than a small dog.

In those moments the other long-coated man ran forward, drawing from beneath his own coat a revolver, a Colt Franklin five-shooter, long and dull, oiled gray. "Hold up there, nigger!"

The other man cried out, "For God's sake don't shoot *me!*"

When Manwell saw the pistol aimed at him, and heard the man cock back its hammer, the powerful black man ceased his struggles, and his harpoon clanged to the public room's plank floor.

While the man with the pistol held it pointed at Manwell's face, his partner withdrew from his coat a pair of iron cuffs, with which he secured Manwell's hands at the small of his back.

The man with the pistol kept it pointed at Manwell while he turned his head and shouted to the silent, stunned room. "This negro is a fugitive slave. Pursuant to federal law he will be returned to his rightful owner. Stand clear!" The man waved his pistol and, in response, feet shuffled as bystanders made way. "Stand clear!"

"Hold where you stand, slave hunters! Or I shall fill your bellies!" The innkeeper, a small and thin old man whose bald head was wreathed with a monk's halo of bristling white hair, shuffled forward out of the bar's dark shadow. In each hand he held a pepperbox pistol, their multiple barrels open toward the two men like steel honeycombs.

The man who had handcuffed Coalbeard stepped away from him and the man with the pistol lowered it.

The innkeeper said, "My son has gone to fetch the marshal. This man is no runaway slave. We shall see about this."

The man who held the Colt nodded. "We know the law, old man. It is you abolitionists who will see."

When Russell, the Deputy U.S. Marshal arrived, the first thing he did was to remove the firearms of all concerned and place them on the bar. Then he turned to the man who had held the pistol. "It is your sworn testimony that this man is a fugitive slave?"

"It is. He escaped his owner in Cumberland County, Tennessee, two months ago. I recognize him."

George stepped forward and touched the marshal's elbow. "That is a lie! I say there is no slave in Tennessee—there is no slave in this union—who possesses such a facial aspect as this man! Mr. Russell, you know as well as I that on any street in this town at any hour of the day you may encounter men of dark skin of the south seas and of Africa. And none are or were ever slaves!"

The marshal turned to the innkeeper. "Josiah, just because a law is new, it is no less the law. And upon my oath I have therefore been bound since last fall to enforce the Fugitive Slave Act. And it says that on sworn statement of any white man I am bound to stand aside and allow him to reclaim his property."

"These men have not come to New Bedford to apprehend runaways. They have come to kidnap free men and enslave them." Josiah the innkeeper went to Manwell and took hold of the man's great arm. "Mr.

Russell, it is plain that this man has been chosen and kidnapped simply because he is strong of limb."

"Josiah, you summoned me to enforce the law. Now you would have me do otherwise because neither you nor I find the law to our liking."

"Very well. When he is brought before a magistrate this wrong will be righted."

The marshal said, "He will not be brought before a magistrate. He has no right to speak in his own defense. No black denounced as a runaway has that right."

The innkeeper barked a bitter laugh. "Well, at least there's no harm in that!" The innkeeper spat on his own floor. "This man could not speak in his own defense if he were allowed to. He is so foreign to this land that he could not pronounce Cumberland County, Tennessee, much less deny that he has run away from it."

And so the two slave hunters were allowed to haul their bewildered prize away.

Afterward, the marshal said to the innkeeper, "You know I believe as you do, that slavery is a sin before almighty God."

The Englishman, who had hovered in the corner watching the play unfold, said, "Then what are men of good conscience to do?"

When the marshal turned and looked upon the Englishman, he stared. Then he said, "I do not know you, sir. But in good conscience I warn you that a negro of your light aspect and erudite manner is prized by slaveowners as a house negro. Equally as is that brawny harpooneer. I expect that this Fugitive Slave Act will attract to New Bedford more like those two, in the way that blood in the water attracts the shark. I do not wish to be the unwilling party to further sin. I counsel you to leave New Bedford immediately."

After the marshal left, George bent and picked up Manwell Coalbeard's harpoon and sighed. "I was charged to return with a harpooneer, not a harpoon."

George, Josiah the innkeeper, and the Englishman peered out through the window into the street. In the fading light, they saw the two slavehunters advancing toward the inn's front door again.

Josiah took George and the Englishman by their arms and hurried them back through the bar and to the inn's rear door. The innkeeper took the harpoon from George, handed it to the Englishman, and said, "Mr. Weeks, as a man of good conscience, I have a suggestion that may solve a problem for each of you."

Watson, the *Corinthian*'s first mate, stood blocking the way to the whaler's gangway with his arms folded across chest. He looked the Englishman up and down as he said, "Mr. Weeks, Manwell Coalbeard, the harpooneer who you were sent to fetch, is a Marquesan. This man appears as much white as negro. And he certainly does not appear strong enough to stab out a whale's heart."

The Englishman raised the harpoon. "If I am not Manwell Coalbeard, why do I possess this? I assure you, sir, one true-aimed harpoon is worth three hurled forcefully to the wrong target."

The man who had become Manwell Coalbeard, and who now stood on the brink of a voyage to California much more roundabout and less pleasant than aboard a steamer out of New York, said, "And Mr. Watson,

I put it to you, in America, what white man in his right mind would impersonate a negro?"

George glanced up at the Corinthian's afterdeck, where her master paced. "Mr. Watson, we can still make the tide. The captain will be displeased if we are delayed further."

The first mate sighed, then stood aside and welcomed aboard George, and then also the *Corinthian's* new harpooneer.

THIRTY-NINE

Shepard turned to Kate in the dark, narrow cross aisle on the Aquatic Park Bathhouse's lower level and sighed. He peered at the rusty harpoon in his hand and said, "This thing tells us nothing about Manuel Colibri that we didn't already know. And it certainly doesn't change the disposition of his estate. Nothing in this collection of his has taught us anything, so far."

"Then put it down. Let the ranger repack it. We'll go back to your place. After you massage the circulation back into my extremities I'll teach you plenty." Kate led Ben by one hand from the dark toward the main aisle's light.

In the main aisle, a white server's jacket flashed in front of the cross aisle's narrow opening, its wearer carrying an object. The draft from the main aisle carried to Kate the sound of a sharp metallic clang and the pungent odor of something that wasn't *hors d'oeuvres*.

Ben jerked her back from the door by her wrist so hard that she rolled an ankle.

"Ow! Shepard! What the—?"

Ben pressed her back flat against the wall of crates as he clamped his big hand over her nose and mouth so hard that she couldn't breathe.

"'Oppit!"

Ben hissed in her ear, "AK-47. Gun oil."

Kate stiffened as adrenaline shot through her like an electric shock.

Ben whispered, "You hear it and you smell it enough you never forget it."

From the hallway Kate heard women scream, then heard running feet.

Ben stared hard into Kate's eyes as he slid his hand away from her mouth and maneuvered his body past her. "Stay in here in the dark. Call 9-1-1."

"I—"

He stabbed a finger into her cleavage. "Do it."

As Ben turned to the main aisle she grabbed his sleeve with both hands, leaned her weight back, and whispered. "You idiot! Some lunatic out there's got a machine gun."

In the distance Kate heard the first rattle of gunfire.

"Yeah. Well, I've got a harpoon." Ben tore his arm free, shoved her back into the cross aisle so hard that she lost a shoe, dropped her clutch bag, then he was gone.

The damn flashlight was gone, probably with Shepard. She knelt and felt along the floor for her bag, couldn't find it, and so not her phone either.

She realized that not only was Ben out there but so was her father.

Gunfire crackled again, followed by the sound, first of glass shattering, then of screaming.

Kate kicked off her other shoe, then tiptoed barefoot

on the freezing concrete and peeked out into the main aisle. It was empty in both directions, except for three female servers who huddled alongside the catering truck outside, weeping but apparently unhurt.

"I *said* this party was stupid." Kate ran, limping and barefoot, up the outside stairs toward the gunfire.

When Kate emerged back into the main party room, people cowered everywhere, behind museum exhibits and overturned auction tables. A bayside window's frame held only knife-edged triangles of shattered glass.

In the room's center stood a man with curly brown hair, wearing jeans and a white server's waistcoat. He had his back turned to Kate and his head was bent over a black rifle with a wooden stock that he held in one hand.

With his other hand the man slammed a curved black ammunition magazine against an opening in the gun, forward of its pistol grip handle. Twenty feet in front of the man a woman wearing a red dress lay on the floor, her body sheltered behind a kneeling man wearing a tuxedo. "Dad! Shit."

The gunman seated his magazine, then raised his weapon to his shoulder and aimed at Kate's father and at Julia Madison, behind him.

Kate stood alongside the table where the wine glass that she had set down earlier still stood. A bald older man, who knelt behind the table with a gray-haired woman, grabbed Kate's ankle and whispered. "Get down!"

In that instant Kate realized that Shepard stood twenty feet behind the gunman and fifteen feet to her right.

"Hey!" Shepard shouted at the gunman, then hurled the harpoon at the man's back. The iron rod spun through the air, then its blunt end struck the gunman between his shoulder blades and staggered him.

The gunman spun and swung his rifle's muzzle toward Ben.

Kate started forward, but the bald man clung to her ankle, tripped her and dragged her behind the table. She stomped the top of his pink head with her bare sole. "Fuck off!"

Kate scrambled to her knees and peeked, eyes just above the tablecloth, past her wineglass.

In that moment three security men, pistols drawn, burst from the stairwell thirty feet to the gunman's left rear.

Ben had made it across ten of the twenty feet that had separated him from the gunman when the man fired.

Blam-blam-blam.

Ben staggered sideways as blood sprayed from the left side of his head. A droplet landed red and warm on Kate's forearm as she screamed.

In the same instant the three security men fired, each crouched and with two hands on his pistol. Gunfire exploded and never seemed to stop.

Their first shots struck the gunman's torso, and his eyes seemed to widen as each successive impact struck and buffeted him.

The head shots seemed to strike all at once.

An explosion of red mist obscured the man's face and blood splattered the room's ceiling, thick and heavy, like somebody had shaken a laden paintbrush.

Something arced slowly through the air toward her,

splashed down in her wine glass, and floated there like a lump of gray sushi.

The rifle dropped from the man's hands, clattered to the floor amid a sudden, deafening silence broken only by scattered sobs. The man's body crumpled, deadweight.

Ben lay on the floor facedown and motionless, the left side of his face drenched blood red. He lay six feet short of the dead man whom Ben had failed to reach in time to save himself. Screaming, Kate scrambled across the floor toward Ben on her hands and knees.

Across the room she saw her father and Julia Madison stir, wobbly but animated.

She reached Ben at the same instant that one of the security men did. He holstered his pistol as he knelt, then slid his fingers onto Ben's throat while he peered at the left side of Ben's head.

Another security man came and stood over them, pistol still drawn and pointing at the ceiling. As the standing man swiveled his head around the room, he asked his kneeling companion, "Whaddaya got?"

Already Kate heard sirens shriek, then die outside the building.

"Hard-headed son of a bitch. It looks like one round grazed his skull and took a chunk off his ear."

Kate tugged the kneeling security man's jacket sleeve. "He's alright?"

The security man looked Ben over, head to heels. "I make it two rounds unaccounted for besides the one that grazed him. But I don't see any other blood. The medics'll go over him nose to toes. But if this is the only hit he took, I'd say he's just in for a hell of a headache, a night of observation, and some stitches. You his wife?"

Kate shook her head. "Friend."

The kneeling man patted Shepard's motionless shoulder. "Well, lady, this is a good friend to have."

Kate's father knelt beside her and hugged her as she began to shiver.

"Katy?"

"I'm fine, Dad."

"How about Shepard?"

"They think he'll be okay. Maybe. Julia?"

"Shaky. Not a scratch. Katy, Shepard saved our lives."

"I saw."

Kate looked up and saw that a crowd of party guests had emerged from hiding and stood stunned, silent, and peering down at Ben.

Uniformed paramedics elbowed through the crowd, separating Kate from her father, and laid out their gear while the security men moved the crowd back.

A paramedic who knelt alongside Ben nudged Kate gently and said, "Ma'am, I'll take good care of him. But I'm gonna need a little more space."

"Sure." Kate stood, then limped backward on her sore ankle. Her knees began shaking as her head lightened. She turned, leaned forward, both hands splayed atop the table behind which she had sheltered.

The bald man who had tripped her, and thereby likely saved her life, still knelt behind the table, and peered up at her. He asked, "You okay?"

Her wine glass also remained where she had left it. The sushi lump afloat in the glass was probably, she realized, a fragment of the dead man's brain. Tendrils of red had diffused from the drifting human tissue, and curled out through the Chardonnay. And thus had turned the wine that she had drunk into blood. It occurred to Kate that it was the reverse of communion. Then, as she fainted, she repaid the bald man's kindness by vomiting on his head.

"Kate?" Shepard peered down at her as she lay on her back. A bulky beige bandage covered the top of his left ear and his face looked fresh-scrubbed. His tux jacket was gone and his pleated white shirt was open to the waist.

She splayed her fingers and ran them down his bare chest. "Finally we're getting somewhere."

Ben smiled down at the shirt, stained with dried blood. "I think my tux deposit's a goner. Kate, you've been out for an hour." He pointed at a tube that snaked up from her arm to a hanging IV bag. "You were dehydrated. They gave you a mild sedative with the saline. When the bag's empty and they've checked you over one more time, I've cleared you. You're free to go. I was scared to death for you."

"Me? I puked and fainted. You got shot."

"Nicked."

Kate raised her head and realized that she lay on a gurney, now in a corner of the same room in which she had fainted and in which hell had broken loose.

In the room's center a bustle of people in various uniforms clustered around the gunman's now-covered body. Kate asked Ben, "Any idea who he was?"

Ben said, "Pretty good idea, actually. When he came in past the catering truck he didn't just bring his AK. He was carrying a valid Nevada driver's license. No prior criminal record. He never served in the military, which relieves me. He was a landscaper at a country club near Lake Tahoe." Ben paused. "*And* he was carrying an eight-page handwritten manifesto folded up in his pants pocket."

A uniformed cop tapped Ben's shoulder and held out a sheaf of papers. "Mr. Shepard? Here's the printed transcription of the manifesto you asked for, sir. Scans of the original pages have been sent to your phone."

"Anybody else know about it?"

"The chief. And my immediate supervisor. And you. That's it, sir."

"Let's keep it that way for a while."

"Yes, sir." The cop nodded, then left.

Kate raised her eyebrows. "Cops call you 'sir,' now? And I can leave a crime scene because *you* cleared me?"

"Petrie called the mayor. I'm his personal representative on site. Until our pros get here at midnight, then I turn into a pumpkin. Suddenly he's a genius for sending me to a party."

"Well, he did send you. That's a fact. And now you're a hero. That's a fact, too."

"I brought a harpoon to a gunfight. Like you said in the basement, that makes me an idiot, not a hero."

"It was a crisis. You rose to meet it. That's what heroes do."

"In a crisis I sank back to the level of my training. That's what actual human beings do, Kate."

She cocked her head. "Ben, that's actually kind of profound."

"That's actually just a cliché every infantryman's repeated a thousand times." Ben frowned as he flipped through the pages that he had been handed. "I should have seen this coming."

"What?"

"Kate, this guy's name was Jerry Chisolm. He moved to San Francisco from Reno eight months ago. And apparently brought his AK, which he bought legally as a Nevada resident, with him."

"But why?"

"That's not clear. What is clear is that he resumed participation in the Catholic Church after he got here. And he claims in his manifesto that he was directed to do God's work here tonight."

"Directed by who? What work?"

"Directed by who is up in the air. The work was to kill Julia Madison to put the brakes on life-extension research. His manifesto's title is 'Eternal Life is a Gift from God, Not a Conceit of Man.'"

David Powell elbowed his way through the police and when he got to Ben and Kate his lips were tight and he looked pale. "They've kept your father and Julia and me upstairs for an hour asking questions. Kate, are you alright?"

She smiled at him. "Fine. Where were you when the shooting started?"

"Supervising the people trailering that damn stupid boat. This is all my fault. But we can't plan a world against the spectre of one disturbed individual."

Ben shrugged. "Mr. Powell, one disturbed individual killing somebody identified with life-extension research is one disturbed individual. Another one trying to kill somebody else identified with life-extension research is a very big coincidence."

David laid his hand on Ben's arm. "You're not going to slander an entire faith just on the basis of a theory like that?"

Ben shook his head. "It's not even a theory. Just a

very big coincidence. And I'm not going to do much of anything about it. If DHS determines that it has a role in this, I won't be in charge of it."

A detective took David Powell aside, and Ben said to Kate, "Is it safe to say that your plans for the rest of tonight are on hold?"

"Well, if they're going to put you in the hospital overnight I'm sitting up with you."

Ben shook his head. "I may weasel out of the hospital stay. I probably need to get back to my laptop. Petrie's going to want flattering sound bites he can give out to America in time for the morning shows. Besides, you and your father both need each other's company tonight."

Ben lifted her gently to a sitting position, leaned forward, eyes closed.

Kate turned her cheek, and as he hugged her he drew back. "What's wrong?"

"Shepard, the first time I kiss you I don't want us to remember that I tasted like barf."

FORTY

"Aaahh!" Something woke Kate, shaking and sweating, in her darkened bedroom and she sat straight up, heart pounding. She hovered there, disoriented between sleep and wakefulness, for unnumbered seconds.

Finally, she rubbed her left hand up her bare right arm and persuaded herself that the droplet of Ben's blood that had fallen on her forearm was not creeping up her arm and engulfing it like a swarm of ants.

She was home in bed. She was safe. Her dad was safe, asleep and snoring down the hall. Ben was safe. Or was he? The wound on his ear may have been "just a scratch," but it had bled like hell. And there was the concussion.

She realized that what had awakened her was a glow that haloed her nightstand like it was a streetlamp in the morning fog. Her C-phone lay as she had left it, face up. The phone's silent alert screen had lit and announced the recent arrival of a text. She lunged for the phone, peered at the screen and realized that her hands were shaking.

Why wouldn't they shake? As the nightmare fell away,

real world memory awoke and she realized that what she had actually experienced had been as terrible as her nightmare. And this nightmare was kindled by witnessing the violent death of someone she didn't even know. How the hell could Shepard, and Roland Garvey, and other people in that line of work remain sane?

She focused on her C-phone's screen. The new text wasn't from Shepard. It wasn't even marked of high importance. Kate read the message, then reread the title line aloud. "CAS. California Academy of Sciences! Ha!" She punched in Shepard's number with both thumbs.

His number rang three times.

Ben yawned. "Kate?"

"I woke you."

"Not exactly. It's eight oh three Eastern. But it's five oh three here. Are you okay?"

Crap. What the hell had she been thinking? "Are *you* okay? How are you feeling?"

"I have a little headache. But they released me."

"So, are you free today?"

"I'm not in charge of anything, if that's what you mean. But Petrie knows I'm as close as my C-phone."

"Ben, I know what CAS is!"

"Oh. That's great."

"Well? Aren't you gonna ask me what it is?"

She heard him yawn again. "California Academy of Sciences. I figured it out last night. I was waiting to call so I wouldn't wake you."

"Well, I hope you weren't planning on waiting until too late, because I have an invitation for a personally guided tour for us at 10:30 a.m."

"You know, we don't deserve VIP treatment because we were in the wrong place at the wrong time."

"Calm down. The invitation has nothing to do with last night. An astronomer wants me to do an article about the search for extraterrestrial intelligence. I'll pick you up at 10:00."

There was a moment of silence.

"Could you make it eight?"

"Oooh! You're inviting me up two hours early. Need some room service?"

"Unfortunately, no. I also figured out last night that CJM H1 probably refers to the Contemporary Jewish Museum."

"Excellent. We'll go there after lunch."

"I booked a before-hours appointment at the CJM at nine."

She blew out a breath in the darkness. "Of course you did."

The Contemporary Jewish Museum was wedged in among taller buildings in the Financial District. The museum's face to the world was a pair of asymmetrical, multistory glass and steel crystals. They looked like giant cobalt-blue dice, thrown so that one came to rest point-up against the low, red brick existing building that housed most of the museum.

The volunteer docent who led Ben and Kate to the assistant director's office was a chubby woman in her fifties named Amy Stein. She wore her hair boy-cut and dyed jet black, and wore a silver ring through a piercing in the right side of her nose. A circular decal on the lid of the C-Pad she carried depicted a skull, divided by a white lightning bolt into a red hemisphere and a blue hemisphere. Around the skull were the words "GRATEFUL DEAD."

As Stein walked them through empty, echoing galleries with diagonally angled walls she asked Ben, "Are we next on the list after the bathhouse museum?"

Ben shook his head. "I have no reason to think there's a particular problem with your museum, Ms. Stein. That's not the reason we're here."

"But, I mean, we're always on the list. We're Jews. The last five thousand years haven't exactly been smooth sailing for us. You know?"

Ben said, "Frankly, this museum seems as secure as any I've been in over the last couple days. But of course you should err on the side of caution."

"Well then, how do we get one of those guys?"

"What guys?"

"The undercover guys."

"There was no undercover guy."

"Then why doesn't Homeland Security release his name? I heard he stabbed the guy to death with a ballpoint pen."

Ben raised his eyebrows at Kate, then said to the docent, "Some details are being withheld. But no. That didn't happen."

"Well, that's a relief. Because that sounded like excessive government force."

The museum's assistant director was slim and quiet. As he led Ben and Kate up a flight of stairs from the museum's lobby to its second floor he said, "H1 isn't a catalogue number. We have virtually no permanent collections or exhibits. But Mr. Colibri did make those items an indefinite term loan. Accompanied by a generous cash contribution. Which we decided to apply to an unusual exhibit themed around those items."

Kate said, "Unusual because H is for 'History?' And this museum focuses on the contemporary?"

The assistant director shook his head. "The cubes you saw that form the museum's façade are stylized representations of the Hebrew letters that form the word 'Chaim,' 'life.' As Amy undoubtedly told you, as she tells all her guests, history has not afforded the Jewish people smooth sailing. But most of our exhibits celebrate Jewish *life*, rather than illuminate Jewish tragedy. Unfortunately, as historical as this exhibit is, the 'H' doesn't stand for 'History.'"

He stopped at the entrance to a vast, angular white-walled space that enclosed a stark maze of head-high, portable white wall panels. The panels displayed black and white photographs interspersed with associated objects.

The exhibit's introductory panel announced:

CHILDREN'S ART AND IMAGES
FROM THE HOLOCAUST

Only a few of the photographs were paired to objects.

H1 turned out to be such a pair, hung side by side on the maze's central panel.

The object was a six-pointed Star of David, obviously fashioned from a tin can's lid. A scrap of cord strung through a hole punched in one star point formed a necklace too small for any neck but a child's.

The object's description read:

> This folk art object's provenance is established by the photograph at left. The artist's identity and fate is unknown.

The black and white photograph had been enlarged to the point of graininess, and mounted, raised and frameless, on plastic foam. It showed in the distance a group of nine uniformed men, hands on hips, peering down at a bonfire's ashes. The distant party faced the camera, and in the foreground, the backs of two jacketed, round-helmeted soldiers framed the shot. The bare hand of the shorter of the two soldiers gripped his rifle stock, and threaded through his fingers was the string necklace from which was suspended, unmistakably, the tin can Star of David.

The photo's description card read:

> On April 12, 1945, American Supreme Allied Commanding General in Europe Dwight Eisenhower (background, far left) inspects Ohrdruf, the first Nazi labor and concentration camp discovered and liberated by American forces during World War II's final weeks in Europe.
>
> Eisenhower publicized the camp's horrors by a personal visit, accompanied by the press, "in order to be in position to give first-hand evidence of these things if ever, in the future, there develops the tendency to charge these allegations merely to "propaganda."

Ben and Kate stared at the image and the necklace as the assistant director said, "I'll never forget that. And I wasn't even born when that image was made. I wonder whether there are enough years in any lifetime to forget something like that."

FORTY-ONE

Pfc. Charlie Schwartz knelt, wheezing and protected behind a tree as big around as a garbage can. Charlie raised his carbine, and covered the Little Professor as the corporal crept forward, noiseless amid leaves soaked by the April rains. Charlie doubted there were any Krauts left ahead to hear them no matter how loud they were. They hadn't seen so much as a German soldier's retreating backside in days.

Charlie dug through the breast pocket of his field jacket for a smoke, and then swore as he remembered he had thrown away the empty pack an hour before.

He looked 'round at the misty, dripping forest as though he expected to find packs of Camels dangling from the trees of central Germany. Not that smokes grew on trees back home, either.

Up ahead, the Little Professor dropped to his knees and took cover behind a fallen tree. He brought his own carbine up to cover Charlie, laid it across the log, muzzle forward, then unfolded his map and laid it alongside his carbine. Then he windmilled his arm for Charlie to leapfrog forward, and also to come alongside him, for a meeting and a break.

As Charlie ran he watched the Little Professor lay out the accessory packs from a couple of C-rations, and also two cans of peaches, from the crate that Ed Peck's mother had sent him.

Everybody in the platoon preferred the canned peaches to any canned choice in any C-ration, and Ed Peck had no use for his peaches. Ed's mother's crate had caught up to the company, along with the rest of the mail, the day after a German mine blew him in half.

Charlie looked forward to the break, not so much because he was tired, but because the Little Professor didn't smoke. So he would always trade the cigarettes in his C-rations for the chocolate in yours.

Charlie coughed into his hand as he ran. They said smoking cut your wind. But if that was true Uncle Sam wouldn't put cigarettes in your C-rations, would he?

The forest ended five yards ahead of the log behind which the two infantry scouts huddled. The open ground beyond was not natural, but had been clear cut, and it was studded with stumps. Fifty yards from the Kraut-made tree line a barbed wire fence stood fifteen feet high.

A couple feet in front of the wire somebody had planted a row of Christmas tree seedlings, straight as a die and no taller than Charlie's knee. Charlie's mother had always reminded him when she scrubbed the front walk of their house back home in the Bronx that good Germans were house-proud.

Fifty yards to the left and right of the scout pair's position in the woods, guard towers made of timber and planks rose. Then the fence line continued in both directions until it disappeared into the morning mist. Inside the fence, rows of rain-blackened wooden barracks rose from bare-scraped Earth.

A light morning breeze drifted across their backs toward the fence, and no sound or movement was audible or visible either in the woods or beyond the fence. Charlie whispered, "It can't be a border."

The Little Professor rattled his wooden spoon around the inside of a silver can that moments before had held peaches in syrup. He nodded at his map, and then shook his head. "It's not marked on the map. But we're in the middle of Thuringia, so it's not a border. It's a camp of some kind."

"Training camp?"

The Little Professor shook his head. "The observation windows and firing ports face in. POW camp. Or a civilian prison."

Charlie dragged on an Old Gold from one of the accessory packs, and then watched his exhaled smoke drift toward the fence line. "There's no guards in the towers."

"No machine guns or searchlights, either. Maybe the camp guards heard something we haven't, took their equipment, and beat it."

"You think the war's already over, Manny?" Charlie stared at the Little Professor. He was short, with dark hair and eyes, and skin the color of the beer that the English called bitter. Everybody called Manny the Little Professor because he seemed to know a lot, especially for a Spick.

Not that anybody in the company knew for sure that Manny was a Spick, or just what he was. Manny, which was the only name anybody knew him by, had gotten separated from his unit. So had thousands of other GIs, as Blood n' Guts Georgie Patton had used his guts and his soldiers' blood to race the Third Army across France, then across the Rhine into Germany, so fast that the fuel convoys, and even the mail, couldn't keep up.

Corporal Manny had filled a hole in Charlie's platoon, created when, everybody hoped, Jimmy Thibodeaux just got left behind taking a crap. Manny didn't just know things like what Thuringia was, he pulled the exhausting and dangerous job of scout duty, out front on the run and under constant stress, over and over without showing fatigue or griping. So nobody cared much who he was or where he came from. Though somebody said he had mentioned California once.

Manny shook his head in answer to Charlie's question. "The war won't last longer than a few more days. But if the camp garrison had abandoned a POW camp I'd expect to see prisoners dancing out in the yard, or that gate over there would have been left wide open when they all scattered."

"Then what do we do?"

"Some of the POW camps are supposed to be garrisoned with diehard Nazis. It's not our job to go in there for a look around and wind up the last ambush victims of World War II. We'll sit tight 'til the rest of the company comes up. The captain may have more information about what this place is and whether we clear it or we bypass it. And at least he'll have more firepower. You take the first thirty minutes." Manny rolled his body so that his back rested against the log behind which they sheltered, tipped his steel pot over his eyes, and was asleep within a minute.

"Manny!" Charlie hissed into his dozing corporal's ear as he nudged Manny's shoulder.

Charlie pointed beyond the wire fence. In the empty space between the barracks row and the wire a small child, a little girl, limped, crying one word, over and over.

"Charlie, you *sprechen Sie*. What's she saying?"

"What it sounds like. 'Mommie.'"

The little girl fell, rose, then stumbled on, from barracks to barracks.

A man, an animated skeleton really, filthy, naked and hollow-eyed, came and leaned against one barracks' door's jamb, watching vacantly as the child limped on to the next barracks.

"Manny, what the hell is this place?"

Charlie's Corporal didn't answer, but snatched up his carbine, vaulted the log that had insulated the two of them from the camp, and ran across the open space between the wood line and the fence line.

Charlie called, "Manny! The Krauts might have mined that!"

"The Nazis wouldn't waste mines on people who are already dead to them. Get the lead out, Charlie!"

It took them a quarter of an hour, hacking with their entrenching tools and bayonets, to breach the wire, then another ten minutes searching buildings, one of which was piled to its ceiling with starved corpses.

Finally, they found the little girl. She was as filthy

as the few living skeletons of men who peered out at them from the barracks they passed, and just as skin-and-bones as the adults were. Though she still wore what had once been a blue dress and kneesocks that had once been white. Charlie was no judge of kids' ages. She could have been anything between four and seven.

When she saw the two of them, she ducked into a shed, and they found her cowering in a dark corner. The place stank even more of slaughter than the rest of the camp did.

Manny went to one knee and inched toward the child. "Charlie, ask her her name."

The girl just stared.

"Tell her we won't hurt her."

The little girl shrank further into the corner.

Manny reached behind him and extended his palm. "Gimme your peaches, Charlie."

"What?"

"I already ate mine. I know you saved yours for later."

"But—"

"I'll give you a month's worth of smokes for them."

When Manny got the little can open she lunged for it. He pulled it back and said, "Charlie, tell her if she eats it all at once, it will make her sick."

Manny fed her the peach syrup with the wooden spoon from his accessory pack, a drip at a time, then the peach slices, cutting each into small bits with the spoon's edge.

"Marthe. Danke."

"What?"

"Manny, her name's Martha. She says 'thank you.'"

Charlie squinted around the dim-lit shed, then frowned as he stepped to a butcher's block in the shed's center then peeked into a washtub alongside the block.

Charlie leapt back, gagging. "Manny! They broke corpse's jaws on this block, to get the gold out of their teeth."

Manny lifted the girl. "Let's get her out of this place."

As Manny, Charlie, and the child emerged into the daylight Buddy Walters from Second Platoon rounded the corner of the adjacent building, double time, rifle across his body at port arms.

When he saw them, he stiffened. "Captain sent me to find you two." Tears streamed down Walters' cheeks. "I swear to God this is the worst place I ever been in my life. There's sheds with bodies stacked in 'em like logs. And burn pits with pieces you can't even tell what they were." He pointed at the little girl's right kneesock, which was bloody from top to ankle. "Medic should have a look at that leg."

The captain and the medic and the rest of company HQ stood huddled in an open space, more or less a parade ground, in the center of which stood a gallows.

Manny carried the little girl to the medic, but when he tried to place her hand in the hand of the smiling man she clung tight to Manny's neck.

"Charlie, tell Martha this man is a doctor. He will make her feel better. She's safe now."

As she let go of Manny and let the medic carry her, she tugged something from around her neck. She spoke to Charlie as she pressed the object into Manny's hand.

Manny opened his hand and found a tiny tin star on a loop of string.

"Manny, her mother made that for her to keep her safe. But now you made her safe. So you need it more than her."

Manny tried to give it back, but she pressed it toward him. He nodded. "Tell her I'll just hold onto it for her until I see her again."

After the medic carried Marthe away, Manny and Charlie took a load off, breathing through their mouths against the hideous stench of death and excrement, which a following wind had disguised when they were outside the camp's fence. They waited while the captain read dispatches, and then knelt over a map spread on the ground, with his platoon leaders.

When the captain finally dismissed his subordinates so they could, in turn, brief their platoons, he turned to Manny and Charlie, and they stood and saluted. "Could you free-spirited gentlemen spare a minute for the business of the Fourth Armored Division?"

Charlie said, "Sir, did you really expect us to sit there outside the fence and just *watch* this once we realized what those fuckers had been doing in here?"

The captain scowled. "No. There's only a handful of adult prisoners left alive in here, and they barely are. It looks like the guards tried to kill off the witnesses and destroy the evidence at the last minute. At least we—you two—were in time to save the little girl."

Charlie said, "Where's division want us to point from here, Captain? Berlin?"

The company commander, still frowning, shook his head. "Nowhere."

Manny frowned. "Sir?"

The captain flicked his eyes to Charlie. "Private Schwartz, the rest of the Army agrees with you. Nobody in the world should sit outside and just watch the things fuckers like these do ever again. So our mission is to secure this charnel house against all comers until the brass bring the world here to see for themselves that we aren't making this up."

Behind the captain's shoulder the medic's helmet, with its red-cross-on-white brassard, appeared. The medic walked to Manny and laid a hand on his arm.

The captain stared at the interrupting medic. "Sergeant?"

The medic tugged Manny and Charlie aside, and stared at the ground.

Manny said. "What?"

The medic frowned and shook his head. "I don't know who did it. I don't know what they did it with. I don't know how any human being could have done it."

"You're saying she was raped?"

"She was half starved to begin with. There wasn't much blood left to lose. The internal hemorrhaging must have been worse than the external bleeding."

Charlie unbuttoned his cuff. "You need a donor?"

The medic shook his head. "Charlie, she's already gone. You were both just too late. We all were."

Manny stared. Then he turned and walked away from all of them, staring down at the little star that the child had given him, its tiny string wrapped around his fingers.

Charlie found Manny twenty minutes later, leaning headfirst against a barracks wall in the shadowed, narrow alley between two of the buildings. His helmet was pushed back so that his forehead rested against his forearm. His free arm dangled at his side, and in his free hand he clutched the murdered child's good luck charm.

"The captain sent me to find you, Manny."

"Fuck the captain."

"We have to set up a perimeter around this place."

"For how long? 'Til the end of the war?"

"No, they're saying the war's going to end in two days, on 6 April. But we're here 'til 8 May. Manny, the brass are coming to expose this shithole to the world. *Ike* is coming himself."

"Fuck Ike. He's too late."

Manny pounded his fist against the barracks wall so hard that the star that dangled from his fingers chimed like a tiny bell. Then he sobbed. "This whole fucking *species* is too late!"

FORTY-TWO

Paul Eustis, wearing his morning coat and striped trousers, led Jack out into the crisp morning and across Powell Hall's upper terrace. There a breakfast table set for three waited, as did David Powell's other guest. Julia Madison stood at the terrace's marble balustrade, staring out across San Francisco Bay. She sipped steaming coffee from a china cup, like the cup into which Paul was pouring coffee for Jack.

Jack eyeballed the three places set around the circular table. The chair that faced away from the view was always David's. David took that one, he said, because he wanted his guests to enjoy the views. But Jack had decided over the years that his boss's principal motivation in seat selection was because that way David could concentrate on his guests' reactions, while they would be less likely to notice any "unfortunate nuances" in his.

Jack went to set his briefcase alongside the chair that looked out northwest, to the Golden Gate Bridge. He paused and frowned, with his eyes on the sterling flatware ranked on the pale pink tablecloth. For some reason he didn't want that chair this morning. He didn't even want to look at the bridge. It was odd. He had known that view for so long, and he had always loved it.

Instead he set his case next to the chair that looked northeast, to the Bay Bridge, then carried his coffee and stood alongside Julia. She stood with her back to Jack as she stared out across San Francisco Bay, which gleamed as sunlight painted it.

The view even more resembled a painting because the terrace's glass wind curtains, their gray frames painted to match the balustrade's color and texture, were up. Electric motors had raised them out of the wells that concealed them.

Julia's dress was a couple shades darker blue than the clear sky over the bay, and Jack noticed her perfume even despite the coffee's aroma. Rather than follow her gaze toward the Golden Gate, he watched a ferry inbound from Sausalito.

When Julia turned to Jack her eyes were red and her smile sagged.

He said, "Short night."

"Horrible night. But you look fine. They say *politics* demands a thick skin. You're such a rhinoceros that Dali would paint your portrait. Or Leutze would paint you crossing the Delaware." She laid a hand on his arm. "You risked your life for me, Jack. Thank you."

Jack shrugged. "Not budging doesn't take much effort."

"Effort no. Courage yes." Julia sighed. "The only thing worse than a stubborn male is a stubborn male who doesn't know how to take a compliment. How's Kate?"

"We didn't talk much last night. But she's fine, I think. She was off with Shepard before I even got up. The last time Katy got up before I did, it involved a pink two-wheeler and Santa Claus."

Julia's smile broadened. "I'd get out of my bed early for Mr. Shepard, too. Unless he was already in it. Are they serious?"

"They've only known each other for three days. But I hope they're serious. All her other boyfriends were jerks."

"My father said all my boyfriends were jerks, too. Especially the one I divorced. Dad was a longshoreman. And a stubborn male in his own right. But at least in that instance being male didn't make him wrong."

Jack smiled. "Some things are the same no matter where we come from."

"I'm not so sure, Jack." Julia extended a hand at the end of a tailored blue sleeve and tapped a long-nailed finger on the retractable wind curtain's glass. The panes vibrated as they held out the chill wind and protected the terrace's warm silence. She said, "Some things are *not* the same for all of us, Jack. The best things in life—breakfast *al fresco* on a sunny morning—may be free. But if the wind blows cold, only the rich can make the wind go away. The rich reshape the world in ways that would never occur to people raised like you and I were raised."

Paul Eustis returned with a serving trolley that he set up alongside the breakfast table. A long cloth covered the trolley's flanks so that the three diners' view would be of matching linen and of a hemisphere of cut flowers, not of anything so utilitarian as a dish. Maybe Julia was right.

Jack pointed at the house manager as Eustis hurried silently back into the mansion. "Sometimes that ability to reshape the world's for the good, Julia. Paul, there, was wounded in Vietnam and when David came across him Paul was struggling with alcohol and with what I think they call PTSD now."

"How does David find these projects?"

Jack shrugged. "Mostly people who work on his cars or tend his gardens or carry his golf clubs. But he found me the old-fashioned way. Ran a want ad in the *Chronicle* for an in-house attorney."

Julia laughed. "I'd hardly call you a project."

David Powell stepped onto the terrace smiling but with his brows knit. "How are you both this morning?"

Jack and Julia turned away from the view and Jack said, "Better than the guy with the gun."

Julia said to David, "Thanks to *your* guys with the guns. Actually, thanks to Ben Shepard. Without his intervention, the security team would have been too late. Neither Jack nor I would be here now."

David asked, "And what about Kate?"

"She's well enough to be out this morning with the man of the hour."

David turned and pointed at the one of two flat-screen TVs mounted in a glass enclosure on the house wall alongside the French doors. "Apparently Arthur Petrie thinks the man of the hour is Arthur."

The left-hand screen was split, with one side showing a high-angle security camera video of the bathhouse incident, run in stop motion. The video showed the gunman spraying bullets around the room, then, after he had cowed the crowd, advancing toward Jack and Julia as he reloaded his assault rifle.

Julia looked away and shuddered.

Then, on the video, Ben Shepard appeared in the lower right corner, distracting the gunman with a thrown object, then charging into the gun's muzzle as it fired and Shepard fell. The video showed the security men entering the room, pistols drawn, then cut away from the gory ending.

Simultaneously, on the split screen, Arthur Petrie spoke from behind a lectern, his words appearing in open caption.

Jack laughed. "He's actually claiming he sent Ben to your party because Petrie smelled trouble."

The screen's other half changed to show what looked like a DHS ID photo of Ben Shepard. Julia pointed, openmouthed, at the script that scrolled beneath Petrie's talking head. "The DHS Cross? There's no such medal. Not that Ben doesn't deserve one. But the purpose of Arthur inventing one is to get himself on TV again, fastening the ribbon around Ben's neck."

David herded his guests to the breakfast table, and while the staff served he said, "I thank you both for joining me, of course. Frittatas hardly compensate for what my stupidity put you both through."

Julia said, "David, it's preposterous to blame yourself for the random act of some lunatic."

"Perhaps. But it's impossible not to, Julia."

Jack shifted in his chair, then pulled his briefcase onto his lap. "Save some blame for me."

David turned to Jack, eyebrows raised. "What?"

Jack patted the briefcase. "David, while you were out of town I did a little snooping in the foundation files."

"I didn't intend that you cross that line. But I know better than to get in the way of your hunches, Jack."

Jack said, "As usual you gave Manuel Colibri a free estate planning opinion via the foundation."

"Of course. You know I've done that for years."

"David, as a result of Colibri's death, the Archdiocese of San Francisco stands to become the owner of Cardinal Systems."

Julia paused with a forkful of frittata between her plate and her chin, her jaw slack. "What? I suppose I assumed Manny was Catholic. And nobody ever thought that he had family to leave the business to. But I never saw *that* coming."

Jack said, "Neither did Colibri. The beneficiary designation probably dated back to what Frank Cardinale wanted back in the 1980s. His wishes hadn't been reconsidered since. Or they had, but were left in place due to tax considerations. And because Colibri didn't plan on dying."

David frowned. "The shooting last night was obviously suicide by cop. But apparently there was no suicide note. There's no reason to associate the dead man to the Catholic Church, Jack."

Jack said, "Well, we have found out that Abney—the bridge bomber—returned to attending the Catholic Church during the months that led up to the bombing."

Julia stared at Jack, eyes wide. "You're actually suggesting the Church suborned assassination?"

Jack shook his head. "No. Kate would skin me if she heard this, but I actually confronted the archbishop of San Francisco about it, and he made it sound as silly as you do, Julia. But Colibri's death does put the Archdiocese of San Francisco in line to own Cardinal Systems. And that will allow the Church to keep the lid on this life-extension research of yours. Which could have been a threat to put the Church out of the heaven business. After all, the two most visible people associated with life-extension research happen to be Manny Colibri and Julia Madison."

Julia raised her eyebrows at Jack. "Well, counselor, if your theory of the case pans out, the archdiocese will be sorely disappointed, won't they?"

David cocked his head. "What do you mean?"

Jack said, "By statute in California, and pretty much everywhere else, a decedent's beneficiary is disqualified if the beneficiary's implicated in bumping the decedent off." He turned to Julia. "But the instrument's a trust, not a will."

Julia sniffed. "Distinction without a difference. I'd take that case."

Jack nodded. "Yeah. Me too."

David paused as he buttered a slice of rye toast and shook his head. "Jack, Christianity's come a long way since Becket was murdered in the cathedral. We all enjoy a good conspiracy theory, unless a judge asks us whether it's been proved beyond a reasonable doubt."

Julia shook her head. "That wouldn't necessarily be the question the judge asks, David. Beneficiary disqualification is a civil matter. The standard of proof to disqualify a beneficiary would only be 'more probable than not,' rather than 'beyond a reasonable doubt.' O.J. Simpson was found not guilty of murdering two people, but he was also found civilly liable for their deaths."

Jack said, "David, Powell Diversified's sitting on the biggest pile of cash in the world just now. This could be an opportunity."

David smiled, then his smile faded. "Jack, as tempting a prize as Cardinal is, it's a leviathan. Even Powell

Diversified is a minnow by comparison." David steepled his fingers. "But, you know, if I could assure that Manny Colibri's work would be carried forward, the acquisition might be worth it. I would prefer that the Powell name be associated with the gift of immortality rather than with all of the family's prior misdeeds."

Paul Eustis stepped onto the terrace and bowed slightly. "Sir, Chief Michaels returned your call. The police department has completed its investigation of the crime scene."

Julia raised her eyebrows at David. "When I was a prosecutor most CEOs didn't call about crime scene investigation details. And if they had called, most police chiefs wouldn't have made time to call them back."

David smiled. "Well, I won't apologize for being the San Francisco Police Officer's Association's largest contributor. But I will apologize for my motives in calling. A one-of-a-kind speedboat that belonged to my grandfather has been exposed to the elements, alongside the temporary pier down at the bathhouse, since last night. And this lovely weather is forecast to turn tonight. It was my hope that if I could regain use of my plaything you two would let me run you across the bay for lunch at the yacht club. If you feel up to it, of course."

Jack furrowed his brow. "I'm sure Julia is too—"

Julia smiled. "No, Julia isn't. Today a boat ride, a glass of Chablis in the sun, and being unreachable for comment for a few hours is my idea of heaven on Earth."

David nodded, grinning. "Done." He stood. "Let me have Paul bring the car around. And I'll text Kate to join us."

David left Jack and Julia to finish their breakfasts.

Julia chuckled. "Kate's and Ben Shepard's idea of heaven does *not* include lunch with the three of us."

Jack smiled, then he pointed at the wall screen, where the weather forecast showed a change from sun to stormy weather by the evening. "Julia, maybe the rich can reshape the world, like you say. But they have to plan their picnics around the weather just like the rest of us."

Julia broke a corner off a scone. "I hardly think that disproves my point. If David buys Cardinal he may be able to decide which of the rest of us gets to live forever. Don't you think that's reshaping enough?"

FORTY-THREE

At 10:24 a.m. Ben and Kate walked from her car past rows of emptied yellow school buses to the California Academy of Sciences' front doors for Kate's 10:30 a.m. appointment. The modern glass and steel building's low roofline was planted with an eco-friendly green blanket of native California plants and was punctuated by seven domes, two of them enormous, and one studded with porthole skylights.

Ben pointed at the building's roof. "My great-grandfather's farmhouse in Kansas had a sod roof. About a hundred fifty years ago."

Kate said, "They rebuilt it green after the '89 earthquake. My dad says now it reminds him of the Tree Huggers' National Monument and Spaceport."

One of the museum's front doors was being held open for them by Dr. Andrea Chaudhury, Hat Creek Radio Observatory's resident astronomer. She smiled. "Kate! I was afraid you'd be tied up with TV interviews or something. You're alright?"

Kate nodded. "Fine."

Then Andrea looked at Ben and her eyes widened. "Wow. Kate said she'd be bringing somebody. But you're that guy."

Kate nodded to Andrea again. "Yep. This is That Guy. Ben Shepard, Andrea Chaudhury." Kate said to Ben, "Looks like your cover is blown. Turn in your ballpoint pen."

Ben shook his head. "I hate this."

Andrea led them, serpentining through lines of schoolchildren, across the building's bustling glass-roofed entry hall. She turned back and smiled at them again, and Ben pointed at the photo on an easel-mounted poster that stood in front of the planetarium ticket desk. A red sticker across the poster read "ALL SHOWS SOLD OUT."

Ben said, "That's you! A celebrity."

Andrea raised her eyebrows. "Me?"

Ben walked to the poster and read it aloud:

"A SHOW ABOUT NOTHING:
THE FERMI PARADOX AND EARTH'S
LONELY LIFE IN THE ORION SPUR
The Morrison Planetarium and SETI Present
Guest Lecturer Dr. Andrea Chaudhury"

Andrea leaned close to Kate, pointed at Ben, and whispered, "I didn't know he was so hot."

"Neither does he."

"Well, I'd be happy to explain it to him."

Kate turned on her C-phone, then displayed its screen to Andrea. "Could I ask you a quick favor? Is there a way to tell whether this is an item in the museum's inventory?"

As Ben rejoined the two women, Andrea pursed her lips, then flipped open the tablet that she carried in one hand. "I'll check the museum catalog." She flicked the tablet's screen with a lavender-nailed finger, then nodded. "TE 21's actually part of a temporary exhibit. We're going right past it."

As Andrea led them to the planetarium entrance she pointed out exhibits with graceful fingers. It seemed to Kate that Shepard was paying close attention. Not that a woman ten years Kate's junior constituted competition. After all, what man would be distracted by a Ph.D. hot enough to sell out a lecture about nothing? Who had flawless *café au lait* skin, glistening ebony hair, and a set of naturals to die for?

Kate hugged Shepard's arm and whispered up to him, "You feel well enough to take an older woman to dinner tonight?"

"I feel well enough for more than dinner, if that's what you mean."

Kate smiled. "Deal."

Andrea paused in front of a seventy-five-foot-tall gray steel sphere, that nearly touched the museum's high ceiling. The Morrison Planetarium was designed to look as though it was rising out of a rippling, floodlit pool, like a friendly Death Star.

Kate's and Ben's astronomer guide led them across a pedestrian bridge that opened onto a railed catwalk that wound around the sphere's base, and led to the planetarium's entrance. A series of plaques along the catwalk's rails were mounted there to educate and entertain planetarium guests while they queued for their show.

The plaques displayed a collection of softball-sized meteorites, and the introductory plaque read:

VISITORS WITHOUT PASSPORTS

Most meteorites originated in the asteroid belt. Some, chemical analysis reveals, originated on Earth's own large natural satellite, the Moon. A very few, recovered from the Antarctic, journeyed here from Mars. All known meteorites originated within our Solar System. Space is so vast, and Earth so small, that it is unlikely that any randomly wandering extrasolar rock will ever reach Earth.

Among the rocky and metallic lumps on succeeding plaques, Andrea pointed out TE 21.

It was slightly larger than Shepard's fist, a lumpy, pocked metallic teardrop, its surface patina smooth and scorched.

The object's description read:

ALLOY XENOLITH
Andes Mountains, Peru
Anonymous gift to the CAS, 2018

This "Pre-Columbian meteorite" was excavated from sediments dating to 1000 A.D., in the high Andes near Lake Titicaca, legendary birthplace of Manco Capac, "the sun god's child" and founder of the Incan nation. Unlike most meteorites, which are composed of rocky minerals or a nickel-iron mix, this object combines the elements titanium, iron, aluminum, vanadium, and molybdenum.

These elements are found in titanium alloy, invented ca. 1910. Titanium alloy is used in the manufacture of such diverse objects as medical prostheses, the venerable C-phone's frame, and spacecraft.

So this unique "meteorite" originated right here on Earth. It returned here when one of the thousands of manmade artificial satellites, that now supplement Earth's one large natural satellite, disintegrated on reentry, and this fragment buried itself upon impact like a speeding bullet.

Andrea laughed. "Alloy Xenolith."

"Why is that funny?" Kate asked.

"I think the term's made-up. I think somebody wanted to spare the donor the embarrassment of describing this probably very expensive 'ancient Peruvian meteorite' as 'space junk.'"

The astronomer led them into the empty planetarium, and turned on the vast sphere's indirect interior lights.

Unlike the planetariums that Kate's father and mother had described to her, this dome lacked a central projector that resembled a giant metallic ant, and beamed points of light against a curved, dark ceiling in order to simulate the night sky.

This open space resembled a Cineplex's biggest theater, with steeply angled stadium seating climbing one wall, facing a vast dome.

Shepard whistled.

Andrea laughed. "The Morrison is not your father's planetarium. It's actually a digital dome projector. My presentation, on purpose, is as much theme park ride as lecture." She seated her two guests in the center of the stadium, then sat in the row just below, then turned back toward them with one arm crooked over her seat back and a remote control in her other hand.

She said, "Kate, I'll just skip through some high points of my presentation. To highlight the ties to what we talked about up at Hat Creek. And also the ties to the lump of space junk that you asked about. The bottom line is that the fact that we haven't found life outside the solar system, and that it hasn't found us, doesn't prove that there's not lots of life out there."

Andrea dimmed the lights, and the dome lit with an aerial view from above of the grass-topped building in which they sat.

Then the image projected on the dome shifted, so that the theater seemed to rotate like a giant spaceship. It then seemed to shoot upward while the museum, then cloud-dappled California, fell away beneath it. In a blink the curved blue and brown ball of the Earth filled Kate's field of vision.

Andrea clicked her remote, and their "ship" paused, floating alongside a slowly spinning, sunlit satellite, the satellite's solar panels outspread like sharp-cornered butterfly wings. The astronomer said, "That exhibit object that you asked about was part of a satellite like this. When the satellite's orbit decayed, it burned up on its return trip through Earth's atmosphere. A few scorched titanium alloy bits survived, and rained down on the high Andes. This meteorite may really *have* been dug out of sediments that were a mud flat on the shores of Lake Titicaca a thousand years ago. But that has to be because this object burrowed into those older sediments. No matter what the sellers may have told the donor."

Andrea hit "play," and the planetarium shot past the Moon, then past Mars, then slowed above a crusty gray ball floating in black space, high above Jupiter's colossal, striped orange surface. Andrea said, "This is Callisto. The Jovian moon whose name your friend Quentin Callisto, the video game creator, adopted. Very likely, beneath Callisto's crust is a liquid water ocean. That ocean isn't warmed above water's freezing point by the sun. The sun's just a pale dot out in Jupiter's orbit. The source of Callisto's inner warmth is probably nuclear radiation in Callisto's core. Life may have evolved in that ocean."

Ben wrinkled his forehead, which looked orange as it reflected Jupiter's light. "But your presentation's about life *outside* the solar system."

Andrea smiled, reached back, and patted Shepard's shoe top. "Come back tonight and I'll give you a full presentation. One-on-one."

Kate crossed her arms and rolled her eyes in the dark. "Oh, for Christ's sake!"

Andrea cupped a hand to her ear. "What?"

"I said, 'Oh, it's an underground lake.'"

Andrea nodded in the dark. "Yes, basically. We currently think liquid water oceans may exist within *six* satellites of Jupiter, Saturn and Neptune. Compared to one habitable hybrid subaerial and aquatic environment on Earth, and maybe one more on Mars, long ago. Aquaspheric civilizations, if they exist, may not beam signals out into space. Are there three times more waterworlds out there than there are Earths? Well, this thin film of moist air and water that we inhabit is awfully fragile. The Solar System's the only example we really know, and here aquaspheres outnumber hybrid environments like Earth six to two."

Ben asked, "What's the Fermi Paradox? In your title?"

"Fermi was a Nobel-laureate physicist who directed the first nuclear chain reaction in 1942. He was also a guy who ate lunch with astronomers. One day when they were all talking about the astronomically high probability that there were hundreds, thousands, billions, of other intelligent civilizations in the universe he asked, 'Then where is everybody?'" Andrea smiled. "Everybody in SETI really hates that guy."

Kate said, "You think Fermi was wrong?"

"We think the negative doesn't prove much." Andrea turned back toward the dome and the theater shot away from Jupiter, and from the Solar System, until the Sun melted into a blur of tiny dots. When they paused again, Kate, Ben and Andrea hung in space, peering back at the Milky Way's familiar pinwheel.

Ben's smile shone in the galaxy's reflected glow. "If we could travel as fast as you just did there, we could test all these theories pretty easily."

"Yep. But we can't." Andrea clicked up a red arrow on the dome and maneuvered it to the dim space between two of the galaxy's bright pinwheel arms. "This spot right here is us. We're between this big white belt of stars, the Orion Arm, and this other big white belt of stars, the Perseus Arm. Our address is this kind of empty black space, the Orion Spur."

Kate said, "If the one arm is the East Coast and the other arm is the West Coast, we're Kansas?"

Andrea nodded. "Flyover country. Empty and boring. If you assume earthlike exoplanets are as common as blades of grass on the Kansas prairie, why would a spaceship cruising on a thousand-year-long journey between the East Coast and the West Coast stop to look at our very commonplace blade of grass?"

Kate said, "So the answer to Fermi is that nobody visits their relatives in Kansas?"

"Partly." Andrea shook her head. "But timing is also an issue. Modern humans have been around for two hundred thousand years. But we've only had the means to even think about looking for other civilizations for less than one hundred years. And at the rate things are going, we may not sustain our interest in looking for them for another hundred years. We haven't even been back to the Moon for forty-seven years."

Ben said, "We may burn out before the other civilizations catch up?"

Andrea shook her head again. "More likely the reverse. Most stars push out particles that surround their system with a magnetic bubble that deflects cosmic radiation. We call the bubble an astrosphere. We call the Sun's bubble the Heliosphere, and we think it's strong, as astrospheres go. So the Earth may have been receiving materially less cosmic radiation than a lot of other planets that orbit other stars. One of the things that jumpstart evolution is mutation. Mutation is stimulated by cosmic radiation."

Kate smiled. "Mankind may be in the slow learners' class?"

Ben smiled, too. "That would explain *so much*."

Andrea nodded. "Lots of other civilizations may have come and gone already. Or they may have come and stayed, but they may have lost interest in examining blades of grass in the middle of nowhere."

Ben's C-phone trilled and he read its screen as it lit his frown in the darkness.

Kate groaned. "Petrie?"

Ben nodded, stood, and walked toward the exit. "Sorry. I have to take this."

Kate said their good-byes to Andrea then caught up with Ben. He stood on the planetarium's entry catwalk with his C-phone to one ear and his hand cupped over the other.

As she approached him, he thumbed his phone off, frowning deeper than ever as he stared at Colibri's lump of space junk. "You know, I was thinking about part of what Andrea said."

"Not the part where she was hitting on you, I hope."

"Don't be ridiculous. I mean the part about why anybody would stop to look at a blade of grass in the middle of Kansas."

"Oh?"

Ben peered again at Manny Colibri's bit of seared titanium. "My great-grandfather was on the way from Maryland to California when his wagon broke down in the middle of Kansas. Once he was marooned there he never left."

FORTY-FOUR

The Navigator made his way aft from the ship's navigation spaces. He was propelled through the ship's aquasphere by his caudal fin's undulations, and around him rose the ship's cylindrical Great Gallery, its diameter a dozen times his body's length and the gallery's length fifty times that of his body.

Ten rows, each row in cross section equal to his body length, ran the Gallery's length fore to aft, and each row was comprised of one hundred squat personal chambers. The ten rows were equidistantly spaced around the Gallery's circumference, and the Gallery's outer surface formed the ship's inner hull. At this late stage in the voyage only fourteen of the one thousand chambers remained occupied. Thirteen excluding his own.

He drifted slowly, parallel to, and within a forelimb's reach of, Row Seven. As he came alongside the entry port to each of the first sixteen chambers, fore to aft, of Row Seven he paused and touched each chamber's vitals panel with the tip of his left forelimb.

The vitals panel of chamber sixteen, like the vitals

panel of chamber one, and like all the rest of the first fifteen chambers' panels, registered unoccupied. This was not of itself troubling, because none of those chambers had been occupied since the first group of the Curious had disembarked so long before.

In fact, ninety-nine chambers out of one hundred chambers in Row Seven were now unoccupied. So were all but twelve of the ship's other nine hundred chambers.

What *did* trouble the Navigator was that each of the first sixteen chambers registered not merely unoccupied but inoperative. He was now certain that the remaining eighty-four chambers would be similarly damaged.

It confirmed his worst fear.

An object had struck the ship, penetrated it from bow to stern straight down the centerline of Row Seven, and then exited the ship through the rear propulsion spaces.

More accurately stated, the *ship*, traveling at two-thirds the speed of light, had struck an object, which had been drifting motionless, in relative terms, through a particularly uncrowded volume of interstellar space.

Really, "object" overstated a particle that must have been a tiny fraction of a sand grain's size. If the particle had been even so large as a sand grain, the kinetic energy generated by a collision at such an unimaginable speed would have catastrophically and instantly disintegrated at least one of the ship's vital systems. The particle must also have been far denser than any sand grain, or else the bow generator's magnetic field would have done its job and brushed it aside.

Now that he understood in general terms the event that had happened, he had to assess, and more tragically to accept, the event's consequences.

When he arrived at Row Seven's sixty-seventh chamber, he paused and gathered himself mentally before he touched the vitals panel and found chamber 7-67 was as dead as all the others in Row Seven. Then, knowing the worst but unwilling to accept it, he rotated the chamber's entry port until it opened.

Inside, she drifted lifeless, as though asleep, and cold and unresponsive to his touch. It might have been possible to determine whether she had suffered because the object had wounded her directly, or whether she had died painlessly in her sleep as the chamber's systems failed. But it didn't matter to the Navigator. The enormity of it was that she was gone. After the fact, how it had happened was unvaluable. Why it had happened was unimaginable.

None of the remaining twelve, of one thousand of the Curious who had inhabited the great gallery's chambers at embarkation, occupied chambers in Row Seven. They would remain asleep and blissfully unaware until he recovered. As for the ship, it would continue to bleed out slowly and inconsequentially, functioning without incident, until he recovered. Then he would sort through a short list of options. None of those options could be executed immediately in any case.

Only then he would rouse the remaining twelve, explain the unexplainable, and prepare them to bear the unbearable.

He reset her chamber to cycle her remains, and then turned ventral-up to drift in a posture of grief.

"I said we shouldn't have continued." The female partner from 4-33 raised her forelimb and turned away from her male.

Her male said, "Those first four disembarkation points weren't different enough to have left home for in the first place. We agreed on that."

8-51 said, "We all knew that accidents happen. And that choosing to travel farther meant choosing greater risk."

8-51's female partner tailed up. "He's right. And there's no changing any of it now."

2-86 said, "Exactly. The Incurious remain at home. The Curious choose the risky path. We all placed the same bet. We bet that another life on another world would suit us better. Now we've simply lost our bets."

4-4 and 4-5, mated twins, rotated, extended their forelimbs toward the Navigator, and spoke in unison so powerfully that the aquasphere in the Great Gallery shimmered. "No! He didn't place a bet at all. And now he's lost more than any of us. So let's all shut up and let him tell us what we have to do next."

They all drifted in silence and stared at the Navigator.

The Navigator turned tail-down. "We have three options. The ship's so badly damaged that we can only choose one. But it's not up to me to dictate which one."

2-2, who rarely spoke, said, "I assume we don't have much time to decide."

The Navigator said, "Actually, if we start thinking in the terms of the available planetary choices' orbital periods, we've got between two years on one of them and three hundred thirty years on the closest one before we arrive at a go-no go decision moment."

8-51 asked, "What kinds of systems are these choices in?"

The Navigator said, "System. We're in a barren spur between two galactic arms and the ship is crippled. We can reach one yellow dwarf that has habitables."

8-51 said, "Habitables? Or inhabited?"

"This isn't the galactic center. It's an empty place where the side of a planet that isn't facing its sun is in darkness."

Somebody burbled in disgust.

The Navigator blinked, and then said, "This particular star's emissions buffer inbound cosmic radiation more than an average astrosphere's do. Usually, limited cosmic radiation means that mutation and consequent evolution are way behind the curve. The possible aquaspherics in the system are satellites that orbit three different gas giant planets. All of the gas giants are very, very distant from the star. Liquid aquaspheres would be under ice, or under rock, or they could be just ice. Assuming they're liquid, they'll be dark environments. They'll be cold environments. If they host life it's likely that life won't evolve even to multicellular organisms for a very long time. But at least those environments will be a *little* like home. And we could get by with a body template that would only modify us for better low-light vision and increased cold tolerance."

8-51 said, "You're saying those choices would allow us to still be us."

4-33 rolled through a full revolution. "If I have to live in the cold and the dark with bugs just recycle me now."

2-86 turned his flank to the Navigator. "Don't tell me those are our *good* choices."

"The third alternative's closer in, warmer and brighter. But it's a hybrid. The aquasphere probably won't host anything you could have a conversation with for another hundred million years. On hybrids, if intelligence develops it usually develops faster in response to the dynamic challenges of the subaerial environment, not in the aquasphere."

8-51 said, "There might be something we *could* have a conversation with?"

"A rudimentary conversation, maybe. And a conversation accomplished by transmitting sound vibration through a gaseous medium that's impalpable and invisible, but yes."

"Except we'd die in the attempt?"

The Navigator raised his forelimb. "No. Template Forty-one *or* Template Forty-three would sample, then conform us to a compatible local body structure. We would be adapted to subaerial respiration."

2-2 said, "So with this subaerial option we would *not* be us. We would be monsters. But we might have company."

2-86 asked, "For how long?"

The Navigator wobbled his left pectoral fin. "The templates rebuild us, cell-by-cell, but after modification we age no more rapidly than normal. Certainly we should experience lifespans of hundreds and hundreds of this planet's orbital periods. Absent external damage, of course."

2-86 said, "You mean absent bigger monsters eating us?"

The Navigator splayed a fin. "Not exactly. Generally the most dangerous species in any ecosystem is the smartest one. And we would be members of that species. Our most dangerous enemies would probably come from among our friends."

The group eyed one another but no one spoke.

The Navigator said, "It's a big decision, and we have time to make it. I'll put you all down for a nap, I'll run some numbers, then we'll reconvene in a year, local time measured on the hybrid."

"And?"

The Navigator said, "And then we'll put it to a vote."

After the Navigator had reconvened the surviving twelve in the Great Gallery the debate had finally progressed to voting. The tally stood at six in favor of one of the aquaspheric moons of the gas giant planets. That choice's supporters favored the least drastic modification of their existing body structure. If that option prevailed, then *which* of the six aquaspheres would be left to the Navigator's discretion, after closer proximity allowed landing risks to be compared. Four votes had been cast for what 2-2 called the hybrid's "subaerial monster option." The hybrid subaerial supporters wanted at least the possibility of interaction with, and existence within, a civilized population.

Only 8-51, male and female, hadn't yet voted.

8-51 male said, "I cast my vote for the hybrid, subaerial option."

She splayed a fin. "That whole idea terrifies me. How can you breathe?"

8-51 turned his eyes to his partner's. "Alright. If you really want the other, I'm with you."

4-33, who had apparently decided that after all she preferred living in the cold and the dark with bugs to dying and being recycled, waved her forelimb at 8-51 male. "You already voted! It's over!"

The Navigator said, "Look. This is too important.

Nobody's vote is final 'til they say it's final." He turned to 8-51 male and female. "So the final total is aquasphere eight, hybrid subaerial four?"

8-51 drifted closer to her mate. "No. I've trusted him with my life so far. I'll do it again."

The Navigator looked around. "Tied. Six to six. Anybody want to switch?"

Silence.

"Okay. Sleep on it. We reconvene and reconsider in—"

2-2 said, "You didn't vote."

"I just drive this thing. I don't have a vote."

Somebody said, "You decide. You're the only one we all trust. All in favor?"

A chorus of "Aye" rippled the aquasphere.

"Opposed?"

Silence.

The Navigator said, "If that's what the group wants. Alright. But I haven't decided yet." Any of the alternatives would require templating. Rebuilding an individual from brain to backfin cell-by-cell, organ-by-organ, and memory-by-memory took longer than that hybrid alternative planet took to orbit its star once. Then when the ship came within investigation range the ship would fine-match the templated bodies to the most appropriate local lifeform.

8-51 asked, "When will we know what you've decided?"

The Navigator said, "I have to program the template before I join you in the medical. You'll know when the medical transfers us all into the lander."

Then the Navigator turned and drifted forward to the Navigation spaces. One thing he hadn't mentioned to the group, because there was no reason to upset them, was that the lander's bay had also been in the path of the particle that had crippled the ship. The lander's diagnostics showed no damage, but most of its systems couldn't be tested until it decoupled from the ship. The debate might be moot if the lander had been damaged.

The ship itself was dying. No matter what, it lacked the capacity to do more than drift once it carried them close to one single destination within the yellow star's system. Thereafter, the yellow dwarf's gravity would eventually draw the great vessel in, and the star would consume it. But if the lander had been damaged they could all be consumed in the descent no matter which destination the Navigator chose.

Behind him, he heard the others still debating.

2-86 asked 8-51 female, "Which way are you betting?"

8-51 female, who had bet her life on her partner's judgment, said, "If I were the Navigator? He's just lost the only one who mattered to him. I'd take the risk on a new life instead of crying about the old one. And, if he died, on a reunion with her on the other side."

2-86 said, "There is no other side."

8-51 female displayed her dorsal fin. "That's not what *I* choose to believe. You like to bet. What will you risk on that?"

"I don't have anything left to risk. None of us have. We've all just bet everything on the Navigator's judgment."

FORTY-FIVE

When Ben and Kate emerged from the California Academy of Science into the midmorning sunshine that beat down on San Francisco, Ben stared up at the sky. "You know, Colibri's helmet didn't turn out to be what he thought it was. His good luck ship carving was probably bad luck. His harpoon's inventor lost out on a fortune for lack of a patent, and Colibri's jewelry piece turned out to be tragic. Now we find out that somebody sold him a phony meteorite. Manuel Colibri was a genius. But the longer this investigation goes on, the more it seems like the poor guy was always getting screwed."

"The longer this investigation goes on, the more it seems like he's the only one."

Ben closed his eyes, exhaled, then stopped and faced her. "There's only one more donation item on our list. Then we can take some time together."

Kate sighed. "DRB 833. I suppose you have that figured out, too."

"Maybe. What's a seven-letter word for a place where you can view the complete works of Picasso and Rembrandt but that contains no paintings whatever?"

Kate stared up at the sky. "Shepard, I don't want to play find-the-museum anymore. Just tell me, okay?"

"Well, it's not a gallery. Galleries have paintings."

"Just fucking tell me!"

"A library. It's a library. The University of San Francisco Library has a place called the Donohue Rare Book Room. 833 is the old Dewey Decimal classification for German fiction."

"It's a *document*?" Kate clutched Ben's forearm. "Finally! It's Colibri's will! It has to be."

The Donohue Rare Book Room lurked in a corner on the top floor of the University of San Francisco's main library. It was a dark-paneled, carpeted room that contained three four-chair dark wood study tables and walls lined with glass-fronted cases inside which were books. At midday, not a student was in sight, but the librarian was.

Edgar Melbourne, the head librarian, had pink, chubby cheeks. He wore a cardigan sweater and a striped tie held in place by a gold tie clip attached to his shirt halfway between his belt buckle and his collar. One of his incisors matched the clip, and the tooth gleamed when he smiled.

Melbourne said, "Mr. Shepard, we catalog seventeen thousand items, and I've had peculiar requests for some of them from some peculiar places. But the Department of Homeland Security?"

"Specifically, German fiction, if 833 relates to a Dewey Decimal number."

Kate said, "It would have been donated by Manuel Colibri."

Melbourne flashed his tooth as he led them to a case on one wall. "Actually, all I needed to hear was German fiction. We've made some adjustments to the collections recently due to budgetary issues. Only one item of German fiction in our collection I would call genuinely unique. And it is indeed a donation from Mr. Colibri."

Melbourne unlocked the case, slid out a Ziploc plastic container, and held it up to display the cover of a slim, beige pamphlet. The cover illustration was a black and white drawing of a man in a bathrobe and slippers. He stood before an open double door and covered his face with his hands.

Melbourne carried the rarity to his desk and pulled on white cotton gloves. As he slid the pamphlet from its envelope he said, "An inscribed first in the original German of *Die VerWandlung*. The story first appeared in 1915 in an expressionist magazine published in Leipzig."

Ben said, "I don't speak German."

Melbourne raised one finger. "But I'm sure you know *Metamorphosis* by Franz Kafka. It's—"

Kate smiled. "About a man who wakes up and finds he's changed into a cockroach."

"Translators differ. Perhaps some other unspecified loathsome creature. But the man's life does not improve thereafter."

Kate pointed at Melbourne's gloves, then at the yellowed, dog-eared pamphlet. "It's valuable, obviously."

"A signed first of a classic? Always." He cocked his head as he turned the pamphlet in his hands, then pointed at tears, folds, and stains that marred its surface. "But more pristine copies change hands at auction periodically. I suspect that this copy was read and reread often between its publication in 1915 and its presentation for inscription to Kafka in 1917. I suppose what drew Mr. Colibri to this rather mundane example was the coincidence of Kafka's inscription."

The librarian turned around so Ben and Kate could read over his shoulder, opened the delicate book to its first inside page, then drew his gloved finger across faded black-inked handwriting there as he read it aloud. "'*Mit den besten Wunschen an Manuel, der den Schmerz des Menschseins versteht. —Franz Kafka, Praha, 3 Marz 1917.*' Literally, 'With best wishes to Manuel, who understands the pain of being human.' Signed on March 3, 1917, in Prague."

Kate flicked a finger at the pamphlet's pages. "Was there a paper folded inside it or something? I mean, you don't seriously think this could be genuine?"

Melbourne drew back. "Ms. Boyle, this library is not a repository for fakes! This is the donation, the whole donation, and nothing but the donation."

He held the pamphlet up in one hand while he pointed at it with the other. "The handwriting and signature are very characteristically Kafka's. The bleak sentiment is quite consistent with Kafka's well-documented real-life melancholy. And he was, in fact, living in Prague in March of 1917."

Melbourne shrugged. "And successful forgers don't fritter away their time by adding relatively little value to a piece that begins in such mediocre condition as this one. So my professional opinion is that Franz Kafka did in fact write that inscription at that place and time. Whether it was presented in person or sent to the author with return postage I can't say."

Ben wrinkled his forehead. "Don't authors write a specific message if a fan asks them to?"

Melbourne cradled the first edition in his gloved hands. "You mean, 'To Fred, with best wishes for a happy birthday'? Of course they do."

The three of them stared down at the illustration of the despairing man in the bathrobe clutching his hands to his face.

Melbourne said, "But if that's the case here, the inscription suggests that this poor person Manuel's life was no birthday party. In fact, it appears to have been Kafkaesque."

FORTY-SIX

Alongside her extended family, the matriarch waded calf-deep through the great lake's shallows, its water frigid against her bare brown skin. Even in the dry of summer the snow covered peaks that ringed the lake fed melt water into it. Heads and wooden spear tips pointed down, all the adults squinted to penetrate the afternoon sun glare that reflected off the lake's ripples, and hid the fish.

When the matriarch's middle grandchild, playing in the pebbles on the lake's bank, cried out, she looked first at him, then up at the corner of the vast blue sky toward which his small hand reached.

A fireball, like lightning at midday, streaked high above the lake, trailing a tail of cloud, whiter than the tail of a gray fox, but as slender as a reed. The tail fluffed and lengthened as the fireball crossed the sky. As the fireball grew and brightened it changed direction faster than a blink, again and again, like a hummingbird did. Although the fireball seemed to have been flying higher than any bird that she had ever seen. In fact, higher in the daylight sky than anything except the Sun himself.

The matriarch's daughter shaded her own eyes against the sun. "The Sun is dying!"

The matriarch frowned as she shifted her gaze to squint into the Sun. He looked exactly as he had every day of her life.

Even as the matriarch watched, the fireball rushed down, now racing toward them across the water at an altitude no higher than that at which a hawk hunted. Even though the day was so calm that the lake's surface barely rippled, the roar of a great windstorm beat at her ears.

She shouted to the other adults, grabbed at her daughter's arm and led them all, splashing as they ran, toward the shore and away from the approaching fireball's path.

The wind's roar deafened her as she glanced back and saw the Sun's messenger touch the lake's surface, far in the distance.

A great cloud, as though water had been thrown on a cooking fire, erupted with a hiss as violent as the wind roar was loud.

As the matriarch reached the shore, she knelt to scoop up her grandson, whose eyes bulged wide and white in his brown face. He stared at the danger that now pursued them, its roar increasing so deafeningly that the matriarch knew that it approached far faster than they could hope to run.

She flicked her eyes back as she ran. The Sun's messenger skipped toward them, in the way that a flat stone skipped by a child might skip across calm water.

As the fireball closed upon them she saw that it glowed as red as a kindling stick glowed when blown upon, and was not a mass of flame but an object, smooth and round as a waterworn stone.

The fireball reached the shore but rushed on, furrowing rock as easily as a child might stab through sand with a broken branch. Then the object struck the embankment beyond the mud flat at the water's edge and exploded with a great bang, like a sap bubble in a cooking fire's log sometimes did.

Bits of the object, and of rock and soil, arched through the air and thudded into the ground all around her family, like sizzling rain. She fell upon her grandson to protect him, as the others fell upon their children.

Within moments silence returned, broken only by the crackle of dry grass set ablaze, and by the shrieks of wheeling, disturbed birds.

The matriarch's eldest son had sustained an angry, red burn across his back, but otherwise her brood was uninjured. Her middle son waded knee-deep into the lake, bent then turned and raised up a fish, silver and as long as his forearm. He grinned as the silver bellies of other fish rose, and then floated at the water's surface. "They're already cooked!"

Holding her squalling grandson on her hip, the matriarch frowned through the smoke roiling up from the vast and spreading grassfire. She peered at the great gouge that now split the ground and extended from the lake shore until it disappeared into the upslope beyond.

For the moment, the Sun's messenger had improved the fishing here. But, all things considered, it appeared to her that the Sun was very unhappy with them.

❖   ❖   ❖

The matriarch and her brood remained near, but safely upwind from, the great fire for a day, until rain came and snuffed it out. During that time everyone grew fat on all the fish they were able to eat, while her daughters and her sons' mates smoked the fish that they could not eat, to be saved for leaner times.

On the morning before it was time to move on, the matriarch gathered her two eldest sons and led them across the rain-soaked ash that the fire had left behind, then up the gouge that the messenger had cut. The place where the fireball had exploded was no farther from the water's edge than the distance that a middle sized child could hurl a stone.

The place was a scorched pit, scooped back into the slope. In its shadows, shoulder-to-shoulder in the gray ash, like strips of smoked fish, the broken bodies of six men and five women lay motionless.

One man, clad in not even so much as her sons wore, staggered, gasping, toward the rank of the dead carrying a sixth woman's body in his arms.

Once he had arranged her body alongside those of the others, he knelt silently, and as awkwardly as a child.

At last, he sowed a powder finer than sand over them all. Then a flame erupted from his fingertips, and fire engulfed and consumed the dead.

The man turned, stumbled, as clumsily as an infant, past the matriarch and her sons without a glance, as though he were blind. When he reached the shore he plunged into the water, hurling himself facedown, and then allowing himself to sink. After only moments he pushed himself up onto hands and knees, gasping and vomiting out lake water.

Then he struck at the water, first with one fist, then with both, as though the water itself were a beloved old friend who had betrayed him.

Then he did something that seemed to the matriarch most uncharacteristic of a god who carried the power of his father, the Sun, in his fist.

He knelt there in the water, covered his face with his hands, and wept.

FORTY-SEVEN

Ben eyed his C-phone as he sat with Kate in her car in visitor parking outside the University of San Francisco Library. "So now we've seen every item Manny Colibri loaned out to museums after the attempted burglary. No exercised powers of appointment. No wills. No codicils. No smoking guns. What do we do now?"

Kate shook her head. "Well, like you said. All we learned from chasing down that stuff is that Manny was better at picking winners in business than he was at buying *objets d'art*. We know three of the items relate to Hispanic culture. We know, from the pictures of Manuel Colibri that exist, that he looked Mexican or Central American. And we know his name is Hispanic. 'Colibri' is Spanish for 'hummingbird,' and 'Manuel' is certainly a Hispanic first name."

Ben said, "He's never applied for a U.S. passport. But nobody can remember him traveling outside the U.S. either. His social security number was issued based on a birth certificate that says he was born in Kern County, California in 1975."

Kate shrugged. "Any Latino in California who doesn't know how to get a phony social hasn't been paying attention. And the People's Republic of San Francisco's been don't-ask-don't-tell about most identity questions for years."

"Nothing from the Cardinal employees, the ones besides Carlsson, who DHS and the FBI and SFPD were able to question, turned up much. But then, Manny was in charge of what went into Cardinal's records. So why would we expect anything but the party line from those sources?" Ben bent his head while he texted.

Kate pointed at Ben's phone. "Who are you texting?"

Ben said, "Mick. For the entry codes to Colibri's house. We're kind of stumped here. Colibri may not have left behind any DNA, and his artifact collection and his laptop may not be in his house anymore, but if we go over there and have a look something might click. In the meantime our suspect list, in alphabetical order, starts with Victor Carlsson and ends with the Catholic Church. And from where I stand I don't see a murderer on that list."

"Maybe that's because you're standing too close to him."

"Now who's playing peek-a-boo?"

"Think about it, Ben. Arthur Petrie has enough money to run for president. His business rep is borderline crook. He's got enough ego to run for president. And now because of the bombing he looks like a hero and a genius."

"Not to me. To me he looks like a flamboyant, insensitive ignoramus."

Kate said, "We've been thinking the motive was

money. But what if it was power? Your boss conveniently was far from the action, so he had to rush to the scene. Where he displayed courage and grace under pressure. Reagan was considered a likable dunce. Then he got shot and displayed courage and grace under pressure. Now people like my dad want him on Mt. Rushmore. Petrie's promoting himself for a slot up there too."

Ben shook his head. "Trust me. Petrie may be a dunce, but he's not likable. And so far he hasn't done anything over the top. He's just taken political advantage of events, like every other politician does."

"Like just happening to send you to the bathhouse?"

Ben felt his eyes bug. "So he didn't brainwash just one assassin? He brainwashed two?"

Kate's phone chimed, she raised her index finger while she eyed it, then cocked an eyebrow. "Hmm. A *personal* 'Message sent from the iPhone of David Powell.' Usually David's admin sends his messages. David hopes you and I are feeling better. He wants to know if we want to go for a boat ride, and have lunch with him, and my dad, and Julia Madison." Kate wiped imaginary sweat off her brow. "Whew!"

Ben frowned. "Why the big relief?"

"Dad hadn't told David about his Catholic Church suspicions, because Dad kind of light-fingered the Powell Foundation's files to get the details about Colibri's estate. He was going to tell David about it this morning. Obviously Dad's big reveal didn't bother David. What's your preference for the lunch invitation?"

Ben said, "I don't want to share you."

"Perfect answer, Shepard. Where are you taking me for dinner?"

"It's your turn to pick the place."

"Another good answer. Hottest table in San Francisco is *Small World*."

Ben wrinkled his forehead. "What kind of—?"

"It's Insectarian."

Ben made a face.

"Don't be a racist hick. Insects are delicious. It's a responsible, sustainable diet embraced by most of the non-white world."

He turned and stared at her. "So is wheat, but you won't eat that. You *do* see the inconsistency?"

She lifted her chin. "I thought it was my choice."

He nodded. "It is. But let's agree that you chose the place," Ben pointed at her, "because you insist on controlling this relationship. Not because anybody in this relationship thinks anybody else in it is a racist hick." He paused and drew a breath. "Have you actually tasted one of those 'delicious' bugs? Ever?"

She looked out the window. "The reviews are really good."

"Last night you wouldn't kiss me because you'd vomited. But you're fine with maggot breath the first time we, you know?"

Kate sat silent. Then she snorted a laugh.

"What's suddenly funny?"

"'You know?' Shepard, nobody's called it 'you know' since 1951. I propose a truce on the following terms. Skip the fancy dinner. Grab a quiet lunch. Then we go back to your hotel room and you-know our brains out."

Ben pointed to the accelerator pedal. "You have to press that to make this thing move."

❖   ❖   ❖

Ben stared at Kate as she sat across from him at the Buena Vista, head down while her slender fingers flashed across her C-phone's screen. The waiter had cleared their lunch dishes, and her Irish coffee glass sat at her elbow. They had gotten the same table that they had shared what seemed like years before but had in fact been only three days earlier.

Kate looked up, then touched her lip. "Whipped cream?"

He smiled. "No. You look perfect."

Bing.

Bing.

Their C-phones chimed simultaneously and as Ben frowned he peered at Kate's screen. She exhaled. "False alarm. It's just Mick. He's attached the entry codes and the other information about Colibri's house that was attached to the DNA report."

Ben said, "Oh. You mean that now you want to—?"

Kate stared at him. "Shepard, I believe we've established what I want."

Ben's phone trilled and vibrated in his pocket.

Kate narrowed her eyes. "And you spending the afternoon on the phone, advancing Petrie's conspiracy, isn't it."

It rang again.

Kate turned her head, arms crossed, and stared out at the sidewalk.

Ben really didn't have to look at the caller ID.

He sighed as he held the phone to his ear. "Yes, Mr. Secretary?"

"Shepard, I'm sitting here with the speaker of the house in his office at the Capitol. The resolution passed both houses with bipartisan supermajorities."

"Resolution, sir?"

"Creating the DHS Cross for Valor. You'll be the first recipient."

"Mr. Secretary, with respect, I didn't—"

"Practice that modest tone for the ceremony."

"Sir?"

"Don't they get CNN out there?"

"I've been busy with my liaison responsibilities. What ceremony, sir?"

"Here. Nine Eastern. The morning shows are covering it live."

Kate stared at the ceiling, shaking her head.

"Sir, I'm not sure whether I can find a flight."

Petrie said, "Heroes don't fly commercial. I'm sending a plane."

Ben smiled in Kate's direction. "Do heroes get to bring a guest, sir?"

"I set you up for an exclusive interview with *Dateline* on the flight back. The jet'll be packed out with the anchor and the crew. By the way, how's the ear?"

"A little sore."

"I mean how does it look?"

"The dressing's pretty thick."

"We'll see what make-up can do about that. Heroes should be wounded in the right places."

"Sir, I really would prefer not to do this."

"Shepard, you're standing in for thousands of DHS employees who never get to stand in the spotlight. But today every one of them is proud to be associated with you. Are you telling me you'd rob them of this moment? To satisfy your own selfish desires?"

"Uh. No, sir." Ben squeezed his eyes shut, then opened them. "Where and when do I meet the plane?"

"Sit tight. I'll let you know. And I had them check you out of wherever you're staying. There's a lot for you to do back here." Petrie hung up.

Ben said, "Kate—"

Kate waved her hand and her eyes glistened. "I heard. Still think he sent you to the bathhouse coincidentally?"

Ben shook his head. "I disagree he's masterminding a conspiracy. But I agree this is too much for me." He raised his phone.

Kate asked, "What are you doing?"

Ben moved his thumb to speed dial Petrie. "Calling him back and resigning."

"No you aren't!" Kate lunged for his phone but he snatched it away. She said, "In the first place, Shepards don't quit any more than Boyles do. In the second place, Petrie's right. You are a hero. And tomorrow you *will* be standing in for all those DHS employees he just guilted you with. But you earned that medal. Not just last night. You'll be standing in for people like Roland Garvey, too."

Ben shook his head. "Kate, I don't want a medal. I want to stay here. With you. Kate, I—"

Kate raised her palm. "Don't say that word! Ben, you think I'm special. But really all I am is different from you. The chance that two random people thrown together under stress for three days are that kind of a fit is less than one in a million."

Ben stabbed his finger into the tabletop. "Your parents sat in this same place and in three *hours* they knew."

"They *were* one in a million. Ben, as of tomorrow, you're going to be the Face of the Franchise. Maybe we should see whether I look all that special to you a couple of weeks from now."

"Kate, why are you trying to talk me out of you?"

Kate stood. "I'm not. I'm trying to talk *me* out of *you*."

"Again, why?"

"Because I'm scared. Ben, it took the astronomer with the large natural satellites about sixty seconds to hit on you. There'll be a million more like her chasing you by tomorrow morning. Considering my track record, I'd rather not start with you in the first place than get dropped by you when you realize how many options you have."

"Kate, you're just upset in the moment because we can't catch a break." He reached across the table for her hand, but she stepped back.

"Don't." Kate breathed, wiped her eyes. "Give me some space. Give us both some space."

Ben blinked back tears, then she turned and was gone.

Twenty minutes after Kate left Ben, Mick Shay sat down across from him at the table in the Buena Vista.

Mick pointed at the empty beer bottle in front of Ben, as well as at the full one alongside it. "I gather this is why you texted for a ride to the airport."

"Thanks for coming. My driver and I had a little falling out." Ben raised his phone. "But I'm about to call her and try to make it right."

"Kate?" Mick shook his head. "Too soon. Any man who has the last word in an argument with an Irish girl's just havin' the first word in the next one. I know. I been married to two of 'em."

"And divorced from two of them."

"Proving my point." Mick tipped up Ben's empty beer bottle and read the label through the lower half of his bifocals. "I see you don't favor the house specialty."

"It turns out they didn't invent Irish coffee here. They invented it in the Dublin airport."

"Mr. Shepard, Irishmen knew how to pour whisky into coffee long before Dublin had an airport. The first time somebody shows off that they know something's not always the first time they knew it." Mick laid a newspaper on the table. "Brought this with me when I walked up from the Pier. Thought we might need something to pass the time." He pointed outside at the darkening late afternoon. "The weather that's comin' in tonight's supposed to blow through fast, but it's gonna be bad. So bad that nothin's gonna be flying in these parts for a few hours. So my bet is that your airplane will sit in Washington awhile before it heads out here."

Ben turned his empty beer bottle and read the label. "How many of these should I drink before I call her?"

By the time twilight arrived, the wind off San Francisco Bay whipped pedestrians' clothing as they struggled, heads bent, past the Buena Vista's windows. True to Mick's prediction, DHS had texted Ben that the plane had remained on the ground in Washington.

Mick nursed his first beer as he traded Ben the *Chronicle*'s national news and business sections for its green sports pages. The waiter had just brought Ben his third beer, which would be one above his normal limit, as Ben flipped the national news' inside pages.

A *Washington Post* story reported political analysts' surprise that low-key efforts to get Petrie's name on primary ballots in key states had been underway for months.

The business section's compendium of developing stories noted speculation about what would become of Cardinal Systems once Victor Carlsson, the presumptive management heir, returned with the rest of the management team.

A related story reported lights turned on, and observed to be burning late, on the three floors of Cardinal headquarters that housed its legal staff.

A longer, unrelated analysis piece focused on the extraordinary cash hoard Powell Diversified had accumulated in recent months, and speculated on possible acquisition targets.

Something Ben couldn't put his finger on nagged at him. He shook his head to clear it.

Mick looked up from the sports page. "Something wrong, Mr. Shepard?"

Ben cocked his head. "What did you say about Irish men?"

"That they lose arguments with Irish women."

Ben shook his head. "After that. That Irishmen knew about putting whisky in coffee before they admitted it."

Mick shrugged as he leaned forward and traced a line in a sports story with one finger. "So?"

Ben motioned their waiter over, then raised his untouched third beer. "Could you take this away and bring me a black coffee?"

FORTY-EIGHT

After Kate walked away from Ben at the Buena Vista she drove south toward Palo Alto.

Her initial plan was to lock herself in her apartment's bedroom, sit cross-legged on her bed in her underwear, then cry while she ate full-fat chocolate chip from the carton until she puked. Five minutes down the 101, she decided that plan would work no better now than it had when Jimmy Kocurski had dumped her in high school.

Plan B was to quit *Gizmo*, stuff the Corolla with her possessions until the suspension bottomed out, chuck the rest, then move in with Shepard, support him until he graduated law school, then get dumped for a blonde tobacco lobbyist with buns of steel. Those two plans bookended the varied and equally ridiculous plans with which she had dealt with all the equally failed relationships she had been part of between Jimmy Kocurski and Kirk the Jerk.

Somewhere on Interstate 280 South, Kate checked back in to reality.

Reality number one was that she couldn't move back to Washington until she whipped her father's denial issues about her mother's suicide. She now knew from bitter experience that phoning from Washington every Sunday, and flying out each Christmas, yielded unacceptable results.

Reality number two was that if Ben Shepard found some hottie whom he preferred during a few weeks' separation from Kate, then better the train wreck never happened.

But what if it was reality number three? Kate had thought since she was five that happiness was a Pulitzer. Now she knew that it was what her parents had. What if she and Ben were the real death-do-us-part deal? If that was true, then she still needed to get her dad straight first. Then she needed to get her job at the *Post* back. Or find something else in D.C., anything, really, that would allow her and Ben to live happily ever after. Which meant that her immediate plan should be to kick the crap out of the Manuel Colibri story and rebuild a résumé.

Kate cut from the left-hand lane to the right, across traffic, then shot off the next exit two feet behind one eighteen-wheeler and ten feet in front of another one, that howled at her.

She reversed direction and entered 280 headed north back toward the Golden Gate. As she drove she asked her C-phone to set a course for the address of Manny Colibri's house. Then she considered phoning Shepard. But by now he had been dropped off in a VIP lounge to await a private jet and a news crew. It left her nothing to do but watch for cops ahead and concentrate on the road, which seemed like a ridiculous waste of drive time.

When Kate finally drove across the bridge into Marin County she clutched the steering wheel so hard that her fingers quivered. Traffic was light, perhaps because commuters had left the city early to beat the weather. But so far the weather wasn't living up to the dire predictions.

According to her C-phone's nav app Manuel Colibri's home was a waterfront address on Belvedere Island, with south-facing views.

Kate knew Belvedere Island. Everybody in the Bay Area did. Belvedere Island was a municipality one square mile in area, whose two thousand crazy-rich residents looked back from a distance upon San Francisco, upon the Golden Gate, and upon all things unwhite and unRepublican.

As Kate pulled up to the gates that protected Manny Colibri's house from the world, but had not protected *him* from it, she craned her neck to see the tops of the stucco walls, which had to be fifteen feet high.

Kate keyed in the entry code and the bank-vault-solid entry gates swung back. She let the Corolla idle downhill into Manny Colibri's courtyard. Across the low contemporary box's roofs and across the bay the red beacons atop the Golden Gate's towers flashed, and left of the bridge San Francisco's spires soared, and its lights twinkled on its hillsides.

Kate parked in the courtyard and clicked through the attachments that Mick had sent to her C-phone. According to the building permits, the place rested upon quakeproof, shock-absorbing foundations. Its bay-facing glazing was both proof against bullets and capable of shuttering itself within ten seconds in case of a "Climatic Event." And a system of drains large enough to walk through would conduct storm and tidal surges harmlessly away from the structure.

Kate stepped from her car as, far out in the Pacific, the faint thunder of an impending "Climatic Event" rumbled. In the deepening twilight, Kate shuddered. "God, Shepard. Where are you when I have to go into a creepy dead guy's house?"

The code opened the house's double doors, which were brass, and taller than the top of a basketball backboard.

The interior lights came up as she entered, indirect, glowing and neither too bright nor too dim.

The far wall of the house's main room was glass, floor to ceiling, and framed the view out to the city and to the bridge across a broad terrace that ended in a sleek pier. As Kate walked toward the glass wall, a barred fence beyond the pier's end, that blocked entry to the compound from the seaward side, sank itself out of sight beneath the water's surface. It no longer obstructed the view from the now-occupied great room.

The wall to the right of the view contained a glass fireplace twenty feet long and four feet high. As Kate walked around the low white sectional in the room's center, toward the wall, the fireplace silently lit.

She whispered, "Holy crap, Manny. This house really does take care of itself."

As she crossed the room, and up a step to the open kitchen the AC hushed on, though the place had felt comfortable enough when she entered. Kate ran her fingers across the kitchen counter's stone, which lit at her touch, translucent blue from below.

Kate returned to the great room and sank into the soft, impeccably white sectional. As she peered above the fireplace to her front, a panel above the mantle hissed open, revealing a shallow, lit recess within which was hung a gilt-framed oil painting of a sailboat filled with passengers, tossed by a storm.

"Damn!" Kate snapped a photo of the painting with her C-phone, then uploaded it to an app called InstAppraisal. While she waited she stepped to the painting and wiggled its frame. It moved like it was just hung on a nail, and no alarms sounded.

When her phone chimed she raised her eyebrows and read aloud, "*The Storm on the Sea of Galilee*; Rembrandt Harmensz van Rijn, ca. 1633; Stolen 1990. Estimated minimum market value if recovered, $US 40 million." She whistled.

As Kate stepped sideways from the painting, another panel, this one waist-high, slid aside and revealed an empty, lighted glass case. Kate touched the case's thick glass and whispered, "So this is where you kept all that old crap."

Suddenly it all fell into place for Kate, with such force that she staggered back and plopped down again onto the sofa.

Manuel Colibri kept a Rembrandt worth forty million bucks here in his house, exposed for the taking to anyone who simply walked up to it. But he had dispersed to safer venues a hodge-podge of ancient artifacts. Even though their aggregate appraised value was lunch money compared to the Rembrandt.

Kate fixed her gaze on the display case, and on its soft-lit, now-empty shelves.

The black-market Rembrandt was probably a great investment. But as such it was just an aesthetically pleasing stock certificate.

Those objects on those shelves were not investments. They were the priceless physical memorials gathered throughout a lifetime. A lifetime so long that only someone who had lived it would believe such lifespans were possible.

A fragment of a spacecraft, wrecked in the high Andes simultaneous with the appearance on Earth of the sun god's child. A story, imagined on paper, of a soul condemned to live alone in a grotesque body, which was only too true. A conquistador's helmet, scarred in the battle that marked the Incan nation's bloody death three hundred years later. And forty years after that, on the opposite side of the Atlantic, a votive ship that hadn't saved mankind from centuries of combat over different visions of a god whom no combatant had ever seen. Two and a half centuries later, a killing tool forged in New Bedford, Massachusetts, by a man who had likely been born as someone's property. And finally a simple tin star that proved that a thousand years of conflict had taught mankind nothing.

Kate snapped her head back against Manuel Colibri's sofa cushions, as though punched in the jaw.

Shaking her head, she said softly, "Manny Colibri, you poor marooned spaceman. Did you ever imagine that after a thousand years your story would end like it did?"

In the silence someone whispered, "It hasn't ended just yet."

"Aaahh!" Kate felt her eyes bug as she crabbed backward across the sofa, away from the whisper that came out of the darkness.

The figure who emerged from the shadows limped toward Kate, dragging one leg. As his face came into the light it was clear that reports of Manny Colibri's death had been exaggerated.

But maybe not by much. The unlined bronze face was the face that Kate recognized from the few photographs of Manuel Colibri that she had seen. But the face was now thin, caked with dirt, and twisted in pain. Colibri wore a black tracksuit, but the fabric of the leg that he dragged had been cut away. The bare leg's skin looked ordinary, the dried blood on the skin dark red-brown. But the bone that was visible where the skin had been abraded away was black and crystalline.

Kate sucked in her breath. "You're not human!"

Colibri limped toward her, then paused an unthreatening distance away and leaned on his sectional's arm.

"Kate, I've lived a dozen lifetimes in this skin. You have yet to complete one lifetime in yours. I would argue that I am, in fact, more human than you are."

"You know my name."

Colibri lifted a C-phone. "Your father and Ben Shepard are right. The eyes may be the window to the soul, but a smartphone is the window to everywhere else. Every C-phone's encryptions have a backdoor. And I have the key."

"You asshole. You eavesdrop on everybody?"

"Not at all. In fact never. On anybody. Until someone tried to kill me. After Ben Shepard's name appeared in the news as a connection to the investigation I decided it was reasonable that a victim keep up to date on whoever tried to kill him. Without announcing that he remained available in case they wanted to finish the job."

Kate pointed at Colibri's leg. "How bad is that?"

Colibri grimaced. "Bad. But the leg's not the half of it. This body is rather more durable, even against a trauma like a three-hundred-foot fall and a subsequent cold, stormy swim, than a standard-issue human body. Once upon a time, the leg injury could have been repaired with the equipment that survived my arrival here on Earth. But even in the best of circumstances the present damage to my internal organs would have been problematic. And now, after a thousand years, what I'll call my 'first aid kit' has finally met its match. This body and I aren't going to survive longer than a few more days."

"We need to get you to a doctor."

"Kate, trust me, a body whose DNA is too alien and too dissimilar to register in standard forensic testing is beyond help from any trauma center designed to heal humans. My time's running out. I'd like to make the most of every minute of it that remains. If you will help me."

Colibri turned back toward the house's bedroom wing, wiped sludge from one arm, and pointed toward the kitchen. "Entering and leaving one's own home via the storm drains is a messy and painful proposition. Would you mind making us tea while I go back to my bedroom and clean up a bit?"

"Then what?"

"Then, if you have a moment, we'll talk. I'm sure

you have questions. And after so long in this body I am more than ready to answer questions while I still can. You're the first person who has been prepared to believe me in a thousand years."

Colibri, whoever or whatever he was, limped into the darkness and left her alone. Heart pounding, Kate found Colibri's kettle, filled it and set it on his cooktop to boil. As she searched through his cupboards for tea and mugs, she dialed her phone, then wedged it between her ear and shoulder.

FORTY-NINE

Jack Boyle waited in the twilight in the Aquatic Park Bathhouse's deserted parking lot. David Powell walked toward him, holding on to his yachting cap so that the swirling wind that tore at the yellow crime scene tape that still surrounded the bathhouse wouldn't blow David's hat into San Francisco Bay.

Jack stood at the passenger's side door of the big Bentley that Paul Eustis had left parked after he drove David, Jack, and Julia down here earlier.

Jack had just packed a tired and tipsy Julia Madison into a cab bound for her home, while David had remained at the temporary pier to be sure his motorboat's mooring would keep it secure until he summoned a crew to winch it into its trailer.

Jack stretched and belched. The day had extended far beyond lunch, fueled by wine, cognac, and conversation animated by David's excitement at the prospect of a big deal.

David, with Julia's and Jack's encouragement, seemed

poised to make a run at Cardinal Systems. In fact, he grasped immediately the nuances of a potential acquisition that would have taken a lesser mind months to comprehend. David wasn't merely a smart businessman, he was a nimble one. He assimilated and acted on situational changes as quickly as anyone Jack had ever met.

David breathed heavily after the uphill walk from the beach, and as he reached the Bentley's driver's side door Jack heard the jingle of Mozart from David's pocket.

David drew his iPhone, raised his eyebrows as he peered down at its screen, then smiled. "It's Kate."

"Well, tell her she's too late for lunch."

David said, "Tell her yourself. I'll put her on speaker."

"David? Is my dad with you?" Kate's voice quavered.

David cocked his head. "Very much so. I'm here at the bathhouse with your father and you're on speaker."

Jack said, "Katy, are you whispering?"

"Dad, David—Manny Colibri's alive!"

Jack frowned. "Did Shepard get you drunk?"

"No. Seriously."

David's face appeared pale in the light cast by his phone screen, and the phone seemed to quiver in his hand. "Kate, what evidence suggests *that*?"

"The evidence of me sitting in his living room talking to him right now."

Jack frowned again. "You've been smoking dope, haven't you? I told you it was hallucinogenic."

"Dad, shut up. Manny escaped from his car as it sank. He swam ashore. He's hurt and he's been hiding out here."

Jack said, "Hiding from what?"

"From whoever tried to kill him, I suppose."

David said, "Where did you say you are?"

"With him in his house."

Jack said, "Katy, if he's hurt you need to call an ambulance."

"Dad, paramedics can't handle Manny's problems. If I say more than that you'll *totally* think I'm high."

David said, "That's amazing news." He paused. "Wonderful news. And Manny's concern for his safety is understandable in light of recent events."

David asked, "Kate, who else knows about this?"

"Manny, obviously. Me. Now you two."

David furrowed his brow. "Jack, if there's a question of the best medical help, I should be there with Manny to pull the necessary strings." He laid his hand on the Bentley's door handle as he said. "Kate, you sit tight. Jack and I will be right there."

David consulted his iPhone, then frowned. "Jack, Manny's place is over on Belvedere Island. The bridge traffic shows as terrible. With the weather coming in I don't think we can rely on a helicopter."

"Then I guess we fight the traffic."

David shook his head. "I have a better idea. We'll take the Bearcat. It's probably the fastest way across the bay anyway."

Over the speaker, Kate said, "You two can't go out in that old boat. There's a storm coming."

David said, "Kate, I've run Miami-Nassau in a cigarette boat when the Atlantic was far worse than tonight's forecast. I'll take good care of your father."

Kate said, "Gotta go."

The line went dead.

David raised his eyebrows. "Well."

"Sounds like you may need to find another acquisition, David," Jack said.

David said, "Jack, while I get the first aid kit out of the Bentley's boot, would you go down to the dock and unpack the survival suits out of the bag in the Bearcat's aft cockpit?"

Jack frowned. "David, Katy may be right. It might be less risky to just send the local cops over."

David unlocked the Bentley's driver's side door and matched Jack's frown. "Local cops can't charter a helicopter or get a top-ranked trauma specialist out of bed. Life is about taking risks for things that matter, Jack."

Fifteen minutes later, the Bearcat pounded north across San Francisco Bay toward Belvedere island. The wind numbed Jack's bare face and hands, but the bulky red neoprene suit, that matched the one David wore, kept the rest of Jack warm. Jack pressed his palms against the forward cockpit's dash to hold himself in place as the boat bucked through the cold dark night. He didn't want to test the survival suit's capability by bouncing out of the speedboat's cockpit into the bay.

So far, the storm was just wind, waves, and spray. But even so, there seemed to be no other marine traffic crazy enough to go out for a joyride. With luck, they would be safely docked at Colibri's before the storm really hit.

As they thundered north, Jack glanced toward the Golden Gate. Looking at the thing still disturbed him, for some reason.

The odd thing, though, was that although David had said the traffic northbound on the bridge was a mess, the yellow headlight stream seemed to be sliding across the bridge span as fast as ever.

Something, not just Jack's odd reluctance to look at the bridge, nagged at him. Just an aggregation of little things, really. Everything David Powell did had a purpose. Neither money nor physical nor mental energy were ever wasted. When David had mentioned that he was going to get the first aid kit out of the Bentley's trunk, he had already chirped the trunk lid open with his remote. But then David had still unlocked the driver's side door.

The only unusual item that Jack knew of that was kept in the Bentley's tidy and pristine cabin was the loaded pistol that Paul Eustis kept in the glove box.

Paul had put it in there two years before.

That had been a day after Paul had been driving David and Jack to another of the interminable hearings about the bathhouse renovation, nudging the Bentley through a demonstrator gaggle blocking the street in front of City Hall.

David had lowered his window to engage the angry crowd in a reasoned debate, a habit Jack had always discouraged without success. One of the protestors, just some kid, really, had thrust a pistol through the open window, pointed it between David's eyes, and pulled the trigger.

Whether the hammer had clacked down without result because the pistol was empty, or it just misfired, they never knew.

After Paul had sped the Bentley away, scattering demonstrators cursing and pounding the Bentley's fenders as they jumped aside, David had sat pale, trembling, and wide-eyed in the Bentley's rear seat.

It was the most uncontrolled emotion Jack had ever seen him display. After a few moments, David's face hardened and he whispered aloud, "What do I have to do to please these people? Kill somebody myself?"

FIFTY

As *Fianchetto*'s bow cut through San Francisco Bay toward the still-distant lights of Belvedere Island, David Powell adjusted her throttle and savored the big Hispano-Suiza's responsive change in pitch. The old engine's deep, arrogant rumble carried him back to a time before raspy modern engines had devolved from their ancestors.

Similarly, he thought, events had now borne him inexorably back into his family's past. His great-grandfather, born of the impoverished union between a failed gold rush forty-niner and a prostitute, David forgave for clawing his way to a small fortune. But even though David's grandfather and father had built that small fortune into a large one, the arrogant, unforced transgressions by which they built it had come to repel him as he matured and discovered how his family had really paid its bills.

Yet his own lifetime, playing life's multidimensional chess games by the world's rules, and gifting back to the world the fruits of honest victories, had not yet earned David the world's forgiveness for his ancestor's sins.

The gift of immortality would have—still would, he corrected himself—change everything. David knew that because he simply knew people. He had always been able to see not just his own next moves in the chess game, but everyone else's.

Except for Manny Colibri. No matter how David had tried to motivate, coerce, or outwit that enigmatic little man, Colibri had clung tight to his control of the gift of immortality that could settle David's debt to the world. It was as though Colibri played life's chess game not merely in all the dimensions that only David saw, but in some additional dimension that even David couldn't see.

And so, finally, David had been forced to play out the game in the way that his ancestors had.

But human pieces on the great board didn't move as predictably as wood or ivory. Abney misdesigned his bomb, and miswrote his suicide note. Chisolm's attempt at murder had proved mere suicide. But in the end as effective as a completed murder would have been.

David looked over at Jack Boyle, clinging to *Fianchetto*'s hull, fully concentrated on the objective ahead, where his daughter waited.

David frowned. As a child, his favorite chess pieces were the knights, because while limited in range their L-shaped ability to leap over any obstacle infused them with an eccentricity that delighted him.

On David's chessboard, Jack had always been his knight. Tenacious to the point of pugnacity, undeterred by any obstacle, and as solid and incapable of duplicity as if he were carved from ivory.

Yet when Abney's failure had forced David to improvise and reshape the board in a new strategy, the adjustment seemed elementary. Like any sound combination, involving Jack accomplished multiple objectives. Frame the Catholic Church *and* resuscitate his loyal knight. But the loyal knight had refused the obvious offer of Abney's connection to the Catholic Church. And had forced David to risk advancing Chisolm, another pawn. That offered pawn sacrifice had succeeded. But now Colibri, somehow, had returned to the board, threatening a game already won.

David pressed his elbow against his waist and felt the pistol through the survival suit's spongy neoprene. There was still time, space, and material enough to salvage not just a draw but checkmate in this most immortal of all games. Although for the first time in David's life he was being forced to step onto the board personally.

David looked again at Jack, who sat, chin out, eyes slitted against the storm, and oblivious to the frigid rain coursing down his wind-reddened cheeks.

As David's grandfather had taught David at the chessboard, you had to sacrifice pieces to win. Even if they were your favorites.

FIFTY-ONE

Manuel Colibri sat on his sectional in his great room as he sipped the tea that Kate Boyle had made for the two of them. The house had shuttered the view out to San Francisco Bay in response to the deteriorating weather, and the big room was silent, except for the rasp of Manny's own breathing in his ears.

The simple human comforts of a shower and a clothing change, combined with the aid kit's last gasp, both relaxed Manny and eased his pain. He had answered Kate's questions for the last ten minutes. But after a thousand years, this body would last only perhaps a day or two longer.

The lander's first aid kit had never been intended to sustain a retemplated body at all. Even as he had modified the kit, it had barely repaired and rejuvenated this peculiar body enough to survive a thousand years of normal wear and tear, as well as to survive four, now five, assassination attempts, two shipwrecks, and other accidents and violent crimes too numerous to recall.

Kate Boyle pointed toward the empty, lit glass wall safe. "So the necklace that the little girl gave you was the last object that you kept in there?"

Manny nodded as he watched his inquisitive guest. By eavesdropping over the few days since he had made his way home, he had come to know and to trust Kate Boyle, and Ben Shepard, and their respective strengths and weaknesses, more than he had trusted any human beings he had known in years. And now Kate's perceptiveness and insight had led her to know Manny in a way that no human being, even Manny's wives, had been able to know or understand the truth of him over the course of the last thousand years.

Kate said, "After the others were killed when the lander crashed you became Manco Capac. You founded the Incan nation."

"Yes." Then Manny shook his head. "But I was no nation builder. It took me years just to learn to breathe properly. Fortunately, God's child passes the audition just by showing up. The Inca were barely more than a handful of matriarchal family groups, at least during the early years of my so-called reign."

"But what happened during a thousand years that took you from god to janitor to billionaire?"

Manny shrugged. "The 'Capac' part of Manco Capac means 'warlord.' That was never my idea. You—we—are a violent species. After the second time my rivals murdered my wife in my bed while they were trying to kill me, I realized that in human society the nail that stands the tallest is the one that gets hammered down."

"Better live janitor than dead god?"

"Basically, yes. Moving on from one identity to the

next is simple once you've done it a few times. And in the days before photography and fingerprinting there was nothing to it. And I wasn't giving up much. Frankly, the difference in real amenities between kings and peasants, especially a peasant immune to human disease and senescence, wasn't much until the last hundred fifty years or so. But securing my personal safety didn't secure me against heartbreak. Kate, I have buried eleven wives here on Earth. I loved every one of them with all of my heart."

"Wives? Then you—?"

Manny smiled. "My marriage equipment works indistinguishably from any other human male's. Except that the only females my sperm could have impregnated died the day the lander crashed. I did raise sixty-one children, who my wives had by other men, either before or during our marriages. I loved each of my children as though they were my own. And I mourned their deaths as deeply as if they had been my own. And as deeply as I mourned the deaths of my wives. So greatly, in fact, that I haven't chosen that path for the last hundred years."

"But there were good times? Interesting times? You met Franz Kafka. Did you meet anybody else I'd recognize?"

Colibri shrugged, cast his eyes to the ceiling. "After the *San Lorenzo* grounded in 1588, I made my way to England via the Netherlands. It took a few decades to become fluent in English and comfortable with the customs. I worked as a valet along with another young man. He was a subsizar—a student valet working his way through school. Rather in the mold of your father and of Ben Shepard. My coworker, as he would be called today, possessed an extraordinary mind. That was in the early 1660s. At Trinity College, Cambridge."

Kate's eyes widened. "You and Isaac Newton did other peoples' laundry together?"

Colibri shrugged again. "Among other jobs. Flush toilets as we know them were then still nearly a hundred years in the future. Kate, I assure you, nostalgia for mankind's environmentally unintrusive past is misplaced."

Kate wrinkled her forehead. "Wait. Did you—?"

Manny smiled and shook his head. "No. I may have made a couple of suggestions about the calculus. There is a certain commonality to mathematics as a descriptor of the physical universe. But gravitation and the rest were strictly Isaac's."

"You're not impressed with mankind's past. But according to Nolan Liu you weren't impressed with the direction of our future, either. Is that why you stepped out of the shadows and took over Cardinal? To buy up all the life-extension patents and retard life-extension research? The way a patent on the toggle harpoon could have retarded whaling?"

Colibri sipped his tea, then smiled. "Over a thousand years I have learned a few things. But if you're suggesting that the sun god is angry with his children . . ." He shook his head. "Let's be clear, Kate. I'm a castaway, not a policeman sent by the interstellar community. There *is* no 'interstellar community.' How could there be when it would take some members of the community three thousand years to travel to the annual potluck supper? I was a sort of tour bus driver. I transported members of our race, who elected an expatriate lifestyle from among various alternative styles created to relieve population pressure. The Curious, as they're called, embark on a one-way journey to continue their long lives in distant and often unknown places. They aren't colonists. They aren't conquerors. They're just more curious than the other, incurious citizens who stay home."

"But your civilization does know something about what else is out there, beyond your home?"

Colibri nodded. "A galaxy's countless civilizations do come into contact with one another from time to time. Over enough time, a body of shared knowledge develops about how civilizations progress. And about the consequences of taking one critical fork in the developmental road, instead of another."

"So the galaxy isn't against us?"

"Nor is the galaxy for us. Kate, the galaxy doesn't care about us any more than the blades of grass on Ben Shepard's Kansas prairie care about another blade of grass. The only ones who care about mankind's future are mankind."

"But mankind is approaching a critical fork in the road?"

Colibri nodded. "Several. After thousands of years of bashing one another with war clubs and musket balls, nuclear weapons have given us the power to destroy ourselves. Now, within the next century, we will face an additional challenge. We will either tear ourselves apart because some of us can live forever while some of us can't, or we will adapt to that reality."

"There's the Singularity. Maybe we'll adapt by uploading ourselves into computers."

"A minority of civilizations have made that choice. The problem for sentient beings living as disembodied electrons in a machine is that the beings *know* that.

And they are as dissatisfied as you or I are dissatisfied by a video game compared to unscripted, palpable reality. Most civilizations that have tried to perpetuate themselves inside machines, even mobile machines, have perished."

"And all the things that worry Nolan Liu about human immortality? Unjust inequality of lifespans, perpetuation of evil, the dilemma of population stabilization, cultural stagnation. They're real?"

"I'm afraid they're very real. Compared to some sort of galactic norm, human technology remains way ahead of human social development."

"What are our odds?"

"As things stand? No better than fifty-fifty. Give us a hundred years to learn to live with ourselves, and with our planet, and we may have a better shot."

"So that's why the Golden Gate Project? Lock down life extension until we've had breathing space? Until we can handle living forever?"

"That was my vision. Obviously, this body won't last long enough to see whether it would have worked."

"What did your body look like before?"

Manny shrugged again. "I was born into the sea. But don't visualize whales or dolphins. To me, cetaceans are only marginally cuter than they are to native humans like you. Think of me as having been a person-sized tadpole with two arms that end in prehensile appendages, and two eyes that face forward, just like yours. And of course equipment to speak and hear and breathe within a liquid medium."

"You feel like a cockroach in this body? Like in the Kafka story?"

Manny paused for breath. He felt himself weaken,

even compared to his weakness when his conversation with Kate had begun. "Once I did feel grotesque, yes. At this moment I feel as human as, and even more vulnerable than, you do."

"If somebody blew me off a bridge I'd feel vulnerable too. So you've been hiding out here trying to figure out who tried to kill you?"

"And hiding every time I've had visitors. Until you. I feel as though I know you."

"Because you've been snooping through my phone? And through Ben's?"

"As you discovered, Victor Carlsson was reluctant to build in backdoor eavesdropping capability. Not because he cared about privacy but because he cared about selling phones."

"So he tried to have you killed?"

Manny shook his head. "Victor correctly never saw me as a threat to his ambitions. And as a practical matter he got what he wanted, a C-phone as unhackable as his competitors' phones were. Which means that *I*, and only I, did have access to his phone. So I'm certain that he didn't try to bump me off. And that was a wise choice on his part. Any new owner will find him insufferable and he knows it."

"My dad doesn't believe your phones are unhackable. So he doesn't carry a phone. And it turns out he's right. Obviously you couldn't snoop on him."

"I couldn't snoop on David Powell, either. He carries an Apple iPhone. If the other brands have backdoors built in, I don't know how to open them. So you and Ben were my window on David."

Kate sat back and cocked her head. "David? Why did you need a window on David?"

"When David took me under his philanthropic wing, he was solicitous and generous. I gather that he's been that way with many up-and-coming entrepreneurs. He offered suggestions about estate planning, addressed my concerns about security of some of my possessions."

"The donations?"

Manny paused for breath and nodded. "Then David approached me about accelerating, or simply acquiring outright, the Golden Gate Project. I believe he genuinely sees life extension as an unalloyed blessing. And I think he believes that bringing that blessing to mankind would expiate his ancestors' sins in a way that even the most generous conventional philanthropy can't. The view that life extension would be an unalloyed blessing is hardly radical. ELCIE promotes it every day."

"But you turned David down?"

"Repeatedly and firmly. Although I certainly didn't tell him *why* I thought I knew the future better than most people did. My last experiment with honesty as the best policy almost got me burned at the stake." He paused, sighed, and closed his eyes. "But the result here appears to have been equally dire."

Kate frowned. "You think *David Powell* may have had something to do with the bombing?"

"The notion only seems irrational until you study it. Much of human nature, and of nature itself, is like that."

Kate shook her head. "David's ancestors may have been crooks, but he's been nothing but nice to everybody I know." Kate gritted her teeth. "But if you're right, I should tell you that I may have screwed up while you were in the shower just now."

Kate's phone trilled, so loud in the silence that she

jumped. She eyed her phone's screen. "This call is from Ben Shepard. Is it alright with you if I take it?"

Manny sagged back against the cushions, drowsy even from the exertion of his conversation. He waggled his hand and nodded without opening his eyes.

Manny listened as Kate put Ben on her phone's speaker.

Ben said, "Kate? I know you want your space—"

"Are you back in D.C. already?"

"I'm sitting with Mick in the Buena Vista. Petrie's plane's still in D.C. waiting for the storm here to pass through. Kate, I need to ask you something very important."

"And I need to tell you something more important."

"Kate, you said that your father was worried about telling David Powell about the connection between the Catholic Church and Manny Colibri's murder?"

Manny sat up and watched while Kate gathered Manny's tea mug and her own, along with her phone, and stood. She said, "Yeah. Ben, about that murder—"

"You're *sure* Jack didn't mention the Church connection to David before this morning? And David was surprised?"

"Positive. Dad practically stole the files from under David's nose. Ben—"

"Stay with me on this, Kate. Like Mick said earlier tonight, sometimes people act like they know things after they actually knew them. Last night David Powell asked me whether I intended to 'slander a whole faith.' If your dad hadn't told him, and I was sitting on the manifesto we found in the shooter's pocket, why would David know to ask me that?"

Kate carried the two mugs and her phone to the

heated sideboard near the terrace door where she had placed the teapot, then refilled the cups. "Maybe lots of reasons. Not least of all that Petrie may have done it in the library with the candlestick."

"David Powell belongs to the country club at Lake Tahoe where the bathhouse shooter worked."

"Ben, you can quit playing Clue. Manny Colibri's alive. Injured, but alive."

"What?"

"I'm standing here pouring him tea." She held her phone out toward Manny. "Want to say hello?"

"I'm—"

"So am I. But it's true. As for all your coincidences, I'll ask David in a few minutes."

"What?"

"I called David and my dad and told them that I'm here with Manny. They're both coming over across the bay in that ridiculous speedboat of David's."

"Kate, can Manny be moved?"

"He was walking a couple minutes ago."

"And you drove there?"

"No. I parachuted in. Ben, who lit your hair on fire?"

"Kate, you and Mr. Colibri get in your car. Now. Drive to the nearest police station. Don't stop even to dial 9-1-1 until you're in the car and on the way."

Manny saw the French door that led in from the terrace, alongside which Kate stood, and which had unlocked when it detected her proximity, open.

Kate froze as a hand, at the end of a bulky red sleeve, thrust through the open door and the pistol that the hand held was pressed behind Kate's ear. The gunman's other hand reached around from behind Kate, grasped her phone, and thumbed it off.

FIFTY-TWO

Cold metal pressed behind Kate's ear and nudged her to turn around slowly as she recognized the newly-familiar smell of gun oil.

Kate turned and faced David Powell. His grim face was two feet from hers, and the black, glistening pistol that he gripped was pointed between her eyes.

Beyond the open door through which David had entered Kate saw her father out on the terrace. He stood stiffly, wind-driven mist fluttering the baggy, red, hooded neoprene survival suit that he wore, twin to David's. Jack's hands were tied in front of him with nylon rope, a blue bruise showed above his left temple, and a cord tied around her father's neck was also tied around David's waist.

Kate said to David, "What the hell?"

Jack croaked, "Katy, stay calm. Do as he tells you. This will be alright."

"Dad! What happened?" Kate's heart pounded.

Jack said, "He coldcocked me with the pistol when

418

we got out of the boat. Next thing I knew I was on the ground with my hands tied with mooring ropes."

Crap. Shepard was right again.

Jack said, "Katy, I knew David was manipulating me from the beginning. That's just what he does. But this time I didn't see why he was doing it."

Kate narrowed her eyes at David Powell. "You dick. When that poor vet you brainwashed didn't leave behind a body and conspiracy evidence, you had to find somebody who would look for both of them. But somebody you knew. Somebody who had the smarts to figure things out. And somebody who was predisposed to take a flamethrower to the Catholic Church. So you used me to get my dad to do it."

Manny Colibri coughed, then spoke to be heard over the storm. "David, I suspected you from the moment my car hit the water. But I still don't understand how your simple plan went so wrong."

"Manny, once you turned me down and I had a peek at that trust document, the plan was obvious and, as you say, simple. But even a simple plan can't survive execution by simple people. Particularly when they don't know they're part of a plan. Poor, suicidal Abney's bomb failed to leave your body behind. His suicide note failed to explicitly implicate the Catholic Church."

David waved his pistol and herded Kate and Manny onto the covered portion of Colibri's terrace. There, David sat them, along with Jack, backs against the house wall, lined up like elementary schoolchildren during a fire drill.

Kate said, "The guy at the bathhouse last night. Obviously, you recruited him just like you recruited Abney. You're a goddam one-man CIA. But why?"

David, pistol in one hand, knelt and rummaged with his other hand through a large canvas bag that had been left just outside the terrace's door. "Why mobilize Mr. Chisolm? Because you and Mr. Shepard and your father weren't finding a body or a conspiracy fast enough."

Jack narrowed his eyes. "A good lawyer knows the answer to a question before he asks it. You knew the Church was the Cardinale Trust's beneficiary. You knew how to disqualify it. And you knew who was stupid enough to pin the blame on the mackerel snappers. But David, you son of a bitch, you actually expected Julia to be *killed* last night."

"Every plan changes on the fly, Jack. This one still works with Julia alive as well as with her dead. An attempt on the life of yet another public figure associated with life-extension research by a Catholic-brainwashed automaton will cast enough suspicion on the Church that it will be malleable. Everything was working splendidly until Manny, here, turned up earlier this evening."

David looked away momentarily, at the worsening weather, keeping his pistol trained on them. Then he consulted his phone. "We have a few minutes before the storm peaks."

Kate said, "Then what? Shoot us all when the thunder covers the noise? Because if that's the best you got you're gonna be complaining about the mattress in your cell for a long time."

David shook his head and laughed. "Jack, she has your attitude to a T. I will miss you both." He turned back to Kate. "No, Kate that is not 'the best I got.' All I need now in order to acquire Cardinal is what I needed before. Manny dead, as an apparent result of the Catholic Church's action. If the Church looks bad enough it will gladly let me quietly buy it out of an embarrassment. Without that advantage, even Powell Diversified couldn't be sure of winning the war for control of Cardinal. So when the storm reaches its height, and therefore no one is paying close attention, I will take my boat, and the three of you, out to the Farallon Islands. There your father and I will strip Mr. Colibri naked. Then we in our survival suits will hold him gently in a tidal pool until he expires from exposure, drowning, or both. When his body is discovered, the fact that he survived as long as he did will be surprising, but will hardly change anyone's mind about what and who killed him."

Jack said, "David, you know I won't do that."

"Jack, what I know is that you won't watch your daughter bleed to death." David walked to Kate and pointed his pistol at Kate's inner thigh. "If you refuse to cooperate I will shoot Kate and sever her femoral artery."

Kate said, "You're just gonna kill us both and dump us in the ocean no matter what happens. We know too much. If I leave blood all over this patio you'll have lots of explaining to do. So go ahead."

"If you insist." David pressed the pistol against Kate's leg and she clenched her teeth.

Jack said, "Christ, David! Stop! I'll do what you want. So will Katy." He turned to Kate. "Katy, as far as the world's concerned, Mr. Colibri's already dead. And he looks to me like he's going to die anyway."

David withdrew the pistol and sighed. "You see? Kate, your father is every bit as predictable as my unbalanced assassins were."

As she sat alongside her father she felt his shoulder press imperceptibly against hers. He had a plan.

Jack said, "I suppose you want Kate to tie Colibri and me up for the boat ride."

David paused. "I am making this up as I go, Jack. But I am the one who's making it up, not you. So no. Actually, Kate will *un*tie you first. Then you and Kate will carry poor Manny into the Bear Cat's cockpit. After Kate reties you, *I* will tie Manny. Gently. Rope burns on his wrists or ankles could complicate the narrative. Which I imagine you hoped for."

After Kate and Jack had settled Manny into the boat's cockpit, Jack sat down alongside the smaller man, then scooted himself against the open cockpit's far side, against, and concealing, a pouch there. From the pouch the boat's old brass flare pistol protruded. Jack's plan became clear to Kate.

As Kate tugged the buddy line from her father's survival suit's chest pocket, then wrapped it around his extended wrists, she locked eyes with Jack and he blinked twice at her.

She tied her father's hands with exactly the same knots that had proved her the least-competent outdoorswoman in Girl Scout history.

Kate knelt in the boat's cockpit, lifted her father's bound hands, then turned her head to David. "Satisfied?"

With his pistol's barrel, David waved her to climb forward into the front passenger's seat, then tugged at Jack's tied wrists. Then David gently wrapped unresponsive Manny Colibri's wrists and ankles with mooring line.

The ridiculous thing was that if David got away with this, Manny Colibri's autopsy would raise so many questions that David's grand plan might fail anyway. Of course, telling David that would only give him time to correct his plan on the fly, which he had already done twice.

In the distance, lightning split the sky as it arced between the clouds and the Golden Gate's north tower. Thunder cracked as David cast off the boat's mooring lines then clambered into the boat's driver's seat.

Kate glanced back at Colibri's house as cold rain pelted her face and the boat pitched in ever-higher waves.

On the opposite side of the house's security wall, reflecting off the raindrops, she saw the glow of flashing blue lights. Her heart leapt. Cops! Of course! Ben had called the cops.

David peered up at the house. "Uninvited guests. Pity Manny won't be here to greet them."

As the motorboat rumbled away into the night, Kate turned and peered back at Colibri's house. Its lights, and the blue lights' flashing glow, disappeared behind sheeting rain.

Ben had tried. But now it was up to the Boyles to beat the crap out of the world, again.

Kate sat next to David Powell, nauseous and bruised as the boat bounded through massive waves toward the Golden Gate.

As Powell, pistol in hand, concentrated on the sea ahead, Kate glanced behind her. Colibri remained bleary, but her heart skipped as she saw her father wriggle one hand free, then grasp the flare pistol and slip it into his survival suit's chest pocket. Jack nodded at Kate.

The Boyle family mutiny was on. But when? The

flare pistol offered one shot. She had no idea what effect a flare would have on David, even assuming it hit him right between his lying, murdering eyes.

The Golden Gate's glow loomed ahead of them, faint through the rain, then high above them. She stared back at her father and saw his face grim in its light, then the bridge disappeared behind them into the storm. Now the only views ahead came and went like snapshots, revealed by the lightning.

Neither she nor her father knew how to drive a boat. Fighting David now would probably just precipitate a shipwreck and drown all hands. The storm was supposed to blow through fast, and at least the Farallon Islands were *land*. She sat, tense and still in the darkness and waited.

Kate didn't know how many minutes they had traveled seaward beyond the Golden Gate, through the storm and the darkness, when she glanced back at her father once again, and he nodded again. Beside her father, Colibri hadn't appeared to stir.

Kate turned and faced forward again as lightning flashed. In the waves, no more than fifty feet dead ahead of them, something huge and rounded moved across their path.

The impact as the boat struck the object hurled her forward against the dash, and her forehead slammed against it.

Kate thrashed in breathtakingly cold water, face up in howling darkness. A wave slammed her so hard that it flipped her facedown, and she swallowed so much brine that she choked and coughed it out.

She righted herself. What the hell had happened? Where was the boat? "Dad?"

She screamed again, her voice useless against the storm, and got slapped by another wave.

Beneath the water something bumped her leg.

She shuddered. White sharks. The Farallons were full of white sharks.

The object bumped her again and she screamed. This time it contacted not just her lower leg, but her side, and slid along her, smooth and alive.

She twisted and saw a black mass that rose above the waves and, in a lightning flash, smooth, cauliflowered glistening skin, that passed by oblivious to her.

In the storm and the darkness, David had rammed a migrating whale.

She reached out in a muscle-memory guided back stroke and her numbing fingers struck another object. This one was dead and hard, and narrow enough that she grasped it. She rolled to face the object and saw that it was a mahogany plank fragment perhaps two feet long.

In the frigid, heaving sea she instantly felt even colder. There was no boat to come 'round and pick her up. No boat to swim back to. The collision had shattered David's wooden speedboat. It was on its way to the bottom of the Pacific.

What had the guide, on the boat that carried the robot, told Bowden, the coroner? Unprotected in this water, the cold that Kate already felt would kill her in minutes. Even if a lifetime's labors in warm chlorinated pools had left her a strong enough swimmer to keep herself afloat.

The whale was gone now, and she was totally alone in the Pacific Ocean's black vastness.

She thought she detected a flicker of light and her heart skipped. The light flashed again. She stroked to a wave's crest, saw the flicker a third time, and swam toward it, harder.

The water-activated strobe on the shoulder of her father's survival suit was faint, and had only guided her to him from a few yards away. But when she reached him, as he lay on his back, paddling, in the waves, she clung to the buoyant red suit and sobbed.

Jack had gripped unconscious Manny Colibri, and he floated face-up against Jack's body. Jack's right arm was laced under Manny's arm and across the smaller man's chest, while Jack paddled with his left arm.

Kate shouted, "What about David?"

Jack, his head shrouded in the suit's rubber hood, shook it. "He went flying when the bow hit the calf. The hull just ran up and over the whale's back. Then the *boat's* back just broke, and it shattered into pieces. The cow was seaward of her calf. I don't know whether she was hurt."

"I hope Powell's already in hell. Dad, can you swim?"

"I don't think so, honey. But this suit floats. Katy, what are you doing?"

"Hooking your buddy line to Manny, and to me."

"Why?"

"I'm gonna tow you both to shore."

"That's impossible."

"That's the only plan I got, Dad."

"Honey, if you can swim for it, just do it. Maybe somebody will pick us up."

"Dad, don't be stupid." Stupid is my department now.

The cold had completed the work of numbing her flesh. Now it had begun to eat her bones.

Kate Boyle had not swum further than from one side of a resort pool, to reach a *pina colada* on the other side, since her fingers had contacted the touch pad at the end of her last collegiate race.

Now, she would attempt to swim miles through frigid waves so high that she couldn't see their tops. And while towing the weight of two bodies that might as well already be dead.

When she topped the first wave crest she glimpsed, through a break in the storm, the red, flashing beacons atop the Golden Gate's towers.

They were so far away that, even though the distance between the towers was eight tenths of a mile, the beacons seemed to have merged into a single crimson dot.

She plummeted into the wave's trough, climbed the next one, and this time the bridge's lights were completely obscured by the storm's dark barrier. The lights were extinguished as completely as was her hope.

Maybe Ben had been wrong, and Manny Colibri had been right. The Golden Gate wasn't just a bridge. The Golden Gate was a metaphor for the end of life.

FIFTY-THREE

"The waves are ten feet high, Mick!" Ben clung two-handed to the grab bar as he stood exposed to the storm on the port side of SFPD Marine 1's fly bridge. Cold, wind-lashed rain streamed across the clear goggles that Ben wore, and the dark night was a blur illuminated only by the boat instruments' glow and the occasional lightning flash.

Each wave seemed to tip the boat back on its stern, then pass, and plunge the boat's bow deep into the sea, over and over. Relentlessly, the boat's big diesels, buried deep in its hull, drove it west through the storm, toward the Pacific Ocean beyond the Golden Gate Bridge.

Mick peered through the rain coursing over his own goggles, and he leaned left as he clung to the boat's wheel. "I make those waves twelve to *fifteen* feet high, Mr. Shepard. I hope you're right about all this!"

As soon as the call that Ben had made to Kate at Colibri's had dropped, and she had failed to answer two redials, Ben had forced Mick to run with him to Hyde Street Pier and Marine 1. By the time they were aboard the boat, Ben's DHS clout and insistence prodded one of Belvedere Island's on-duty police officers who Ben phoned to visit Manuel Colibri's home. The officer had reported Kate's Corolla parked on the driveway apron inside the estate's security fence, the house lights on, two mugs of warm tea on a sideboard, and otherwise nobody home and nothing amiss.

Ben shouted back, "I'm right about enough of this, for sure."

The MLB 47 passed beneath the Golden Gate, into the darkness and toward the less-sheltered waters beyond.

Ben snugged his life vest, then tightened the chin strap on the crash helmet he wore. He tugged at the heavy weather harness, strapped over his waterproof coverall, which secured him to a D-ring on the bridge's side rail. The vest, helmet, harness, and coverall were twins to the ones that Mick wore. Mick's caution announced to Ben that, however underutilized Marine 1 had been during Ben's previous trips around San Francisco Bay, tonight's conditions were pushing the motor lifeboat to its design limits.

Mick said, "Well, if you're wrong, I think they call this piracy."

Ben shook his head. "No. Piracy has to be perpetrated on the high seas. We're in jurisdictional waters of a sovereign power. I think this is grand theft."

"Well, that's much better. Ben, either way, if it turns out that Kate and Mr. Colibri just took a walk, the department won't call it early retirement when I leave."

"Well, I'm AWOL from a national news crew and a

cabinet secretary, myself. Mick, Kate and Mr. Colibri didn't take a walk. The only acquisition target in the world that would justify the cash that Powell Diversified was holding is Cardinal Systems. But every investment banker on Earth knew Cardinal wasn't for sale. And it wouldn't be for sale as long as Manny Colibri was in charge. Only somebody who knew Manny Colibri wasn't *going* to be in charge would plan differently. And last night David Powell slipped and let me know that he knew the Catholic Church stood between him and Cardinal, even if he got rid of Manny Colibri."

"That doesn't mean he's on his way to the Farallons."

"David needs two things to get his plan back on track. One, Colibri's dead body. Two, Colibri's body found dead in a place and due to a cause consistent with the Church's involvement in Colibri's murder. Like you said, that means the body has to turn up in the Farallon Islands. And the perfect time to drown Manny Colibri and leave him washed up there is when the weather's so lousy that no one will be watching."

"If he plans for Kate and her father to disappear too, we may already be too late."

Ben peered up at the radome atop the mast behind them. "The radar show you anything?"

Mick shook his head. "Nothing that could be them."

"They couldn't have vanished without a trace."

Mick regripped the wheel. "Tug called the *Conestoga* vanished without a trace in rough seas near here in 1921. They didn't even identify the wreck 'til four years ago."

Ben shook his head. "Some crappy little tugboat sinking a hundred years ago means they've sunk?"

"I'm just telling you no small craft shows on the

radar. And that crappy little tugboat was a state-of-the-art one-hundred-seventy-foot-long oceangoing tug bound for Hawaii with a trained U.S. Navy crew of fifty-six."

"Any other good news?"

"GPS says we just passed Point Bonita lighthouse."

"What's that mean?"

"That we're out of the Golden Gate Channel now in the unsheltered Pacific ocean."

"Stop telling me this stuff."

"Stop askin'."

Ben shut up and squeezed his grab bar tighter.

As they thundered along Ben peered out into the port side darkness while Mick kept focused ahead and to starboard.

Suddenly, lightning flashed, the diesels' roar changed pitch, and the boat slowed.

"Mick! Don't slow down!"

Mick pointed ahead. "There's something out there." He reached past the wheel with his left hand. "I'm gonna hit the spotlights."

Two vast bulks, smooth and reflecting the MLB's forward-facing spotlights, loomed amidst the waves in the near distance.

Ben said, "Whales?"

"The calf's back's been gored. But look at the cow."

"Oh jeez." Ben shook his head. "No. No."

A splinter of brown mahogany plank protruded from the larger whale's flank like a harpoon.

"How bad do you think, Mick?"

"Can't say. Those old woodys are solid. But if Powell was running as fast as that rumrunner could go..."

Mick shrugged. "That cow may be wearin' the biggest piece of that boat that's left."

"Kate's close by, then."

"Sure." Mick paused. "I'll turn on all the lights. You get the handheld spotlight from the starboard stowage bin. And we got FLIR."

Ben raised his eyebrows. "Forward Looking Infrared? On a police boat?"

"Eat your hearts out, Coasties. I'll try to maneuver in some kind of pattern so it'll do us some good. And I think I better radio this in now. The Coasties respond to distress calls, even when they come from pirates and boat thieves better equipped than they are."

Ben turned to detach his harness so he could climb down to the deck to get the spotlight, but Mick caught his elbow and spun Ben back to face him. "Ben. There's no telling how far these two whales have moved away from the spot where the boat hit them. A Gray can make ten miles an hour if she's trying to get away from something. And we don't know how long any survivors have already been in the water. That water's deadly cold. And this sea is worse than rough."

Ben stared at Mick as he swallowed a lump in his throat. "You're saying..."

Mick paused, then he released Ben's arm and laid his hand on Ben's shoulder. "I'm sayin' we'll stay here all night if we need to. And all day, every day too, for as long as you want, son."

Ben turned again to leave the bridge and Mick pointed at the harness attachment D ring on the bridge rail to which Ben's line was attached. "Keep reattaching your heavy weather belt as you go. 'Cause I can't stop steerin' to come fish you out or we'll capsize."

FIFTY-FOUR

For Kate, lucidity was now an infrequent visitor. Sleep and warmth, however, were old friends who waved her toward them, whispering in the darkness just beyond her vision. She knew that she was cold, but she could not specifically feel cold. In fact, she could not be sure that her limbs were there to feel or to move.

Except that she was counting something. One, two…

She was counting something. One, two. Two. There were two people with her somewhere who depended on her to keep counting. One, two—after two there was more. She knew that. She just didn't know what.

She rose and fell and as she rose and fell she counted. One, two. For some reason that was important.

She rose and there was a light.

She fell, and the light was gone. But the light meant something.

The next time she rose she saw the light again. Faint, distant. The light triggered lucidity, and also what she vaguely remembered as an adrenaline rush.

The light, faint and distant, meant there was someone or something there in the darkness in addition to her.

The shore? Or a vast ship bearing down upon her blindly, to crush and drown her? Or rescue? Two. Two strokes. Two people attached to her as if by an umbilical cord. Her father. Her father was attached to her by a rope. The rope she had tied badly on purpose. So the Boyle family could mutiny.

The pistol. The flare gun. Her father had taken the flare gun.

Kate rolled over to backstroke and saw her father afloat on his back, a few feet distant, connected at the end of the buddy line that attached him to her and to the other guy. The other guy was somebody she knew. The barely visible strobe light on the shoulder of her father's blubbery red suit was as weak and as weary as he looked. The sea tossed both of the men, moment to moment, from wave crest to trough and back again.

She managed to reel them in to her, hand over hand, her limbs clumsy and numb. Her father's face poked skyward out of the opening in the suit's hood, his skin chalk and his eyes vacant.

"Dad?"

He slid his eyes in her direction and stared. He blinked, said nothing.

"Dad, do you still have the flare gun?"

He didn't answer.

She pulled herself closer to him, clawed open the flap that secured the suit's chest pocket, then thrust her hand inside, but withdrew her hand empty. Her hand was nearly useless now, no more able to flex and grasp than a raw pork loin that someone had sewn to the end of her arm. Again she thrust and her hand came out empty. Then on the third try she grasped something.

When she saw the gun's tubular barrel in her hand, she tried to scream for joy, but the sound died in her throat.

Kate moved the pistol deliberately, from one numb hand to the other, held it close to her face, and examined it. There was a flare cartridge the size of a fat sausage inside the pistol's squat metal barrel. A spring loaded hammer at the barrel's closed end had to be cocked, then the user would point the pistol's open end at the sky, pull the trigger, and send up a flare. If one could stab a dead finger attached to a dead hand inside the metal loop that guarded the trigger.

She transferred the one-shot pistol to her right hand and pressed the pistol's grip into her palm, moving as cautiously as if the gun might explode.

She hissed through clenched teeth as she forced her stiff fingers to close around the pistol's grip.

A wave pounded her shoulder so hard that it stunned her. The pistol spun free, hung, tumbling slowly in the spray above the waves, then splashed into the heaving ocean and vanished.

She thrust her hand beneath the surface, screaming. There was nothing.

She sobbed, pounded the waves with one half-formed fist. It just wasn't fair.

"Kate?"

The faint voice was not her father's, but it was familiar.

She turned her head.

Colibri bobbed alongside her father, his dark eyes tired but alive.

He lifted his right hand out of the water.

From his right hand the flare gun swung, dangling from his little finger, which was entangled in the gun's trigger guard loop.

Kate shrieked, paddled a stroke to Colibri, and grasped the flare pistol with two hands.

Unable to paddle, she sank beneath the waves into total blackness. Arms upraised out of the water as she sank, she felt for the pistol's hammer, cocked it back with her thumb, and pressed the trigger.

It seemed nothing happened. The flare could have been a dummy. It could be wet. Or she hadn't done it right.

Then she felt the pistol kick back against her palm and red light flashed above her head.

She scissor kicked once, broke through to the surface and as she gulped a breath saw the flare arc, glowing red, up into the sky. Before she could draw a second breath, it plummeted back into the waves and disappeared.

Around her, the storm's howling darkness remained impenetrable. The waves remained brutish and random. And the cold simply remained. Nothing had changed.

She resumed her strokes, even as she felt the rush of adrenaline, and of alertness, and of hope, ebb.

One, two.

One . . .

She couldn't remember what came after one anymore. And she didn't care.

FIFTY-FIVE

On the motor lifeboat's heaving fly bridge, Ben clung to the handheld spotlight with one hand and to the port side grab bar with the other. He turned the spotlight in the direction of the red spark that he thought he had glimpsed from the corner of his left eye.

His straining eyes, half blind behind rain-smeared goggles, got scant help from the tiny cone of illumination that the handheld spot jabbed at the darkness. The boat's other lights created a pathetic island of light amid waves that soared twelve feet between trough and crest. Of the array of antennae and equipment that sprouted from the boat's mast platform behind and above his head, only the searchlights were worth anything in this maelstrom, and they weren't worth much.

Still, he was sure the flash that he had seen hadn't been a trick of light played by the goggles.

He lurched across the bridge deck to Mick and shouted in his ear. "Mick, did you see it, too?"

Mick stared ahead, both hands gripping the motor

lifeboat's wheel. "Can't see much but straight ahead, Mr. Shepard. Port side has to be your territory."

"Turn the boat. I saw something."

"Saw what?"

"A red light. A flare maybe."

"Where away?"

"Left and behind us. Eight o'clock."

"Coming to port, aye."

"Well? Do it!"

Mick adjusted the big, horizontal wheel minutely. "Mr. Shepard, I did my master chiefin' in the engine room, not on the bridge. I'm not the helmsman Captain Ahab was. And I don't want us endin' up where he did."

"Mick, please."

Mick said, "Long as I keep the bow into the swells, she can ride a twelve-foot sea. But if I'm careless, and a big wave takes us abeam, she'll roll on her back like a mutt with fleas."

Ben clasped his hands. "Mick, I know Kate's alive out there. I can feel her. I'm begging you, turn the boat. Turn the boat now!"

Mick sighed, then adjusted the wheel. "This boat's designed to go straight. She doesn't turn fast no matter how much we want her to." Mick pushed the starboard throttle forward and throttled back the port engine. "She'll turn tighter if I steer with the throttles *and* the rudders."

The heaving boat began to pivot around its center, and for an instant the deck tilted beneath Ben's feet. Then the MLB leveled.

Mick whispered, "Atta girl."

Boom!

The boat heeled onto its port side. Ben's viewpoint

went in an instant from upright to prone, his shoulder struck the bridge rail, and then he was somersaulting in slow motion under shockingly frigid water. He tried to gasp in a breath and got a throat full of sea water.

Submerged, Ben thrashed and spit blindly for what felt like minutes.

Then, as though a great hand had hoisted him, he was out of the water, gulping air, tumbling.

He struck something solid and found that he lay facedown, straddling the fly bridge's port rail. He rolled back inside the bridge's confines, fell onto the fly bridge's deck, and sat, coughing, with his back against the bulkhead.

Mick sat opposite him, gasping.

"Mick. We capsized?"

Mick pointed at his throat and nodded. Then he coughed and said, "Wave took us abeam. Boat jerked us back up like a couple puppets by the heavy weather harnesses when she righted."

"How long were we under?"

"Book says she rights in six to twelve seconds. Felt longer to me." Mick pulled himself back into the starboard coxswain's chair.

"Are we sinking?"

Mick peered at the instrument panel, frowned, then pressed his palm to the panel. "I can feel the dewatering pumps running. But they're electric. The diesels are dead."

"Why wouldn't they be dead?"

Mick shook his head. "They're designed to run *upside down* for at least thirty seconds." He frowned deeper. "The rudders can do a little to keep her bow into the swells. But without maneuvering power, you and I'll be takin' another cold shower momentarily. And I don't know how many rollovers Textron built into her. Ever seen a diesel up close?"

"I've worked on combines since I was five."

Mick faced the boat's bow and grasped the wheel with both hands. "Go make Kansas proud, Mr. Shepard. And be quick."

Ben felt his way down the ladder from the fly bridge, slipping on its rain-slicked rungs, unclipping and reattaching his harness as he went. In one moment he expected to be swept away. In the next he expected to be pinned beneath the capsized boat and drowned.

When he staggered into the survivor's compartment and secured the hatch behind him, he realized that the electrical system may have been intact, but the interior lights were off. He groped his way deeper and deeper through the boat's dark, unfamiliar interior spaces, guided only by the handheld spotlight's beam.

The engine room resembled more an engine crypt, a tiny pit, at or beneath the waterline, in the boat's stern. The engine room was accessed through a tiny, angled hatch that led back and down from the survivor's compartment. While the boat's dewatering pumps may have done their jobs admirably by Mick's standards, Ben found himself ankle-deep in sloshing seawater. Head bent and crouching, Ben used one hand to steady himself against one of the tiny, pitching compartment's bulkheads while he aimed the spotlight with the other.

He examined the two diesels. Volvos. He shifted his right foot, and slipped on something on the deck, invisible beneath the water. He bent, fished the object from the cold brine, examined it by the spotlight's beam, and breathed, "Aha!"

When Ben finally clambered back up the exterior ladder to the fly bridge, he clipped his heavy weather harness's line to its D-ring as Mick yelled over his shoulder. "Well?"

"I slipped on a wrench down in the engine compartment. There was a toolbox sliding loose on the deck. Either the box wasn't secured, or it broke loose and spilled when we capsized. It probably knocked an alternator wire loose. I disconnected everything, tried to blow things dry, reconnected them, then reset the breakers. Not rocket science."

"Good. We don't have time for rocket science. That's on me. I was workin' on the port engine when you phoned and I didn't police up my mess before I came to see you."

Ben pointed to the controls. "Well?"

Mick pressed the diesels' starters.

Rrrrr.

Rrrr.

Mick whispered, "Come on! Come on!"

On the third try both diesels coughed, then sputtered, then rumbled to life. As the engines idled, Mick clapped Ben's shoulder. "Close enough to rocket science, Mr. Shepard."

Ben shouted, "Any other damage?"

Mick frowned as he eyed the magnetic compass forward of the starboard steering station, and oriented the boat toward the heading where Ben had reported the light.

Mick said, "The diesels are balky, but for the moment we've got engine power. We've got lights. We can maneuver. I expect we can even make coffee. But whatever we do now, we may have to do it on our own. Textron don't guarantee the third party electronics. Radio's gone. So's the FLIR and the rest of it. So's my phone. What about your phone?"

Ben dug inside his rubberized coverall, then through the soaked pockets of his clothing underneath, until he retrieved his C-phone. The screen lit at his touch, and he pumped his fist. But after a few seconds he frowned into the screen's light. "No service. No phone, no text, no internet. The internal apps and widgets work fine. We can take selfies all night."

Mick nodded. "Get to the gunwale and look sharp, then. Let's rescue some people and take their pictures."

"There!" Ben's heart skipped and he pointed. In the distance a tiny light flickered. It shone, then disappeared, then reappeared, as it rose and fell with the furious swells.

When Mick brought the boat close enough, Ben fumbled down the ladder to the deck, and then to the starboard side recovery well, a notch as long as a human body, cut down into the boat's deck rail. When kneeling in the recovery well, a rescuer on deck was barely two feet above the waves, and could reach down and pull in a person floating in the water alongside the boat.

Ben saw three persons out there in the waves. Just tiny, bobbing heads, really. One, the source of the flickering light, floated face-up, wearing one of the red survival suits that Ben had seen, so many lifetimes before, amid people wearing tuxedos and gowns and listening to chamber music. A feeble strobe light winked from the suit's shoulder.

The other two inert people in the water looked unprotected against the sea.

When the distance to the three of them closed to ten yards, Ben realized that the person in the suit was Jack Boyle, and that Jack clung to the other two with an arm around each as he floated. One of the others was dark-headed. That had to be Manuel Colibri.

The third person was Kate. She lolled, her skin luminous white in the night, her eyes closed, and her head laid back against her father's chest.

Ben grasped the safety line that secured him to the boat, then leaned out and cupped his hands around his mouth. "Kate!"

He could scarcely hear his own voice above the storm. There was no response.

Ben gathered up a life ring, secured it by a line to a D-ring in the hull, and frisbeed it, two handed. It landed two feet from Kate. He thrust both fists in the air. "Yeah!"

It was the most accurate throw he had made in his life. "Kate! Kate, grab it!"

The three heads bobbed in the waves, motionless, unresponsive, unconscious at best. The waves slapped the life ring away from them.

Ben shook his head as tears welled in his eyes. As the corners of his mouth turned down, his lip quivered. Tears poured out and mingled with the cold rain that coursed down his cheeks.

After all this. After all he had done, he had done too little. Again. "No. No."

He peered down into the heaving, dark water. He narrowed his eyes as he hated the water like it was an evil, living thing.

His heart pounded and a cold mass seemed to swell in his stomach. "Not this time." Ben drew a breath, held it, and jumped.

FIFTY-SIX

Ben stood, shivering, exhausted, drained of emotion, in Marine 1's survivor's compartment. He wore dry coveralls that he had found packed in plastic, along with blankets, in the forward compartment's locker, and he leaned against the survivor's compartment rear bulkhead as he waited for the coffeemaker secured there to brew cocoa.

The deck beneath his bare feet scarcely pitched. The storm had moved east, and the sea upon which the motor lifeboat now drifted was rapidly smoothing to glass in the darkness.

A few feet from Ben, down in the MLB-47's engine room, Mick labored to restore its still-balky diesels.

Ben turned and knelt alongside Manuel Colibri, who lay face up on the compartment's deck, swaddled in blankets. He was comatose, though his pulse, respiration, and even body core temperature measured near normal. Ben's quick physical exam of Colibri had demonstrated that he was, however, anything

445

but normal. It had taken a few minutes of shock and disbelief before all the clues he and Kate had tracked down fit together. Then Ben understood just who—or what—Manny Colibri was. So there was no telling what his vitals should have been.

Alongside Manny Jack Boyle sprawled, eyes closed. Jack was covered by his own set of blankets. Ben knelt again and pressed two fingers against Jack's throat. The pulse Ben felt in Jack's carotid artery was strong, and his body temperature continued to feel normal to the touch. With the exception of possible frost bite in his exposed fingertips, and bumps, bruises, and exhaustion, Jack seemed stable.

Ben stood, blinked and drew a breath. Then he knelt alongside Kate. Her body lay face-up atop one blanket on the deck, wrapped in two more. Her cheeks were as pure alabaster as they had appeared to him the first moment that he saw her. Her eyes were closed.

It had taken Ben untold minutes to thrash through the waves to the three of them, then to drag them back to, and then secure them, one by one, with lines alongside the pick-up port.

And then precious minutes longer to wrestle first Kate, then Colibri, then Jack in his survival suit, up to the deck's relative safety.

Ben's own numb fingers had trembled and he had shivered uncontrollably as he had stripped her wet clothes off her. Her unconscious body's core temperature had measured ninety-one degrees Fahrenheit, so hypothermic that it had ceased even to shiver.

Even after minutes of skin-to-skin warming had restored, for a time, a flickering consciousness, she stared, unable to perform so simple a task as adding one plus one when he had asked her. Then she had lapsed back to unconsciousness.

Ben bent over her and pressed his cheek against hers. "Kate?"

Her lips trembled, then she said, "Shepard, how did I get naked under these blankets?"

He smiled and felt tears well in his eyes. "You're feeling better."

"I bet you are too, you pervert." She tried to lift her head, but Ben laid his palm on her forehead and kept her flat. "Your circulatory system's probably still dilated. Stay flat or you could have a stroke."

Kate said, "How's my dad?"

"Better than you are. That survival suit was worth every penny David Powell intended to deduct for it."

"What about David?"

Ben shook his head, shrugged. "No sign."

Kate managed a weak snort. "Good. The bastard. Ben, Colibri's an alien. I mean a real one. He's been stranded on Earth for a thousand years. He thought human beings weren't ready to live to be a thousand yet. David tried to kill Manny because David thought we *were* ready, and killing Manny would be doing the human race a giant favor."

Ben nodded. "After I took a look at Manny's leg, I put things together and figured most of that out." He thumbed his C-phone, frowned. "The C-Doc app says you may not be out of the woods yet." He stood, carried an insulated hot cup of cocoa to her, then cushioned the back of her head while he dribbled the warm liquid between her lips. "Sip. Not too fast."

"The human race isn't out of the woods yet, either, I'm afraid."

Ben and Kate turned to Manny Colibri, who had struggled upright.

Ben stepped to him and peered into his eyes. "How are you feeling, Mr. Colibri?"

Manny laid a small, trembling hand on Ben's forearm. "Better than I would have been but for you, Ben. Thank you." He nodded to Kate and to Jack. "And thanks to you both, also."

Jack opened his eyes, sat up, and nodded toward the hot cup remaining on the bulkhead. "Is anybody drinking that?"

Ben handed the cup to Jack and he sipped, then Jack turned to Manny Colibri. "What kind of bullshit have you been feeding my daughter?"

Colibri smiled weakly as he pulled his blanket away to display his crystalline black leg bone. "This kind."

"Jesus fucking Christ!" Jack's eyes bugged as he choked on his cocoa.

Colibri nodded as if half-asleep. "Ben, Kate, after the additional injury caused by this ordeal I only have a few hours left, at most."

Kate shook her head. "No."

Colibri waved his hand. "After a thousand years, in *this* body alone, it's fair to say that I've lived a full life, Kate. And it's also fair to say that I'm tired. There's really only one open question for me."

Jack, his mouth still open, said, "The estate?"

Colibri closed his eyes. "Jack, after a thousand years I finally realize that I'm the wrong guy to choose mankind's future."

Ben asked, "What do you mean?"

"Mankind should decide whether mankind is ready to live forever. I'm not a god. I'm a passerby."

Jack raised his eyebrows. "You're going to leave it up to the mackerel snappers after all?"

"Point taken, Jack. Frank Cardinale was a remarkable, and generous, and devout man, and at first I simply honored his vision as a good friend should. But I had always found his philanthropic choice of the Archdiocese of San Francisco narrow and problematic. But when one expects to live forever succession planning is easily deferred."

Jack said, "Problematic? I'd call the Catholic Church's track record worse than problematic."

Colibri smiled. "I'd call the track records of *all* of mankind's controlling institutions—religion, government, the captains of industry—problematic. Mankind has excelled at blood and murder in the service of greed and of abstractions since long before the conquistadors eradicated the Inca for gold. And before men were condemned to die in the galleys for the heresy of counting the days of the year differently. For all I have watched mankind grow and all I have seen us invent, it seems that the lessons we have really learned are how to design deadlier harpoons and more efficient concentration camps."

Ben asked, "Then what's the answer?"

Colibri grimaced and doubled over.

Ben stepped quickly and laid a hand on the small man's shoulder. "Sir?"

Colibri straightened, waved Ben off. "I'm alright for the moment. Ben, do you think I might have a little water?"

Ben carried a cup to him, Colibri drank, then said, "There may be no answer. And mankind may not survive long enough to find the answer even if it exists.

I have only hours. Ideally, I would leave the decision in the hands of people who I know, and who I believe to be intelligent, courageous, and of good character."

Mick Shay stepped into the survivors' compartment, wiping his fingers with a rag. He looked around the compartment, raised his eyebrows, and smiled. "We're feeling better, I see."

Ben pointed at the engine room. "Are the diesels feeling better?"

Mick shrugged. "Another hour, maybe."

Colibri sighed. "I may not even have that hour." He pointed to the phone in Ben's hand and said, "Ben, would you mind pulling up the Cardinal InstaWill app on your C-phone? You'll find it under Self-help."

Ben wrinkled his forehead as he thumbed to the app. "Sir, I don't think—"

"On the contrary, Ben. You do think. And very well. So does Kate, as I have learned over the last few days."

Kate looked from Colibri to Ben. "What's going on?"

Manny said, "Kate, if I had been more foresighted perhaps there were alternatives. A worldwide search. Some sort of international commission. However, now my options are limited. But frankly, given world enough and time, I don't think I could make a choice in which I would have greater confidence." He looked up at Ben and nodded. "If you would be so kind?"

Ben thumbed his C-phone and the app appeared onscreen. He knelt in front of Colibri and extended the phone in front of Colibri's face so that its camera recorded the small man's words while a teleprompter-like display scrolled on the screen in front of Colibri's face, so that he could read or paraphrase. The words he spoke were then transcribed into text.

The dying interstellar voyager spoke into the camera.

"It is now the very early morning of January 11, 2020. My name is Manuel Colibri. I was born forty-five years ago in Kern County, California, as my birth certificate reflects. I now reside on Belvedere Island in Marin County, also in California. I am a single man and have no living relatives or other natural objects of my bounty. I am also trustee of the Frank Cardinale Trust, dated and effective July 1, 1983, and possess the expressly unrestricted power of appointment therein granted to me as trustee. This is my will and also my exercise of that power of appointment. It revokes all prior wills, codicils, and appointments." Colibri waved Ben to pause the recording while he motioned Mick and Jack to step into the picture, then the video and transcription resumed.

Manny continued, "I do hereby leave to my friends Katherine Marian Boyle, a single woman who resides in Palo Alto, California, and Benjamin R. Shepard, a single man who resides in Washington D.C., in equal shares all of my assets, notably and particularly all of the stock of Cardinal Systems. Ms. Boyle and Mr. Shepard shall be coexecutors of my estate and shall serve without bond."

He paused for breath. "I am presently aboard a police boat in the Pacific, a short distance west of San Francisco. It is my wish that if I die here, as I likely will, I be buried at sea immediately."

A box appeared on the screen, and Manny used his finger to sign and date.

Then he turned to Mick and Jack and asked each of them to sign as witnesses.

Each of them read out recitations that they had been asked to be witnesses, had seen Manny sign, believed him to be of sound mind and memory and under no duress, and stated their full names and addresses.

Then they signed and dated their own boxes.

Manny nodded and Ben shut off the recording, then tucked his phone back into his pocket.

Kate sat up, holding her blanket to her bare chest, and peered at Manny Colibri, openmouthed. "Are you nuts?"

Ben said, "Kate! Lie down!"

"Shepard, did you hear that?"

Mick scrambled into the forward compartment, returned with a coverall, and looked away from Kate as he handed it to her.

As Kate, beneath the blanket, wriggled into the coverall, Manny said, "Kate, if you and Ben choose to, you now have the absolute power to alter the arrangement any way you choose. No strings attached. Except I very much want you to bury me at sea immediately upon my death. An autopsy would give a whole new meaning to the expression 'illegal alien.' That could undermine my wishes."

As Kate zipped the front of her blue coverall, she said to Jack, "Dad, he can't give away a trillion dollars just like that. Can he?"

Jack shrugged. "Katy, it's in writing. It's signed. It's attested by two witnesses, who happen to be a cop and a member in good standing of the California Bar. And if anybody tries to contest it, a judge can watch the whole thing on TV and be sure the decedent meant what the document says."

Kate shook her head. "The human race doesn't want me maintaining its future. I don't even change my car's oil on time."

Clang.

Above all of them the hatch that led from the survivor's compartment to the deck slammed against its stops as the cold night air spilled across the compartment.

Silhouetted against the darkness, in the open hatchway, a figure slumped against the hatchway's edge. David Powell's bulky red survival suit dripped seawater that trickled down the two-step ladder that led into the compartment, and the suit's shoulder strobe flashed.

Powell's face was death-white in the strobe's light, his hair was plastered to his head, and blood trickled from a ragged gash in his forehead above his left eye. His right arm hung at his side, but his trembling left hand held a pistol that he pointed down at them.

Ben recognized the pistol as an M1911 service .45, the sidearm the Army had used for decades. The 9 mm Beretta that finally replaced it, that Roland Garvey had used to put the dog out of its misery so long ago, didn't hit as hard as a .45. But Ben was sure that the .45 worked just as well when wet as the Beretta had.

FIFTY-SEVEN

Jack Boyle, now seated on the survivor's compartment floor alongside Manny Colibri, turned and craned his neck so that he faced David Powell, who stood staring down at Jack, Colibri, Shepard, Mick Shay, and at Katy, who now sat up on the compartment's deck.

David clutched the pistol that he had removed from the Bentley's glove box, and that David had clubbed Jack with as the two of them walked from Colibri's pier toward his house. That moment's inattention Jack forgave himself. But his failure to have seen that David had set him up from the beginning he could not forgive himself.

Jack said, "David, give it up. It's over."

David shook his head. "Jack, you're usually brighter than this. As long as Manny, here, winds up drowned in the Farallons, and all the rest of you disappear, nothing has changed in a way I can't control."

As David focused his attention on Jack, Jack watched from the corner of his eye as the policeman, Mick

Shay, inched toward an adjustable wrench that Mick had set down when he had wiped his hands.

Bang!

David's shot struck the wrench and spun it out of Shay's reach. The ricochet glanced off the policeman's knuckles, bloodied them, then sang off the forward bulkhead.

Shay yelped and grasped his bleeding knuckles.

David grinned. "Anyone else? Lady and gentlemen, my grandfather taught me to shoot, and not just whales. I have eight more rounds; there are five of you. And I assure you I need only one apiece."

Jack turned his palms down. "David, think it through. Your grandfather, your father, taught you *that*, too. The sun comes up in a few hours. There are probably a half dozen freighters waiting to enter the bay within a few miles of us. They've probably already noted this boat on their radars. Hell, the Coast Guard has shore radars. This boat's not invisible. And if the SFPD hasn't noticed it's missing yet they will soon enough. What are you going to do if you do manage to kill us all and dump our bodies? Make a run in a stolen police boat for Canada? Mexico? Hawaii? At twenty-five miles an hour?"

David waved his pistol at Manny Colibri. "Jack, he's wrong! He was trying to hoard the Holy Grail. Do you know how many millions of lives we could prolong with that technology that he intends to sit on? Jack, I could even the score forever."

Jack said, "Then make your case to the world, David."

"Plead not guilty by reason of good intentions?" David barked a laugh. "I don't think they teach that one even at night school. Unlike you, unlike those two other misbegotten losers who failed me, I'm not easily suggestible."

Katy said, "David, you have no idea what you're talking about. On so many levels. Trust my father's insights and instincts. They've made you millions."

David's eyes were wild, now. He was weighing the truth that Jack had just told him. A simple plan had gone wrong, then gone wronger, and now was irretrievable.

David was realizing that, for the first time in his life, the remaining possible moves in this chess game all led to checkmate. And all that was left to him was to lash out at anything within his reach.

Jack saw Ben Shepard, his eyes on David's trigger finger, inch closer to David. But Ben was too far away and would have no more success than Mick Shay had.

David tossed his head, laughed again and said to Katy, "Now that is amusing, Kate. This plan would have gone smoothly *except* for your father. I made the mistake of trusting the insights of a man too blind to see his wife was dying before his eyes. As for your father's instincts? This man was so insensitive, so pigheaded, that when she needed him most to save her from herself he ran away. He might as well have driven her to the bridge himself, then pushed her off."

Jack snapped his head back at the words as though they were a physical slap. He blinked. And in that moment all the memories crashed back into the forefront of his consciousness.

He remembered the moment when he finally realized that Marian's decline, so subtle at first, was symptomatic of something more sinister. He remembered his disbelief at the initial diagnosis, his rage at the specialist at Stanford when the man had confirmed it.

And then Katy was there and he realized that the worst was only getting worse. And in his rage and his frustration at a problem that he couldn't beat the crap out of, he had run away. Not far, or for long. But he had run away, nonetheless, and it had been too far, those hours too long.

And then Jack remembered Katy as she stood there with tears streaming down her cheeks, and behind her through the big bay window the blue lights flickered as they stopped traffic on the bridge.

And he remembered the note that Kate held out to him, her fingers trembling.

Katy sat there on the police boat compartment's deck, shook her head and whispered, "Oh, Dad."

Jack saw his daughter's lip quiver. Ben Shepard inched toward David. The kid was still too far from David to reach him.

But in that moment it wasn't about distances and angles.

It was simple, irrational, rage, pent up and blind, at himself, at the world, and at the old friend gone mad who threatened to hurt Katy.

Jack spun around, then lunged up the ladder at David Powell, tackling him around the thighs. "You son of a bitch!"

David fired once, and Jack screamed at the shock as the bullet smashed his arm. Then Jack's momentum carried him and David, who toppled backwards, out onto the deck.

In the darkness, Jack sat astride David and pounded at David's face with his uninjured hand, balled into an awkward fist.

David heaved Jack off him, kicked Jack's torso. The two men wrestled, prone on the deck in the cut-away recovery well, across which Shepard had thrust them all up onto the boat.

As David and Jack struggled, Jack glimpsed Shepard, crabbing on hands and knees toward them, across the deck.

David held the pistol, but Jack grasped David's gun hand by its wrist, with his own uninjured hand, so that the pistol jerked back and forth in a mortal tug of war. The pistol fired again, then a third time.

David straddled Jack, then David tore his gun hand free and aimed the pistol at Jack's face in the instant that Shepard launched himself at David.

Shepard's shoulder struck David's back, knocking the older man's arms wide. The pistol spun through the air, splashed into the now gentle Pacific swells, and disappeared.

David staggered to his feet on the rolling deck, clutching his thigh, his fingers glistening as red as the survival suit from blood that poured from a new wound.

David, his eyes wide in astonishment, looked down at Jack. "You son of a bitch, you're not supposed to shoot me." The knee of David's injured leg buckled, he lost his balance, and toppled backward into the dark water.

FIFTY-EIGHT

Ben ignored David Powell in the water and knelt alongside Jack Boyle. The older man writhed on his back on the afterdeck, cursing through clenched teeth, and clutched his right arm above the elbow.

"Dad!" Kate screamed as she scrambled to her father. Her eyes bulged as she saw the blood pouring out of his arm between his fingers. Kate gasped, "Oh, God! Oh, God!"

Ben gently shouldered Kate aside as he said, "Okay, Jack. Let's see what we got." Ben tried to pry Jack's fingers away to examine the wound, but Jack screamed.

Jack grimaced, struggled to his feet still clutching his arm, and hissed. "I'm okay. I think the bullet broke my arm. And it feels like the bastard kicked me in the ribs, too."

Mick hurried to Ben's side, supported Jack, and said to him, "Take it easy there, young man. Let's get you back inside by the aid kit where I can dress and splint that arm and have a look at things in the light."

"Help me!" David Powell's scream drifted to Ben from the water.

Kate and Ben turned to the recovery port and stared out into the night. Ten yards from the boat Powell's shoulder strobe blinked.

As Ben unfastened a life ring from its mounting and paid out its line to fasten it to a D-ring in the rail, Kate stood in the recovery well, leaned with her hands on her knees, and shouted at David Powell. "Help *you*? Two people are dead because of you. Manny Colibri's dying because of you. You just tried to kill me and my dad, too. And now you just shot him. Stay out there and freeze to death in the dark, you fucker!"

Ben grabbed Kate by her shoulders and turned her to face him. "Kate! I know how you feel. But we can't!"

She leaned close to Ben and whispered, "I know. But we can scare the shit out of him first, can't we?"

She sighed, crossed her arms and nodded at the life ring that Ben held. "Go ahead. Throw it. But if you hit him in the head with it, I'll make it worth your while, sailor."

It took two tries before Ben got the ring within ten feet of Powell and the wounded man paddled toward it.

Aft of Marine 1, her bow now pointed south as she drifted parallel to the distant coast, a gray whale's black back rose silently out of the rolling sea. It was followed by another, then a half dozen more, then others, all undulating through the swells.

Humid breath exploded from their blowholes as they packed together and labored south. The whales parted only enough to avoid the motor lifeboat's mass, some passing to Marine 1's port, others to starboard.

The sea displaced by the whales' great bodies spread in wakes as the whales that passed between David Powell and the boat rocked it. The wakes washed the life ring back against Marine 1's hull, and simultaneously washed David Powell farther seaward.

When the last whale had vanished, the sea rolled on exactly as it had before the first one appeared. Except that the yards that separated Ben and Kate, aboard the immobile lifeboat, from David had widened into an unbridgeable chasm. He had become a pale speck on the dark sea.

Kate and Ben stared, transfixed and powerless, while he drifted away. Powell's screams dwindled to sobs and the strobe light on his survival suit faded to a spark flickering in the Pacific's black vastness. Finally all trace of David Powell vanished and the view west was only silent darkness.

Numb, Ben recovered the life ring and coiled its line. "Do you think somehow, on some level, the whales...?"

Kate shook her head as she stared. "Like Manny told me, the universe isn't against us. The universe isn't for us. The only ones who care about the human race are us."

Mick climbed up out of the survivor's compartment, stepped aft and leaned against the floatation chamber. He laid out flares from the MLB's pyrotechnics kit, then fired them, one by one, into the night. As the last flare fell, then died, just a smoke trickle on the swells, Mick stepped close to Ben as Kate stared at the darkness. She refocused her eyes on the two men, and frowned.

Mick kept an eye on Kate as he whispered, "Ben, there's a problem with Jack."

❖   ❖   ❖

Kate knelt alongside her father as he lay on the survivor's compartment deck alongside Manny Colibri. Blankets covered both men, but Jack's feet had been elevated with pillows and his arms were outside his blankets. Jack's right forearm was streaked with dried blood and his upper right arm was wrapped above the elbow in white gauze, and splinted. A blood pressure cuff wrapped Jack's left arm.

Mick leaned close to Ben. "The round that struck his right arm did break it, then exited. It must hurt like hell. I gave him a sedative."

"Bandage seems to have stopped the bleeding." Ben turned to Mick. The old sailor's face was tight. Ben frowned. "In fact it stopped the bleeding too well. What else is wrong with Jack?"

Mick shook his head. "Ben, he was complaining about a broken rib. When I checked I found an entry wound on his right side near the base of his rib cage. Barely even bleeding. Almost missed it. It was so small I thought it was just a nick from a fragment of the bullet that broke his arm."

Ben said, "There were three rounds fired. Powell caught one, the second broke Jack's arm."

Mick nodded. "There's no exit wound I can find. Jack's rib probably broke up the third bullet. He's slippin' deeper into shock every minute. His BP's so low he's gotta be leaking inside. Who knows how many pieces of that bullet cut him up, or where they wound up. Ben, it's bad."

"So what do we do?"

Mick shook his head. "We're dead in the water. We got no radio. We got no phone. I just shot up all the pyrotechnics we got. Even if somebody saw 'em, after this storm the Coasties and the emergency choppers probably got their hands full elsewhere for too long."

"Is he coughing blood?"

Mick shook his head. "And he can breathe. Wherever he's bleeding out from I don't think a lung's collapsed or his stomach's cut open."

"Anything on board we can rig to transfuse him?"

Mick shook his head. "It's a lifeboat, not a trauma center. I got some extracurricular morphine tucked away in the kit, because this ain't my first rodeo. But Ben." Mick laid his hand on Ben's arm. "This *is* Jack's last one."

The beginning of tears blurred Ben's vision as he watched Kate stroke her father's pale face and gray hair. She whispered to Jack while he gritted his teeth.

Ben said, "Mick, get me that morphine."

Ben knelt alongside Kate and peered down into Jack Boyle's taut face, while Kate looked at Ben with her lips pressed tight together.

She said to Jack, "You picked a hell of a time to recover from hysterical amnesia."

Ben said, "Jack, hang in there. Mick's working on the diesels and he sent up some flares." He held up Mick's syringe. "I've got something here for the pain. If they have to airlift you out it could get rough."

Jack nodded but waved away the syringe as he patted Ben's forearm. "You're a good man, Ben. Good men make bad liars. I know I'm dying."

Kate choked on a sob and shook her head. "Dad, no."

Jack relaxed his face. "It's alright, Katy. If any father can pick his reason, dying to save his child's as good as it gets."

Kate kept shaking her head. "No. No."

Jack said, "Maybe your mother's waiting for me. She and I both have a lot to catch up on. And now you and I are caught up, too."

"Dad, stay here. You always said heaven's crap. Bait for the suckers. A crutch for their survivors. A billion to one shot."

"I'd rather take a billion to one shot at eternity with your mother than live forever with her on one side and me on the other. Katy, the life we made together was perfect." He reached up and brushed her cheek with his fingertips. "The life we made was you."

Kate held his fingers against her cheek while her tears trickled across them.

Jack turned his head toward Manny, who lay alongside him. "Let's ask Manny. He's been telling me his story. What about it, spaceman? All those millions of civilizations. All those billions of years they lived and they died. What's the truth?"

Manny turned to Jack. "You're asking me whether the soul carries on when its time in this universe ends?" He turned his dark eyes to the compartment's ceiling, as though he saw beyond it. "Some of those civilizations out there believe it does. Some believe it doesn't. But nobody's found any empirical evidence out there yet, so none of them have ever really known. By definition the unprovable can't be proved."

Jack said, "Where do you think you're headed, then?"

Manny managed a small smile. "I lost my partner a thousand years ago. I'm more ready than you are to take that billion to one shot. Jack, it's the nature of faith to believe the unbelievable."

Jack touched Manny's shoulder. "Good. Then maybe we'll see you two at the newcomer's barbecue."

Kate bent and kissed her father's forehead as her tears fell on his cheek. "I love you, Dad."

"I love you, Katy. We both do." Jack Boyle closed his eyes.

Two hours later, Mick emerged again from the MLB's engine room and chucked a wrench into the open tool box on the survivors' compartment floor. He said to Ben, "I know I got it this time." He jerked his thumb upward. "I won't push her hard, but I'll get topside and we'll make for port."

Kate still sat silent beside her father's body. At last she wiped her eyes, then pulled the blanket over his face.

Ben laid a hand on Mick's arm. "One more thing before we leave here, Mick. Manny's gone, too."

Mick raised his eyebrows as he glanced at the small, blanket covered body on the compartment's deck. "If we bury him at sea there'll be explainin' to do."

"If there's an autopsy there'll be more. And all three of us will have to live with breaking a promise to a dying friend."

Mick and Ben carried Manny Colibri's body, zipped into a line stowage bag and weighted with spare parts, up onto the deck and laid it gently in the starboard side recovery well.

As they stood alongside the body, Kate stood behind it, looking out across the water, then closed her eyes.

She said, "I didn't really know Manny Colibri. But in an important way I knew him better than anyone in the past one thousand years knew him, because I knew where he came from. Even though I'll never see that place. And neither will he see it again. He lived a remarkable life, even though nobody else on Earth will know how remarkable. And he died as well as a thousand-year-old man can. I think that there is no place on Earth where Manny Colibri would feel more that he had come home than in the sea."

Kate opened her eyes, then nodded at Mick and Ben. Manuel Colibri's body slipped into the gently rolling water and disappeared.

Kate and Ben stood side by side at Marine 1's bow, grasping the waist-high bow rail, as the boat sailed slow and straight toward the center point between the Golden Gate's towers. On the lifeboat's fly bridge, Mick steered as they bore Jack Boyle's body home.

Kate said, "You missed your plane to Washington."

Ben said, "Not really. My phone dried out ten minutes ago and I emailed Petrie my resignation."

Kate nodded. "You and Washington never fit. Which says more about Washington than about you."

"You either. And now you've found your story that can change the world. You just can't tell it."

Kate said, "I don't suppose we'll be contributing to Petrie's campaign. Maybe to Julia's though. And there's Carlsson and all the rest of it to deal with. But that's all *small* stuff. Ben, what's the right way for mankind to go?"

Ben shook his head. "I don't know. But we have time to figure it out together."

Kate laid her hand over Ben's. "Maybe we have forever."

In the east, beyond the Golden Gate, orange fire streaked the sky as the sun rose.

ACKNOWLEDGEMENTS

Thanks, first, to my publisher, Toni Weisskopf, for the opportunity to write *The Golden Gate*, and for the wisdom that made it better. Thanks also to my editor Tony Daniel for insight and patience, to my copy editor J.R. Dunn, for perfection, and to the talented Dave Seeley for a subtle, superlative cover illustration. Thanks also to worldly wise Corinda Carfora and Christopher Ruocchio for telling the world, to Jennifer Faries for a superbly designed book cover, and to everyone at Baen Books for their unending support and enthusiasm.

Thanks to the following, in alphabetical order within category, for their assistance in keeping the many factual aspects of this complex story accurate. Any errors in those areas are mine and not theirs.

Regarding the Textron MLB 47 motor lifeboat, Bay Area police procedures and coordination, certain Homeland Security issues, and things nautical in general: SFPD Officer James Griffin Barber; SFPD Sgt.

Keith Matthews, of the SFPD Marine Unit's Marine Patrol and Homeland Security Unit; and Lt. Mark Solomon, retired, founding officer-in-charge of the SFPD Underwater Recovery Unit.

Regarding the heliosphere, the Fermi Paradox, extrasolar planets, the Orion Spur, meteorites from Mars and elsewhere, the concept that "Space is freaking awesome," and things astronomical in general:

Brian Fields, Chair and Professor of Astronomy and Physics, the University of Illinois; Zoltan G. "Zolt" Levay, Image Processing Specialist, Hubble and James Webb Telescopes, the Space Telescope Science Institute; Dr. Scott Sandford, Senior Research Scientist, NASA Ames Research Center; and Grace Wolf-Chase, Astronomer, of the University of Chicago and the Adler Planetarium.

Regarding the Aquatic Park Bathhouse:

Gina Bardi, Research Librarian, and Susan Greider, both of the United States National Park Service's National Maritime Historical Park.

Regarding the Contemporary Jewish Museum:

Janine Okmin, Associate Director of Education, and Ms. Nina Sazevich.

Regarding the Oakland Museum of California:

Ms. Lindsay Wright.

Regarding rare publications and the University of San Francisco Gleeson Library's Donohue Rare Book Room:

John Hawk, Head Librarian and Head of Special Collections and University Archives.

Regarding details of, changes to, and the history of, San Francisco's tech industry, tech culture, and neighborhoods:

David Buechner, CCIE, VCP; Scott and Michelle Richards; and Vera Sparre.

And for their valuable time and invaluable insights, very special thanks to readers SFPD Officer (and author) James Griffin Barber, David Buechner, Robert Richards Buettner, and Scott Richards.

Finally and forever, thanks to Mary Beth for everything that matters.

ABOUT THE AUTHOR

Robert Buettner has been General Counsel of a unit of one of the United States' largest private companies, a National Science Foundation Fellow in Paleontology, has prospected for minerals in Alaska and in the Sonoran desert, served as a U.S. Army Intelligence Officer, as a Director of the Southwestern Legal Foundation, and has practiced law in thirteen states and five foreign countries.

A national best-selling author, he was a Quill Award nominee for Best New Writer of 2005 and his debut novel, *Orphanage*, called a classic of modern military science fiction, was a Quill nominee for Best SF/Fantasy/Horror novel of 2004. *Orphanage* and its seven follow-on novels have been compared favorably to the works of Robert Heinlein.

The Golden Gate is his first novel set in the near present.

He lives in Georgia with his family and more bicycles than a grownup needs.

Visit him on the web at *www.RobertBuettner.com*.